The

of the Game

Books by Jennifer Dawson

The Name of the Game
The Winner Takes It All
Take a Chance On Me

Published by Kensington Publishing Corporation

The Name
of the Game

JENNIFER DAWSON

ZEBRA BOOKS
KENSINGTON PUBLISHING CORP.
http://www.kensingtonbooks.com

ZEBRA BOOKS are published by

Kensington Publishing Corp.
119 West 40th Street
New York, NY 10018

All Kensington titles, imprints, and distributed lines are available at special quantity discounts for bulk purchases for sales promotion, premiums, fund-raising, educational, or institutional use.

Special book excerpts or customized printings can also be created to fit specific needs. For details, write or phone the office of the Kensington Sales Manager: Attn.: Sales Department. Kensington Publishing Corp., 119 West 40th Street, New York, NY 10018. Phone: 1-800-221-2647.

Zebra and the Z logo Reg. U.S. Pat. & TM Off.

First Printing: October 2015
ISBN-13: 978-1-4201-3429-2
ISBN-10: 1-4201-3429-9

eISBN-13: 978-1-4201-3430-8
eISBN-10: 1-4201-3430-2

10 9 8 7 6 5 4 3 2 1

Printed in the United States of America

To the Rini Girls
Mom, Aunt Be-Be, Aunt Grace,
Kristen, Jordyn, Samantha, & Ivy.
I am forever grateful to be blessed with
your never-ending love and support.
I think Grandma is proud of her little flowers.

To my editor Esi and my agent Courtney.
Thank you for not throwing up your hands, screaming, and
running from the room when this book was a total mess.
If it wasn't for your support, patience, and guidance,
this book wouldn't have been possible.

Chapter One

"How can you drink that stuff?" Gracie Roberts wrinkled her nose at the offending protein shake in James Donovan's hand. Of course, his drink of choice wasn't her business, but whenever she was around the stuffy professor of forensic anthropology for more than five seconds, she couldn't resist the urge to antagonize him. In her defense, as a baker, his obsession with health food went against her nature.

How could she trust a man who didn't eat sugar?

One brown brow rose as he stared at her, not speaking. Behind black, wire-rimmed frames, his cool, ever-green eyes studied her in a way she could only describe as dismissive. The standard expression he wore in her company.

When they'd met eighteen months ago, they'd taken one look at each other, and it had been instant dislike.

Which was strange. In her thirty-three years she'd rarely met a person she didn't like. She loved people and people loved her right back. Her momma had always said she'd been born with more charm than should be legal.

Why, Gracie hadn't had a nemesis since the eighth grade, when Katie Womack told Greg Holbert that

Gracie had lice, so he'd take Katie to the spring fling instead. But in the end that turned out to be a godsend because now Katie was saddled with five screaming children and Greg cheated on her with a bottle blonde in the next town over.

Good riddance.

She eyed the professor with matching disdain as they squared off, prepared for yet another battle. Living hundreds of miles apart meant she should be able to avoid him, but he came with her best friends. Since Gracie loved her friends she was stuck with James. When she'd volunteered to come up to Chicago and help Cecilia Riley move into the fabulous house she'd bought with her fiancé, she'd known she'd have to endure the presence of her nemesis, but it didn't make it any easier.

She sighed. The things she suffered for friendship.

She glared at him. "What are you looking at?"

A flickering once-over. "Not a thing."

She shouldn't engage him, but found it impossible this bright, sunny morning. Everything about him irritated her. He'd forsaken his normal geek-wear of tan slacks and a polo shirt, which made him look like a customer service rep for GEICO, for jeans and a vintage-inspired, faded blue *Empire Strikes Back* T-shirt. The cotton stretched over his broad chest and flat abs, emphasizing all those hard muscles he'd worked to hone.

She planted her hands on full hips she'd been told belonged on a 1940s pinup model, and glared at his offending drink. "Why don't you drink chalk? I'm sure it tastes better."

"This drink contains the perfect blend of protein, carbohydrates, and vitamins." James eyed the powdered-sugar doughnut resting on a paper plate at her fingertips. "Which is more than I can say for that fried, sugary monstrosity you're calling a breakfast."

How dare he?! Doughnuts were universally loved. Only

sickos and crazies didn't like them. Gracie opened her mouth to blast him, but before she could, his older brother came to his rescue.

Shane held out his hands like a referee breaking up a couple of prizefighters. "Let's not start another round of the food wars. It never ends well and it's going to be a long day."

Next to him, Cecilia, nodded. "We appreciate the help this weekend, but it's only been an hour and you've bickered nonstop."

Disgruntled, Gracie pointed at James. "He started it."

He gave her the disapproving scowl he reserved for her. "*You* started it. I was standing here minding my own business."

"You insulted my doughnut!" A stray blond curl flopped into one eye and she pushed it behind her ear even though it never stayed put.

"After you turned your nose up at my shake." James crossed his arms over his chest and his biceps rippled.

For a second, the corded muscles running the length of his arms distracted her, but she quickly regained focus and snorted. "Shake! That's an insult to shakes. Real shakes are made with actual ice cream. And I'm not talking low-fat frozen yogurt either. I'm talking—"

A loud, piercing whistle filled the air and Gracie covered her ears.

Cecilia's four-carat diamond ring flashed, nearly blinding Gracie, as she sliced a hand through the air. "Please. You two are giving me a headache."

Shane slid a big hand around Cecilia's waist, pulling her close. "And I'm the only one allowed to make her upset." He leaned down and kissed his future wife's neck.

Between Shane and Cecilia getting married, and Gracie's friends Mitch and Maddie Riley being newly-weds, the constant love fest had started to grate. While she was overjoyed they were happy, it forced Gracie to bear witness to their public displays of affection all too often.

And Gracie was big enough to admit she was a tiny bit jealous. She loved herself a little PDA, only she had no one to PDA with. The year anniversary of her unintentional celibacy had come and gone and she was starting to get twitchy. Abstinence hadn't been the plan. She loved sex. She'd dated plenty, only no one had flipped her switch enough to get her into bed.

She shot a sidelong glance at the professor, always so proper and reserved. He probably thought kissing in public was as disgusting as doughnuts. Hell, he probably only had sex in the missionary position with the lights off. Anyone that uptight would be a complete dud in the sack. Of that much, she was sure.

Not that she thought about what he was like in bed.

When Shane's tongue flicked over Cecilia's skin, Gracie's brows pinched together. "Hey, stop that." She jerked a thumb at the professor. "You're going to give him nightmares."

Shane sucked on Cecilia's neck, his teeth scraping over the soft flesh. Gracie couldn't blame her friend one bit when Cecilia's eyes practically rolled into the back of her head.

Unlike his brother, Shane Donovan was not the kind of man who fucked with the lights off.

James sighed, a deep, heavy sound of the resigned. "Once again, you've managed to lose me."

Shane lifted his head and grinned at his younger brother. "She thinks you're a prude, Jimmy."

James scowled for several seconds, and then shook his head as though Gracie was just too silly for words. He picked up the box labeled "kitchen" off the counter and started toward the door, saying over his shoulder, "You make a gazillion dollars. Why aren't those movers you hired taking care of this?"

That . . . was actually a good point. "Hey! He's right."

"Holy fuck, you agreed with him." Shane craned his neck and called after his brother. "Did you hear that, Jimmy? She agreed with you."

"I'll mark it down in my calendar and drop dead of a heart attack," James said wryly and out the door he went, thus concluding round 513 of their on-going battle.

"That's it? That's all I had to do?" Gracie grinned at Cecilia. "Think of all the time I've wasted."

Shane narrowed his green eyes. At first, Gracie had thought all the Donovans shared the exact same eye color, but James's were different. A cool, crisp ever-green amongst the rest of the clan's warmth.

"Do you have to antagonize him?" Shane asked.

Indignant, Gracie placed a hand over her expansive cleavage. "Me? What did I do?"

"Don't play innocent. You bait him. You've been bait-ing him since the day you met." Shane slid a hand onto the counter behind Cecilia, and when her friend shiv-ered a little, Gracie suspected he'd worked his fingers under Cecilia's black top. Again.

Gracie sighed.

Cecilia nodded. "I'm afraid he's right."

Gracie rolled her eyes. "Ugh. I miss the days when you guys didn't constantly agree with each other."

Cecilia grinned at Shane, her sleek ponytail perfectly in place even though they were doing manual labor. "I'm trying, but I can't seem to work up a good mad."

Shane tugged her mane of caramel-colored hair. "I'm sure you'll think of something soon."

"How about the fact that you don't have movers?" Gracie asked. After spending last night hearing *way* too much, she wasn't sure how much longer she could stomach their ooey-gooey love. Between them and the stuffy professor, her body couldn't decide if it was stuck in a voyeuristic fantasy or *My Fair Lady*.

Shane's hand settled on Cecilia's neck. "The movers will be here in thirty. Ce-ce wanted to take care of the important stuff herself."

Determined to show her friends the enthusiasm they deserved, Gracie smiled at the happy couple, pushing aside her pettiness. "It's hard to believe six months ago Cecilia cried on my couch over you. Now look at you guys, moving in together and getting married."

Cecilia's expression held nothing but complete adoration as she gazed at her fiancé. "Pretty crazy, huh?"

Shane brushed a kiss over her lips, and Gracie looked away.

In six months Cecilia had changed her entire life around. She'd gone from a shut off, work-obsessed woman stuck in a job and life she hadn't wanted, to the vibrant woman she was now. She'd quit her job as her father's political advisor, disowned said father, made amends with her brother and mom, started a new business as a PR consultant specializing in image repair, and fallen in love with Shane.

Gracie couldn't even manage to get herself laid. Which was pretty much her fault since she kept turning men down. Good men. Hot men.

She shook her shoulders. Enough of that. She had a great life. Sex and companionship weren't the key to happiness. She had everything a woman could want: a thriving business, great friends, and a beautiful home she shared with her brother.

She was a self-sufficient, empowered woman. Men were secondary. Nice to have but certainly not vital.

James strolled back into the room, moving with an easy grace that irritated her. She'd be hard-pressed to pinpoint why she'd taken a dislike to him. Other than his addiction to health food and exercise, there wasn't anything the least bit objectionable about him. Like his testosterone-laden alpha brothers, he was handsome enough—in a bookish sort of way.

At six-two, he was the shortest of the three Donovan boys, and while he had a body that rivaled his brothers', there wasn't anything threatening about James. He was an ordinary guy. Nothing exceptional. Nothing objectionable. With most men, especially harmless men, she went out of her way to flirt and flatter, but for some reason she couldn't do that with James. It was something about the way he looked at her, as though he was on to her. Had figured her out. Only, she couldn't figure out what he understood that she didn't.

"What?" James asked, startling her out of her thoughts.

Her stomach did an unwelcome little jump, as it sometimes did when he gave her that hard glare and his jaw got all stern. She waved a hand. "Oh, nothing."

He pointed at one of the boxes on the kitchen table. "Are you going to get to work, or stand there?"

Gracie huffed. "Um, I was here an hour before you."

A quirked brow. "But did you do anything?"

"You are such an ass." Gracie shook her head at the ceiling. How would she survive this day? Let alone the whole weekend?

"You're getting repetitive." James cocked his lean hip against the island countertop and took another drink of his disgusting shake. "You've already told me that twice today."

Gracie searched her mind for a proper comeback only to find herself flummoxed. Another reason he irritated her. While she'd never admit it in a million years, she often got tongued-tied around him. She made men like him nervous, not the other way around.

Ignoring him, she whirled around to Cecilia. "Do you see what I have to put up with?"

Cecilia pressed her lips together to suppress a laugh.

Shane, however, did not have the same problem. "You did kind of start it."

Cecilia elbowed him in the ribs and shushed him before crooking her finger at Gracie. "Come on, let's go start on the bedroom."

Shane grabbed Cecilia's wrist and tugged her back, bending down to whisper something that made color splash onto her cheeks before letting her go. Cecilia wobbled, then righted herself, a secret smile on her lips. "We'll just have to see about that, now won't we?"

Shane gave her a long, slow once-over. "Yeah, we will."

Gracie rolled her eyes. God help her. See, this was why she had sex on the brain. It was their fault.

Cecilia spun on her heel, head held high. "Come on, Gracie." As she passed, Shane smacked her on the ass and she yelped. "Hey!"

Shane laughed and Cecilia glowered, although the huge grin on her lips gave her away. Gracie sighed, a bit wistful, as she followed her friend up the back staircase.

Nobody had smacked her ass in, like, *forever.*

James Donovan watched Gracie climb the back stairs, her fantasy-inducing ass encased in a pair of tight jeans that clung to her showgirl legs, in annoyed awe. The sentiment pretty much summed up his yearlong, animosity-filled acquaintance with her. The tight red T-shirt she wore displayed her hourglass figure in all its lush glory, and he'd about broken into a cold sweat as soon as he saw her.

If it was just her body it would be one thing, but her face was equally compelling with those dancing cornflower-blue eyes and wild mess of blond curls that refused to stay tamed no matter how many times she tucked it behind her ears. She was an odd mix of heart-stoppingly cute and wickedly sexy.

His jaw clenched. The kick of desire he felt bothered him. James's mind and body had been under control for a long time, and his attraction to the blond sex goddess was a reminder of parts of him better left behind.

He wished for the thousandth time she'd meet someone. She dated plenty, but as far as he could tell, discarded men like used tissues during the heart of flu season.

When she'd stopped seeing the sheriff she'd been involved with when he'd first met her, James had been sure she'd hook up with one of his brothers. Women like Gracie *always* went for guys like his brothers. At first he'd assumed Shane, because they'd hit it off so well, but that hope had been dashed as soon as Cecilia had shown up.

At his sister Maddie's wedding, his younger brother, Evan, had been all over Gracie, but to James's surprise she'd rebuffed his advances with that good-natured charm she turned on everyone but him. James still didn't understand why. Evan hadn't heard the word no since he was fourteen. His brother was a six-five, star NFL wide receiver. He'd been to the Pro Bowl. And while she flirted with him shamelessly, she hadn't acted. Gracie remained stubbornly unattached. Which irritated him more than if they were actually sleeping together; if Evan had sex with Gracie, she'd be off the table and his problems with her would be solved.

"Are you going to do something about that?" Shane's voice interrupted his thoughts.

James jerked his attention away from the staircase

Gracie disappeared up and rested his palms against the marble countertops. "I don't know what you mean."

His older brother's green eyes narrowed. In that moment, with that particular expression on his face, he looked the spitting image of their father, and James experienced the dull ache of loss that never went away, no matter how much time passed.

"The tension between the two of you is becoming annoying."

"It's not tension," James said in a cool, well-modulated tone. "It's dislike. There's a difference."

Yes, they might have an undercurrent of chemistry, but it was crystal clear neither wanted anything to do with it.

He certainly didn't. He liked his women rational.

"Bullshit. Stop beating around the bush and take care of it before you get a permanent case of blue balls."

"Charming as always." James kept his face relaxed and impassive. He'd made damn sure no one knew the extent of his lust for Gracie, but of course he didn't fool Shane. "In case you haven't noticed, she's not a fan."

"For a smart guy you sure are stupid."

It was easy for guys like his brothers. They saw something they liked, and they went for it, consequences be damned.

James liked a little more planning than that. And while he'd put the insecurities of his youth to bed years ago, he was careful about his relationships. James raised a brow at Shane. "At a bare minimum I require my partners to respect me."

Shane grinned. "Respect is overrated. Take her to bed and get it out of your system."

An image of tangled sheets and a naked Gracie

filled his mind, but James shook it off. "Mind your own business."

"I don't understand you at all."

That was pretty much par for the course. James had never been like the rest of them and never would be. Their baby sister, Maddie, might be the tiny one in the family, but she was all fierce and spirited like his brothers. James accepted a long time ago he was the odd man out, and he'd given up wishing he could be like them the night of the car accident, when his father had died and his sister had lain in a coma.

His siblings were impulsive. James was the reasonable one. They didn't get it and he didn't blame them. It was hard to explain to people who thrived on risk that he liked his life orderly. Neat. Discipline and structure had helped him survive and become the man he was today. It had saved him and he had no desire to go back. He liked his life boring and predictable, even if it meant nobody understood him.

Yes, like any red-blooded man, he'd like to go to bed with Gracie and lose himself in her body and all that heat. But he'd examined the situation from all angles and saw no practical reason to satiate his desire. If, on the off chance she agreed—a highly unlikely scenario as she'd made her dislike crystal clear—it would be a disaster. Their personalities were at complete odds and it would end with her hating him more than she already did.

Sex was the only upside.

While it was a considerable upside, in the end it would do more harm than good. Instinct told him that not knowing how she'd feel under his hands and mouth was a good thing. The last thing he needed was the memory of what it felt like to slide inside her. Or how it would feel when she came.

He shook his head to clear the illicit thoughts. In the end, they were oil and water. Incompatible in every way that mattered to him.

"Stop thinking and just do it already." Shane's exasperated tone matched the expression on his face.

James didn't bother to explain what his brother would never understand. "Don't we have boxes to move?"

"Chicken shit," Shane said.

"Smart," James corrected.

"Well, if you won't do anything about the situation, at least stop rising to the bait. She wants a reaction."

"I'm fairly certain she doesn't want anything from me." James turned around and picked up a box, thinking through Shane's statement.

Why *did* he fight with her? He didn't fight with anyone else. As far as he could tell he was the only person Gracie didn't get along with. Was arguing a way to engage her? To hold her attention?

He couldn't dismiss the idea entirely. Not when he thought about how her sharp tongue made him hard. She might lay down the kindling, but he added the flame.

He must have a motive for engaging in repartee with Gracie. A motive he'd have to analyze at a later date when she wasn't around to distract him.

But to Shane's point, not rising to her bait was a concrete action he could take. He'd be around her the whole weekend. More than enough time to see the cause and effect of being cordial. He could be nice and polite for forty-eight hours. He turned the idea over in his mind, examining it from different angles, and couldn't see the harm. It would be a good test of her reactions, and his own. To see if the antagonism between them was habit, or the only way to deal with the subtle and inconvenient attraction that he fought against and she flat-out ignored. Once he conducted his experiment, and examined the outcomes, he'd come up with a reasonable hypothesis and course of action.

He'd ignore Gracie's barbs and be pleasant to her. He managed civility with colleagues and students at his university downtown every day; surely he could apply the same strategies here.

It was only a weekend. How hard could it be?

Chapter Two

Five hours later Gracie was exhausted, and cursing Cecilia's big closet. She eyed the shoebox on the top shelf in the back corner, hovering out of her reach. She stood on tiptoes, stretching her five feet, six inches to maximum height. Her fingertips brushed the box, which pushed it farther out of her reach. "Shit!"

She tried again but the shoes stayed firmly out of her grasp.

"Here, let me," a deep voice said from behind.

She screeched, whirling around to see James leaning against the doorframe. She placed a hand over her pounding heart. "You scared me."

"Sorry." He straightened. "Let me help you."

She eyed him with suspicion. "Why?"

His jaw hardened, his mouth opened, but then he shook his head and his features relaxed. "Because I'm taller than you and thought it would fulfill my daily chivalry quota."

She resisted the urge to stick out her tongue. Childish, but he brought out the worst in her. She cocked a brow. "I bet you do have a quota, along with a checklist."

"Correct. I store it in my analytics software." His voice was totally deadpan.

"You know what's sad?" She planted her hands on her hips. "I don't think that's a joke."

"I never joke. I have no sense of humor." Expression stoic, he crossed his arms over his impossibly broad chest.

"So I've noticed."

He shrugged. "It's not on the checklist."

Not quite the response she'd been looking for. She frowned. When forced to spend time with the professor, their sparring matches were the one thing on which she could depend.

But he hadn't risen to the bait since their argument that morning.

The man had been downright nice. Which, strangely, turned out to be as irritating as when he argued with her. More so, if she was honest. She couldn't start being nice to him now; it threw off their whole dynamic, and then where would she be?

She gave him an overly sweet smile. "Do you think I need a big, strong man to come to my rescue?"

"No. Just a taller one." His voice was so mild it raised the fine hairs at the nape of her neck.

"Don't be cute." Wow. Now didn't she sound petulant? She should be rejoicing in his cease-fire, but instead she kept pushing his buttons, hoping for some kind of reaction she knew what to do with. She should have him lapping out of the palm of her hand, but he never played by the rules.

He straightened and his chest seemed to expand, spreading the *Empire Strikes Back* logo on his T-shirt ominously over his broad muscles. With a sigh, he took a step toward her.

The urge to step back roared to life. How silly. She had nothing to be nervous about. He was a geeky professor.

He advanced on her with a look in his evergreen eyes she'd never seen before. He looked . . . determined.

She gulped.

His long legs ate up the floor separating them and her heart rate sped up, her mouth going dry as she fought the desire to retreat.

This was James. The most harmless man on the planet.

He'd eaten a salad for lunch. A salad! With lemon juice and olive oil for dressing, while the rest of them ate Italian beef sandwiches.

She squared her shoulders, tugging at her top. She was not nervous. She didn't get nervous.

He stopped inches from her. He was close. Closer than he'd ever been. And they were alone. She couldn't even hear the distant sounds of the movers.

She didn't know how the silent pact started, but they had always made sure they were never left alone together. And here he was, changing the rules.

She sucked in a breath. Oh no. He smelled good. Like work and leather and man. They'd been doing manual labor for hours; how could he smell so good? Suddenly he seemed too tall. Too broad. Her vision of him expanded as he stretched outside the box where she kept him. Throat dry, she swallowed. "What do you think you're doing?"

"I'm being helpful." He smiled, and to her shock one dimple deepened his left cheek. Where had that been hiding?

It occurred to her she'd never seen it because he never smiled at her. He only glowered. The glower she could handle, the dimple she could not.

Heat radiated off him, warming her from head to toe, making her stomach jump, suspiciously like arousal. This was not a turn-on. If *he* turned her on she needed to have sex ASAP. She frowned. "Stop it. You're being annoying again."

His gaze met hers. This close, his eyes were startling green mixed with hints of blue, thus explaining their cool undertones.

His attention drifted to her mouth, and to her dismay her breath caught. She crossed her arms over her chest to hide what felt like nipple tightening, tapped one foot, and pointed at the shoebox. "Well, what are you waiting for?"

His lips quirked. "I thought my help annoyed you."

If he could play it cool, so could she. She shrugged. "You're here. Might as well make yourself useful."

"I suppose you'll have to suffer through the torture." He shook his head, his full mouth creased in feigned sympathy. "However will you sleep tonight?"

With a scornful twist of her lips, she said, "I can assure you, when I'm lying in bed at night, you're the last person who comes to mind."

It was a lie. She did think of him sometimes, but only to ruminate on how much he maddened her. Nothing else. Well, okay, she had, on occasion, imagined how horrible he must be in bed. But that barely counted.

He didn't speak, just stepped closer, his expression filled with a healthy dose of skepticism.

Was he trying to intimidate her? Because it wouldn't work.

She had years of practice handling men. A skill she'd developed quickly when she'd turned fifteen and developed double-D breasts seemingly overnight. The first time a man hadn't been able to tear his gaze from her cleavage, her momma had sat her down and they'd had a long talk about how Gracie had to be careful. She had taken the lesson to heart and learned to stay one step ahead of men ever since.

She raised a brow. "Is there any particular reason you're standing right on top of me?"

One large hand slid onto her hip, making her jump. The heat of his palm seemed to sear right through her, leaving an imprint on her skin through her jeans. "You're in my way."

"What?"

His fingers squeezed her hip, sending a jolt of something she refused to name ping-ponging through her. He bent his head, and when he spoke his voice was low. "You're in my way."

And then he pushed her to the side.

She swayed, the imprint of his hand still branding her skin. With ease, he picked up the box and handed it to her with what looked a hell of a lot like a smirk.

Her mouth fell open, but before she could say anything, Cecilia called out, "Gracie?"

Heat fanned over her neck, splashing onto her cheeks.

A moment later Cecilia stood in the doorway of the closet, cell in hand. She glanced back and forth between the two of them. "What's going on?"

Gracie held the shoebox with an iron grip. "Nothing. Nothing at all. What could be going on?" The words tumbled too quickly from her lips, making her sound guilty when she had absolutely nothing to be guilty about. He'd helped her. That was all. She cleared her throat. "What's up?"

A small smile on her lips, Cecilia's brows rose. She held up her phone. "That was Maddie. They left Revival early and will be here in an hour. We thought it would be fun to go to dinner tonight before the craziness of the weekend starts. Just the six of us."

The six of them. Mitch and Maddie. Shane and Cecilia. Her and . . . She shot a sidelong glance at the man standing silent next to her.

James.

"What about Evan?" she asked, in a hope-filled voice. If he went too, it would be less like couples and she'd have his flirting to distract her.

Something flashed in James's expression, but it was gone before she could decipher its meaning.

"He's got a team charity event tonight," Cecilia said.

Ugh! Her mind frantically flew through the names of other friends who might attend, but she kept her mouth shut as it would be too obvious she didn't want to be James's date. She cast another discreet glance in his direction. He studied her with a sharp gaze behind his black frames. She hastily looked away.

She'd spent all day with him. She had to see him all weekend. She didn't want to go to dinner with him too. "I don't have anything to wear."

"You can borrow something of mine," Cecilia said.

Ha! Gracie probably outweighed her friend by at least thirty pounds. She eyed Cecilia's small chest. "Let's ignore the fact that I couldn't fit one leg into any of your clothes; they're all packed away."

Cecilia waved her hand. "We have reservations but we can change them to somewhere casual and you can wear what you have on."

Gracie wrinkled her nose. "You want me to wear clothes I've moved in all day? No, thank you."

"Come on, it will be fun. Shane knows the owner of this new place and already got us a prime table. I promise you'll love it." Cecilia turned to James and held her hands in prayer, her cell sticking out like a steeple. "You're in, aren't you?"

His vision flickered over Gracie, then he smiled at his future sister-in-law. "Sure, I'm in."

"Great! It's our treat to repay you for all your work." Ce-Ce beamed a smile at him before shifting her attention to Gracie. "Please? I have a black dress that I'm sure will work."

Gracie looked her friend up and down. "Does it stretch?"

Cecilia grinned. "Enough to give everyone a heart attack."

Fantastic. But how could she say no without looking like an ingrate? She sighed. "All right."

"I'll go call Maddie." And with that, Cecilia was off, leaving Gracie alone with James.

She swung around to face him. "What did you go and do that for?"

"Do what?" James asked. Was that amusement in his voice?

Gracie pointed toward the now empty doorway. "Do you really want to go to dinner with the love brigade?"

One brow rose up his forehead. "Afraid people will think we're a couple?"

"As if. Nobody in their right mind would think that."

He stiffened. "This isn't about us. It's about Shane and Cecilia."

"There is no *us*," she hissed.

He stared at her for a long, uncomfortable moment before shrugging. "Suit yourself. Don't go."

Then he walked away without a backward glance, leaving her alone in the closet.

Something squeezed tight in her chest. Something that felt a lot like loneliness. Which was silly. She had everything she needed. Her life was perfect.

* * *

James sat with Shane and their brother-in-law, Mitch, in the mess of his brother's new living room, surrounded by boxes the movers had left, while they waited for the girls to finish getting ready.

"Nice place you've got here," Mitch said, examining the spacious room with its high ceilings, his beer clutched loosely in one hand. "Although both of you moving the day before your engagement party seems like biting off more than even you can chew."

Shane shrugged and glanced up the wide staircase leading to the second floor. "Ce-ce didn't want to wait."

Mitch eyed him with that speculative lawyer's expression he wore. "My sister is hardly the impatient type."

Shane grinned. "I guess she couldn't wait to shack up with me."

Mitch shuddered as though the room had taken on a sudden chill. "I'm not sure I'm ever going to get used to you and my sister."

Shane cocked his head, grinning. "What are you talking about? I'm the traumatized one. I'm still having nightmares of when you and *my* sister stayed with us last time. Seriously, man, if you're going to do that kind of shit, get a hotel room."

Mitch laughed, scrubbing a hand over his jaw. "Don't pretend you weren't trying to outdo me."

James shook his head at the both of them. It was just his luck that Mitch and Shane were the two most competitive men on the planet. And now, involved with each other's sisters, James was forced to endure endless discussions about who was more disgusted over the near constant displays of affection exhibited by the couples. They never seemed to grow tired of the game and constantly ribbed each other.

While James was disgusted by both of them, he gave a slight advantage to Mitch, since Maddie was his sister too, after all. He had to agree with Shane that it was rather disconcerting to walk into a room and catch his brother-in-law's hands up his sweet sister's top.

The bastard never even apologized.

James returned his attention to the television, where he'd covertly changed the channel from a baseball game to a history documentary about the invention of the nuclear bomb. Too busy giving each other shit, Shane and Mitch hadn't noticed. As an MIT professor droned on, James's mind wandered back to where it had stubbornly wandered all day. Gracie.

He'd replayed their exchange in the closet. He'd done his best to be nice to her. He'd been helpful and affable. He'd ignored her barbs, refusing to rise to the bait, although it was damn hard with that sassy mouth of hers. He hadn't missed the flare of awareness in her, but so far, being congenial hadn't lessened the tension. If anything, it seemed to grow, and she'd become more agitated. He could only conclude pleasantness didn't have an effect on her behavior. He tapped a finger on the remote.

Or maybe he hadn't given it enough time.

While the results might be inconclusive, the experiment had taught him one thing: he'd been right to never be alone with her.

They sparked. He supposed it was a good thing Gracie was the most stubborn woman on earth. With all her talk about him being a geek, and her agitation about his dietary choices, she'd never admit they had chemistry.

She'd go to her grave insisting she hated him. He suspected she even believed it. As a teenager he'd watched as his brothers dated girls like Gracie, and he knew the score. He was hardly her type. While a part of him itched to prove her wrong, her rejection of him as a potential partner suited him fine. They were fundamentally incompatible. And he preferred his sexual encounters to mean something.

Eventually she'd meet someone. Or he would. Someone more suitable to his personality, who would build the strong, grounded relationship he desired.

Before he could contemplate any more, his baby sister came bounding down the stairs in a flirty little red dress. The color should clash with her auburn hair, but didn't. She beamed at her husband and plopped down on his lap.

Shane grimaced. "There are plenty of available seats."

"Don't listen to him." Mitch slid his arm around Maddie's waist and placed a hand inappropriately high on her thigh. "Well, don't you look gorgeous, princess."

She leaned in and kissed his neck. "Thank you, so do you." She whispered something in his ear and a second later Mitch laughed.

Shane scowled. "Jesus, Maddie, I heard that. Now I'll think about it all night and end up impotent."

"I certainly hope not," Cecilia said, making her way down the stairs. She wore her caramel-colored hair loose and was dressed in skinny black pants, a stretchy matching top, and heels at least four inches high. On her tall, lean frame she looked every inch the sophisticated rich girl she was.

Shane took one look at her and shrugged. "Problem solved."

Cecilia grinned and moved into the kitchen. "It's a mess, but I know where the wine is. I made sure of that. I'll open a bottle of red. Does anyone else need anything?"

If James drank, he stuck to red wine with all those

good antioxidants, and he suspected he'd need a few drinks to get through the evening. "I'll take a glass."

"Where's Gracie?" Mitch asked.

"She was last in the shower," Maddie volunteered before saying to Cecilia, "I'll take a glass too."

James's mind flashed to a naked Gracie with water streaming down her lush body, and shook off the thought. Images like that were not productive.

Cecilia came over and handed him a glass of deep red wine before passing one to Maddie. Moments later she returned with her own and settled herself into the crook of Shane's arm, plastering her body against his. Now both couples were on the couch, staring at their partners adoringly, and James contemplated Gracie's earlier question about wanting to be around them.

In retrospect, she had a point.

They were rather annoying. And this dinner did leave them the odd couple out. The awkward fly in the love-fest ointment. Usually there were other people around to act as a buffer, but tonight, with only the six of them, the contrast between their dislike for one another and the couples' infatuation would be the elephant in the room.

It was one night. For his brother. And it would give him a chance to continue his experiment.

The rest of the weekend they'd be around friends and family, and James wouldn't have to talk to her. It wouldn't kill him to spend an evening with Gracie and, as he'd said, this wasn't about them. It was about Shane and Cecilia. After all his older brother had done for their family, James would swim through shark-infested waters if it meant securing Shane's well-deserved happiness.

His brother had saved them from the streets after their father died. Their mother had been overcome with grief and needed all her time for Maddie's rehab after the accident, so they'd been near destitute. Shane had taken on all the burdens of their family, working himself to the bone, until he became insanely successful. Most people only saw the man he was today; they had no idea how hard those early years had been. Or how tirelessly Shane had worked to hold it all together.

James marveled at his brother's strength and determination. He'd used it as a model for turning his own life around. Sure, he'd never be rich like Shane and Evan, but he was well respected in his profession. He had the admiration of his peers, law enforcement agencies all over the country hired him as a consultant, and he had secured tenure at one of the most prestigious universities in the country. In the world of academia he was at the top of his field. James owed that to Shane, who'd paid for college, put food on the table, and kept their family together and thriving.

If Shane wanted him here, James wasn't going to let a blond-haired vixen get in his way.

And then said vixen walked down the stairs and knocked the wind right out of him.

Maddie whistled—a long, low, wolfish sound. "Damn, Gracie, you look like a dominatrix."

James couldn't help but agree, and could only stare at her in stunned silence.

Gracie's black minidress molded to every curve of her body, clung to her waist and hips as though it was painted on, and ended so high on her thighs James started to sweat. The plunging neckline displayed a jaw-dropping amount of cleavage and Cecilia had been right when she'd said it would give people a heart attack. James's heart pumped so hard he was in an anaerobic state. Matched with black knee-high boots, red lips, and wild, blond curls, she did, in fact, look quite formidable.

"See, I told you it would fit," Cecilia said, her voice smug with satisfaction.

Gracie ran a hand down her stomach, and shifted in her boots. "There isn't room to spare, even with the spandex."

James lost track of what they were saying, unable to tear his attention away from the woman in front of him. She looked so delicious, so unbelievably sexy, he'd have to beat the men away with a stick. James frowned. He shouldn't be having those thoughts.

She didn't belong to him and never would.

"What are you looking at?" Gracie demanded, breaking into his inappropriate thoughts.

"What?" he asked stupidly.

She straightened her shoulders and put her hands on her hips. "You're wearing that disapproving look you have. If you don't like the dress, blame your sister-in-law, not me."

He stiffened as everyone turned toward him with speculation on their faces. Unlike Gracie, James hated being the center of attention. That's why he wanted a nice, quiet girl who hated scenes as much as he did. He shook his head. "You're paranoid."

Maddie shrugged. "Well, you were kind of glaring at her."

James narrowed a dangerous gaze on his sister. The little traitor. "I was thinking about something that had nothing to do with her. She happened to be in my line of vision."

Shane chuckled and Cecilia gave him a little nudge.

"Ha! See, she saw it too. It's not in my imagination."

Gracie punctuated each word with a jab of her finger in his direction.

He gritted his teeth and thought about his plan to be agreeable this weekend. He prided himself on discipline and follow-through. They were the cornerstones of his life. Plus, an experiment was only sound if testing was conducted properly. Yes, she was a challenge, but a little challenge built character. She would not get the best of him.

He gave her his most pleasant smile, the one he reserved for alumni parties when faced with a large donor to the university. "You look quite nice, Gracie."

"Whatever! I don't need your approval." She flounced away and a second later the bathroom door slammed shut.

Mitch shook his head. "God, you're an idiot."

"What? I complimented her." James took a sip of his wine—well, a gulp, really. She was the unreasonable one here, not him.

Cecilia raised a brow. "You told her she looked nice."

What did they expect? For him to fawn all over her? *Nice* was a safe compliment, and fit his criteria for pleasantness. "Yeah? So?"

Maddie huffed, shaking her head like he was too stupid to live.

James adjusted his glasses and sighed. Hoping for a little male camaraderie, he looked back and forth between Mitch and Shane. "What's wrong with nice?"

Before they could answer, Gracie stomped back into the room, her boot heels hard, angry jabs on the newly stained, wide-planked wood floors. "You don't tell a woman she looks nice. Grandmas are nice. Puppies are nice."

"That's the stupidest thing I've ever heard." He

cringed at the condescension in his tone. Unfortunately, old habits died hard. He took a deep breath and reminded himself to stick to the plan. He could salvage this situation.

"I am not stupid," she said, her tone filled with venom.

"Don't twist my words." Anger stirred hot in his chest and he squashed it down. He would not give in. He was in control here. He drained his glass, much faster than he should have considering his light lunch this afternoon.

"How can you be so clueless about women?"

In that moment, more than anything, he wanted to show her just how wrong she was about his supposed cluelessness. "I can assure you I've told plenty of women they looked nice without them throwing a hissy fit."

Two splotches of pink stained her cheeks. "I am not throwing a hissy fit."

"Most women would say thank you and go about their business. But not you—no, you have to make a big deal about the fact that I'm not fawning all over you."

On the couch the two couples' attention bounced back and forth between James and Gracie as though they were watching a tennis match. He should stop. He needed to stop. He was a calm, reasonable man. He did not do scenes. He had an experiment to conduct.

"I don't want your stupid fawning. *Nice* is not a compliment!" She stood there, magnificent chest heaving, looking like a bull waiting to charge.

"*Nice* is a perfectly acceptable compliment," he insisted stubbornly, even though logic dictated he apologize and get this over with.

"You might as well say I look horrible," she yelled.

Something snapped and he stood up, pointing at her. "Don't even give me that load of crap when you don't give a fuck what I think."

"You're right, I don't," she shouted.

"Let's calm down," Shane said.

"Stay out of it," James said, cutting a menacing glare at his brother before shifting back to Gracie. "Then what are we arguing about?"

Her chin tilted. "Nothing. Forget it. Let's go."

"Fine," he said, all his good intentions shot to hell.

She stomped past him. "This should be fun."

He gave her a snide once-over. "I'm sure it will be real *nice*."

Chapter Three

Gracie stood against the wall in the trendy, River North restaurant's bathroom while Cecilia and Maddie looked at her with twin frowns.

Cecilia sighed, the sound exasperated. "I thought you were going to be nice."

After a near silent car ride, Gracie was still trying to figure out what happened. Why had she baited him into an argument? He'd been agreeable all day, and she'd jumped all over him. Yes, normal people understood a woman didn't want to be told she looked nice, but she'd overreacted. And he'd yelled at her. Honest to God yelled.

How did she explain to her friends that he'd been helpful and pleasant and it drove her irrationally insane? On the defensive, she blinked and sputtered. "But you agreed with me."

"Well, yeah, until you took it too far," Maddie said.

She *had* taken it too far. She'd known that while it happened, but she hadn't been able to stop. He just made her so mad.

"You're so awesome with everyone else," Cecilia said, lines of disapproval bracketing her mouth. "Why can't you be as warm and lovely to him as you are with other people?"

Wasn't that the million-dollar question? Gracie'd had the best intentions. Getting ready with her girlfriends had put her in a good mood. They'd laughed, traded makeup, and been downright girly as they had gotten ready for the night ahead. After a couple of hours with Cecilia and Maddie, Gracie had felt human again and found she actually looked forward to a fun evening. After squeezing herself into Cecilia's spandex dress, she'd twisted and turned in the mirror and determined she looked pretty awesome. She'd walked down those stairs feeling kick-ass.

But then he'd frowned at her. And, if she was honest, it gave her the excuse she'd been looking for all day to bait him. Which didn't make any sense. She should be happy he'd started treating her like she was a regular person. Only, she wasn't, and she didn't know why. So she'd acted out and he'd given her exactly what she'd been looking for, and now she was more confused than ever.

She wished she'd never agreed to come for the weekend. She wanted to go home to Revival, curl up on her couch and watch bad TV in sweat pants.

She nibbled on her lower lip and shrugged sheepishly at her friends. "I'm sorry. I'll apologize."

Maddie nodded. "Thanks. You don't have to like him, just be cordial."

Gracie tried to smile, but it wobbled a bit at the corners. "I will."

Maddie and Cecilia shared a private glance, and Gracie was struck by how in sync they were. She used to bridge the gap between the two women, but they didn't need her anymore. They were bonded together, through friendship and family, in a way that would always exclude

Gracie. The petty thought brought tightness to her throat.

Maddie raised a brow and Cecilia shook her head. With a little shrug, Maddie nodded in affirmation and the silent conversation ended.

Gracie didn't have a clue what they'd just discussed. She placed a hand over her heart. "I'll apologize. Okay?"

Something shimmered in Cecilia's gaze. "We just want you to be happy."

Gracie's head snapped back. Where was this coming from? "I am happy. I said I was sorry. I said I'll apologize. What more do you want?"

Another glance between the sisters-in-law before Maddie said, "Nothing. It's all good. Let's have a fun time tonight. This is supposed to be a celebration."

Gracie straightened, smoothing down her dress. She would not be one of those selfish people who ruined her best friend's engagement. From this second on she'd be a joy to be around. "I promise I'll be good."

"Thank you," Cecilia said, but her expression didn't ease.

Maddie pointed to the door. "We should get back."

Gracie jutted her chin toward the stall. "You go on, I'll be there in a second."

Cecilia stepped forward and put a hand on her arm. "Are you okay?"

She would be, as soon as they left. She needed a moment to compose herself. She waved her hand at the door. "Yes, yes, now go before your Neanderthal fiancé comes looking for you and I get in more trouble."

"You sure?" Cecilia asked.

Gracie blew out a breath of exasperation. "For God's sake, Ce-ce, I'm just going to the bathroom."

"Okay," Cecilia said but didn't look appeased.

Thankfully they relented, leaving her alone. Gracie

took a deep breath and blew it out. She opened her purse and scrounged around for her makeup bag. She'd freshen up and put on her best smile. Even if it killed her she'd be on her best behavior and as warm as she could be with James. Once she got home, this odd unrest she felt about him would flitter away in the Revival wind. She'd bake her favorite salted caramel cupcakes and all would be right with the world.

She pushed her phone out of the way, and when it illuminated she saw she had a text from her brother.

She unlocked the screen and swiped the icons until she read the text message from Sam, who'd stayed back home an extra day to take care of his bar. **You okay?**

She smiled and some of the pressure in her chest eased. **I'm fine.**

A second later the phone rang and she shook her head, laughing. "I'm fine!"

"What happened?" Sam had a *gift*, as their momma used to call it, of sensing trouble. Being thicker than thieves, and still living together in the house their mom had left them, he had the annoying habit of knowing when she was distressed.

Gracie sighed. She could deny it, but there wasn't any point. Sam would guess anyway. "Nothing. I had a run-in with the professor and now everyone is mad at me. I'm hiding out in the bathroom."

"What'd you do?" Sam's amusement carried over the line.

She expelled a long breath, feeling lighter and more centered with every second she talked to him. She didn't understand how it worked, but Sam sometimes seemed to shift a person's emotions; a trait that served him well as the owner of a bar. He'd defused many bar fights without even raising his voice.

A chuckle bubbled up inside her for no particular reason. "Why do you think I did anything?"

"History."

"I might have been a little bitchy," she admitted. Sam wouldn't judge her. He was her family. The only family she had, and they stuck together.

"You need to stop this, Grace," he said, sounding like their mother.

"Yeah, yeah, I know. I promise I'll be nice."

"Good. I'll be there tomorrow so you won't be alone."

She blinked back the sudden swell of tears as he pinpointed in thirty seconds why she was distressed. She did feel alone. In the bedroom, as she'd gotten ready with Maddie and Cecilia, she'd managed to forget, but the incident with James brought it all back. She felt out of step with them.

She took a shaky breath. "I hate you."

Sam chuckled in that lazy way he had. "Everyone does. I'll see you tomorrow."

The idea of seeing him soothed her. "Thanks."

She hung up and looked at herself in the mirror. Her cheeks were stained with pink, her eyes a bit too bright, but other than that she appeared her regular old self.

It was time to face the music and eat some crow.

Even if it was like glass going down.

The trendy hotspot was packed, the din of the crowd an octave over reasonable. As Gracie walked through the restaurant on her way to the bar, where everyone was waiting, the energy crackled around her. Chicago had an electricity that couldn't be matched in Revival, where everything was lazy and serene and everyone knew everyone. In Revival, she couldn't sneeze without the whole town taking notice, but here, in this vast city with its skyscrapers and endless lakefront, a person could get lost. As much as she loved the small, cozy town she called home, at times the thought appealed to her.

A million years ago she'd dreamed of leaving Revival and moving to the big city, but then her mom had gotten sick with the cancer that would eventually take her life and Gracie couldn't bear to leave. After her mom died, Gracie hadn't wanted to leave Sam alone, and eventually the dreams faded until they were nothing but the memories of a young girl. Now, she no longer thought of leaving. Revival was home. Her rock.

She shook her head, ridding herself of the past and focusing on her immediate future. The bar was packed and she wormed her way through the crowd, searching for her friends. A man leered at her chest and licked his lips. *Ick.* She skirted away before he could get any ideas, turned and froze.

James stood there with her friends—dressed in his black pants and matching V-neck pullover—looking almost trendy with his hands shoved into his pockets. Tonight, he didn't look anything like the geek stereotype she'd boxed him into, but that's not what stopped her cold.

The woman he smiled down at did.

A tall, strikingly beautiful woman, with cool Grace Kelly blond hair and the poise of a dancer, spoke to James, her hand on his arm.

He threw his head back and laughed at whatever she said.

Gracie's stomach dropped.

The woman's chin tilted as she gazed at James adoringly.

"Gracie, over here," Maddie called, breaking her from her trance.

She squared her shoulders. Big deal. She didn't care if

he talked to a woman. Besides, it was probably nothing. Maybe a friend of Shane's and Cecilia's. And even if it was something, it didn't mean anything to Gracie.

James's dating life was none of her concern.

With purpose, she strolled across the space that separated her from the group, and James looked her way. His expression flickered, then smoothed back over.

When Gracie joined the group, Cecilia covered her arm with her hand. "Everything okay?"

"Of course," Gracie said, pushing her hair out of her eyes. Not willing to stand there like an idiot, she turned toward the woman with James and held out her hand. "I don't think we've met. I'm Gracie Roberts."

"Lindsey Lord." The woman shook her hand. Her fingers so delicate Gracie worried she'd crush them.

Gracie plastered on her best smile. "It's a pleasure to meet you. Are you joining us for dinner?"

Lindsey's hand fluttered to her décolletage and non-existent chest. The muscles of her shoulders were sinewy and supple, and as far as Gracie could see, the woman didn't have an ounce of fat on her. Gracie was positive the woman didn't eat cupcakes and hated her instantly on principle alone. "Goodness, no, I'm with people. But when I saw James I had to come and say hello." Voice cloying, she beamed at him, her teeth perfectly straight and impossibly white. "It's been far too long."

Lindsey was definitely flirting, quite overtly.

Not that Gracie cared; she was just surprised. Sure, he was cute. And, yes, he had a spectacular body, but he was hardly a rock star like Lindsey's gaze seemed to indicate.

Gracie assessed Lindsey Lord with a critical eye. She must like her men on the sedate side.

Which sucked for her, but had nothing to do with Gracie. A sting of pain radiated from her palms and she realized she was digging her nails into her skin. She relaxed her fingers.

The hostess came up and said to Shane, "Mr. Donovan, your table is ready."

Shane straightened, sliding his arm around Cecilia's waist, as he glanced back and forth between James and Lindsey.

What was that about?

James nodded. "Go ahead, I'll be there in a minute."

Shane frowned, obviously reluctant to leave his baby brother.

James's brow rose and he tilted his head toward the waiting hostess.

Cecilia elbowed him and Shane gave up, turning.

Maddie looked back over her shoulder as they started walking, and waved. "It was nice to see you again, Lindsey."

"You too," Lindsey said, her attention already returning to James.

Who was that woman? Why did the Donovans all know her?

As they were led through the crowded restaurant, Gracie trailed behind, unable to resist looking back. James didn't notice as he focused completely on Lindsey, smiling in a way he never smiled at Gracie.

Wait. Gracie blinked, her heart speeding up. Was she his girlfriend? Were they, like, a couple? But nobody had ever mentioned him having a girlfriend. Maddie had never mentioned it. Cecilia hadn't. God knew James had never said anything. Surely, at some point, *someone* would have said *something*. Gracie's mind searched frantically through a year's worth of conversation only to discover she hardly knew anything personal about the professor.

So it was possible.

But then why wasn't she joining them for dinner?

As soon as they'd sat down, Maddie worried at her bottom lip as she looked back to where James still stood. "I hope that's not trouble."

Gracie's ears perked up. What was this? She quelled the urge to twist around and check out what he was doing. She cursed her choice of a spot. Damn it. She couldn't see anything.

Shane peered over Gracie's shoulder to where his brother stood, and scowled.

What was going on? What was he frowning at? She gripped her menu. She had to know. Not because she cared, but because she was curious. She'd always been a curious person. Her momma had always said as much.

"I'm sure he'll be fine. That was a long time ago," Shane said.

Okay, that sounded like the past. But Gracie couldn't be sure with the way they'd looked at each other, with those sweet smiles. Or the way Lindsey fluttered her thick lashes at him. And the tilt of James's body into her frail frame.

Gracie needed to know what they were talking about right now. But she couldn't very well ask. She scanned the table and settled on her target. Mitch. After living next door to him for so many years in Revival, she'd been friends with him longer than anyone else at the table. She picked up her water glass, cleared her throat, and zeroed in on him. She narrowed her eyes, staring at him until he sensed her and glanced in her direction.

Ask what's going on. Ask what's going on. Ask what's going on. A frantic chant in her head.

Amber eyes dancing with amusement, he raised a brow. "What?"

Stupid man. She sighed and tilted her head fractionally at his wife.

Mitch stared at her for ten full seconds and then

comprehension dawned, lighting his expression. He poked Maddie's waist, and pointed in Gracie's direction. "Gracie wants to know what's going on."

The rat bastard. She huffed. "You're the worst friend ever."

With a sly smile, he shrugged. "Turnabout is fair play."

"What did I ever do to you?"

"Do you want a list?"

Since they'd known each other since childhood, when Mitch and Cecilia would come visit their grandparents in Revival every summer, Gracie wasn't surprised he had a standing list of grievances.

She shifted her attention toward Maddie. Cover blown, she might as well ask all the questions burning a hole in her gut. "Who is that woman?"

Maddie glanced around and leaned forward.

Gracie held her breath. It was his girlfriend. Gracie could feel it in her bones.

"Lindsey and James met in graduate school," Maddie said.

Gracie experienced a sinking in her stomach.

"They were together for five years. We thought they were going to get married, but then one day she wasn't with him for Sunday dinner," Maddie continued, ripping Gracie away from the questions racing through her head.

Gracie released her pent-up breath. Not a girlfriend. An *ex*-girlfriend. But, still, there were obviously feelings there. Or were there? She got along famously with Charlie. They even flirted sometimes. It was possible to have a good, nonsexual relationship with someone you used to sleep with. She was living proof of that.

But she didn't look at Charlie like she wanted to eat him for dinner.

Gracie blinked, realizing Maddie was still talking.

"We asked what happened, but all he would say was that they were no longer together. He refused to say why the relationship ended." She turned her extremely cute but worried face toward Shane. "Has he even seen her since then? Or is this the first time?"

Shane shrugged. "I have no idea. You know how he is."

Questions burned in Gracie's brain, but, afraid they'd tumble out and reveal her unnatural curiosity, she pressed her lips together and prayed Maddie would fill in the silence. When she didn't, Gracie coolly turned her attention to the menu. "Interesting."

"What's interesting?" James asked from behind her, making her jump, thus explaining why Maddie hadn't elaborated. He slid into the empty seat next to Gracie.

Silence filled the table as they all looked at him.

He raised a brow.

Gracie waited for Shane or Maddie to say something, but they didn't.

The silence grew.

"What's going on?" James asked, his tone filled with suspicion.

"Nothing," Maddie said, straightening in her chair.

More awkward silence.

Something broke inside Gracie and, per usual, her mouth ran away with her. "We were talking about you and your ex-girlfriend. They're worried you're going to freak out over seeing her."

The whole table gaped at her, and heat crawled up her neck. She tilted her chin and said before she put any thought into it, "And what kind of name is Lindsey Lord? Is she a stripper?"

James blinked at Gracie, a smile threatening at the corners of his mouth. He raised a brow. "Stripper?" The idea of the refined Lindsey circling a stripper pole was laughable. Lindsey was so far from anything resembling a porn star, the notion was preposterous. She was refined, highly intelligent, and very well respected in her field. "She's a physicist at the University of Chicago."

Gracie frowned and waved her hand through the air. "Same difference."

James laughed, and her eyes widened in surprise. "Hardly. But I can assure you I'm not about to freak out."

Shane drained half a glass of water before he said, "Yeah, you never do."

Maddie leaned forward, her expression concerned. "Do you want to talk about it?"

"There's nothing to talk about." James turned to his menu, hoping to close the subject. They'd assumed Lindsey had ended their relationship and left him heartbroken, and he'd never bothered to disabuse them of the notion. The truth was, he'd broken up with her and let people fill in the blanks as they chose. His rationale had been twofold: he'd wanted to protect her privacy, and it freed him from explaining his unexplainable actions.

After five years together, Lindsey had wanted to get engaged. It made sense. On paper, she'd been perfect for him. She was smart, beautiful, and accomplished. They had the same interests, same educational background, were both in academia, and had the same values and life goals. Lindsey was about as perfect for him as a woman could get, but something had been missing. Every time he'd planned on buying an engagement ring, he hadn't been able to walk into the store.

He'd searched his mind for what it was and couldn't come up with a sound justification for his apathy. The only thing he'd been able to pinpoint was that he'd never looked at her the way his dad had looked at his mom. An abstract reason, but true, nonetheless. His world had been pleasant when she'd been around. He'd enjoyed her company. But the sun didn't rise and fall because of her, and in the end, it wasn't enough.

No one had ever guessed he'd been the one to break her heart. She'd been devastated, he'd felt horrible, and letting people think she'd dumped him seemed the kind thing to do.

Despite what his family believed, he'd seen her numerous times since the breakup, although it had been a while. Not so long that he didn't recognize her flirting, or the way her lashes fluttered at him. If he chose, tonight after dinner, he could go to her house and she'd let him in. They'd go to bed and the sex would be great. They'd talk and laugh. Share stories about students and colleagues. Discuss papers they'd written and fall right back into the old rhythms of their relationship. But, in the morning, he still wouldn't look at her the right way, and he wouldn't be able to explain why, any better than the first time.

"Not true," Gracie said, stirring him from his thoughts. "You freaked out at me."

James turned to the woman who was equal parts nightmare and fantasy. "I think that's a bit of an exaggeration."

Gracie shook her head, her curls flying. "You were definitely mad."

"You provoked me." Mad wasn't the right word. She frustrated him. He'd never been attracted to someone he had nothing in common with. Who disliked him so intensely. How could he barely be in the same room with her without an argument, and still want her?

She sighed, a deep, resigned sound. "Yeah, I did and I'm sorry."

Surprise lit through him. Had he heard her right? From the corner of his vision he could see the two couples watching them with rapt attention. He shrugged. "I might have overreacted a little."

"I pushed," she said, a smile flirting over her lips. She tilted her head toward the couples. "Maybe, for the sake of the lovebirds, we could call a truce?"

It had been his goal all day, so why didn't it sit well with him? He nodded. "I'd like that."

Their gazes locked, and a glimmer of something passed between them, before she jerked her attention away and picked up her menu. "It's settled then. What's good here?"

As usual, everyone started talking at once.

James returned to his own menu, scanning the items, not really paying attention to the food or the conversation. Her desire to call a truce sat like a thorn in his side. He'd accomplished what he'd set out to do this morning, but at an unwelcome cost.

The truth.

A part of him liked how she baited him, because deep down he'd wanted to believe it meant something. When he'd stayed behind to talk to Lindsey, it hadn't been to catch up with her. He'd wanted to see if Gracie might get jealous.

Lindsey was a beautiful woman, and he couldn't deny he'd wanted Gracie to see that he wasn't quite the geek she thought he was. That, while she believed he sat in his basement playing *World of Warcraft*, in reality he was as capable as any other man of landing a pretty girl.

But, as with all his plans with Gracie, it had backfired. While she seemed interested in his relationship with Lindsey, and her barb about Lindsey's name rang with a hint of jealousy, she now wanted to drop the hostility. After being nice to Gracie all day, now that she'd met

Lindsey she wanted to call a truce. He pondered what it meant. Why did she have to be such a difficult read? He didn't have this kind of trouble with other women. In fairness, with another woman, he'd ask her to explain and expect a straightforward answer. An option not available to him and the vexing Gracie, where every conversation, no matter how simple, turned into a raging fight.

So, with direct communication off the table, he could only apply the Occam's razor principle to derive the most logical conclusion. Gracie, like him, wished he'd meet someone, thereby rendering their chemistry moot. Thus, when she met Lindsey, she'd determined James no longer posed a threat and she could therefore relax.

It was the simplest, most straightforward reason.

He should be happy about this turn of events. In fact, this worked in his favor, since they were as incompatible as two people could be. Even if attraction existed, there was no future there. The thought of all her chaos in his well-ordered life was enough to give him hives.

Now that things were settled he'd be able to have a nice, cordial relationship with her. He'd treat her like he treated his coworkers. Since she'd decided to stop baiting him, he, in turn, would stop thinking about her sassy mouth. He'd force himself to stop thinking about ways he could put all that energy she had to good use. Or what it would be like to—no, stop.

No traveling down that road. He'd spent years mastering the art of discipline, and he'd apply the same principles to his relationship with her.

Eventually his willpower would win. It always did.

Gracie had given up on sleep and crept downstairs to sit in the bay window of Shane and Cecilia's new house.

She hadn't wanted to stay, insisting that the couple should be alone on their first night, but they'd refused to listen. Seeing how Mitch and Maddie stayed as well, Gracie didn't have a great argument for going to a hotel.

She sighed. Her body was exhausted but her mind wouldn't let her rest, so here she was, in the dark, amidst half-empty boxes.

The city skyline was lit up, still awake and alive despite the late hour. Back home it would be pitch-black and dead silent, the sky filled with nothing but a million stars. She stared up into the sky, gray with light pollution, and missed the comfort back home.

Tonight had confused her. She'd kept her promise and been nice to James. Some of their antagonism seemed to have broken. She should be thankful. But she wasn't.

And the thing she hated most was that she couldn't stop thinking about him. She'd been lying in bed, staring at the newly painted ceiling, unable to stop replaying every interaction she'd had with him today. Sure, she focused on the things that annoyed her—like how he'd had ahi tuna for dinner and berries for dessert, while she'd gorged on molten lava cake—but she didn't like how she couldn't stop.

"I thought I heard you," Cecilia said, and Gracie about jumped out of her skin.

"Shit!" she exclaimed, looking over her shoulder. "You scared me."

"Sorry." Cecilia came over to the window seat alongside her. "Shane says he's going to put a bell on me so he knows I'm coming."

"I guess all those years of ballet make you sneaky," Gracie said, scooting into the corner to give her friend more room.

Cecilia laughed. "I guess so."

Gracie gave Cecilia a sly smirk. "Although, if Shane doesn't know you're coming, he's doing something wrong."

A wistful, love-soaked expression floated over Cecilia's face. "Nothing wrong there. The man is a deviant."

Not surprised at all, Gracie grinned. "You lucked out, Ce-ce. I wonder how the professor got so straitlaced."

She cringed. Why on earth had she brought him up?

Cecilia cocked her head to the side. "What makes you think James is straitlaced?"

She blew out a long breath. Stupid. "Please. Look at him. He's wound so tight he's bound to be a dud in the sack."

"His ex-girlfriend looked more than willing to take him back," Cecilia said.

Gracie shrugged, turning her attention to the window, silently cursing herself for bringing up James. The image of him smiling down at the pretty Lindsey irritated her in a way she refused to contemplate. "The skyline sure is pretty. So different from Revival, don't you think?"

Cecilia was silent for a long time before she sighed. "Gracie, why don't you just admit it?"

"Admit what?" Her heart rate kicked up a beat.

"You're attracted to James." Cecilia's words were blunt, hard blows to the chest.

Gracie's head snapped back and she scowled. "I am not!"

She wasn't. He bothered her. Everything about him irritated her. She scowled at Cecilia. "Don't confuse tension with attraction. It's not like you and Shane."

"But it is *something*. Come on, admit it. You don't think he's the least bit sexy?"

Gracie could only stare at her, openmouthed. "Of course not."

Yes, she conceded that he was quite good-looking,

and he looked pretty hot tonight, but he wasn't her type at all. And he was *not* sexy.

Cecilia shrugged. "I think you're lying to yourself. You like him, Gracie. You're just too stubborn to admit it."

"How could you possibly think that? Can you even imagine?"

"Let me ask you this: How long after meeting James did you break things off with Charlie?"

Gracie couldn't believe this. She shook her head. "They have nothing to do with each other. I broke things off with Charlie because I was tired of coasting. Things had gotten routine and comfortable. It's just coincidence the events coincided."

"Hmm . . ." Cecilia's voice trailed off, and she tucked her long legs underneath her.

"What?" Gracie asked, cringing at the defensiveness in her tone.

Cecilia smoothed down her tank top. "When's the last time you went on a date?"

Gracie blinked, then blinked again. "I went out with the new football coach."

"But you turned down a second date."

"So?"

"I'm just saying, you haven't gone out with anyone since you met James, and that seems a bit odd."

"I live in Revival, where I've known everyone since birth. New people are hard to come by, but I've dated plenty. I just haven't met anyone who interests me. Simple as that." Gracie watched the lights blinking on the top of the John Hancock building. There was no relationship between her dry spell and James. None at all. She'd never been great at commitment. Unfortunately, she was like her father that way.

"What about sex?" Cecilia continued her probing, looking for meanings where there weren't any.

"What's that?" Gracie laughed, meaning to sound breezy, but instead the sound came out a bit choked.

"You know Charlie would take care of any itch you have, and you've told me often enough he's great in bed, so what's stopping you?"

"Not James." Gracie frowned, blowing out a deep breath. "I don't want to fall into that pattern again. Is that so hard to understand?"

"Nope, not at all." Cecilia looked at her, her face soft in the lights of the window. So different from all the hardness she used to carry around with her. "I guess I'm wrong."

"You are." She was.

Gracie did not have the hots for the professor. She thought of the flare of awareness she'd experienced in the closet when he'd stood so close to her. The way she'd dug her nails into her palm when he'd smiled at his ex-girlfriend. The idea that kept slipping into her mind of them in bed together, maybe even right now.

No. She refused to even think about that. Absolutely refused.

Chapter Four

Gracie pulled up to the Donovan family's brick bungalow and turned off the ignition. The modest house was located in a tight-knit neighborhood on the South Side of Chicago and looked nearly identical to all the other bungalows lining the street, except for the brightly colored balloons next to the door.

She got out of the car and walked up the steps. Today's event was at Shannon Donovan's house. The mother of the groom had wanted a close-family-and-friends celebration before the official engagement party tonight. Gracie blew out a deep breath. Another day with the Donovan clan, and a new opportunity to change her ways with the professor.

As she'd been here before, she knocked on the door and then walked in.

An explosion was followed by a sound of rapid machine-gun fire, so loud it had to shake the plaster off the walls of the small foyer. Gracie peered into the small living room to find James playing a video game with a chubby, angel-faced boy around twelve or thirteen.

Neither of them glanced in her direction.

Controller in hand, James's attention was riveted on

the flat-screen television. The line of his jaw was hard, his cheekbones defined, as he concentrated on the game.

"Flank him. Go. Go. Go," James yelled, gesturing wildly with his controller.

Gracie had never seen him so animated before. The sight was riveting.

The boy's arms flailed as his thumbs frantically worked across the controller. "To your left."

One of the guys in military garb on the screen moved and James said, "You've got it, take the shot."

The other animated soldier dropped to one knee and shot, filling the screen with the splatter of blood and brains flying through the air before the screen cut to another scene.

"Yes!" The boy whooped, his face alight with the thrill of virtual victory.

"Did you see his head explode?" James grinned, leaning back on the floral brocade couch. The feminine fabric highlighted the masculinity of his face, the broadness of his shoulders in a black waffle-knit shirt.

Gracie couldn't help but be charmed at the excited expression the professor wore. She'd never seen him look so carefree or unreserved.

The boy looked at James with complete adoration, a sweet smile on his round face. "That was awesome."

Gracie stepped into the room and leaned against the doorframe, finally making her presence known so she wouldn't be caught gawking. "That was some impressive splatter."

They looked at her.

James's gaze flickered over her body. "Gracie."

She fought the urge to stiffen at his cool tone. It was a casual brunch, so she wore jeans and a black scoop-neck knit top that highlighted her blond hair and curves.

She'd made damn sure she looked good, covering the shadows under her eyes with concealer.

"Professor," she returned before beaming at the boy. His mouth hung open as he gaped at her. "Aren't you going to introduce me to your friend?"

James's mouth quirked as he noticed the boy's stunned expression. Gracie thought she detected an eye roll but she couldn't be sure.

James jostled the kid out of his daze and said, "Gracie Roberts, this is my cousin, Declan."

Gracie walked over and stuck out her hand. "It's a pleasure to meet you, Declan."

The boy turned scarlet as his sweaty palm slid into hers. "Thank you, ma'am."

Gracie waved. "Ha, *ma'am* makes me feel like I'm a hundred years old. Call me Gracie." She jutted her chin toward the television. "Nice shooting. Maybe later you can show me how it's done."

Declan flushed an even deeper shade of red, jerking his gaze toward the professor. "James did all the hard stuff."

Gracie shrugged. "From what I saw you delivered the kill shot."

James smiled at her, a real smile, one that flashed the mysterious dimple, and Gracie's heart gave a hard lurch. In a split second, like the sudden strike of lightning, she saw it. The sun streamed through the window, highlighting the gold in his hair, and she saw the man she'd been refusing to acknowledge since she'd met him. The one everyone else saw. The man Lindsey Lord looked at like a god and Cecilia thought sexy.

The man who called to some deep, secret place inside her. The attraction that pulled at her while she focused instead on all the things about him that irritated her.

The world swung and she blinked, taking a step back. Oh no.

The smile transformed into concern and he stood, walking toward her. "Are you okay?"

She nodded even as a swell of heat washed through her. *No. No. No.* Not him. Anyone but him. He was all wrong for her. He was her best friend's brother. He was secure and stable.

He was coming closer. Too close. Awareness flared, impossible to ignore.

He was going to touch her. A second later he gripped her arm and she gasped. "You're as white as a sheet."

A jolt of electricity shot up her arm. He was one of those solid-relationship guys who mowed the lawn and had five-year plans. She straightened and squared her shoulders. "I'm fine."

He didn't eat carbs! Or sugar! Flour was a part of her life. She was a *baker.*

His forehead creased. "Are you sure?"

"Yes," she said, her voice too breathless. He needed to stop touching her. She needed space to get a handle on this. She blurted the first thing that popped into her head. "I have the cake in my truck."

His hand dropped away and she could finally breathe. "I can go get it."

James's black shirt stretched over his broad chest. Her fingers twitched as a startling visual of tracing her hands over the lines of all those muscles filled her mind.

Oh no. Where was his geek-wear? She needed a pair of chinos, stat. She cleared her throat. "It's a two-man job; you'll need help."

He nodded. "Are you sure you're okay? You look a little shaky."

"I'm great. Just tired." Her gaze snagged on his mouth, his full mouth, but instead of focusing on what a horrible kisser he'd be, she could see it. Feel his mouth moving over hers. She sucked in a breath. "I'm used to sleeping in my own bed."

Expression filled with disbelief, he was clearly perplexed by her behavior. He started to say something, but Evan came in and his mouth snapped shut.

He stepped away.

Out of the corner of her vision, she saw James's face smooth over into the cool remoteness he always seemed to wear whenever she was around.

"There she is." Evan bounded over to her and swept her up in his powerful arms, giving her a big smacking kiss on the lips. "How's my favorite girl?"

Thankful for the distraction from her troubling thoughts, she laughed and swatted the pro football player and resident wild-child away, relaxing into the easy flirtation. "Ah, if only I could believe you, but after last week's game you told that pretty reporter with the red hair the same thing."

"But with you I mean it." Evan grinned down at her. At six-five he was built like a Greek god crossed with, well, a pro football player. With the Donovan family's green eyes and dark brown hair, he was about as gorgeous as a man could be. Considered one of the best wide receivers in the game, he was a media favorite, with all his crazy antics and a new supermodel every week.

He loved to flirt, and she flirted right back. "You're a liar, but I still love you."

Since they'd met he'd made it plenty clear he'd take her to bed without even the slightest encouragement. He'd whispered outrageous things in her ear. Hugged her. Teased her. They'd gotten drunk together on more than one occasion, and yet she'd never given him the opportunity to make a move. Why?

He was a hot-as-hell, wild, testosterone-soaked, NFL Pro Bowl-er. Women lined up for a chance to be in his

bed. So what the hell was wrong with her? Sure, it would
be a fling, because there's no way Evan was a settling-
down kind of guy, but he'd be the best kind of fling.
They'd have fantastic, sweaty sex and still be friends
the next morning. So why hadn't she jumped at the
chance to get between the sheets with the notorious
Evan Donovan?

She turned and her gaze collided with James's. His
arms were crossed, his expression had turned stormy,
and his jaw was firmed into a hard line.

Heat spiked across her skin and her belly jumped.
Cecilia was right.

It was because of *him*.

It was one of those crisp, sunny, early fall days and
they'd been able to sit outside instead of being piled
into his family's bungalow. James sat on the back stoop
with his thirteen-year-old cousin Declan and watched
the intense game of half-court basketball going on in the
alley.

Shane passed the ball to their cousin Pat, teenage super-
star and Declan's older brother. Pat swung around one
of his cousins and slam-dunked the ball, hanging on to
the rim attached to the two-car garage, in exaggerated
showmanship. The two brothers couldn't be more opposite. James had declined playing in favor of sitting
with Declan. Out of all his family members, this barely
teenage cousin was the most like him, and James understood all too well how it felt not to be athletic in a family
full of sports fanatics.

Even now, with all his exercise and training, James
wasn't actually *athletic*; he was merely in excellent shape.
There was a difference. He could play a decent game of
basketball but only because he'd been forced to play

with his brothers growing up. He wasn't good, merely passable.

Of course, now he could outrun both Shane and Evan. But that was just putting one foot in front of the other; it took practice, not skill.

Declan shifted on the step and James looked at him, realizing he wasn't watching the game. His cousin stared wistfully at Gracie, who sat with a group of the girls at a round picnic table. A small smile lifted the corners of James's mouth. Gorgeous blondes were apparently another thing they had in common. James nudged him and tilted his head toward Gracie. "She's probably a little too old for you."

The boy turned a particularly bright shade of crimson and he scuffed the toe of his black Converse on the step. "Is she your girlfriend?"

James had been taking a sip of his iced tea, and the question was so startling the liquid went down the wrong pipe, and he started to choke. He coughed, shaking his head as a strangled laugh clogged his throat. When he was finally able to speak, he asked, "Where would you get that idea?"

Declan shrugged. "She's always looking at you."

James frowned. While Gracie had acted strangely today, he was sure it didn't relate to him. "I think you're mistaken."

"Dude, she looks at you, like, all the time," Declan said.

James glanced over at her, but her attention was on the table, not on him.

He didn't see the point in arguing when the obvious sat right in front of them. "Well, she's not my girlfriend. She lives next door to Mitch and Maddie down in Revival."

"You should go for her," Declan said, his voice ringing

with all the wisdom of a teenager. "If a girl like her looked at me that way, I'd go for her."

James squinted back at the table of women. This time Gracie was looking his way.

Their gazes met.

Locked.

Held.

She jerked her attention away.

James rubbed his jaw. What in the hell was going on? Since she'd gotten here she'd been acting strange, almost jittery, but he couldn't imagine what that had to do with him. Before he could contemplate the situation further, Peter, Declan's father, came over and pointed toward the basketball court. "Why don't you go out there and play?"

Beside James, Declan stiffened. "I don't like basketball."

Peter shook his head, frowning. "Come on, it will do you some good. Get you away from those video games."

James's hand tightened on his iced tea glass. This was a common occurrence, and unfortunately it prompted a flashback to his own childhood. He remembered the awkwardness and embarrassment too well to be remotely objective.

"Dad," Declan said, his tone taking on a whine, "I don't like sports. I'm not good at them."

"How are you going to get good if you sit on your butt all the time playing video games?" his father asked, exasperated.

James understood his uncle's good intentions. Declan was overweight, didn't get enough exercise, and probably ate nothing but junk food. He also had the pasty look of the die-hard gamer. In Declan's dad's mind, playing sports was a way to get his son to exercise. A tactic James had been subjected to a thousand times growing up. What Uncle Peter didn't understand, considering he'd been captain of the football team in high school, was that those comments only increased the kid's awkwardness and insecurity. The more he pushed Declan, the less inclined he'd be to play anything. And worse, it plummeted his self-esteem into the toilet.

Unable to keep his mouth shut, James jostled his younger cousin. "I'd rather be dead than play basketball. Never saw the point of all that running around just to throw a ball into a tiny hoop."

Declan's expression flashed with gratitude and relief, only to cloud a moment later when his dad said, "Yeah, but look at James. He used to be just like you. Take a lesson from him."

"He's fine," James said, his tone flat. Embarrassing the hell out of the kid wouldn't help matters. If Peter was smart, he'd do what James did. At least once a month, he took Declan out and made sure he got active in things James knew he enjoyed. He didn't force him to play the sports he hated, and Declan never once complained about having to use his muscles.

"All I'm saying is it wouldn't kill you to play a little basketball," Peter insisted.

James's jaw hardened.

"Sorry to interrupt," Gracie said from behind Peter, the distinct purr in her voice that meant she was about to manipulate someone. "But earlier Declan promised to show me how to play *Halo*." She beamed at Peter, her smile so dazzling it was blinding. "You don't mind, do you?"

If he didn't know she'd scratch his eyes out, James would have kissed her on the spot.

Peter's attention dropped to Gracie's chest, stretching the confines of her fitted top, and coughed. "Um . . . no, of course not."

Gracie grinned at Declan. "Basketball bores me to

tears, too. I mean, I'd much rather kill things with a sniper rifle, wouldn't you?"

Declan grinned back, the worship written across his face.

Bottom lip puffed out in a pout, Gracie fluttered her lashes at Uncle Peter, who looked a little stunned. "I hope you don't mind, but I've been stuck on level thirty, for like, forever. Declan promised he'd help me beat it."

Unable to contain his wide smile, James shook his head. Right at this second he would have done anything for Gracie. She'd made a kid who desperately needed a boost of confidence feel like a god.

"Sure, go ahead, son." Peter gave Gracie a long, perplexed look, then walked away.

Declan jumped up and waved her over. "Come on, Gracie."

James pointed toward the back door. "Go set it up; she'll be there in a minute."

Declan ran into the house with surprising speed, probably expending more energy in that brief minute than he had all day. When the door shut, James turned back to Gracie and stood, then walked down the couple steps to stand at her level. "Thank you."

She blinked, and a faint pink stained her cheeks. "You seemed on the verge of losing your temper."

"I was." James was surprised she'd noticed, until he remembered Declan's assertion that she watched him.

The question was, why? Was she plotting his murder?

She flashed a smile, a real one this time instead of the sex kitten one she'd used to distract Peter. "I thought maybe I'd come to the rescue. You were already mad last night; we can't have you go two days in a row with outbursts."

He narrowed his eyes, trying to read her. What was going on in that head of hers? "Last night was only a minor slip."

Her head tilted to the side and she swallowed. "I seem to bring out the worst in you."

The conversation was filled with tension. Something had changed between them, but he didn't know if it was for the better. On the surface, they were being nicer today than in their whole acquaintance, but there was a subtle awareness that hadn't been there before. Or maybe they were too accustomed to spitting nails at each other and this awkwardness was all they could hope for.

Blue eyes wide, she bit her bottom lip, sucking it between her white teeth. Illicit images of her down on her knees, looking up at him, filled his mind. He gritted his teeth, willing the wayward thoughts away. He said carefully, "I don't know about that."

She sucked in a harsh little breath, then pointed toward the back door. "I should go in."

He studied her face but could read nothing. He nodded. "Sure. Thanks again."

"My pleasure."

Neither moved.

Their gazes held.

Tension thickened the air.

She cleared her throat. "Um . . . see ya."

He wanted to press. To ask her what she was thinking, but didn't. Maybe later, after he had more time to think. "You will. See me later, that is."

"Right," she said, turning to go into the house.

When she hit the second step he called after her. "Gracie?"

She froze and looked back over her shoulder.

The sunlight hit her hair, casting her in its golden glow, making her absolutely breathtaking. "Would you do me a favor?"

"What's that?" She turned to face him.

He smiled, hoping to put her at ease, and shoved his

hands into his pockets. "Don't make Declan fall in love with you. He's young and I'm not sure he can take it."

Slowly, she nodded. "Sure."

Not quite the sassy retort he'd expected. He followed her up the steps.

Her gaze roamed over his chest, and her breath hitched just the tiniest bit. "I've got to go play some *Halo.*"

This was definitely awareness. "Gracie."

"What?"

He smiled. "It's *Call of Duty.*"

She squared her shoulders. "Huh?"

"The game you're ready to play, it's called *Call of Duty.*"

"Oh, okay." Then she turned and practically ran into the house.

He could only stare after her as the door slammed shut, wondering what to do about this strange turn of events.

Chapter Five

The engagement party was in full swing and Shane and Cecilia glowed with happiness. The rooftop restaurant they'd rented out had floor-to-ceiling windows with spectacular views of the lake and Navy Pier. As this was a party for Chicago's power couple, the weather cooperated so guests could enjoy the expansive balcony and watch the weekend fireworks over the water. The venue and view was spectacular, and Gracie supposed it came with the territory when a corporate mogul marries the daughter of a senator.

Everything was perfect. Gracie couldn't be happier for them, but she also couldn't wait for the night to be over. While the guests filed in at a seemingly endless pace, she stood at the table that held the cake she'd made, fussing with the flowers and placement of the candles, even though they were already flawless. Normally she was a social butterfly, but she couldn't work up the energy tonight, and adjusting the decorations gave her something to do with her restless hands.

All day she'd been off-balance. Cecilia had asked her what was wrong. So had Maddie. Mitch. Shane. Evan. Even Maddie's childhood friends, Penelope and Sophie, had asked. The only person who hadn't asked was Sam, but that was only because he already knew. She tried to talk herself into acting normal, but now that she'd discovered the truth, she had no idea how. She'd avoided James like the plague because every time he'd gotten within two feet she'd started blushing like an awkward teenager. She could barely even talk to him. Ironically, she couldn't stop watching him, her changed perspective casting him in a new light. He'd caught her more times than she cared to count and the tension grew with every long-held, questioning stare.

"You've outdone yourself," a deep, smooth voice she recognized said from behind her.

Thank God, she finally had a distraction. She looked over one bare shoulder at Charlie Radcliffe: Revival sheriff, best buddy, and former friend-with-benefits. Per usual, with his black hair and midnight eyes he looked gorgeous. Charlie was the very definition of tall, dark, and dangerous, but as beautiful as he was to look at, he no longer made her stomach jump. She smiled, then turned back to admire her handiwork. "Thanks, I'm happy with it."

An understatement. She was thrilled with how the cake had come out. A gorgeous three-tiered, Tiffany blue and black creation with an elaborate flower design that was both sophisticated and modern. The hours she'd spent perfecting the cake were worth it, because it was the most beautiful thing she'd ever made.

Charlie slid an arm around her waist and she leaned into his strong frame, relaxing a little just being in his company. He kissed her temple. "I always said you were an artist."

She pulled away and looked up at him. "Thanks. And how are you? I feel like I haven't seen you in a year."

It had only been a couple of days, but home seemed a million miles away.

He grinned and tucked a lock of hair behind her ear. "I saw you last week when we played cards. You kicked my ass and stole all my money. I remember it vividly."

She laughed and smoothed down the fabric of her red dress. A strapless number that hugged her curves in all the right places and ended at her knees. "That's right. My winnings bought me this dress."

"Then it was worth it," he said, his gaze traveling down her body. It was a familiar, flirty look, the kind they shared frequently. Once upon a time it would have meant something sexual, but these days it was pure comfort.

She sighed, a bit wistful it hadn't been enough. Unlike the professor, Charlie was exactly her type. They had amazing sex, and they'd always had fun, which suited her perfectly. Everything between them had been pure ease, but toward the end it had stopped being enough. At the time, she'd believed it was because she wanted what Mitch and Maddie, and now Shane and Cecilia had, but after she'd rejected enough guys she'd come to the conclusion that maybe she wasn't cut out for long-term commitment. Once her relationships started heading in that direction, she lost interest.

Unbidden, her attention drifted to James to find him watching her. Standing in a group that included his brothers, she saw only him in his white fitted dress shirt rolled up to his elbows, and slate-colored flat-front pants.

Their eyes locked.

Held.

A flush spread over her chest, infuriating her.

His gaze drifted over her body, traveling down, then up, before lingering at her mouth.

Stomach jumping, she sucked in a breath.

Attention on her, he took a drink of his wine, looking at her from over the glass the whole time.

It had been like this all day. Thick silences. Held glances.

They hadn't fought. Other than that moment on the steps, they'd barely spoken. But these looks had set her on fire.

She bit her bottom lip.

She needed to stop.

She released the air pent up in her lungs and put a hand over her fluttering stomach. With a force of will, she turned away to find Charlie studying her with that cop's expression he wore.

Busted.

"What?" She knew right away she'd come off as defensive and far too obvious.

He smiled. "Took you long enough. I was beginning to think you'd never figure it out."

"I have no idea what you mean." She straightened her spine.

"Come on, let's go." Charlie took her hand and pulled her toward the outdoor veranda already crowded with people. "We'll get you some fresh air."

Resisting the urge to look over her shoulder at the man who plagued her thoughts, she let Charlie drag her outside. The cool air washed over her hot cheeks, but instead of calming her, it made her more aware that her skin burned for the professor.

Without a word, they worked their way through the people until they stood next to the balcony railing. She blew out a long breath as they looked out over the lake in silence.

Finally Charlie said, "You'd don't get this view in Revival."

"No, you don't." She pointed up at the night sky. "But you don't get the same stars here."

He followed her gaze. "True."

On the pier, the Ferris wheel spun in slow rotation, the

lights glittering. Not wanting to think anymore about James, she focused on the man next to her. Better to probe his secrets than hers. "Do you miss Chicago?"

His shoulders stiffened as they always did whenever she asked him about his past. "Sometimes, although I traveled so much I'm not sure it ever seemed like home."

Once upon a time Charlie had been with the FBI. When he quit he'd followed Mitch, his childhood friend, to Revival and joined the small police department. A year later when the old sheriff had retired, he'd been elected to the position he'd held ever since. In all the years they'd slept together, Charlie had never spoken of his reasons for leaving the bureau, no matter how much Gracie pried.

She put her hands on the rail, the cold metal against her fingers, steadying her. "Are you ever going to tell me why you left?"

"It doesn't matter," he said, stubborn as ever. "So when did you figure it out?"

She'd asked one question too many and now the topic was back on her. She evaded. "Figure what out?"

"That all that snarling you do at the professor is really fear?"

Her brows slammed together and she swung on him. "I am not afraid! He's the most harmless man I ever met."

Charlie snorted. "Hardly."

She bit her bottom lip to keep the rash words from flying out of her mouth. She needed to play this cool. She waved a hand and put on her most breezy smile. "Please, you're delusional. Can you even imagine?"

Charlie's eyes narrowed. "Yeah, I can, quite easily."

"That's ridiculous. We're totally incompatible." Okay, so she realized she harbored some sort of feelings for the guy, but that didn't change the fundamental truth.

He was the exact opposite of the kind of man she wanted. He wasn't wild or spontaneous. He cared about propriety. He was overly controlled. Intellectual. Analytical. Logical. A fitness addict, a health-food freak. And a hundred other things she didn't want.

She couldn't sleep with him. Besides Sam, her friends were the closest she had to family. She couldn't risk ruining her relationship with them when she knew perfectly well things would never work out with James.

Charlie shook his head and the wind blew through his dark hair. "Still doesn't change the fact that our days were numbered after he showed up."

She planted her hands on her hips. "He has nothing to do with us."

He smiled at her, trailing a finger down her cheek. "I know your reasons and you were right. We had great chemistry, but we've always been more friends than anything else." He smoothed her hair away from her face again. "You deserve what they have, Gracie. I want you to have it."

Something deflated inside her and she leaned into his strong chest. A moment later he wrapped his arms around her. She sighed, taking comfort in his warmth. "You know I'm not like that. Did I ever pressure you for commitment?"

Charlie rubbed her back. "Not even once, but that doesn't mean you shouldn't get what you deserve."

She didn't know what to say to that, so she rose to her tippy toes and kissed him on the cheek. "You're a good friend."

"You too, honey." He winked at her. "I'm not going to lie though, I still miss the sex."

She laughed and swatted his arm. "I'm not going to tell Felicia Hayes you said that."

He had the good grace to look chagrined. "You know about that, huh?"

"Duh, we live in Revival."

"Were you jealous?" He gave her a wicked grin.

"Did you want me to be?"

He held his thumb and forefinger an inch apart. "Maybe a little bit."

"I was, a little." It was the truth. While he'd never brought the other woman around, when Mary Beth Crowley, head of the junior league and local gossip-monger, had told Gracie, she'd experienced a twinge of remorse. She tilted her head. "I didn't know you thought that about the professor."

"Honey, I knew the second you started arguing with him that we were over."

"That's the stupidest thing I ever heard."

He laughed, shaking his head. "You're so clueless."

"I most certainly am not!"

He put his hand on her chin, and gave her a gentle smile. "Gracie, in the time I've known you there hasn't been a member of the male population you haven't flirted with. Old and young alike. As far as I can tell, James Donovan is the one exception to the rule. I don't need to be an ace detective to connect the dots."

She lowered her gaze and sighed. "I didn't connect the dots."

"That's because you're stubborn and never ran across a guy who threatened you."

"He doesn't threaten me," she shot back, said stubbornness rearing its ugly head.

He grabbed her hand. "Come on, let's go back in."

"Hey, are *you* jealous?"

He grinned. "Hell, yes."

Laughing, she bumped her hip into his as they started walking toward the door. As soon as she entered the crowded room, her gaze skipped around, searching until she landed on James.

He talked to two women. A pretty, long, lean brunette and a cute strawberry blonde. The redhead said something and he threw back his head and laughed.

An image of reaching for him and licking his throat filled her mind. What would all those muscles feel like under her tongue? She breathed out an exasperated sigh. She had to get this under control. She needed to remember nothing had changed.

He was still the wrong man for her.

All the noise, combined with the sudden shift in his relationship with Gracie, had made James's head ache. Things had gotten increasingly strange between them as the day wore on. She hadn't snapped at him. Or rolled her eyes. Instead, she kept looking at him. They'd exchanged long, lingering looks, heavy with portent and ripe with sex.

As the day wore on he'd grown increasingly bold, letting his gaze roam over her body, pause on her mouth. He'd watched as her fingers played over her throat, as her tongue flicked over her lips.

And when she'd gone out on that balcony with Charlie, an irrational, possessive urge to stop her about burned a hole in his gut.

The illogical emotion irritated him. She wasn't his. And never would be. Now, if he could figure out a way to stop obsessing over her, he'd be all set.

Needing a break from the party, he weaved his way through the restaurant and out into the quieter hallway. He breathed a sigh of relief as the noise buzzing in his head quieted.

"James," his great aunt Belinda, on his father's side, called from down the hall. She raised a hand and walked toward him as fast as her eighty-five-year-old legs would carry her.

Unfortunately for James, she was surprisingly quick. He waved at her, and being a bad nephew, veered down a long corridor leading to the elevators.

She called after him, "James. Oh, James, dear."

The old woman had a slight case of dementia that was acting up this evening. No matter how many times he told her he was a PhD, not an MD, she kept getting confused. Thirty minutes ago she'd cornered him to discuss her bunions. God only knew what she'd bring up next, and James didn't intend to wait around to find out.

"Be right back, Auntie." He disappeared around the corner, jogged to the exit sign, and slipped through the door before she rounded the corner.

He stepped into the stairwell and froze in surprise.

Gracie sat on the steps, her head in her hands. She lifted her face and James frowned at the faint shadows under her lashes.

She blew out a long breath.

The door closed with a resounding thud.

She was as gorgeous as ever and made his throat go dry.

Their gazes locked, then slid away.

"Are you following me?" She shifted and crossed her legs, smoothing the wrinkles from the clingy fabric.

A sudden urge came over him to slide his hands up her dress to stroke across her thighs. To spread her legs, fall to his knees on the step below her and scrape his teeth along her skin. He pressed against the door, the cool metal seeping through his dress shirt and bringing him back to the subject at hand. "I'm hiding from my great aunt."

"Why's that?"

"Shane called me *doctor* and now she thinks I'm, well, a doctor." He slid his hands into his pockets, fingering the sharp edge of his keys. "She has a list of ailments I definitely don't want to discuss."

Gracie's gorgeous lips tilted slightly at the corners.

"What are you hiding from?" he asked.

She bit her bottom lip. "Why do you think I'm hiding?"

They were alone. For the second time in twenty-four hours. The small space was filled with the tension that had plagued them all day. He shrugged. "Since I've known you, I've never seen you be anything but the life of the party."

She stared at him for several long moments before she finally tilted her head to the side, sending her wild mane of curls tumbling over her shoulder. "What did Declan's dad mean when he said you used to be like him?"

Out of all the things she could have asked him, this was the last thing he expected. He paused; this wasn't something he liked to discuss. He pointed to the spot on the stairs next to her. "May I?"

Her throat worked as she swallowed hard before nodding. "It's a free country."

Maybe he'd been wrong before. Maybe it was time to stop avoiding the situation. Maybe he needed to start applying the same principles with her that he utilized in his relationships with other women.

He'd been playing her game since he'd met her, but maybe it was time to stop. "What's changed since yesterday?"

It was the type of direct question he would have asked any woman. He didn't do well with hints and suggestions, instead preferring direct communication.

She started, as though he'd slapped her. She shook her head. "Nothing. Nothing at all."

He raised a brow. "Really? Because you haven't called

me a geek in the last twenty-four hours, and I'm sure that's a new record."

Her knuckles whitened as she clasped her hands tighter. "I'm abiding by our agreement to call a truce."

He dropped his attention to her mouth, lingering there longer than was polite. "You didn't make any sarcastic comments when I passed on dessert at my mother's."

Her pink tongue snuck out to swipe along her bottom lip. "It's your body. What do I care if you treat it like a temple?"

He chuckled, and her blue eyes darkened as she crossed and recrossed her legs. He grinned. "I ran ten miles today."

Her shoulders straightened and her expression flashed with her customary fire. "That's disgusting. You're sick in the head."

He laughed, and straightening from his position against the wall, took a step toward her.

She sucked in a breath. "What are you doing?"

He gestured to the space next to her. "I'm sitting down."

Another faint flush stained her cheeks. "Oh . . . okay."

He took a seat on the step and his thigh brushed hers. She tensed, but instead of giving her space, he decided not to move.

She didn't shift away, but he suspected that was more pride than instinct, because every muscle in her body seemed taut.

She watched him defiantly, a challenge in her eyes, but her chest moved in shallow, rapid breaths.

He could kiss her and she'd let him. The tension was so off the charts, all hell would probably break loose. The image was all too vivid and he pushed it away. Sex would not solve anything. If she was an ordinary woman maybe he could let passion take over, but that wasn't possible. Gracie's life was too intertwined with his own.

But what they were doing wasn't working, and someone needed to be the logical one in their non-relationship. He placed his elbows on his knees and laced his fingers together. "I'm having a difficult time finding my way in this truce of ours."

"What do you mean?"

He looked at her, but she stared down at her tan heels as though they were the most fascinating shoes she'd ever seen. In a soft voice, he said, "I don't want to fight with you anymore."

Her throat worked as she swallowed. "Me either."

He opted for as honest as he could manage at the moment. "But I don't know how to be friends with you either."

She glanced at him before looking away. "What does it matter if we like each other?"

"We'll be seeing each other for years to come. Wouldn't you prefer they weren't filled with animosity?"

She nodded. "Yeah, I would."

"So we want the same thing?"

"Yes." Next to him, her thigh muscle was rigid. He resisted the urge to stroke her leg and soothe all that tension obviously beating away inside her. "Have any ideas on how to be friends?"

The laughter that bubbled from her seemed to surprise her. "Not a one."

Their eyes met, and everything stilled between them.

It was right there, hovering, and he could practically feel his lips on hers. But he didn't take the opportunity. Instead he said, in a voice far too filled with smoke and desire, "I've never made you laugh before. I like it."

She yanked her attention away, focusing on the door

that led back to the party. "We should go back to the party."

"We should."

Neither of them moved.

Along the hard muscles of his thigh, her softness pressed against him. His fingers tightened as he fought the urges pounding away inside him.

They sat like that, thigh to thigh, breathing jerky and uneven, shoulders touching, for so long he finally understood the expression "cut the tension with a knife." The air between them was sharp, suspended, as unspoken desire, long checked, roared to greedy, demanding life.

When he could stand it no more, he stood and turned to face her.

She looked at him, her blue eyes hungry and confused, mirroring his own knotted emotions. He put his hands in his pockets. "I don't want to argue anymore."

"I know. Me either." She licked her lips. "We'll have to figure the rest out."

"I hope so."

"Other people seem to like you, so I'm sure I'll get the hang of it one day." She smiled, and it dazzled him just like it dazzled everyone else.

Christ.

He cleared his throat. "Enjoy the rest of the party."

"You too."

They got caught in another long, tangled look that, in the heat department, could rival any sex he'd ever had.

And, just like that, he understood.

The animosity. The constant arguing. The baiting. He'd assumed it was annoyance due to their many differences and incompatible personalities and the pesky attraction that lurked between them. But he'd been wrong. It was more than mere attraction; the chemistry was powerful, almost tangible. Unlike anything he'd ever experienced before.

It defied reason and logic.

His gaze dipped to her lush, red mouth, already wet, parted, and waiting for him. Before insanity could consume him, he took the only reasonable path available, and got the hell out of there.

Chapter Six

The click of the heavy door reverberated in Gracie's ears as James left without a backward glance. Without the warm press of his body next to her, the cold concrete seeped through the thin fabric of her dress, making her aware of just how hot her skin was. She blinked at the gray landing.

What was *that*?

They'd been making an effort. Had gone an entire conversation without snapping, but at what cost? Without the animosity, the sexual tension between them was off the charts. Sitting there next to him had made her so hot, at one point she thought she might spontaneously combust.

She sucked in a breath and blew it out with a long exhale. She couldn't be his friend. All her normal interactions with men didn't apply. She couldn't flirt outrageously.

She remembered when she'd first met Charlie. As soon as they'd laid eyes on each other, Gracie had known it was on. They'd circled each other, their innuendos increasingly bold, until she'd plopped herself into his lap and whispered an invitation that would make Mae West proud. They'd been in bed about thirty seconds later.

She tried to envision employing the same tactics with James and cringed, unable to picture it. She couldn't act like that with him.

This was James. Even with the heat in his evergreen eyes that made her question everything she'd ever believed about him, she couldn't imagine it.

The door opened and she swelled with hope that James had come back to finish what they'd started. How had this happened? Was it only yesterday that she'd been content and secure in their antagonism?

A second later she deflated when her brother stood in the doorway. He flashed his trademark lazy smile. "I thought I'd find you here."

Back home he wore nothing but jeans and T-shirts, but tonight he was quite handsome in black pants and a French-blue dress shirt. She put on her brightest, happiest expression. "Need a break from all the fawning women?"

As their momma had always said, he had the face of an angel but the devil in his eyes, and women itched to get under his good-natured facade. They never did, but it wasn't from lack of trying.

Sam plopped himself down on the steps next to her. "What are you hiding from? It's not like you to slink away by yourself."

She shrugged. "It's been a long weekend and the crowd is getting to me. I'm ready to go home."

"Sounds plausible," he said, voice a slow drawl. "Now tell me the truth."

Shoulders sagging, she sighed. "Isn't being tired enough?"

"Sure, if it was true. But I think you finally figured out that you have the hots for the professor, and you're not happy about it," he said, his tone matter-of-fact.

She wrinkled her nose, shaking her head. God, it sounded worse than she'd feared. "I don't want to talk about it."

Sam chuckled and swung his arm around her shoulders, pulling her close and giving her a noogie. She swatted him away. "Hey! Watch the hair."

"There's not a damn thing I can do to mess up that mop of yours." He leaned back, resting his elbows on the steps behind them.

Needing to change the subject, she focused on their genetic disparity. She poked his ridiculously flat stomach. "Do you know how unfair it is that you got the thin genes?"

He rolled his eyes. "Don't play that card with me. So what are you going to do about it?"

"Do about it?" Maybe if they didn't speak his name she could pretend they were discussing a different man. "There's nothing to be done. We're hardly compatible."

Sam straightened, scrubbing a hand over his blond stubble. "You'll feel better if you take some action."

"Like what?" James would be in her life forever. It wasn't as easy as just sleeping with him. As much as she hated to admit it, the idea of him bringing someone like Lindsey Lord to Thanksgiving dinner was like a jab to the stomach. They'd never even kissed and she was already jealous of the shadow woman sure to be sitting across from her one day. She gritted her teeth.

She wasn't even a jealous person.

Sam shrugged. "I'm not sure, but I know you. And you'll feel better if you stop stewing. You never were a good stewer."

Gracie couldn't see a solution. She blew out a long breath.

Sam bumped her shoulder, and pointed toward the door. "We should go back to the party."

She sighed. "Oh, all right."

Two minutes later they stood talking to Shane and Cecilia, but Gracie was already distracted, searching the crowd for James.

Damn it.

In a blink of an eye he'd become her center of focus. Which was crazy, but she found herself unable to stop. She bit her bottom lip when she spotted him across the room, talking to Charlie, of all people. They were locked in some sort of discussion.

Well, now, wasn't that every girl's fantasy come to life. The cop and the professor. All that stern authority. The hard, measured stares. She shivered. How many of James's female students had fantasies about him? Pictured him turning all that careful control on them?

Throat dry, Gracie swallowed hard.

Charlie nodded his dark head in agreement to something James said, and then laughed. Were they talking about her? Probably not.

Unobserved, she could drink James in, following the lines of his broad shoulders, the lean back, and flat abdomen.

"Excuse me," a man said.

She jerked her attention back to the conversation to find Sam, Shane, Cecilia, and an older man she didn't recognize all staring at her. She straightened, ignoring the heat filling her cheeks. "I'm sorry."

The unnamed man held up a piece of cake. "Did I hear Cecilia correctly that you made this cake?"

Gracie cast a questioning glance at Cecilia, who nodded. She turned back to the man. "Yes, I did."

"This is the best cake I've ever had." He took another bite as though to emphasize his point.

She never got tired of compliments about her baking, especially considering she was self-taught. When she'd been younger she'd had dreams of going to pastry school, but she'd never had the chance. She smiled broadly. "Thank you. I'm so glad you're enjoying it." She held out her arms, presenting her friend. "You can thank Ce-ce. It's her favorite."

Cecilia shook her head. "I picked the flavor, the rest is on you."

The man juggled his plate into one hand before reaching into his pocket to pull out a business card. "I'm Ron Sorenson. My daughter is turning sixteen and I'd like to talk to you about doing a cake for her birthday party."

"Gracie Roberts." She took the offered card, running her finger along the edge, her heart swelling with pride. "Thank you, that's a lovely offer, but I don't live in Chicago."

"I don't care," the man said, a determined expression sliding over his face. "I'll pay extra for the delivery. My wife insisted I find out who you were and demand your services." He smiled and gave her a wink. "She's not a woman you say no to."

Gracie laughed, slipping the card into her small purse. "I'm sure we could work something out. How about I give you a call on Monday to discuss the details?"

"Wonderful." He took another bite of the white raspberry cake and his eyeballs practically rolled in pleasure. He turned to Shane and Cecilia. "You're lucky to have found such a gem."

Cecilia nodded, looking sophisticated and elegant in a shimmery blue-white dress, her hair piled on top of her head. "We love her too, and not just for her baked goods."

"Thank you," Gracie said, smiling. "My momma taught me everything I know."

"You're not professionally trained?" Ron asked.

It was one of her biggest regrets, but such was life. She'd made her choices and wouldn't change a second of the time she'd spent with her mom. "I suppose that depends on your definition of trained. But I didn't go to culinary school. I've always done my own thing."

"You do it quite well." He pointed to her purse. "Don't forget Monday."

"I won't."

He walked away and Gracie turned to Shane and Cecilia. "Ha. Look at that. Knowing you guys is paying off already."

Cecilia pointed after the man. "Do you know who that is?"

"It's Ron Sorenson," Gracie quipped.

Shane slid his hand to rest on Cecilia's hip. "He's the mayor's chief of staff."

"Oh, well, that's fun." Gracie got the impression she was supposed to be impressed, but, knowing little about Chicago politics, his name didn't have much impact. "I promise to make his daughter a birthday cake she'll never forget."

Cecilia shook her head. "You don't understand. His daughter's sweet sixteen party will have two hundred of the most influential people in Chicago attending. This could be huge for your business, Gracie."

The implications finally struck her and she glanced at her brother.

He smiled. "Sounds pretty cool."

Gracie's brows furrowed. "But I don't live in Chicago. My business is in Revival."

"Maybe it's time to expand," Shane said, with all the practicality of a man who'd never encountered a business problem he couldn't handle.

"It's one cake." Besides, she wasn't equipped to handle a large influx of customers. She'd designed her business around Revival. She worked out of her house in her lemon-colored kitchen with all the commercial appliances she needed. She made cupcakes for little girls' birthday parties, and cookies for the PTA. Her business was successful, profitable, and small. The way she liked it.

Shane pointed at the business card in her hand. "One cake for a very connected politician."

She waved her hand. "Let's not get ahead of ourselves."

Before anyone could speak, a woman said from behind her, "Excuse me."

Gracie turned to see a refined woman in her forties standing there in a champagne cocktail dress.

"Virginia, it's lovely to see you again," Cecilia said, putting her hand on her fiancé's arm. "Shane, you remember Congressman Dalton's wife."

Smooth as silk, Shane extended his hand. "Of course, always a pleasure."

Gracie would bet money Shane had no idea who the woman was, but no one would ever guess. That's why they were a great couple. Shane and Cecilia complemented each other and made it look effortless.

Gracie's attention slipped to James. The two women he'd been talking to earlier had joined him and Charlie. Her stomach twisted with jealousy. Who were they?

Over the strawberry-blonde's head, James looked up and caught her gaze. Instant heat. Her lower belly jumped. With a hard swallow, she turned back to the conversation.

"Congratulations on your engagement," Virginia said, then turned to Gracie. "Did I hear you made this cake?"

Chapter Seven

Gracie sat in the car in front of James's townhouse, heart pounding so hard she feared it might burst from her ribs. What in God's name was she doing?

After the party, she'd gone back to Shane and Cecilia's, and as everyone retired to their separate rooms, she'd paced the floors like a caged animal.

All night their gazes had locked across the room, over and over again, like some sort of magnetic force had drawn them.

Then, somewhere mid-pace, the solution dawned on her. So simple and straightforward it about slapped her in the face.

Sex.

She'd been looking at it in the wrong light. If she slept with him the tension would break and all this angst would be over. A one-time deal would get them over the hump, and take care of the awkwardness of their new-found truce. With all the heat they'd generated all evening she'd forgotten one very important fact: they were fundamentally incompatible. She preferred her sex wild, impulsive, and dirty. Three words that in no way described James. He was just too . . . neat and controlled.

And really, the man didn't eat cupcakes, so how crazy could he be? The way she figured it, he probably had a set routine:

Kissing—seven minutes, twenty-five seconds.

Foreplay—subsection A: nipples. Five minutes on each side.

Foreplay—subsection B: clitoris. Two minutes of gentle stroking followed by light, circular pressure.

He'd be methodical and plodding, as he was with everything else. Even if he was decent in bed, it wouldn't be her preference, and he'd be off the hook. The more she'd thought about it, the more convinced she became it was the solution to this fiasco. Sleep with him and the tension would be over.

They could have a good laugh at how unmatched they were, and she could finally treat him like every other guy.

It was easy as cherry pie. She'd stolen his information from Cecilia's contact list on her computer and snuck out of the house without a backward glance.

Only now, sitting in front of his house, nerves bouncing in her stomach, she seriously questioned her sanity.

This was the only solution that made sense. She yanked the key out of the ignition. She was taking action. Come morning, her dry spell would be over, and she'd have Professor James Donovan out of her system once and for all.

The last person James expected to see standing at his front door at half past midnight was Gracie. Maybe he'd finally gone off the deep end and he'd started hallucinating? He blinked but she was still there on his stoop. Standing there in all her spectacular glory in the red dress that had taunted him all evening.

"Gracie?" He opened the door wider and took a step back.

She nibbled on her bottom lip, shifting on the balls of her feet, then pointed at the doorway. "May I come in?"

What could she possibly be doing here? With the way things had gone between them tonight, he half expected her never to talk to him again. He waved her into the foyer. "Yes, of course."

She squared her shoulders, then marched past him. A woman on a mission.

A small smile quivered at his lips. "This is an unexpected surprise. To what do I owe the pleasure?"

She dropped a large purse on the leather bench and swung around, planting her hands on her generous hips. Her *Playboy*-worthy breasts jiggled in the silky material of her strapless dress. He'd been trying all night to figure out how the dress stayed up when it appeared as though one crook of his finger would send the fabric sliding to the floor.

She blew out a breath, sending a curl flying. "I've been thinking about this truce of ours, and it's not working."

He closed the door, blocking out the cool night air. He couldn't argue with her there. "Maybe we just need time."

A frown marred her full mouth. "I want things to be normal."

"What's normal?"

"With you?" She gestured at him like he exasperated her to her wits' end. "I have no clue. But I've had it."

The evening's turn of events clearly had her on edge, and he couldn't say he blamed her. The sharp arousal had driven him crazy, inducing him to fantasies of yanking her into some dark closet. "Had what?"

"I've had enough of *this*." She waved her hand around wildly in the space between them.

Despite his best intentions he felt a smile twitching at his lips, which he quickly repressed into a firm line. An evil part of him wanted to toy with her, to pretend confusion, but she seemed too agitated. And that response would be inappropriate, designed to provoke and tease, which wouldn't help their current predicament. "Maybe it's not possible for us to be friends, but I think we haven't given it enough time."

She covered her face with her hands and hung her head. "What am I doing?"

He itched to go to her but didn't dare. They were a powder keg waiting to explode and it was better not to add spark to the detonator. "Maybe we need to start with the basics."

"How?"

He smiled, hoping to put her at ease. "I've seen you with other men. So go ahead, start flirting. Dazzle me with your smile and sweetness."

"You're impossible!" She clenched her hands into fists at her sides, as though trying to keep from punching him in the face.

"Too much, too soon?" He carefully studied her, rubbing a hand over his jaw.

"I'm serious!" She pressed her fingertips to her temple. "Argh, this is so frustrating! This isn't going the way I planned. Which is pretty much par for the course with you, Professor."

It struck him how often he'd felt the same way about her. He always had the best intentions, but they never worked once he got in the same room with her. He gave her a wry smile. "I can relate."

She sucked in a breath that expanded her chest and her hands fell to her sides. "I've been thinking about this all night and I don't see a lot of options other than to spit it out."

"Please do," he said, without the foggiest clue where this would lead.

She seemed to contemplate for several long moments before drawing in another deep breath. "It seems like there's something between us, even though we don't want it there."

He nodded. "Yes, there is."

That seemed to bolster her confidence and she stood straighter, her chin tilted. "I think we should deal with it, once and for all."

"And what do you propose?" he asked, both dreading and anticipating the answer.

"I don't see any other way to solve the problem. As you pointed out, our lives are only becoming more entwined. But I think there's too much tension. We need to fix it. . . ." Expression stormy, she shook her head. "Deal with the source of the problem."

James couldn't argue with her logic. He raised a brow. "And how to you propose we do that?"

That stubborn, wayward curl flopped over one eye and he clenched his hands to keep from tucking it behind her ear. A moment later she pushed it away and squared her shoulders. "I think we need to hit the sheets. Like a Band-Aid, rip it right off."

He just stood there, staring at her like a big dope.

This whole mess made Gracie twitchy.

Still, he said nothing.

Feeling defensive, she planted her hands on her hips and demanded, "Well?"

Adam's apple bobbing, James swallowed hard. The muscles in his forearms flexed, and the veins running up his wrists momentarily distracted her, before she managed to refocus.

He shook his head, as though waking himself from a

stupor. He stepped back, gesturing toward the open expanse of his house. "Come on, let's go sit down."

From the foyer she craned her neck to peer into the place he called home. The loft had timber rafters, rich, wide-planked hardwood floors, and fifteen-foot ceilings. It was decorated with warm browns, reds, and greens. The professor was cold and controlled; everything should be gunmetal gray and industrial. It should not be warm, lush, and inviting.

The disparity between her expectations and reality made her uneasy. Heart rate kicking up a notch, she resisted taking a step back and escaping through the front door. "For what?"

Behind those black wire frames, his cool, evergreen eyes narrowed. "Should I just take you against the wall and send you on your way?"

A flash of heat, followed by a trickle of ice, slid down her spine. Well, fine, if he wanted to be all calm and collected about this transaction, so be it. She squared her shoulders and held her chin high. "I apologize. Lead the way."

He frowned but said nothing, leading her into the big open space.

The room was even better than it had looked from the foyer, and his view from his great room was breathtaking, with large bay windows overlooking the Chicago skyline. And his kitchen. She shivered. Open and connected to the main living area, it was a cook's dream, and she couldn't resist running her fingers over the cool marble. "This isn't what I expected."

"What did you expect?" His voice was as smooth as the river that ran behind her house on a day with no breeze.

Someone had gotten his composure back.

Unfortunately, it wasn't her. She wanted to put on her normal facade, or at least say something to throw him off-balance, but the truth was, nerves got the better of her. Which irritated her. Sex didn't make her nervous. She put her hand on her belly. "I expected more industrial and sleek."

"I don't like closed-in spaces or cold metal." He walked over to the fridge, stained to match the dark wood cabinets. "Would you like something to drink?"

She fought an urge to snap at him, for no other reason than he acted like she'd suggested a walk by the lake instead of a night of hot sex. Bound and determined to rectify this situation, she refused to give in to temptation. The professor wasn't the only one with discipline. She cleared her throat. "Water is fine, thank you."

He opened the fridge and pulled out a bottle of water, a small smile curving the corners of his mouth. "Don't go getting all civil on me now, Gracie. I'm not sure I can take it."

She snatched the bottle from his hands. "You get irritated at me for being irrational, but when I'm polite you criticize. There's no pleasing you."

A muscle jumped in his jaw. "I was teasing."

"Ha!" She flounced over to the chocolate couch and plopped down onto it, biting back a moan. It was even more comfortable than it looked, the suede butter soft against her bare skin. Pure heaven. She could roll around on this couch for days, but she stayed upright, crossing her legs. "We both know you don't have a sense of humor."

He shook his head, walked to the camel-colored club chair, and sat down. He crossed his legs at the ankles and laced his fingers over a stomach that should be declared illegal. "I assume you're nervous and thus will excuse your rudeness."

She blew out an exasperated breath. Calm. She needed to be calm. All this pent-up sexual energy messed with her brain. Once they got this over with she'd be back to normal. She was sure of it. Then they could get on with the business of being friends.

He sat across from her, looking more likely to go to sleep than make a move on her.

She sighed. Now that her decision was made, she was antsy to get it over with. She glanced meaningfully at the open staircase that most likely led to his bedroom. "Can we just get on with it?"

"Do you have somewhere you need to be?" he asked.

Most men would have pounced on her the second she'd made her offer, but not the professor. Although, she could look at his lack of action in a positive light, as it confirmed she'd been right about the way he took his sex. "No, I just don't want to waste any more time."

He was silent for several long moments before his head cocked to the side. "I'm not sure how sleeping together is a viable solution."

God, couldn't he understand how on edge she was? She threw up her hands. "Why can't you be a normal guy? I'm offering you sex. Can't you just take it and quit talking about it?"

He raised a brow. "If I was just a normal guy and you were just an ordinary woman, we wouldn't be in this situation, now would we?"

The silence stretched out between them like an endless chasm. The heat permeated the air until it felt thick and humid. Finally, she couldn't take it anymore and blew out a hard breath. "I suppose there's truth to that."

She braced herself for some sort of smugness, but he leaned forward and put his elbows on his knees, calling to attention the wide expanse of his broad shoulders and hard cut of his jaw. "While there's always been attraction between us, this tension is new. What is wrong with talking it through?"

A splash of heat spread over her chest. He'd said it out

loud. There'd be no pretending it didn't lurk between them now. A silly notion considering she'd just propositioned him for sex, but she'd made that sound more like scratching an itch. More about taking one for the greater good of the team. "I'm sorry, I'm not sure what you want to discuss."

"How about the fact that we rub each other the wrong way? How we're entirely different people? How we're going to have to see each other for the next fifty years?"

All good questions if she'd proposed dating, but she hadn't. "I'm not suggesting we get married. I'm suggesting we have sex one time so we can move on to our truce."

"I think your way has consequences we need to examine." Voice calm, he sat there with his fingers loosely clasped, like he didn't have a care in the world.

This conversation made her head ache and she pressed a fingertip against her temple. What kind of guy examined the consequences of sex? You offered. They took. Easy. Only James made it complicated. She drained half her water, wishing for something stronger, before putting it on the coffee table between them. She sighed. "We already have a terrible relationship. It will only help."

"And how do you figure that?"

Exasperated, she let out a little screech. This conversation was exactly what drove her crazy about him. "For the love of God, it's just sex. It won't even be good sex. So let's get it over with and go on our merry way."

His expression flashed before turning cool. He sat back in his chair and studied her in that level-eyed way he had. "What makes you think it won't be good?"

Okay, she needed to stop hoping to get a rise out of him. Most men rose to the challenge when their sexual prowess was questioned. But, of course, James didn't play by those rules. No, James wanted to talk it out. She brushed imaginary lint from her dress. "Poor word choice on my part. I'm only suggesting we'll be as incompatible at sex as we are at everything else."

He placed his elbow on the arm of the chair, rubbing his fingers in a slow motion, as though contemplating something tactile. His lips quirked. "I see. I think this is becoming clear. So you're assuming the mediocrity will cure the fixation."

"Well, maybe not mediocre." Her belly heated. She thought of all those long, lust-filled glances. The desire skipping between them in the stairwell. Too hot to be truly horrible. "I'm sure it will be fine."

"I assure you, you're mistaken."

Her breath caught in her chest. That sounded confident. She recalled the way Lindsey Lord had flirted up at him with adoration. Instinct told her to keep quiet, to change the subject, but her mouth ran away from her. "I'm sure you're skilled. But I'm equally sure we won't like things the same way."

"Do tell."

Was that amusement in his tone?

She should back down, but a demented compulsion made her continue. "Well, come on, when's the last time you had sex not in the missionary position?"

Okay, the corners of his lips definitely quivered with contained mirth. What was so funny? She'd insulted him, for heaven's sake.

He rubbed a palm over his jaw. "What do you have against the missionary position?"

She blew out a breath. "Nothing."

"So let me get this straight. If I'm reading between the lines, you want me to disappoint you sexually for the sake of the truce. Is that correct?"

"Why do you have to put it like that?"

"How would you like me to put it?"

She crossed her arms and huffed. "Why are you making things difficult?"

"Why do you always evade questions with more questions?"

Unable to sit still a moment longer, she flew off the chair, sexual frustration and exasperation building like a pressure cooker inside her. She lapped around the room while he sat quietly in the chair, watching her with that intense expression of his.

Screw this. She stalked over to stand in front of him. "Look, are we going to fuck or not?"

His gaze traveled over her body at a slow, leisurely pace. "Do I have a choice in the matter?"

She crossed her arms over her ample chest to cover the rapid tightening of her nipples. "Don't even try to pretend it's a hardship."

Behind his wire frames, his eyes narrowed on her cleavage. "Wanting you has never been the problem, Gracie."

"Good—" She started toward him, but he grabbed her wrist, cutting her off.

"But I'm afraid my answer is no."

Chapter Eight

In complete shock, Gracie could only stare at him, her mouth hanging open. She couldn't have heard him right. Was this some sort of joke?

After what seemed like an eternity of standing there, staring at each other, she managed to sputter, "No?"

He nodded, his grip on her wrist falling away. "I don't think it's smart."

"You don't think it's smart?" Repeating his statements seemed all she was capable of as her brain refused to function.

He'd said no.

To her.

He'd refused. How was that even possible? She'd never heard of a man turning down sex. And, well, she'd certainly never been turned down. But here he was, saying no.

"Correct," he said, not elaborating.

"What? Why?" She could not believe this. This was so like him. Of course he'd refuse. He was the professor. He never did anything right.

God, she was so stupid. Instead of the humiliation burning a hole in her gut, she latched on to the anger.

He, on the other hand, appeared completely at ease. "I don't like casual sex. I don't believe in one-night stands. It's meaningless and, call me old-fashioned, but I think sex should have meaning."

"You have got to be kidding me." She could not believe this. She wanted to scream.

"Afraid not." He spoke calmly, as though they discussed weather patterns over the Atlantic.

Somehow she'd managed to find herself attracted to the only prude left in the United States. Wasn't that just her luck? With as much sarcasm as she could muster she said, "Well, you can forget about a marriage proposal, because that's never going to happen."

He narrowed those green eyes and she thought she detected a flash of anger before he leaned back in his chair. "I don't need a marriage proposal, Gracie. But I do require something basic you and I don't have."

The humiliation wormed its way through her anger, poking hole after hole until it lay tattered at her feet. She'd never considered this. She'd assumed that as soon as she offered, they'd be in bed. Getting him out of her system. The idea that he'd say no never even entered her mind. She straightened her shoulders, determined to put on a good show. "And what, pray tell, is that?"

He stood and instinctively she took a step back, still stung by his rejection.

He sighed, shaking his head as though he found her too exasperating for words. "At bare minimum I want the person I sleep with to at least like and respect me."

His words were a direct hit and all the fight drained out of her.

He was right.

She'd come over here to use him and now she was pissed he'd said no. Her shoulders slumped. The truth hit her like a two-by-four. She'd convinced herself this was the only way to resolve their issues, but she wanted him. Like, wanted, wanted him. And he'd rejected her. To her horror she felt the back of her throat grow tight. Oh dear God, no.

"Understood," she managed to squeak out before spinning on her heel and walking toward the door.

She had to get out of there, and she practically ran to escape. Grabbing her purse from the bench, she grabbed the door handle, twisting it open. The cool, late summer air splashed her face, smelling like freedom. She pulled open the door wider, only for it to slam shut. She blinked James's strong hand into focus.

Desperate to get out, she said in as calm a voice as she could muster, "You've made your decision. There's nothing more to say."

"I don't want you to leave like this. You shouldn't drive when you're upset."

His voice was so damn soft, so damn understanding, she wanted to punch him. But she settled for clenching her hands into fists. "I'm not upset."

"Yes, you are. Now stop this so we can talk."

She wanted to deny it but didn't have the strength. "There's nothing to talk about."

He put his hands, warm and strong, on her bare upper arms. For a brief, crazy second she wanted to lean into him and melt. The insanity of the notion had her stiffening her spine.

"Gracie, come sit back down and let's talk about this."

"No."

"Stubborn," he whispered close to her ear.

She clenched her teeth. "You said no. You were right to say no. It was a silly idea."

His fingers tightened on her shoulders and she flinched. "How do you expect to sleep with me when you can't stand me touching you?"

"Don't be ridiculous." She didn't know what else to say. "It doesn't matter."

He turned her rigid frame. She could have demanded he let her go, and she understood him well enough to know he would. He wasn't the kind of man to overpower. But her lips stayed stubbornly closed as she leaned against the door and looked past him into the warm space he called home.

"Maybe I was a bit abrupt. Let me try again." His hand slid up her arm and curled around her nape.

She shivered, her flesh breaking out in undeniable goose bumps at his touch. She refused to look at him. She'd let him have his say and then be on her way, never to think about this disaster again.

His thumb brushed over the curve of her neck, as though he was trying to soothe her, which only made her tense. "If I ever have the pleasure of sleeping with you, I want you in my bed because you want to be there, not because you're trying to get me out of your system. Is that so hard to understand?"

Oh, she wanted to be there, but didn't know how to admit it. Not now, after everything. And old patterns died hard.

She could feel his gaze on hers, compelling her to look at him, and she found she couldn't resist the pull. Those fine shards of blue intermixed with the green were bright, burning with some sort of cold fire. She could only shake her head. "Who are you?"

"If you ever want to find out, you know where to find me."

"What are you saying?"

"I'm not rejecting you." His attention drifted down to her mouth, lingered, then rose. Still wrapped around her neck, his fingers exerted no pressure, but his skin was hot, burning. The imprint of his touch would linger far after he let her go.

Pulse kicking up a beat, she swallowed. "What do you call it?"

"Adjusting your expectations." At his words, her belly dipped with anticipation.

She needed to get out of there. "I have no idea what that means."

His thumb stroked over her neck, up the line of her jaw, then pressed under her chin until her head tilted. "We may not live in the same city, but between trips to Revival to visit Maddie, and your trips here, I've seen how you operate with other men, and I sure as hell know what makes you so damn irritated with me."

She had an uneasy feeling she didn't want to hear this, but was too stubborn for her own good. "And what's that?"

"You can't control me and you hate it."

His words nailed her to the wall. He was right. Her relationships with men had always been easy, and she'd been in complete control. Her smile easy and wide, but she'd always protected herself. That was the way she liked things, but no matter how hard she tried to put James Donovan into a box, he refused to conform.

He smiled, a small lift of his lips that hid his dimple. "If it makes you feel better, I can't control you either and hate it just as much."

The confession shocked her and she sputtered, "You do?"

"Yes." His gaze drifted down to her mouth again. "I like order. And calm. You're chaos and fire."

Her breath caught and held, as sex seemed to fill the space between them. She opened her mouth—to say what, she hadn't a clue—but before she could get any words out his lips covered hers.

Stunned, she stiffened, frozen with surprise.

His lips moved as his fingers tightened on her throat. Desire shimmered through her, dimming the humiliation that had left her cold.

The man could kiss.

Mouth hot when she'd expected cool, he coaxed her into a response she didn't want to deliver but couldn't resist. Lashes drifting closed, her surprise melted away as desire took over.

His tongue flickered against her lips, seeking entrance, and she forgot everything. Forgot his rejection. Her stubbornness. Forgot all the ways they were wrong for each other.

All she remembered was this kiss, delivering what those long, lingering looks had promised all day.

She opened, tilting her head to grant him access. His tongue slipped inside to tangle with hers. She kissed him back, getting lost in the feel of his mouth as her breath quickened.

His lips were sure. Slightly demanding. Not what she expected. Or wanted. But she couldn't stop.

The kiss changed. Transformed from gentle exploration into something hot and greedy.

Unbidden, her hands slipped over his shoulders to curl around his neck. A low rumble that vibrated against her lips made her moan.

He shifted, his hands sliding down her back to her hips. He pulled her closer, his head slanting to deepen the angle of the kiss. She rose on tiptoes, needing *closer*. So much closer. She gasped as his strong, hard chest brushed her breasts. His arm locked against her waist as his other hand tangled in her hair. He fisted the curls and tugged, forcing her into a deeper response.

Her blood heated. Her body roared to greedy life. Her purse dropped to the floor. She wrapped her body around his, needing more.

He delivered, kissing her deeper. Harder.

He shoved her against the door.

All at once, everything between them grew hotter. More frantic.

She tightened her fingers in his hair and pressed her now aching breasts against him.

Their labored breathing filled the foyer.

So good. Too good.

He kicked her foot to one side, and she gasped at the unexpected display of dominance. Her body going into hyper drive.

Yes. Yes. Yes. How long had it been? Too long. Maybe never. Because it was him, and some part of her had been craving him since the day they'd met.

He gripped her thigh, yanking the skirt high. His palm a brand on her skin, sending a trail of fire in its wake.

She arched.

He lifted her leg and hooked it on his hip.

His hard cock slid between her inner thighs, sending a frisson of pleasure exploding through her.

She rocked, desperate to relieve the ache. He grabbed her wrists and raised them above her head, pinning them to the door before he devoured her mouth.

And he did devour.

He consumed.

Feasted on her.

And she was helpless to do anything but let him as he held her trapped against the door. Captive.

He created an inferno, an unquenchable hunger, and she went a little mad. Twisting frantically beneath him in an effort to get closer. She rocked hungrily against his erection, moaning into his mouth.

He growled low in his throat, then tore away, and stepped back.

She wanted to scream.

They stared at each other, both panting for breath in choppy, uneven gasps. His hair was disheveled, his green eyes blazing, his mouth swollen and wet.

She'd never, ever been kissed like that.

She started to tremble. It scared the hell out of her.

Thank God he'd stopped. Because if he kissed like that, she'd been wrong about his performance in the bedroom. With him, she was always wrong.

She needed to escape. So she could think.

She flushed on top of her already overheated skin. Flustered, she blinked and pointed to the door. "I need to leave."

"Yes," he said, his voice a husky rasp that stroked over her flesh, inflaming her. "That's probably for the best."

"Umm . . ." She picked up her purse. "See ya."

"Tomorrow."

"Huh?"

He sucked in air, as though he'd run one of his marathons. "Tomorrow. Breakfast."

Shit. She'd forgotten. Why hadn't she remembered when she'd concocted this stupid plan? "Oh . . . ummm . . . okay. Bye."

Shaken to the core, she didn't wait for a response. She spun and ran out the door as fast as her legs would carry her.

James sat down at the large table in the crowded restaurant, already weary. This was the last event of the engagement weekend and he couldn't wait until it was over. All he wanted was to lie on the couch and read in utter silence and gather the tattered remains of his discipline and self-will.

He needed peace. To regroup and think. Get his thoughts organized. And he wouldn't get it until Gracie Roberts was back on the road to Revival.

The image of that hot, straining kiss, where he'd struggled with his control in the face of the reality of her—far more intoxicating than he ever would have imagined.

What had possessed him to kiss her like that?

He settled into the seat, and his vision shifted to the woman in question. Their eyes caught and held. She jerked her attention down to the menu.

His brother Evan sat next to Gracie, his arm casually draped around the back of her chair. James clenched his jaw and tried to ignore the stab of jealousy.

That should be his arm. The notion irritated him and he picked up his menu to occupy his mind. He had no business thinking such possessive thoughts. Yes, he'd kissed her, but it changed nothing. He had no claim over her and it was inappropriate to contemplate breaking Evan's arm for daring to touch her.

Of course, that didn't stop his fingers from twitching.

He nodded at the group. "How's everyone this morning?"

Mitch and Maddie, Shane and Cecilia, Sam, his mom, the mother-of-the-bride, Charlotte Riley, and his eccentric great aunt Cathy all sat around the table as well. There was a chorus of good mornings but his mom frowned at him. Her blue eyes narrowed in that motherly way she had. "You look tired."

He was tired, having been up far too late, his mind filled with images of a certain blond bombshell who kissed like the devil. What bit of stupidity lurking in his brain had possessed him to touch her? Now, just like he'd anticipated, his brain didn't work properly and he'd lost out on some much-needed sleep.

In a calm voice that betrayed nothing, he said, "I'm fine."

"Didn't you sleep well?" his mom pressed, still with that look of concern. She wore her faded strawberry-blond hair in some sort of clip, and her cheeks had a healthy glow, as though she'd exercised that morning. In a buttery yellow top she looked downright radiant. Better than she had in a long time.

"I slept fine," he lied.

He'd been so close to losing it. Ten more minutes and he would have taken her against the wall. Right after he'd thrown down the gauntlet and made his big speech about her actually having to like him, he'd been ready to pound into her, consequences be damned. She had no idea how close she'd come to obliterating his control. After she'd left he'd gone running, and five miles had done nothing to calm his emotions.

Since his mother still watched him like a hawk, he said, "You're looking particularly well."

A smile lit her face and she shifted in her chair. "Thank you."

"He's right," his sister said, giving their mother a long perusal. "There's something different about you."

"I'm happy my daughter is married and my son is on his way. What else could a mother ask for?" Shannon Donovan asked. She held up two fingers. "Two more to go."

God help him.

Thankfully he was saved from a response when his eighty-eight-year-old great aunt Cathy snorted. The older woman, who had never had children and buried all five of her husbands, accompanied his mom to most get-togethers so she wouldn't get too lonely.

A second later Evan joined her. "Not everyone wants to settle down, Mom."

James contemplated his brother's hand that still rested on Gracie's chair.

He didn't like it. It took all his discipline to fight the urge to tell him to move it or suffer the consequences. He shook his head. Suffer the consequences? Hell, he was turning into Shane.

Gracie frowned at him, and he realized he was glaring and relaxed his expression. She shifted in her chair, angling her body away from Evan, and James's muscles eased fractionally. She tucked a curl behind her ear and went back to paying elaborate attention to her menu. Today she wore a powder-blue V-neck top with buttons down the front. He wanted to rip them off.

He was in trouble.

That kiss had rocked his world. Unlike Gracie, he'd never tricked himself into believing kissing her would be anything other than a disaster, and he'd been right. Now he couldn't think about anything but getting his hands on her again.

"You didn't run one of those marathons this morning, did you?" Aunt Cathy asked, her cackling voice shaking James from his thoughts.

"What?" he asked, lost in the conversation.

Aunt Cathy, who still fancied herself a teenage girl, prided herself in keeping up with all the latest trends. Today's outfit was a pair of skinny jeans and a One Direction T-shirt. "You're not tired from running one of those marathons you're so fond of?"

James glanced down at his watch. "It's nine thirty, Auntie. Twenty-six miles takes me a little longer than an hour or two."

"All that exercise isn't healthy, boy," she said.

James picked up the glass of water and toasted her. "Medical science would disagree."

She waved a gnarled, dismissive hand in his general direction. "Ha. I'm eighty-eight. I smoke, drink, and eat whatever I want. I'm proof those scientists don't know what they're talking about."

Even though he knew better than to argue with her, he felt compelled to point out her recent diagnosis. "You've developed emphysema, which is why you're not supposed to smoke anymore."

She huffed. "Just a touch."

Shane chuckled. "I think that's like being a touch pregnant, Auntie."

"That's not the point, boy," the ornery old woman

said. She'd had five husbands and put every one of them in the grave; in her mind that made her the expert on everything. "The point is it's not right for a man to worry about calories."

It continued to elude him why everyone gave a damn about his eating and exercise habits. He liked to take care of himself. In most circles this was a good thing. But not his family, who'd taken it as something they needed to fret about.

He sighed, shrugging at Evan, who'd finally moved his hand off Gracie's chair. "Evan exercises way more than I do."

"That's for his job," Aunt Cathy said. She lasered her intent focus on her youngest nephew. "You wouldn't exercise if you didn't have to, would you?"

"No, ma'am," Evan said, all lazy and sly.

"See," Aunt Cathy said, her expression rife with satisfaction.

His mother put a hand on her arm. "Let James be."

Aunt Cathy shrugged and glowered at James. "I liked you better the other way, boy."

Gracie's head shot up and she zeroed in on him, the questions clear in her expression.

"Auntie, you know there's no use trying to convince him to be a couch potato," Shane said, rescuing James from a response.

Fortunately, the waitress came to the table to take their orders and James ignored the snort of derision when he ordered an egg-white omelet.

"You okay?" Maddie asked as they washed their hands in the restaurant's bathroom.

"Sure, of course," Gracie lied. She didn't know what she was, but okay wasn't it. She'd contemplated making an excuse and heading back to Revival this morning, but in the end she couldn't do it. Running away was not her style and she wasn't about to start because of the professor.

Her friend pressed. "You sure?" Maddie looked lovely in a white top and fitted jeans, her red hair loose. The green eyes she shared with her brothers shone with happiness and Gracie could barely stand to look at her. She was a breath of fresh air, in direct contrast to how Gracie felt after a horrible night's sleep. The only things that gave her any satisfaction were the dark circles under James's eyes, indicating he hadn't slept any better than she had.

They'd suffered alone, but at least they'd both suffered.

Gracie beamed her brightest smile. "Of course, what could be wrong?"

"I don't know, you've been quiet since yesterday and that's not like you."

Gracie shrugged. Under normal circumstances she'd confess everything to Maddie. Share every detail about the kiss and the emotional upheaval she currently internalized, but how could she? James was Maddie's brother. Yes, Shane and Mitch routinely gave each other shit about sleeping with the other's sister, but that was different. Gracie was pretty sure Cecilia and Maddie weren't plopping down and comparing notes. Besides, the thought of some girl talking about Sam the way Gracie thought about James was enough to give her the heebie-jeebies. "I'm good. I'm just tired and ready to get back home."

Maddie glanced at her in the mirror, her expression concentrated and speculative, but finally she shrugged. "Okay. But you'd talk to me if you needed to, wouldn't you?"

"Don't I always?" Questions about James burned in her chest. Namely, what exactly had Great Aunt Cathy meant when she'd said she liked James "the other way"? It was the second time a family member had alluded to James being different in the past, and Gracie was near desperate for answers. But of course she couldn't ask.

Maddie's face clouded. "Lately it doesn't seem that way."

That's because I can't stop thinking about your brother. Or the way his mouth felt against mine. Gracie turned away from the sink, dried her hands, then turned back to her friend. She gave her a big hug. "I'm fine, I promise."

"Okay, as long as you're sure." Maddie squeezed back.

"I am. Come on, let's get back." She needed to figure out a way to get James alone and confront him about last night. She needed to make sure he understood that kiss had been a mistake. Last night, she'd lain awake in bed, staring at the dark ceiling, and had never been so grateful to be rejected. If he kissed like that, once would never be enough. Her plan only worked if it was a disappointment, which clearly wouldn't be the case.

Sex with him could only lead to disaster.

As luck would have it, the gods were smiling upon her, and twenty minutes later James's car and hers were the last ones in the valet line. Thankfully, Chicago's busy streets didn't allow for lingering, and everyone had said their good-byes and driven away. Gracie tapped her foot anxiously as Cecilia waved before climbing into their Mercedes. As soon as Shane and Cecilia had driven away Gracie took a big breath and turned to James. "About last night."

Brow cocked, he cast those cool, evergreen eyes on her. "About last night."

She cleared her throat, cursing the nerves jumping in her stomach. "I think we can agree it was a mistake."

"Was it?" That voice, that smooth, steady voice.

"Yes." There, she sounded quite certain.

His gaze dipped to her mouth. "Then why do I want it again?"

"Stupidity," she quipped.

To her shock, he laughed. A real laugh that made his dimple flash and her heart skip a beat. "I'm not going to argue with you there."

She stubbornly ignored how his hair ruffled in the breeze. "That's a first."

The smile stayed on his lips even after the laughter faded away. "I've discovered there are other ways to occupy you besides arguing."

Heat. How could there be nothing but heat after all this time? She swallowed hard. "Don't even joke."

"Who's joking?" He stepped closer and she had to look up at him.

What had possessed her to wear ballet flats today? Oh yeah, her feet had been killing her after all the time she'd spent in heels. And she hadn't anticipated him towering over her. On the defensive, she said the first dumb thing that entered her brain. "Look, it was an okay kiss, but that's as far as it goes."

"Just okay, huh?" He appeared amused versus insulted.

"Yes," she said, her throat Sahara-desert dry.

"Liar."

"I am not." She jabbed a finger at his chest. "I didn't need more than a kiss to know I was right about you all along."

"That I'm a complete dud." Again, with that bemused expression.

Why couldn't he be normal and be insulted? "Exactly."

His gaze slid over her. "Your pulse is pounding."

The observation made her hyper aware of her rapidly beating heart. "Wrong."

"Your pupils are dilated."

With the sun, she could hardly blame the weather. She gave a nonchalant little shrug.

"And you can't stop thinking about that kiss."

She licked her parched lips. He was far too observant. "How can you be this much of an egomaniac when I'm rejecting you?"

He took another step forward. The brightness of the day made his eyes so bright and compelling she couldn't look away. "I've had mediocre kisses before, and that wasn't one of them."

"Maybe you just lack experience."

His expression flashed. "It's so much easier for you that way, isn't it? Pretending I'm some bumbling professor with patches on his tweed sports coat, who doesn't know his way around a woman's body. But you can't quite buy it, can you?"

He was acting different. Or was he? She couldn't tell. All she knew was she was confused and needed to get away from him, only her feet were glued to the sidewalk. "You're delusional."

"Is that so?"

He was so frustrating. He didn't fight like a regular guy and it threw her off-balance. And she hated feeling off-balance. One more mark against him on an already long list. So why did she want him so damn much? "Yes, that's so."

The valet sped to the curb with her SUV. She pointed to it. "There's my car. See ya."

With a sigh, he shook his head, grasped her arm, and pulled her close. His mouth covered hers and everything else ceased to exist.

It was a hard, demanding kiss. He took complete control, giving her no other option but to respond. She wanted to remain rigid, but her body had a mind of its own and her arms wound around his neck.

His tongue thrust, twining with hers. She plastered her chest against his, moaning into his mouth.

It was better than last night. More aggressive. She shuddered. Dirtier.

His mouth was so damn sure. So damn confident. Some deranged part of her had always been attracted to arrogance and his kiss was nothing but.

The noise of the traffic, the people on the street, the wind at her back, all faded into the background. She was lost. She rose to tiptoes, needing *closer*.

His arm tightened on her waist as his fingers tangled in her hair. His tongue rolled over hers, and she moaned, low and deep.

Then he pulled away, leaving her gasping for breath.

He ran a finger over her cheek and down the curve of her neck. He released her and she swayed. Steadying her, he flashed a wicked smile she'd never seen before, turned, and walked to his car, which had pulled behind hers while she'd been locked in his arms.

Both the valets watched them with smug, knowing expressions.

James pulled open the door of his sensible, dark gray sedan. "See ya."

Then he was gone and she could only stare after his car in utter shock.

Chapter Nine

It had been a strange, crazy day.

Gracie hung up the phone, tapping her pen on the pad of paper in front of her. Including Ron Sorenson, she now had five orders from people who'd attended Shane and Cecilia's engagement party.

Five. And it was only Monday.

She wasn't sure why she was surprised. She had confidence in her baking abilities. She might not be a professionally trained pastry chef, but she'd worked her ass off perfecting her craft. When she'd made the cake for Shane and Cecilia's party, all she'd been thinking about was her love for her friends and how she wanted to create something spectacular for them. Getting new clients from the party had never crossed her mind. If she had thought about it, she would have assumed all those Chicago people had some couture bakery they all patronized.

She put down the pen she'd been holding and took a deep breath. This was a huge deal. All the potential customers wanted elaborate designs that would stretch her skills as a baker. They'd asked for Web pages and portfolios. Tasting menus and cupcake flavor profiles. Things the good people of Revival never asked for, considering they'd known her since the day she was born. And they rarely wanted artistic. Sure, she did wedding cakes, but most of the town's residents were conservative and liked the traditional, white-tiered cakes she could do in her sleep.

These cakes were for the high society, Chicago power-set Shane and Cecilia ran with. They expected perfection and grandeur. Ideas raced in Gracie's head at the speed of light as butterflies danced a tango in her stomach.

Ron Sorenson's daughter's sweet sixteen party was in three weeks. Crazily enough, his wife had canceled the other cake she ordered because she'd loved Gracie's so much.

She blew out a hard breath. Yes, five orders less than forty-eight hours after the event was a lot, but it was still only five cakes. The deliveries to Chicago would be a bit tricky, but it was doable. It would be fun. Something different that would stretch her as a baker before she returned to her regularly scheduled program.

In the town where she'd lived her whole life, she never got a chance to stretch her wings creatively. And that was fine with her for the most part. She was happy. She had a good life. She knew everyone and everyone knew her. She had a nice, comfortable business. She was busy but not crazy. She made a decent living that allowed her to cover her expenses and still save some money. She had her friends and Sam, and she loved them all fiercely. Yes, sometimes she wished she'd gone on some of the grand adventures she'd dreamed of when she was a girl. But that wasn't the way her life turned out, and she wasn't one to whine, especially when she was so fortunate.

But these orders would be a chance to do something new, to test the skills she'd honed but rarely had a chance to use. She did love a good challenge.

And, the cakes were going to Chicago.

She traced her lower lip with her fingertip, remembering James's mouth on hers. How every cell sparked to life when he'd kissed her. He challenged her.

And scared her.

She hated that he was right. She couldn't control him. He didn't conform to her expected mold. While the men she dated dripped with testosterone, they were vanilla cupcakes with buttercream frosting and sprinkles, something she could handle in her sleep.

She gripped the counter and took a deep breath.

Had she started playing life safe? She thought of all the adventures she'd planned that had never happened. All the things she'd wanted to do that had faded into the background as real life took over.

When she'd graduated high school she'd never wanted to go to a traditional college. Instead, she'd longed to attend a program in Paris. As soon as she'd finished high school she'd started working with her mom, who'd baked for extra money. Gracie also took any odd job she could get her hands on, working two or three jobs at a time. Four years she'd worked her ass off, saving every cent she'd earned until she had the money to apply to the program, pay the tuition, and live for a year in the most beautiful city in the world. When she'd received her acceptance she'd been overcome with joy.

Two weeks later her mother had been diagnosed with stage four breast cancer.

Gracie had never claimed her spot. In fact, she'd never even replied, throwing every letter from the institution into the garbage, unopened. She'd turned her back on her dream and devoted all her energy to taking care of her mom, promising herself that after her mom was better she'd reapply. But slowly her savings dwindled away as she dipped into her stockpile to pay for the things insurance wouldn't cover.

Her mom never got better.

Gracie used the last of the money to pay for her mother's funeral, and never dreamed of Paris again.

Sam had tried to convince her to go, but even if the money weren't gone, she wouldn't leave him. Three years younger than she, he'd been finishing high school, running with a bad crowd, and getting into too much trouble. She needed to stay and make good on her mom's dying wish of getting him straightened out.

She'd never broken her promise.

And she'd never regretted her decision.

She shook her head and straightened. She walked over to her industrial oven and turned the temperature to three fifty.

Maybe it was time for a little adventure. Break out of her comfort zone and do something different. Since that adventure wouldn't include Professor James Donovan, fancy cakes for Chicago high society would have to do.

"So that was the infamous Gracie, huh?" Jane Conway asked, sitting across the large island in her open kitchen.

It had only taken her five minutes to ask. That must be a world record in restraint.

James gave his best friend a droll look. He'd met Jane his first year of college and he'd been trying, and failing, to keep things from her ever since. Despite his best intentions, she'd ferreted out information on Gracie shortly after he'd met her and had been bugging him ever since.

Still sweaty and hot from their long run, he took a sip of his Gatorade and tried not to remember the way

114

Jennifer Dawson

Gracie's mouth tasted. It had been an impulsive move, brought on by her insistence that he would be bad in bed and the kisses that they'd shared hadn't meant anything. Despite what she believed, he wasn't the prude she thought he was, and he itched to disabuse her of the notion. Now he paid the price.

The woman had proved to be as big a distraction as he'd feared. At times when he needed to concentrate he found himself plotting what he'd do to her. How he'd make her beg. Scream his name.

"Earth to professor." Jane snapped her fingers in front of his face, yanking him out of his thoughts. "Damn, I knew you had it bad, but I didn't know it was *that* bad."

"I don't know what you mean. I had a thought about the Jane Doe we've been working on." He did not have it bad for Gracie, she just . . . preoccupied him.

Jane grinned. "Oh really? What is it?"

His mind instantly blank, he blinked. Well, he hadn't thought that through, had he?

He blamed his blond vixen.

Colleagues at the university, James and Jane often consulted on cases together and had recently been called by the Chicago police to help identify the remains of a woman found in the Chicago River. Several pieces of data had stumped them and they'd been working on solving the mystery of what happened to the woman.

Caught in his lie, he cleared his throat and said, "I'm still formulating my theory."

Jane snorted. "Sure you are."

In an effort to change the subject he focused on their late afternoon run, a Tuesday ritual left over from their college days when they'd shared an apartment. Jane was as much a fitness fanatic as he was, and they still trained together a couple times a week. "You knocked a minute off your time. At this rate you'll break your marathon record without any problem."

Jane took a large bowl of fruit from the fridge, a vintage-inspired red number that reminded James of a 1950s diner, and put it on the counter. "You're avoiding."

"You're nosy," he shot back.

He was saved when Anne, Jane's partner, bounced into the kitchen. "Who's nosy?"

James smiled at the petite strawberry blonde. "Your wife."

"You promised to wait for me!" Anne sat on the stool next to him and grinned. "Gracie is *seriously* hot; I don't blame you one bit for crushing on her."

James pinched her arm. "I'll be thirty-four this January. I do not crush on women."

A loud harrumph from Jane's corner. "Please, this is us."

James glanced around the kitchen. "Where are my goddaughters?"

"At their grandparents'," Anne said, rubbing her hands together in maniacal glee. "They can't save you."

Damn it. Gracie Roberts was a subject he had no intention of discussing. Which was precisely why he needed his goddaughters; these two women were downright ruthless when they wanted information. Seriously, they could teach the CIA a few things about torture.

James sighed, a long-suffering sound that wouldn't fool Jane or Anne for a minute. "For the last time, there is nothing between Gracie and me, nor will there ever be."

A few kisses didn't count. Of course, if he were smart,

he'd never have kissed her in the first place. He'd always known once he touched her, he'd turn greedy.

"Don't be stupid," Jane said, using that pragmatic tone with him.

James shook his head. "You haven't even met her."

"Exactly," Anne said, rifling through the fruit bowl and pulling out a bunch of red grapes. "Don't think we didn't notice you kept her far away from us."

"Please, what was I supposed to do, drag her across the room and randomly introduce her to my closest friends? Why would I do that?" He spoke slowly, enunciating each word. *"She's not my girlfriend."*

James grabbed an orange and started peeling as he planned his exit strategy.

Jane shot her partner a sly glance. "Did you see the way they kept staring at each other all night?"

Anne grinned, nodding her head vigorously. Clearly they'd already discussed this. "So perfectly synchronized too. First he'd watch her, in that brooding Mr. Darcy way he has."

James frowned. "I am not Mr. Darcy."

Anne ignored him, holding out her hands like she framed a movie scene. "Then he'd turn away, with a stiff upper lip, and like magic, she'd turn those big blue eyes on him." She pressed a hand to her chest, sighing dramatically. "The longing. But the very best was when their gazes would lock from across the room. All that tension. All that heat."

"Jesus Christ," James said, throwing up his hands in exasperation. Yes, maybe he'd been hyperaware of her all night, but they were clearly exaggerating. "You had a *Pride and Prejudice* marathon again, didn't you?"

"Yes, but that's beside the point." Anne gave Jane a big goofy smile. "Do you remember those days?"

Jane returned the smile with a big goofy one of her own. "I remember them well."

Anne swiveled on the stool. "See, we've been together for ages now, so we need to experience the excitement of new love through you."

"Are you high again?" James asked, shaking his head. "For the last time, there is no new love."

"Well, you and the blond cupcake do a spectacular job pretending to be infatuated with each other," Jane said.

The comment stuck in James's side and didn't sit well. "Don't call her that."

"Oooh, look, he's all protective." Anne giggled, before puffing out her lip in a pout. "I guess that means I'll have to scratch her from my list."

Jane patted her hand. "I told you, honey, you can't have real people on your list. They can only be movie stars or fictional."

James's head was starting to hurt. He shot confused glances back and forth between the two of them. "List?"

Anne threw her head back and laughed. "It's what we long-term couples do to keep up the fantasy that you can still sleep with other people. Surely you've heard of people's lists."

"Yes, but . . ." James sputtered. "You can't have Gracie on your list."

"That's what I just said," Jane reminded him.

What was this irrational spike of jealousy poking him in the ribs? What in the hell was happening to him? Gracie was straight. He had greater threats to contend with than Anne.

Threats? He frowned. Why was he thinking this way? Gracie *was not* his. He gritted his teeth. See, this is why he'd always stayed away from her. He'd kissed her twice and it was already making him stupid.

James shook his head as though it would help rid him of the thoughts. "I'm not participating in this conversation."

Jane sighed. "So explain to me, what exactly is your problem with her? I mean, I know with those big blue eyes, wild blond curls, gorgeous face, and Marilyn Monroe body, there's a lot to complain about."

"And don't forget she bakes." Anne made a gagging noise. "I mean, ick. How can you stand it?"

Jane nodded, her expression serious. "True, true. Did you see that cake? It was horrid. There wasn't even a piece left. I swear I saw a congressman licking the plate, so, you know, stay away from that one."

James could not believe he was being forced to participate in this conversation. As calmly as he could, he countered, "So you're saying being good-looking and making baked goods is the standard for women? Seems a bit at odds with your militant feminism."

"Nice," Anne said, nodding approvingly at him. "But no cigar, buddy."

Jane rolled her eyes. "You may have conveniently come up with an excuse not to introduce us, but we kept an eye on her."

"Which was quite easy, I might add," Anne said.

"Yes, we know you like her, but she belongs to James," Jane said, grinning.

Yes. No. Yes. Hell, James needed another run to clear his head. Or maybe he'd go lift after he left.

Jane turned back to him. "Back to the point. Any fool can recognize she has a warm, magnetic personality. People don't gravitate toward assholes."

"Ha!" James scoffed. "You've never seen her around me. She hates me."

"See," Anne said, pointing at him. "This is why I'm gay. Men are so dense."

James cocked a brow. "Me? I'm why you're gay?"

She wrinkled her cute little nose. "Well, that and I'm not a big fan of the cock."

Jane choked on the water she'd been sipping as she started laughing, and James couldn't help but join in. It's why he loved them. It was hard to take life too seriously when they were around. And, as Jane had pointed out when they first met, he needed that sometimes.

When the laughter finally faded away, Jane sighed. "Oh, James, you have so much to learn about women."

"I know plenty about women." Only Gracie stumped him. With the rest of the female population he had a pretty good track record.

Anne cupped her hands around her mouth and shouted, "She likes you, you idiot."

And that's what they didn't understand. She didn't like him. Yes, maybe she found herself attracted to him, but she didn't *like* him. "You're wrong."

Jane started to speak but he held up his hand and cut her off. "Let's say for the sake of argument you're right. What does it matter? We are fundamentally incompatible."

Anne shot a peek at Jane before shrugging. "People thought Jane and I didn't have anything in common."

"You have different backgrounds. That's not the same thing," James said. Jane came from a well-to-do, stuffy family that ultimately disowned her for falling in love with Anne. A stark contrast to Anne's artistic, hippy family; they'd taken Jane in and accepted her as one of their own.

Jane nodded slowly, her expression pinching with the concern he recognized only too well. "Ah, I see what this is about."

He stiffened. Did they think he was stupid? That he hadn't thought about it? He'd examined this attraction from all angles, and didn't see the point in pursuing the chemistry that simmered below the surface since he and

Gracie had met, and had now reached the boiling point. Nothing good would come from it. "There's nothing to discuss. We have nothing in common. And, I promise you, I'm her least favorite person."

"And it has nothing to do with her reminding you of the cheerleaders you couldn't land in high school," Jane said, her voice soft, without even a hint of amusement.

"Don't be ridiculous," he insisted. Yes, growing up he'd been riddled with insecurity, but that was long behind him. He'd conquered his past and buried the boy he'd been. A fact he was compelled to remind Jane. "I've dated plenty of beautiful women."

"True, but she's different, isn't she?" Jane asked. "You like your women contained and refined. Pliable and agreeable."

James clenched his jaw tight as a muscle jumped in his cheek. She made it sound so boring, and maybe it was, but debating the point didn't help his overall thesis, and he would not be trapped in an illogical argument. "Exactly. And she likes men like Evan. Hence, the not compatible comment."

"You could have fooled me. She didn't know Evan was alive." Jane could be quite ruthless when she wanted to be and today wasn't an exception. "You, on the other hand, she couldn't stop staring at."

Anne put a hand on his arm and offered him her sweetest smile. "Just because we don't want to sleep with you, doesn't mean most women don't. You still don't seem to pay attention to the way women look at you."

"For the love of God," James said, dragging a hand through his hair. "What am I, a sixteen-year-old? I know that. I'm not an idiot; I'm well aware of the attraction. But attraction is not compatibility."

Jane narrowed her gaze, looking him up and down. "Then why aren't you dating? That pretty, dark-haired psych professor has been trying to catch your attention for months."

He snapped back, his spine straightening as he frowned. Yes, that was a good question actually. Why wasn't he? Alison Benson was exactly his type. Smart, beautiful, agreeable, and she did triathlons.

He knew the answer, and she was in Revival, Illinois, haunting him from afar.

Chapter Ten

A week later Gracie slid five drawings across her large farmhouse kitchen table to Maddie. "Okay, which is your favorite?"

Her artistic best friend had recently taken to creating murals for several businesses around town. Word of her talents had spread, and slowly but surely Maddie had fallen into an unexpected career she'd always been destined for. Maddie's opinion was the only one Gracie would trust with the cake design for the Sorensons' sweet sixteen party, which was turning out to be quite a challenge.

The problem lay between the mother and the birthday girl. Tiffany Sorenson wanted a bubble-gum pink debutant ball, but her daughter was a soft-spoken bookworm whose favorite color was black.

During their phone consultation, when Gracie had asked to speak to the teenager, Tiffany had sounded reluctant but handed the phone to her daughter. As Alexandria's resigned voice conveyed her favorite things, Gracie became determined to come up with something exciting for the teenager. Sixteen was too young to hate your birthday.

But, since Tiffany Sorenson was paying, Gracie needed to please her too.

Maddie studied each of the pages in front of her. "I think these two are the best."

Gracie breathed a sigh of relief when Maddie picked her two favorites. "Me too."

"What are you thinking for colors?" Maddie asked, pushing her auburn hair back from her face.

"The mom wants pink. The birthday girl is in that teenage black-only phase, so I was thinking pale, pale pink for the base, with black details."

Maddie tapped her nails on the table, studying the pictures she'd drawn—one design had a stack of books written by Alex's favorite authors, and the other had an open book with Happy Birthday on one side and the girl's Tolkien favorite quote on the other. "I think the open book will create a cleaner look. I worry with the other one, the stack will compete with the sophisticated design on the bottom."

"But is it good?" Gracie worried her bottom lip.

Maddie glanced up from the sketches she'd been studying, a frown on her face. "It's perfect. What's wrong? It's not like you to be insecure."

Gracie shrugged. "I get insecure sometimes."

"When?"

"Like right now." She wanted the cake perfect.

Maddie leaned back in her chair. "But why? You know how talented you are."

"Sure, the people in Revival are great, but these orders are different. These Chicago clients have different expectations. They haven't pinched my cheeks as a baby, or held my hand while my mom was sick. And, well, I don't know . . . things are changing and I'm not sure how I feel about that."

Maddie nodded, and ran her finger over the edge of

the papers. "Maybe you're ready for a change. You've seemed different lately. Restless, not as happy."

"Of course I'm happy," Gracie protested. But was she? She seemed to be struggling with restlessness and couldn't put her finger on why. Maybe it was because all her friends were moving forward in their lives and she was just sort of stuck. "I have a great life and a lot to be grateful for."

"You do, but that doesn't mean you can't want more." Maddie smiled, the soft, warm smile that had endeared her to Gracie since the day they'd met. "I love you, but I miss you."

Gracie couldn't explain the distance, other than petty jealousy. Well, that and lust for her friend's brother, who wouldn't get out of her head for five freaking minutes! "Mads, I'm right next door."

"Maybe I'm being silly, but it seems like you want to talk to me, but something is stopping you."

"I'm fine," Gracie insisted, not sure what else to say. She couldn't admit her infatuation with James and she couldn't admit her jealousy over Maddie's relationship with Cecilia. Both of which were too stupid for words and would upset her friend unnecessarily. "I'm overwhelmed with the logistics for these Chicago orders, but that's it."

Maddie's forehead creased. "Promise?"

Gracie crossed her fingers under the table. "Promise." Needing to change the subject, she asked, "Hey, do you want to go to Big Red's tonight?"

Big Red's was located in the town over, a raucous Western bar filled with rednecks, line dancers, and margaritas the size of her head.

A grin flashed over Maddie's face and some of the concern slipped from her expression. "Yes, I have to get my drinking in now. Mitch is starting to talk about kids."

A pang of envy sat heavy in Gracie's chest, but she'd

never show it. She loved kids, and dreamed of her own, but the problem lay in that pesky little commitment thing with the potential father. She was great with fun, no strings attached, but anything else made her nervous. She made a big show of exasperation, throwing her hands in the air. "That Neanderthal! You just got married!"

"That's what I said." Maddie wrinkled her nose. "Don't get me wrong, I love kids, but I'm not ready yet, especially now that my business is starting to get off the ground. And I just started those graphic design classes over at the community college. There are a million things I want to do first."

Gracie stood and grabbed the batch of cranberry muffins she'd made that morning for this afternoon's Lions Club meeting. She set the plate down in front of her friend and Maddie took one automatically.

Gracie asked, "Did you talk to Mitch?"

"Of course, and he understands. He wants me to accomplish everything on my list, but he's thirty-five now and doesn't want to be an old dad."

Instead of devouring her muffin as Maddie normally did, she picked at the liner.

"And?" There was more.

Maddie shrugged one shoulder. "I went to the doctor the other day for a physical and got 'the talk.'"

"The talk?"

"Yes, the talk. The 'you're married now, when are you going to start having babies because your fertility is heading south' talk."

There was a talk? Gracie had never gotten a talk, and they went to the same doctor. The doctor who, because they lived in Revival, knew she wasn't married, had no prospects, and might never have sex again.

"You're thirty. I thought you had until you're thirty-five." Gracie was thirty-three. Only two years away from the magic number.

Maddie shook her head. "That's what I said. But Doctor Jacobs said that's when you become high risk, but your actual fertility starts to decrease after thirty."

So she was already behind the curve. "That's ridiculous!"

"It is," Maddie agreed, before her expression fell. "Unfortunately, it's also reality."

"Well, margaritas will dull reality considerably." For both of them.

Maddie laughed. "Agreed."

Gracie leaned her elbows on the table. "But seriously, Maddie, the biology of it is only half of the equation. Emotional readiness also matters. Don't let fear guide you."

A lesson she should take as well.

"I won't. I'm done with all that. And Mitch gets it. He knows how long I spent doing things because of other people's expectations, and that's the last thing he wants. But he's been thinking about it. I wish . . ." She trailed off.

"What?"

Maddie smoothed the papers under her hands. "I wish I hadn't wasted so much time trying to walk the straight and narrow. Then maybe I wouldn't have so many things left undone."

"True. But if you'd stayed a wild child you wouldn't be here now. You'd probably be married to some convict and have to face Mitch in court on larceny charges."

After spending her childhood as a wild troublemaker, Maddie had reformed into a model citizen after her father's death, had lived a staid adulthood filled with obligation and too much Catholic guilt, until she'd run away from her wedding and right into Mitch.

Maddie laughed. "You're right. See, this is what I love about you. You always put things in perspective."

Gracie grinned and waved her hand. Advice was so

much easier when directed at other people. "That's what I'm here for."

Maddie's expression once again creased in concern. "But what about you?"

"What about me?" Gracie asked, jumping up, thankful when the phone rang. That didn't sound like a question she wanted to answer. She pressed the talk button. "Hello?"

"Hello, Gracie, it's James." His deep voice rumbled over the line and her whole body broke out in goose bumps.

Her gaze flew to Maddie, who watched her with a big question mark written across her forehead. Gracie swung around and put her hand on the counter to brace herself as she remembered what she'd done this morning while thinking about the last time the professor kissed her.

"Did I lose you already?" he asked. Oh man, when had he started sounding like pure sex?

"No," she squeaked and then cleared her throat. "I'm here. Are you looking for Sam?"

"I'm looking for you."

Surprise raced through her. In all this time, he'd never called and she'd never expected him to, regardless of how hot their kisses were. He'd made himself clear and she knew how disciplined he was.

She could feel Maddie's eyes burning a hole in her back. Determined to play it cool, she asked, "How may I help you?"

"Let me guess—you're not alone?"

"That's correct."

There was a pause over the line. "Is my sister there?"

"Yes." Her throat had gone bone-dry. When was the last time she'd been this nervous talking to a man? She thought back . . . um, never.

He chuckled and it about seared her through the

phone. "Then I'll make this quick. Shane told me you'll be in Chicago to deliver a cake to the mayor's chief of staff."

"Correct."

"On Friday, two weeks from now?"

"Yes." She felt like an idiot. Where was he going with this? She honestly had no idea. Maybe he wanted her to do a cake for some professor thing.

"What time is your delivery?"

"Three o'clock."

"Would you like to have dinner after?"

Was he asking her on a date? Her fuzzy brain, shocked at hearing his voice, found it difficult to string together coherent thoughts. "With who?"

He outright laughed now. "With me."

She gripped the counter. *Yes. Yes. Yes.* "But . . . why?"

"Because I can't stop thinking about you. No matter how hard I try, or how many arguments I make about what a bad idea it is."

"It is a bad idea." A terrible idea, but the more she'd thought about him, the more she knew she had to find a way to get him out of her system.

"I agree. Are we on for dinner then?"

This had disaster written all over it. Her relationship with her friends. The way he refused to eat sugar. That she'd never get rid of him. And someday she'd watch him bring some other woman, who looked a lot like Lindsey Lord, over for Christmas. Her breath came fast. "Yes."

"Will you stay at my house instead of Shane and Cecilia's?"

She had a thousand questions and couldn't ask any of them with Maddie listening to every word. What about sex? Yes, she'd propositioned him, but that was before he'd kissed her and blown all her preconceived notions about him out of the water. "I don't think that's a good idea."

"You can stay in my spare bedroom. I'll be a perfect gentleman."

"That doesn't seem smart." God, she cursed having to answer this call now while stuck with the ability to only deliver vague responses.

"Maybe not, but I was hoping I could persuade you to spend Saturday with Declan and me."

She could only blink down at her hardwood floors. He wanted her to spend the day with him? And his cousin? Her head spun. This was the last thing she'd predicted when she woke up this morning. "I don't know."

"If you stay with Shane and Cecilia, I'll have to come pick you up. Which is fine by me, but you do understand we'll suffer a lot of questions, and every person we know will find out before we even get in the car and drive away."

He played dirty. Damn him. She sighed. "Fine. As long as there's a separate . . ." With Maddie behind her she couldn't say *bedroom* without raising suspicion, so she settled for a less meaningful word. "Area."

"Deal. Then it's a date?"

"Yes." In a daze she hung up the phone.

She had a date . . . with the professor.

In the end, what to do about Gracie had been a spontaneous decision.

James, who thought through every detail of his life with careful, methodical reason, wasn't quite sure what had come over him. In his office at work, sitting at his desk, ready to work on his recent publication about body mass estimation from cranial variables. His research had been organized, his document open, fingers on the keyboard.

The next thing he knew, twenty minutes had passed and he'd written the word *the.*

Instead of working, he'd stared off into space, thinking about Gracie. Her mouth. The flash of her blue eyes when she was mad at him. Which was always. The way her body felt under his palms. And how he didn't think he could live without touching her again. Without tasting her. He thought about what Jane and Anne had said. He either needed to take action or ask out the psych professor who had been tossing him signs so blatant they may as well have been in neon. The kind of woman he always dated.

And there had been no contest. Every time he attempted to conjure up Alison's face, she morphed into Gracie.

Shane had mentioned in passing about Gracie coming to Chicago. James wanted to see her.

No matter how he fought it, she was there, lurking in his thoughts. He was tired of fighting his attraction. It wasn't working. Now that he'd kissed her, everything felt unfinished.

He needed to take control of the situation and finish it.

The idea had popped into his head and before he knew it, the phone was in his hand and he'd Googled her number.

Five minutes later he had a date with the most wanted woman in Revival.

Chapter Eleven

Gracie rang the bell of James's townhome and hoped she wouldn't faint. This was it. In retrospect, agreeing to dinner tonight had been a stupid idea. She'd been up since five putting the finishing touches on the cake. Then she'd driven for hours to make the delivery on time. She was drained, exhausted, and sore.

It had been worth it. The stress and adrenaline and frantic work had paid off because her cake was spectacular. One look at the happy mother *and* daughter told her she'd hit her mark. It came out exactly as she'd envisioned, clean and sophisticated enough for a fancy party, but with the sixteen-year-old's wishes firmly in mind. When the girl had hugged her and whispered a reverent thanks, Gracie's heart swelled.

Gracie couldn't be more proud of her accomplishment. Or more exhausted. Once the cake had been delivered, the adrenaline had seeped out of her, leaving her wanting to curl up in her bed and sleep for a week.

But instead she was here for a date with the professor.

If not for the nerves jumping in her stomach, she'd have fallen asleep on the front stoop. Luckily, she was too tired to contemplate how much she wanted to see him. Or how she'd ached for this day since he'd called her and asked her out. They'd only spoken one other time to go over the details of her arrival, and even though she'd been alone, she'd still been tongue-tied.

Which frustrated and confused her.

Before she could ruminate any further, James opened the door and her throat dried up.

He looked gorgeous. His hair was slightly messy and he wasn't wearing his glasses, so his green eyes seemed to hit her right in the solar plexus. In a pair of faded jeans, his broad shoulders filled out a blue T-shirt with a white police box on it and the words *Trust Me, I'm the Doctor.* Next to him she felt like a bedraggled mess.

He smiled and held out a hand. "Can I take that for you?"

She blinked and froze. Everything would change once she stepped over the threshold.

James took the overnight bag from her hand and opened the door wider, gesturing her inside. "Come in, Gracie. I won't bite."

She waited for the "unless you want me to" pun men normally made after comments like that, but this was the professor, so of course it didn't come. She swallowed hard, urging her feet to move.

They stared at each other for several long moments before she finally cleared her throat and stepped inside. "Thank you for having me."

He grinned and her heart leapt in her chest. "My, aren't we polite today."

She wrinkled her nose. "I'm always polite . . . except to you."

The door clicked behind her as she entered the foyer.

"I guess I'm a lucky man."

"Guess so." Behind her she heard a thump she assumed was her overnight bag.

"I figure you're exhausted." He sounded close. Too close.

She nodded.

He pressed a hot, open palm to the center of her back, which burned through the cotton of her blue top, urging her forward, and she tried not to flinch in surprise. If he noticed her tension, and she was sure he did, he didn't mention it. For all her tightness, he couldn't have sounded more relaxed when he spoke.

"Kick off your shoes and go put your feet up so you can relax. Give me your car keys. I have to run outside and put a permit on the dash."

"Okay." She grabbed her keys from the front purse pocket where she always kept them and handed them to James.

He led her to the couch and nestled her into the corner, running his hands down her jeans-covered legs to lift her feet onto the sofa. It was an intimate, caring gesture and she wasn't sure why she let him handle her that way, other than it was nice. Unexpected.

"How'd it go?" he asked.

"Good," she said, letting her head fall back against the soft cushion. She didn't know if she was dead on her feet or he really had the most comfortable couch in the world. "I have pictures."

"I'll check them out when I get back, but for now, rest. I won't be but a minute."

And then he was gone.

She glanced around the room. His house was so warm and open, nothing like the man himself. Was that true? Or was his perceived coldness another layer of defense she put between them? She let her shoulders relax and her lashes drifted closed. She'd think about it later. For now, she'd sink into these lush, soft pillows and be thankful she could finally put her feet up.

Her lids grew heavy.

She yawned.

Her body eased and she let her mind drift.

"Gracie," a man's voice said from a distant, faraway place.

"Gracie."

She snuggled deeper into the warm haven and mumbled, "Go away."

A deep chuckle pulled her into consciousness. "Come on, open up. I have something for you."

As the voice finally registered, she bolted straight up, instantly wide-awake. "Where am I?"

"You fell asleep." James sat on the couch next to her, the heat of his thigh pressing against her hip.

She relaxed into the cushions. She didn't remember drifting off. "How long was I out?"

"About forty-five minutes."

She scrubbed at her eyes, belatedly aware she wore mascara and probably had smeared it all over her face. She must look a wreck. "I'm sorry, I don't normally come into a person's home and pass out."

"You have nothing to be sorry about. I'm sure it's been a long day. That's why I got you something."

She blinked at him. He got her something? "What?"

He jutted his chin toward the stairs. "It's why I couldn't let you sleep any longer. Come on, I'll show you."

She licked her dry lips, and as though he was a mind reader he held out a chilled glass. "I figured you'd need this."

Grateful, she took the glass and drank. It was delicious. It tasted like water and lemon, but with a hint of something else. Refreshing and crisp. She downed the whole thing, then looked at him quizzically. "What's in there?"

"It's infused with cucumbers and lemon. It boosts energy and helps flush toxins."

Instead of her normal churlishness when he spouted health-fanatic stuff, she couldn't help but smile. Especially when it tasted surprisingly good. "It's delicious, thank you."

Their eyes met. Locked.

Heat filled the space between them.

She soaked in his features. He might not drip testosterone like the men she normally dated, but he had a presence even more compelling.

She swallowed, unable to look away. She wanted his mouth on hers. For weeks she'd been thinking about the way he kissed. Had barely been able to get it out of her mind.

As if he read her thoughts, his gaze dipped to her lips, and those evergreen eyes darkened.

Her lips parted in anticipation. Her breath caught.

He shook his head, then stood, and disappointment washed over her.

He held out an open palm. "Come on."

Her attention slipped to his T-shirt. What did a police box have to do with being a doctor? She pointed to his ridiculously impressive chest. "The doctor?"

He laughed. "It's from *Doctor Who*. Maddie gave it to me last Christmas."

"Who's that?" She took his hand, and when his fingers curled around hers electricity shot up her arm.

"It's a sci-fi show about a time traveler who's only known as the Doctor." He tugged her upstairs. "We can watch it on Netflix if you want to check it out."

"Is it good?"

"It's awesome." He came to a door and opened it. The

bedroom was dimly lit, and soft, soothing music filled the air.

Her heart sped up to a gallop and for one brief moment she thought he was about to take her to bed, but then a short woman in a white shirt and pants stepped out from another door. "I'm ready, Mr. James."

Confused, Gracie regarded him. "What is this?"

"I thought you'd be tired and sore from your day, so I arranged a massage for you." He gestured to the woman standing patiently by a table. "This is Rosa. She gives the best massages on the face of this earth. You'll be in good hands for the next ninety minutes."

Openmouthed, Gracie could only gape at him. "You did this? For me?"

He nodded.

"Why?"

He shrugged, frowning at her. "I thought you would like it."

She shook her head. "It's too much."

"It's not. I wanted to. Besides, I think our dating experiment will go better if you're not dead on your feet."

She couldn't believe he'd done this. She was stunned. Floored. She couldn't be more surprised if he'd offered her diamonds. Hell, this was better than diamonds. It was too much. "I shouldn't."

He cut her off. "Don't deny me."

His words caused a tingle low in her belly. She bit her lip, then put a hand on his arm, hoping to convey her gratitude from this unexpected gesture. "Thank you. This is the nicest thing anyone has ever done for me."

He rubbed his knuckles over her arm and she shivered. "Then you haven't been pampered nearly enough in your life."

She'd never been pampered at all. Men normally focused on getting her naked, not taking care of her. "I don't know what to say."

"Say you'll enjoy yourself and let Rosa work her magic." He pointed to the closed door. "The guest bath is through that door. It's got a state-of-the-art steam shower and a heated Jacuzzi tub. Feel free to use either or both. I put your bag in there while you slept."

He'd thought of everything, and for the first time she found herself thinking maybe an analytical, overly prepared man wasn't all bad. She was so overwhelmed with gratitude she wanted to raise to her tiptoes and kiss him softly on the lips, but didn't dare. Instead she whispered, "Thank you, James."

"You're welcome," he said, his voice gruff. "Now go."

She went, turning herself over to Rosa.

Two hours later Gracie wandered downstairs, her skin pink, damp curls around her face. Rosa had left a bit ago and James had been waiting for Gracie to appear. He laid the book he'd been reading across his stomach and smiled, trying not to wonder if she was naked under that big, fluffy robe. She shouldn't look sexy, but of course this was Gracie they were talking about. The woman could make a burlap sack alluring.

The bags under her eyes were gone. The fatigue that had pinched her face when she'd arrived had also eased. She looked fresh, her cheeks rosy. Makeup-free, her expression held an innocence and vulnerability he'd never seen on her before. She sank into the corner of his couch, farthest away from the club chair where he sat, and tucked her bare feet under her.

"Feel better?" he asked.

"I feel excellent." She smiled, all soft and warm. "I'm so relaxed, I'm Jell-O. You're right; Rosa is a genius. Thank you again."

"You're welcome. I'm glad you enjoyed it. I had a hunch you might, and a good massage never hurts after you've been working your ass off, as I'm sure you have been."

Gracie picked up the end of the tie of her robe and started to fiddle with the edges. "You shouldn't have."

"I wanted to."

She bit her bottom lip and her gaze flitted to his, then away. "Why?"

He picked up the book and put it on the end table next to him. "I wanted to do something nice for you. I wanted to take care of you, because I'm guessing you don't get that often. But I'm selfish too; I didn't want you exhausted." He decided to be bluntly honest. "Besides, if you're going to be preoccupied thinking about a bed, I'd rather it not be because you're dying to go to sleep."

"I see." More fiddling with her robe. "So you're not that much of a Boy Scout."

"Nope. Although I stand by my promise to be a complete gentleman." He still wasn't sure sex was a good idea, but when he'd asked her out he'd decided to stop pretending it wasn't a possibility. Since the weekend of the engagement party, the dam had burst, and he wasn't sure there was any stopping it. Or if he wanted to.

She shifted restlessly on the couch as though she couldn't find a comfortable spot. "You know this is a stupid idea."

"Probably." He couldn't argue with her there. This was not his brightest hour, and surprisingly, he found he didn't care. He needed to finish this with her. He'd play out this weekend and see where they landed.

"We have nothing in common," she said, her voice soft, with none of the sass she normally reserved for him.

"We don't. Or maybe we do, and don't realize it."

"Doubtful."

Even though he agreed, her belief that they were so dissimilar they might as well be different species irked him. Irrational and unfair, since he'd often focused on their incompatibility to manage his attraction. "There's something, though, isn't there?"

She shrugged.

"If there's not, why are you here?"

"Curiosity."

Instead of being defensive, he chuckled. "Is that all?"

"You're distracting me from my point."

"Which is?"

"I hate health food."

He nodded, pressing his lips together to stop the smile twitching at his lips. In his most deadpan voice he said, "In that case, I need to cancel our reservations for the vegan, raw food restaurant I was going to take you to."

Her head shot up, the scowl already lining her lips. "I hope you're kidding!"

He laughed. "Do you really think I know so little about you that I would take you to a health food restaurant?"

She shrugged one shoulder. A habit around him, it seemed.

"You refuse to eat my cupcakes, so it's not out of the realm of possibility."

Ah yes, their war about cupcakes had started not long after they'd met. They'd been forced together at Mitch and Maddie's house and she'd been on a real mean streak, constantly baiting him. And, while it might have been childish, when she'd offered him one of her cupcakes he'd rebuffed her. Somehow the battle had escalated into a full-blown war and now they were in a standoff over her baked goods. Which was as ridiculous as it sounded, but there it was. This weekend he intended to show her he wasn't entirely a tight-ass.

He sighed, like it was a big imposition. "Fine, I'll eat your cupcakes the next time you make them."

She stared at him for several long moments. "You know, most people don't consider eating cupcakes a hardship."

"I'm not most people." He had his reasons for the way he was, why he required so much discipline and control over his life. Other people might not understand them, but they made sense to him. Structure and discipline had saved him at a time when he'd thought he was unsavable, and he wouldn't apologize for it. "For the record, it's not an insult toward you that I eat healthy. I was this way long before I met you."

She twirled the end of the robe about her finger. "Then why does it feel like it?"

"You tell me."

She took a deep breath and exhaled. "I feel like you're judging me."

The comment took him aback; it was so far from the thoughts he had about her, he almost didn't know what to say. "Why on earth would you think that?"

"You yell at Shane for eating Cheetos."

James was lost, unable to understand how the two were related. "Yeah, so? He's my brother. He regularly gives me shit about my eating and exercise. In return, I give him shit about junk food. That's what brothers do."

"So you'll eat Cheetos?" Her expression lit up with what could only be hope.

"God no, do you know the kind of chemicals in those things?" He hated to burst her bubble, but he refused to pretend. Not even for her.

Her face fell and her fingers tightened on the belt of her robe. "See, that's what I mean."

"As usual, your thought processes elude me." He sat forward, putting his elbows on his knees. "What does not liking Cheetos have to do with judging you?"

She opened her mouth, sputtered, then closed it before starting again. "I'm just saying this is why we're not compatible."

"Still not getting it. Are you such a huge fan you require your dates to eat a bag before you go out?" He looked her up and down. "Do you have a powdered-cheese fetish I should know about? Because that might be a deal breaker for me."

Wide-eyed, she stared at him before a smile quivered at her lips. "Of course not. I don't have any fetishes."

"Not even one?" He frowned, finding he liked teasing her. "For a wild girl, that's pretty disappointing. And here I thought I'd learn some new tricks."

She sucked in a breath and shifted, the bathrobe flashing a hint of leg before she quickly covered up. "Don't change the subject."

"I don't even *understand* the subject. I'm trying here, but I don't get how they are related." Subtext had never been his strong suit.

"It's just that . . . well . . . I eat pizza and it ruins the enjoyment if someone's sitting there judging my food choices."

"I eat pizza sometimes too, Gracie. I'm not a robot."

"I've never seen you."

"That doesn't mean I don't. You know what I think? You judge me and assume I'm doing the same. Which I'm not. The only time I've even thought about what you ate was to imagine licking it off you. Nothing more. Nothing less."

That seemed to stump her, and she undertook the serious business of playing with her robe belt again, so he continued. "When I'm training, which I was the last time you spent any real time with me, I eat healthy because it affects my performance. While I might not be a crazy sports nut like Shane and Evan, I'm still competitive and want to better my time. Training for a marathon while filling your body with junk food does not facilitate peak performance. But I'm not a tyrant, nor do I expect anyone else to follow along. Does that clear things up for you? Or is there something more?"

She studied her lap for a long time before she said in a hesitant voice, "So you don't care I'm not a hard-body? That I'm not all buff?"

Why on earth would she think he'd care? Yes, she was curvier than the fashion industry deemed acceptable, in the same way Marilyn Monroe wouldn't be considered fashionable today. And Gracie understood her effect on men. He'd watched her use it to her advantage over and over again. So why exactly would she think he'd want her to be a hard-body? "Gracie, I've watched men trip over themselves when you passed them on the street."

She shrugged. "Yeah, so?"

"Your body is amazing, as you damn well know."

Another shrug. "I saw your ex-girlfriend."

The idea that Gracie might harbor a tiny bit of jealousy over Lindsey was almost impossible to believe. And satisfied him in a way that was entirely immature. Instinct warned him that grinning like a fool was a poor choice, so he kept his expression neutral. "My *ex*-girlfriend."

"But still, have you ever dated anyone like me?"

"Gracie," he said, and waited until her blue-eyed gaze met his. "Most men go their whole lives never even seeing a woman like you, let alone being given the chance to date one."

She scowled, and two frown lines marred her forehead. "You're missing the point. I'm not talking about looks. I'm talking about important stuff, like compatibility. I'm never going to train for a marathon with you."

"Fine. I'll tear up your training schedule. I was

planning on getting you started tomorrow morning at six sharp."

"Don't even joke." She tucked her hair behind her ear. "I'm not going to change for you."

This conversation was making his head hurt. "We're going on a date, and by the end we could loathe each other. Isn't it a little early to start worrying I'm going to try and change you?"

"Maybe you think I'm being silly," she said, picking at imaginary lint on her robe. "But I don't have a big family like you. I've got Sam, and I have my friends, which in case you haven't noticed, are made up largely of your family members."

He scrubbed a hand over his jaw. "I hadn't thought of it like that."

"They're important to me. I don't want to lose them."

He laced his fingers between his spread knees, thinking through her point. "I don't want that either. I only see two options: spend the weekend together and see what happens, or cut our losses and close the door on the attraction."

She shifted again on the couch, blowing out a hard breath. "Why'd you have to go and kiss me?"

His lips twitched. "You have only yourself to blame."

Her expression lightened as sass lit up her eyes. "Me? How am I to blame?"

He threw up his hands, grinning at her. "You propositioned me for sex."

She rolled her eyes. "Well, how was I supposed to know you'd be any good at it?"

In an instant, the mood shifted; tension permeated the air between them. His attention drifted her full, lush mouth he'd been dreaming about. Voice dropping, he said, "You know how you hate all that analytical, over-thinking calculation?"

Her pink tongue darted out and wet her lower lip. "Yes?"

"It can be used for evil."

She swallowed. "I see."

Their gazes met. Heat. An undercurrent of barely leashed desire, biding its time before it sucked them under.

"So dinner." He didn't ask, because there wasn't really a question.

Slowly, she nodded. "Dinner."

Chapter Twelve

The heat of James's palm burned through the thin fabric of the blue dress Gracie wore. All he'd said about the restaurant was that it was fine dining mixed with adventure. With no clue what that meant, she'd worn a V-neck jersey dress that molded to her curves, and simple jewelry.

The restaurant barely had a sign on a nearly deserted street on the outskirts of Wicker Park. If she blinked she would have missed it. They entered the dining room and she came to a dead stop. It was a small place, with about ten tables that were mostly filled. Rap music pumped through the stereo system, the heavy bass a heartbeat that made the air pulse. A waiter came out from the back with a bottle of Jameson and brought it over to one of the tables; a minute later the patrons, along with the waiter, cheered and downed the drinks.

This was not anything like what she'd expected.

Gracie's eyes widened and she craned her neck to look at James. "I thought you said this was fine dining."

"I promise you'll never eat another meal like it." He grinned down at her and her stomach did a flip. After their talk, sex was all she could think about.

"They're playing Run-DMC," she said.

"I know. Our table is over there, in the corner." His hand slid over the curve of her hip and she shivered. They'd stopped pretending the air between them didn't crackle with sexual tension, and every touch was electric.

An empty table for two was nestled into the corner of the room, next to the window overlooking the street. She walked over to it and sat down, still unable to get over the place. The whole restaurant was bizarre, with the heavy beat of bass, dim lighting, and red walls that gave the room a red-light-district ambiance. As they settled into the chairs she asked, "Have you ever been here before?"

This didn't seem like the kind of place a stuffy professor would frequent.

From the kitchen, visible from the dining room, a guy in his midtwenties called out, "Professor Donovan, be right there."

And she was wrong. Well, wasn't James just full of surprises? "I guess so," she said, answering her own question.

He shrugged. "Eli was one of my students before he gave up academics to become a chef, smoke weed, and down whiskey."

Gracie laughed. Damn, he kept doing that. Making her laugh. Making her want him. "This has to be the strangest place I've ever been in."

Even though the music was loud, she didn't have to yell. The room was intimate despite the crowd. They'd done a good job creating a pleasant atmosphere.

"And you haven't even tried the food." From the bag he'd brought with him he pulled out a bottle of red and put it on the table. "You only drink red, right? Zinfandel?"

She nodded slowly. "How did you know?"

"I'm observant." He gave her a long once-over. "And you're a hard woman not to notice."

She sucked in a breath at the heat he kept blasting in her direction. It was torture. He was a sadist. That was the only logical explanation. She didn't know how, but he was seducing her more effectively than she'd ever been seduced before, and he had barely touched her. He hadn't even kissed her.

"What do we have here?" A sly, cocky male voice broke through her lust-filled haze.

Gracie looked into the face of the chef who had called out to James earlier. A cute guy in his twenties, with dirty-blond hair, brown eyes, and a truly devilish smile.

James gestured toward Gracie. "Gracie Roberts, this is Eli Burke."

Gracie shook the younger man's outstretched hand. "It's a pleasure to meet you, Eli. Interesting place you've got here."

"The pleasure is all mine." He drank her in with all the enthusiasm of a puppy eyeing a tasty morsel. "God-damn. You've outdone yourself, Professor Donovan."

James laughed and gave Gracie another heated stare. "I'm thinking I'll keep her."

To her horror, her nipples beaded under the skimpy fabric of her dress. She tugged her hand away from Eli and resisted the urge to cross her arms over her chest.

Eli gave her another appreciative look. "If you change your mind, I'll take her."

"Not even in the next life, boy." James's voice turned menacing, but his expression remained good-natured.

The possessiveness in his tone made her press her thighs together, but the modern woman was compelled to speak up. She gave them both a smile. "Don't I get a say in this?"

James skimmed a glance over her. "No."

Even as the protest rose to her lips, she couldn't help thinking she'd never heard the word *no* sound so hot before. She raised a brow. "No?"

His eyes didn't even flicker. "No."

The twisted part of her liked his presumption. He was evil. And she liked it, far too much. This was bad. Very, very bad.

"Come with me, babe," Eli said, breaking through her thoughts. "I'm a hell of a lot less bossy than the professor."

James gave him a stern glare. "Are you going to feed us, or hit on her?"

Eli laughed. "Both. That cool?"

"I suppose." James reached into the mystery bag and pulled out a bottle of Glenlivit. "Your favorite."

Eli nodded appreciatively at the liquor. "The professor always brings the best stuff. Be right back." He tossed a corkscrew on the table. "For the wine." Then he was off.

Gracie swallowed past her dry throat. "Interesting service here."

"It's an experience." James grabbed the opener and started working on the bottle. "I'm positive you'll love it."

She ran a finger over the tines of her fork. "Where are the menus?"

He smoothly poured the red into a stout glass. "There are none. You eat what they give you."

The night was getting stranger and stranger. "This wasn't what I was expecting when you asked me to dinner."

"Trust me," James said, pouring his own glass of wine. "When you leave here you'll have had one of the best and most interesting meals of your life. You'll also be drunk as hell, but hopefully you'll remember what you ate."

"Drunk? But isn't it BYOB?" Another oddity at a fine dining restaurant.

Leaning over the table, his voice lowered an octave. "I don't think anyone leaves this place sober."

She licked her lips. How could she stand this? "Even you?"

"Even me." His green eyes darkened. He wasn't wearing his glasses tonight, opting instead for contacts. "It's why we took a cab. And why your virtue will remain intact."

"I'm not virtuous." She wanted him. She wasn't going to be able to last the night without attacking him. "And I haven't had anything to drink yet."

"There's no leaving this place sober, and the first time I take you we're not going to be intoxicated. That's non-negotiable." He gave her a cocky smile she'd never seen before. "I can probably be talked into orgasms."

Ready to come right here, right now, she was saved from a response when Eli came back over and plopped three shot glasses on the table. He filled the glasses with the liquor James had brought him. "Bottoms up."

She stared at the shot, understanding why the evening might not end in sobriety. Her gaze met James's. Something hot, almost tangible, passed between them and in that moment she decided to throw any ounce of caution she had left into the Chicago wind.

She picked up the shot and the men followed suit. "Cheers."

"Cheers," they chorused back, and the three of them clicked glasses.

Excited to see where the night took her, she downed the whiskey.

* * *

Two hours later James was on the wrong side of buzzed and Gracie was well into drunk territory. Along for the ride, Eli had not only downed shot after shot with them, but drank with the other tables as well.

James couldn't understand how the guy even saw straight.

But it was all worth it because Gracie's eyes gleamed with pleasure, and it was obvious she was having a great time.

As the night progressed Eli had taken to flirting outlandishly, and she'd done nothing to rebuff the younger man. Happy to play the straight man, as they expected, James continuously rolled his eyes at the two of them.

"Hey, Gracie," Eli said, putting the next course in front of them. There had been so many James had lost count. "You want to go out back for some green?"

Gracie giggled up at the boy, her cheeks flushed. "Are you offering me drugs?"

"Nah, just a little pot." Eli rubbed his flat belly. God bless the young. "To stimulate your appetite."

"For fuck's sake, Eli," James said, realizing his words were slurred. "You're going to get yourself arrested."

Gracie gasped and pointed a finger at him. "Oh my God, he swore." She looked at Eli. "He said fuck."

Eli stumbled a little before righting himself. "She's got you there, Professor."

"I swear sometimes," James said, wondering how he could sound both drunk and stuffy at the same time. A feat only he could accomplish. "I save my profanity for when it's meaningful instead of peppering it into my conversation like you two."

Gracie and Eli looked at each other, then promptly broke into hysterical laughter, holding their bellies as they shook.

Another chef came over. "What'd I miss?"

They continued to laugh and James gave him a somber shake of the head. "I have no idea."

"Time for another shot!" the chef yelled.

Twenty people cheered. Over the course of the evening they'd met everyone in the small restaurant, and as it always did, the place became one big drunken party.

Gracie waved her hands. "I can't. Not anymore."

Eli ignored her and poured another round of shots, then left to make his way around the restaurant to refill glasses. It was a ritual to bring liquor to the restaurant as a gift, and the boys had bottles on reserve.

Gracie leaned across the table. "I can't drink anymore."

James was having an increasingly hard time concentrating on anything other than getting his hands on her.

"Come on," Eli said, crowding everyone together. "Toast."

James stood, weaved a little bit, then grabbed Gracie's hand, pulling her up. She fell against his chest, her warm, lush body pressing against him. He let his hands roam down her back and over her hips. He leaned down and whispered in her ear, "Jesus, you feel even more fuckable than you look."

She gave an erotic little moan, her breath hot on his neck.

"Come on, Professor, you're holding us up," Eli said as the large group crowded together.

James tugged Gracie forward, enfolding her into the circle and stepping behind her. They all raised their glasses.

Adam, one of the other chefs, shouted, "Here's to big tits and the Cubs winning the World Series."

James laughed at the classic Chicago toast. The crowd cheered and then everyone pounded the shots.

James slipped an arm around Gracie's waist, letting his palm settle around her softly rounded belly. He brushed his lips over the curve of her neck. His self-control was shot. "I think orgasms are definitely in order."

She leaned back, her ass brushing his erection. "James."

The crowd started to disperse and James whispered, "You have no idea the things I'm going to do to you."

She spun around, wobbling. She licked her lips. "Like what?"

He gripped her bare arm, pulling her close. "Wouldn't you rather be surprised?"

"Maybe." Her gaze darted around the room. "I, um, need to go to the bathroom."

He jutted his chin toward the kitchen, where the one and only bathroom was. "Do you need help?"

The air was so hot between them they could start a fire. Her nipples were so hard they were visible under her dress, and he itched to stroke them.

"I'm good," she said, the words a pant.

He chuckled as she turned on her heel, in an off-kilter manner, and weaved her way to the back.

He returned to his table, and a minute later Eli came over. "Man, Gracie is hotter than hell."

"Yes, she is." James couldn't help the smug grin from sliding over his lips. And she was his, for at least the next day or so.

"And she's fun as fuck."

James laughed. "She is."

"How'd you meet her?"

"She's friends with my sister."

Eli shook his head, frowning. "Damn, you lucked out. My sister's friends don't look anything like that."

Gracie slid into her seat and put her napkin on her lap. "What's going on?"

James grinned, gesturing at his former student. "Eli was just talking about how hot you are."

"Aww . . ." She batted her thick lashes at the younger man. "Thank you."

Eli's expression turned sly. "Three-way?"

Gracie burst out laughing, shaking her head. "You're incorrigible."

Eli hit James on the shoulder. "What do you say, Professor?"

"I don't share. Ever," James said in a low voice.

Gracie swallowed hard.

"That's a shame. But if you change your mind . . ." He trailed off, his expression filled with hope.

"You'll be the first on the list," James said, not taking his eyes off her.

"Awesome. I'll be back," Eli said, filling their glasses of wine before heading back to the kitchen.

Her fingers fluttered to her lips, then fingered the thin silver chain at her throat. He suddenly couldn't wait one more second to taste her. He stood, grabbing her wrist, and leaned over the table, yanking her to meet him halfway. His mouth met hers, in a hard, brutal kiss that held nothing back and would certainly destroy all her illusions about his sexual incompetence.

Her free hand snaked around his neck. The kiss turned a bit frantic at the edges and he pulled away before he ended up taking her right there at the table. He whispered against her lips, "There's definitely going to be orgasms."

Chapter Thirteen

After closing the place down, Gracie and James crawled into a cab. Her head spun. From alcohol, fun, the excitement of the night, but mostly from James.

He'd taken her on the best date of her life.

She leaned her head against the backseat and studied him as he slid into the cab and gave his address to the driver. In the darkness, the streetlights highlighted his sharp cheekbones, and he was the most beautiful man she'd ever seen.

He caught her staring and raised one brow. "What?"

"You are full of surprises, Professor." Her voice, a low purr, surprised even her.

He put his arm along the back of the seat, twisting to face her more fully. "Why's that?"

Since she'd stepped into his house that afternoon, he'd been nothing less than spectacular and he deserved his due. Later she'd worry about the implications of this date and how they hadn't fought once, but for now, she smiled. Wanting—no, *needing* his mouth on hers again. "That was, by far, the best night I've ever had, by a mile."

He picked up a lock of her hair and twirled it around his finger. "So I've annihilated my competition?"

She was past denying anything, not sure if it was the alcohol or James making her honest. "I don't think you've had competition since the day we met."

He moved closer to her, his gaze dipping to her mouth. "Good."

"You're a lot more arrogant than I would have thought."

His finger trailed down her neck and gooseflesh broke out over her arms. "Is that a good thing?"

Her voice dropped an octave as her breath caught. "What do you think?"

"I think you have the softest skin I've ever touched." He traced a path over her collarbones.

She swallowed hard, her body burning with an ache completely out of proportion to how little he'd touched her.

"I think I'm going to enjoy making you come."

She peeked at the driver, who didn't appear to be paying attention to them as he tapped out a beat on the steering wheel to exotic music playing over the radio. She licked her lips.

He leaned closer, his mouth a mere inch away. "And I think you need a little arrogance in a man."

Her breath came out in little pants. She did. She didn't know why, but she did. "Yes."

His hand curled around her neck. "In this, at least, I understand you."

She nodded, suddenly wondering if he might be the only man who'd ever understood her.

He brushed his mouth over hers. Once. Twice. Three times.

She moaned and reached for him, pressing her lips to his.

His tongue met hers and she was lost. She twined her hands around his neck, pulling him close. He let out a low growl that thrilled her, heightening her desire until she would have done anything. All night had been one slow, torturous, teasing simmer that now came to a boil. He gripped her hips, twisting her to face him. Mindless of her surroundings, she climbed on top of him, not caring they acted like candidates for *Taxicab Confessions.*

She straddled James as his mouth consumed hers, his grip sure and hard, slightly rough on the swells of her hips. Just the way she liked it. When she pressed against his hard cock, they both moaned.

His fingers tightened and she rocked again. Her breath fast. Her nipples brushed against his chest and she gasped.

God. Such delicious friction. She moved again. She needed more. So. Much. More.

His hands roamed up the sides of her body, and his thumbs stroked over her aching nipples.

Yes. Yes. Yes.

It had been so long. And his hands felt so good. She moved in rhythmic circles, riding him. In perfect rhythm he thrust to meet her. Their mouths matched the frantic pace of their bodies.

He pinched her nipples through the thin fabric that separated them.

She throbbed and pulsed with need. Frustrated. Desperate to get closer. She needed skin. She wanted him pounding inside her. Driving into her.

She groaned, a low, needy sound.

He seemed to understand. He rocked hard at the same time he jerked her hips down. She cried out. Any more of that and she'd come. She dug her hands into his shoulders.

Skin. She needed skin. To touch him.

Wanted everything it now seemed like only he could give her.

A loud, long, insistent honk filled the air, ripping her from her sexual haze and plunging her into reality.

James heard it too because he ripped his mouth away and said in an angry tone, "What?"

"You're here, buddy." The cabbie had the rough, gravelly voice of a smoker.

Heat flooded Gracie's already hot face.

James raked a hand through his hair and gave her a little squeeze. "You'll have to move so I can get my wallet."

Still panting for breath, Gracie slid off him and fumbled with her purse as James paid the driver, whom she refused to look at. Grabbing her hand, James led her out of the car and up the stairs to his door.

The sexual haze of lust and desire was so strong she could barely breathe. James was in front of her, opening the door with one hand, his other locked around hers. She clutched his arm like he was her lifeline on a sinking ship. He pushed the door open and pulled her inside before shutting out the outside world and cocooning them into his rich, sensual home, which now looked exactly right for him.

Before she could speak, he pinned her against the wall, his hands locked around her wrists, his mouth on hers.

Blocking out the torrent of emotions crashing around inside her.

His mouth was fierce. His tongue demanded. His lips crushed. It was too much. Too crazy, but she was drowning and speech was no longer a viable option.

She just took it. Took everything he gave her until her body was a melting puddle of liquid lava, ready to be molded into whatever James Donovan commanded.

He growled low in his throat, a hot, primal sound that inflamed her blood.

She was going to incinerate. Be consumed by need.

He locked her wrists together, pulled them over her head, and encircled them with one hand. His free palm roamed down her body and cupped her breast. He played with her nipple through the thin fabric of her dress. Stroking the hard bud. Squeezing. Teasing.

She whimpered, arching her hips in invitation.

He didn't relent. Didn't concede to her wishes. No, he continued his torture until she was mindless. If her mouth had been free, she would have begged. So her mind begged for her. Pleaded in urgent whispers to take her soon or she'd be lost forever.

When at last she believed she could take it no more, he stopped, and his hand continued its evil path. Down the curve of her waist. Over the swell of her hips.

He kicked her foot, forcing her to step wide.

Oh, God, yes. She'd been so wrong. He knew exactly what she wanted. What she liked. How she needed to be handled.

He ground the heel of his hand between her legs, right where she desired it most. She rose on tiptoes, desperate to get closer. He slid his fingers into her panties, gliding over her skin, slick from her wetness. His thumb brushed over her clit and she came.

The explosive orgasm thundered through her with unexpected and unanticipated force. She tore her mouth free, as a cry ripped from her throat.

It wasn't a normal climax. Nothing about this was normal. No, this was violent, crashing, endless waves of pleasure so intense her vision dimmed and her world spun.

"Jesus," he said, his voice hoarse.

Before she had a chance to come to her senses he swung her around, pushing her to the carpeted floor. She tried to form a coherent word but her skirt was shoved up to her hips, her panties pushed to her knees and his mouth was on her.

He licked the hard bundle of nerves.

His tongue moved against her in exquisite torture. No hesitation. No tentative stroking. Just hard, demanding, all-consuming pleasure.

She was going to die.

Break apart and never be put together again.

He moaned, and it vibrated against her swollen flesh. His fingers plunged inside, first one, then the other.

He hit her G-spot.

She let out a low, mewling wail. Like an animal. Like a cat in heat.

He massaged in hard, rhythmic circles as his mouth latched onto her clit.

Perfect, perfect rhythm.

Her hips jerked.

Her body keened.

Another orgasm built inside her, so forceful it threatened to devour her.

"James," she cried out, her hands falling helplessly to the side as she started to rock against his mouth and fingers as though some demon possessed her. "Please, James. Oh God. I can't stand it."

In answer, he increased his pace.

His fingers moved harder.

His lips firmer.

His tongue faster.

Relentless.

Strong strokes built an inferno inside her.

Need coiled tighter.

And tighter.

And tighter.

She burst, climaxing so hard, she lost all sense of time as the contractions beat through her and hot wetness slid down her thighs. She shook in a mindless heap on his floor. Helpless to do anything but ride the waves of the orgasm controlled by James's ruthlessly talented mouth and uncompromising fingers.

Finally, he relented and she went limp. Her muscles lax.

He crawled up her body and she managed to blink at him, her brain still numb from shock and pleasure.

He ran a finger down her cheek; so tender it was hard to believe he'd been so merciless. "You okay?"

"I was wrong," she managed to say. "You're the devil."

He chuckled. "You have no idea."

Her fuzzy brain wanted to follow the thread, but her tongue was so thick, her body so heavy, it drifted away before she could get the words to her mouth.

He gathered her in his arms. "Come here, I'll carry you."

She shook her head, but he ignored her protests and picked her up off the floor. Exhausted, she put her head on his chest and managed to mumble. "Too heavy."

He laughed and started to climb the stairs as though she weighed nothing.

"You're gonna hurt yourself," she said, her brain finally starting to work, although she was too limp to move and lay against him like a rag doll.

"I can deadlift three hundred and fifty pounds. Trust me, you're a feather."

She had no idea what deadlifting was, but he wasn't even breathing hard, so she settled and let him take her where he wanted.

Several unconscious minutes later he placed her on a soft bed. Her body finally stirred to life. She tried to sit up, but he shook his head. "No, stay here, let me get you some water."

Lashes drifting closed, she sank back down into the fluffy comforter.

Her last coherent thought was that James had excellent taste in furniture.

* * *

Dressed in a robe, Gracie crept down the stairs, her head a bit achy from all the alcohol she'd consumed. She was mortified. She'd passed out on James. Again! He'd given her two of the most fantastic orgasms of her life and she'd promptly passed out.

She wanted to die of embarrassment.

In the light of day her confusion over last night had only grown. James was nothing like the man she'd created in her mind. Nothing he did was expected, from the massage he'd arranged for her yesterday, to the place he'd taken her to dinner. How could she loathe him and focus on how incompatible they were if he didn't make any mistakes?

And those orgasms. She shivered. The man was clearly an evil genius. Her stomach flipped. She'd come so damn hard. He'd driven her insane.

As she went down the steps, she saw James already sitting at the table, reading something on his iPad.

He looked up.

Their gazes locked.

She wanted him. She wanted more of what she'd had last night.

As her nipples beaded and her belly leapt with desire, a furious heat filled her cheeks. Why did she keep blushing around him? She was not a blusher!

He gave her a cocky smile that flashed that damned dimple. "And how do you feel today?"

She cleared her throat, sliding into the chair farthest away from him, and said lightly, "Nothing a little coffee can't cure."

He stood, and she about started to drool. He wore a white T-shirt that molded to his magnificent body, and gray sweats. The glasses were back in place, but his hair was messed up, making him appear so endearing her heart skipped a beat.

If he were another man she'd almost slept with, she'd walk right up to him, bold as brass, wrap her arms around him, and seduce him. But she couldn't do that with James. He wasn't like other men. She couldn't seem to control him. Or her attraction to him. And every time he touched her, the world tilted off its axis.

"Black, right?" he asked, sliding the mug in front of her, because of course he already knew the answer.

"Thank you," she said, her voice soft as she wrapped her hands around the warm mug. When he sat back down she flushed again, and wanted to strangle herself. She licked her dry lips. "I'm sorry I passed out on you."

He shrugged, pushing his iPad out of the way. "I'll try not to take it personally that you keep falling asleep on me."

She covered her face with her hands and let out a little shriek. "God, I'm so sorry! I don't know what happened."

"Hey," he said, his tone gentle. "I was teasing. You had a long day, and a lot to drink. It was bound to happen."

She let her hands fall away and blew out a breath. "But I had a massage and a nap. I don't have a good excuse."

"It's fine." He grinned and she wanted to drop her panties, crawl up onto the table and offer herself to him. "I guess I'll have to work harder at keeping you stimulated."

She cocked her head to the side. "You can't be serious. Any more stimulation and I'll have a heart attack."

The grin turned into an arrogant smile. "Really now?"

She straightened, spine snapping straight. "Don't be fishing for compliments."

He laughed. "You'd never give them to me anyway."

By his tone, he'd meant to be playful, but the statement bothered her. It was true. She never gave an inch with him when she'd give other people a mile. And the time had come to rectify that wrong. "I'm sorry."

"None of that. I was joking and I haven't exactly been doling out the praise either." He leaned over the table. "The night we went to dinner with everyone, when I told you that you looked nice. That was a lie. You looked a hell of a lot better than nice. Jesus, those legs and those boots, I had nightmares for weeks."

Breathless, she asked, "Nightmares?"

"I glared at you because I wanted you for myself and I didn't think I'd ever have you."

"I'm here now."

He gave her a long, slow once-over that sent tingles racing down her spine. "Yes, you are."

She cleared her throat. "I didn't know."

"Know what?"

"That you were attracted to me."

"Are you still unclear on the matter?"

She swallowed and shook her head.

His expression darkened. "As much as I'd like to provide you with more proof, we've got to pick up Declan in an hour."

That's right. They were spending the day with James's thirteen-year-old cousin. "Are you sure you want me to come? I don't want to intrude on your time with him."

James chuckled. "I think he'd murder me if I showed up without you. I asked you not to make him fall in love with you, didn't I?"

Her mood lightened considerably and she gave him a galled expression. "Excuse me, I didn't do anything except play video games with him."

"That's more than enough, baby girl."

The endearment, the low tone of his voice, sent instant lust crashing through her. Had the room's temperature increased by twenty degrees? "Don't call me that." The words came out a sputter.

"Why's that?"

"I'm a grown woman." She had no idea what she protested, but the intimacy made her uncomfortable. And hot. Very, very hot.

He smiled, and it was all too knowing. "You're a horrible liar." His vision swept down her body and she pulled her least sexy robe tighter around her frame. "I could practically feel you get hotter."

Damn incorrigible, too observant man. Her mouth fell open. "Don't be egotistical."

He cocked a brow. "Do you want to go out tonight? Or stay in?"

The change of topic gave her whiplash, throwing her even further off-balance. It's what she hated about him. She never got the upper hand. Unfortunately, she'd come to discover it was also what turned her on the most about him.

If she agreed to stay in tonight, she knew what would happen. Well, in fairness, it would happen if they went out too. But if she said she wanted to forgo dinner, she was admitting she couldn't wait. That she was desperate for him.

And it was all the truth. She didn't want to deny it. She might not be able to throw herself at him, but she wouldn't pretend that a night alone with James wasn't what she wanted. She sucked in her bottom lip, then blew out a breath. "Stay in."

His expression flashed. Heated. "Good. Now go get dressed."

She went, grabbing her coffee to take with her. She made it to the top step before stopping to look over her shoulder. Determined to try and gain some upper ground, she gave him a slow smile. One she'd used a million times, which never failed to put a man off his game. "James?"

He glanced at her, the question in his eyes.

"Last night," she purred in her most sultry voice. "It was phenomenal."

"I know." His tone smug and sure.

She sucked in a gasp. Damn him. She stomped up the stairs to the sound of his laughter ringing in her ears. The jerk.

Well, she'd show him. She'd been seducing men since she was old enough to know better and she could sure as hell seduce the professor. By the end of this day she didn't intend to be the only person driven mad with desire.

And wouldn't he be sorry?

Chapter Fourteen

"Where are we?" Gracie asked. Those blue eyes that drove James crazy widened at the line of people on the sidewalk.

Declan popped his head up from the backseat. "You've never been here? It's the best fast-food place in the city."

James grinned at Declan's cool voice. The kid had been salivating all over Gracie since they'd picked him up twenty minutes ago, pulling out all the tricks in his thirteen-year-old book.

Gracie twisted in her seat. She wore her hair in some sort of ponytail, the tendrils curling over her cheekbones. Her makeup was light, but she kept applying some damnable lip gloss that made her mouth look the best type of obscene. Whenever she slathered the gloss over her pouty lips she gave him a sly, half-lidded look as she used slow, deliberate strokes.

Apparently she was in full seduction mode and James couldn't deny he enjoyed every minute, now that it was finally directed at him. She smoothed down a white top that hugged her Marilyn Monroe body, before brushing her hand over her thighs encased in tight, low-cut jeans that accented the flair of her hips and tiny waist.

She should look cute. She didn't.

She looked like sex and sin and he was already contemplating all the mean, dirty things he planned to do to her. Last night had been a precursor. She'd learn soon enough that being thorough and detail orientated wasn't all bad.

She gave Declan her knockout smile and James watched his cousin slip deeper into infatuation.

Right there with ya, kid.

"It's a hot-dog place?" Gracie asked.

"It's the sausage emporium of Chicago," James said, keeping his expression deadpan.

"But you don't eat sausage," she said, her brow wrinkled.

Declan snorted, his face jutting between James and Gracie, blocking his view. "Um, yeah, he does, we come here all the time."

Gracie raised a blond brow. "Really?"

"Don't be so surprised," James said. "I make all sorts of exceptions for delicious things."

She jerked her attention back to Declan. "What do you recommend?"

"Make sure you get the duck-fat fries, they're the best," Declan said, pointing at the growing line. "We'd better go or we'll have to wait forever."

"Duck-fat fries?" Gracie's expression was still twisted in confusion.

James shrugged. "A Chicago delicacy. And he's right, we'd better go. The wait is long but worth it."

She shook her head, the curls fluttering around her face. "What kind of sausage is worth a two-block wait?"

"Trust us, you won't be sorry," Declan said, and slid out of the car.

Gracie moved to open her door, but James grabbed

her wrist and tugged her back, leaning in to flick his tongue over her bottom lip.

She sucked in a breath.

James was starting to live for that breathy little sound. He wanted to sink into her, but resisted. He brushed her mouth again. If she wanted to tease, he'd tease.

An hour later they were squeezed in around a small table Gracie had finagled from two college guys, who'd fallen all over themselves to offer up their seats for a chance to talk to her. James had rolled his eyes at the whole exchange as Gracie dazzled them, flirting with them good-naturedly in that effortless way she had. A man had to have a healthy ego to be around her or he'd die of insecurity within the first hour.

Despite his geek status, James had actually dated plenty of beautiful women, but none of them attracted the type of attention Gracie did. It was hard to pinpoint what it was that attracted so much admiration. She wasn't classically beautiful, but there was something mesmerizing about her. The woman was just sexy as hell. But more than that, she was very accessible. She invited people in with her smile, her warmth and easy laugh.

Today, it was hard to remember why she was so unsuitable for him. Or what exactly he'd been objecting so strongly about.

She took a healthy bite of the sausage she'd ordered with Brie, onions, and truffle oil, and her eyes about rolled to the back of her head. She moaned, picking up a napkin and dabbing her lips as she chewed. When she swallowed, she put her hands on the table. "Holy. Shit."

He laughed, and when Declan laughed too she frowned. "Sorry, I shouldn't be swearing, but that might be one of the best things I've ever put in my mouth."

James wondered if she'd someday include him on that list.

Declan scowled. "I'm in seventh grade. I hear worse than that at the bus stop."

Gracie's lips quirked with amusement, but she nodded in all seriousness, then plucked a fry out of the basket in the middle of the table. "Where do you go to school?"

Declan took a sip of his root beer. "Saint Pats."

"Do you like it?"

Declan shrugged.

While Declan was in the top of his class and had above average intelligence, school was not a good place for him. Unfortunately, James could sympathize all too well, and it was one of the reasons he spent time with his cousin. Declan's painful school experiences mirrored James's own past and he worked his ass off to give the kid a place he felt accepted. A place where he could get out of the house, have some fun and activity without feeling like he was a loser.

James gave Gracie a slight shake of the head.

Of course she didn't miss a beat and gave his cousin a winning smile, waving her hand in the air. "It's Saturday, who wants to talk about school? So, more important subjects, what's your favorite video game?"

Declan's shoulders relaxed and he was off, talking about various games, the pros and cons of different platforms, talking about the latest cult indie game, going into the kind of detail only a true gamer could aspire to.

Gracie listened with rapt attention, hanging on his every word as though he was the captain of the football team describing a big play. She asked questions. Listened. Laughed when he made a joke. And with every passing comment from her, Declan's spine got a little straighter, his expression a little brighter.

And that was the thing about her. What made her

special. She listened. Really listened in a way few people did. In ten minutes she managed to do what James had been working on for two years. She made Declan feel important.

James wanted to kiss her in gratitude.

Gracie took another bite of her sandwich, nodding at something Declan said. After she swallowed she asked, "So who exactly is this *Doctor Who?*"

Declan looked at her in shock, as though she'd never heard of breathing. "You've never watched *Doctor Who?*"

Gracie shook her head, then cocked a grin at James. "Am I the only one?"

"Seems so," James said. "The show's gained quite a bit of popularity recently. Much more accessible than Declan's and my current favorite, Japanese monster movies."

A smile quivered on Gracie's lips.

"We like anime too, but I think you'd love *Doctor Who*. It's an awesome sci-fi show," Declan interjected, waving a fry in the air. "I know—we should have a marathon."

Gracie held up her hands. "Wait a minute. Before I agree, I need to know what I'm getting into, because I'm not a big sci-fi fan and I hate *Star Trek.*"

James looked at her in mock horror. "You hate *Star Trek?*"

"Yes, awful show." A shadow passed over her face. "My dad used to watch it on Saturdays, the old ones."

James realized he'd never once heard her mention a father, although he knew her mom had died from breast cancer and that Gracie had been her caregiver during her illness. The memory clearly wasn't a good one, but since his cousin was there, James let it slide. "*Doctor Who* is the far superior show."

"What's it about?" she asked.

Declan hurried to jump in before James could speak.

"The Doctor travels through time and space in a blue police box, saving the universe."

"Sounds . . . interesting." Gracie smiled.

"I don't think she's buying it," James said.

"Give us one episode to convince you," Declan said.

Gracie held up one finger. "All right, one."

"Hmm . . ." James scrubbed a hand over his jaw and looked her up and down appraisingly. "Which one do you think?"

"'Blink'?" Declan sat back in his chair and mimicked James's gestures, and James contained his smile.

"That's good, nice and scary. What about 'Midnight'?" James said.

Declan nodded seriously. "Good stand-alone."

"Christmas is in a couple months, what about 'A Christmas Carol'?" James said, and Gracie beamed at him, clearly enjoying herself.

"Not a favorite. How about 'Human Nature'?" Declan asked.

James eyed Gracie. "Or we could just go with the classic, 'Dalek'."

Gracie blinked at them, shaking her head. "Do you know the name of every episode?"

Declan gave her a perplexed look, as though it was the strangest question he'd ever been asked. "Well, yeah."

"I see," Gracie said slowly, her lips quivering as she looked at James. "And you?"

"Of course," James answered in his most serious tone. "What kind of fans would we be if we didn't know episode names?"

She shook her head. "That explains the T-shirt."

James grinned. "I'm sorry to say it's not even my only one."

She tilted her cup at his vintage blue T-shirt that a

former student had given him, which read, *Fear the Professor.* "I see we went un-trademarked today."

"I like to keep it interesting."

Gracie shook her head, twisting the curls of her ponytail. "So tell me, how exactly did you decide to be an anthropologist?"

"Forensic anthropologist," he corrected.

She wrinkled her nose. "What's the difference?"

"Dead people—he studies dead people," Declan supplied helpfully.

She blinked, fluttering those lashes at him. "Why did you want to teach *that*?"

It was the first time she'd seemed genuinely interested in his career and shown anything but distain. Progress. "I do more than teach. I also do a lot of consulting."

"For who?"

He shrugged. "Chicago police, FBI, military."

"He's even worked for the CIA," Declan said, excitement ringing in his voice. His cousin forgave James for the dead people when it came to espionage. Not that he had done anything remotely exotic for the agency.

Surprise lit Gracie's expression. "Really?"

"Really," James said. Did she actually sound a little impressed?

"How did you get into the field?" she asked.

"It seemed interesting, and after my dad's death, there was something satisfying about giving people closure when they lost someone." Even though his father hadn't been murdered, he'd died so suddenly, James had struggled after his death.

He'd spent many nights replaying their last conversation in his head and wishing he could go back and say something significant. It hadn't been about anything in particular. A test he had in school that day, his dad hurrying him out the door so he wouldn't be late. James hadn't even hugged him good-bye. Why would he? He'd been a teenager. How could he have guessed that was the last time he'd see his father?

James had started college as a pre-med major, not because he'd wanted to be a doctor but because he liked science and didn't know what else to be. He'd taken a forensics class and it occurred to him how horrible it would be to have a family member disappear and not know what had happened to them. He'd switched majors shortly thereafter and the rest was history.

Gracie straightened in her chair, folding her arms and putting them on the table in front of her. "Aren't you full of surprises."

"It's never been a secret, Gracie." James's gaze dropped to her mouth.

She nibbled on her bottom lip. "What's on the agenda for the rest of the day?"

James smiled. He could become addicted to throwing Gracie off-balance. "I thought we could head over to Extreme for rock climbing and laser tag."

"Laser tag and rock climbing?" Her words were slow and careful.

"Yes, I thought it would be fun." James liked to mix up the things he did with Declan and after sausage and duck-fat fries he thought activity was in order.

Her lashes narrowed as she eyed him suspiciously. "Is this a covert way of getting me to exercise?"

Declan scoffed and grinned at Gracie. "No, it's a covert way of getting *me* to exercise."

"You're both wrong," James said. "It's a blatant way of getting you to have fun. Exercise is just a bonus."

Gracie stood and started gathering up the debris on the table. "Okay, but don't try and trick us into working out. Declan and I are too smart for that."

The boy beamed at her, his round cheeks rosy with pleasure. He gave a definitive nod. "Yeah!"

"You be quiet," he said to Declan before shifting his gaze to Gracie. His attention traveled over her body in a long, slow perusal that had her crossing her arms over her ample chest. He wanted to tell her if she'd wanted to hide her peaked nipples she should have worn a different shirt, but since his cousin was here, hanging on their every word, James said, "I'll get you to work up a sweat one way or the other, baby girl."

The fork she'd been holding fell from her hands. She scowled at him, brushed her hands off, and then her expression turned sly. "I'll make you a deal, Professor. I will play your game, but afterward I'm making cupcakes and you'll have to eat some. Don't you think that sounds fair, Declan?"

Declan nodded in enthusiastic agreement.

She looked at the professor. "Deal?"

James nodded. "Deal."

She jerked her chin toward the back. "I'm going to hit the ladies' room."

"You do that," James said, watching her go.

"I knew it!" Declan said, pointing at him.

"Knew what?" James's attention didn't drift from Gracie's ass, which was probably par for the course with the rest of the males in the room. How could a woman look so fuckable wearing pink Converse?

"I knew she was your girlfriend," Declan said, staring after her departing form right along with him.

James shook his head. "She's not my girlfriend. She happened to be in town and I thought we'd show her a good time."

Declan snorted. "Dude, do I look stupid to you?"

No, he did not, but James wasn't about to make any confessions to his cousin. He shrugged. "She's a friend, that's all."

Declan rolled his eyes in the exaggerated way only a teenager could manage. "Whatever."

* * *

Gracie grinned at James as he sat at his island counter, while Declan talked a mile a minute. The more comfortable the boy got, the more animated he became, and he bounced around the kitchen like the Energizer Bunny as he helped Gracie with the s'mores cupcakes they were making. Declan's choice.

After indoor rock climbing, they'd decided to forgo laser tag, and headed back to James's house. Gracie had gone to the store to get supplies and returned to find the two of them in a heated conversation about some indie game that had just come out.

Declan loved it.

James argued that it was a pale imitation of some game called *Meat Boy*.

All Gracie could think was that it was a strange new world.

"How much cocoa powder, Gracie?" Declan asked, standing there with the container in his hands.

"Half a cup," she said. Out of the corner of her eye, she watched James watch her.

Despite Declan's presence, they'd grown increasingly bold, and Gracie was surprised to find James was a good flirter. Full of cunning innuendo and dry wit that made her so hot, she worried she might spontaneously combust.

James's gaze dipped to her mouth. "Are you sure these are going to be worth it?"

She placed a hand on her cocked hip. "Do you think I'd make you something that wouldn't convert you forever?"

He straightened and patted his flat stomach, flashing those killer dimples at her. "I don't want to eat too many calories."

She understood now he was teasing her, and didn't

take offense. But she did give him a good pout, huffing and waving her arm in exasperation. "By the time I'm through with you, calories will be the last thing on your mind."

"Oh, really?"

"Yes, really." She flicked a glance over him. "You'll be begging me for more."

Declan sighed and turned on the hand mixer James had pulled out from the back of his cabinet. A few minutes later, the cupcakes were out of the oven cooling, the frosting was done, and Declan had run off to the bathroom, leaving her alone with James in what felt like the first time in forever.

She dipped a finger into the creamy chocolate frosting and held out her hand to him. "Try some."

He slowly stood, and walked around the counter to stand in front of her.

Gracie's heart kicked up a notch as she boldly met his gaze.

He grasped her hand, bent his head, and sucked her finger into his mouth.

The hard suction traveled all the way down to her toes. She bit her lip as his tongue swirled and licked the frosting clean. When he raised his head, his green eyes were as dark as moss. "Delicious."

She gulped.

"Save some. I can think of other, more interesting places I'd like to lick." His tone was dark and filled with promise.

The mental image of how talented his tongue was, how he'd brought her to a screaming orgasm, filled her mind.

His attention drifted to her mouth as his hand slid around her neck. "I haven't kissed you today."

Throat dry, she managed, "No, you haven't."

"I need to rectify that." His fingers tangled in her curls, tightening to lift her head up.

"Yes," she said, her voice a hoarse whisper.

He lowered his head and brushed his lips against hers. A light, feathery touch when she wanted so much more.

She rose to her tiptoes, but he didn't deepen the kiss. Instead, he flicked his tongue along her bottom lip. She breathed out, "James."

In answer, his teeth scraped along her wet flesh and her stomach jumped.

"I want you." Another brush of his lips. "But you're going to be the one begging."

Her fingers curled into the cotton of his shirt. "We'll just see about that."

"Yes, we will."

Just as his mouth covered hers, a throat cleared.

They jerked away from each other.

Declan stood, grinning at them, arms crossed. "Just friends, huh?"

Chapter Fifteen

"Come on, have another one." Gracie puffed out her lower lip, letting out the full force of her flirty nature now that Declan had gone home and she was alone with James.

She stood in front of him where he sat on the couch, and offered him a plate of cupcakes.

He rubbed his belly, shaking his head. "Gracie, please have mercy on me."

"Pretty please," she said, her voice a seductive purr. "After all this time, I finally have you right where I want you."

One brown brow rose. "Eating cupcakes? That's where you want me?"

She nodded, grinning at him.

He leaned forward and put his hands on her thighs, tugging her forward.

She resisted, but as she was fast learning, when James was determined, he got his way. He was just a lot quieter about it; sneakier.

He took the plate from her hands and placed it on the side table next to the couch. He met her gaze. "Come sit on my lap and we can negotiate."

She didn't even bother to hesitate. He still wasn't anything like the men she normally dated. Instead, somehow, he was impossibly better. She climbed on top of him, straddling his legs and running her hands down his chest. "So, about those cupcakes."

He'd taken off his glasses again, and his eyes were dark as he trailed his fingers down the curve of her spine. "You're very talented."

"Thank you," she said, her breath catching.

"But I'm not in the mood for cupcakes."

"This isn't much of a negotiation." Heat raced along her skin.

His fingers tightened on her waist. "Take off your top, Gracie."

Two could play this game. She shook her head. "First chocolate."

"Arms up." He inched the fabric up her waist.

"What do I get in return?" She couldn't deny that the near constant verbal foreplay made her weak.

"My mouth on your breasts." He rocked up while pressing her hips down, causing a lightning bolt of pleasure to shimmer through her.

On a gasp, she said, "You're not what I pictured."

"What did you picture?" His palms slipped under her top and slid up her back.

"You know what I pictured."

He smiled, flicking his gaze over her. "Well, you were right about one thing. I do like to fuck in the missionary position."

"That doesn't surprise me, Professor." She kept her tone light, but it wasn't the truth; everything about him surprised her.

A slow chuckle. "I think you'll like it."

"Why do you think that?"

"You'll feel possessed, taken." His fingers squeezed

her hips. "And how long has it been since you've felt that?"

Throat going dry, she gulped. A long, long time. Slowly she raised her arms.

"Good girl," James said, his voice strong and sure.

She shivered with desire.

He whisked the top over her head, but instead of going right for her bra as she'd expected, he just sat there, studying her. Her bra was simple nude lace that supported more than it revealed. He ran his hands up her back. "You have no idea how many times I've pictured you like this."

The comment spread pleasure throughout her whole body. "Have you?"

He traced the seam of her bra with his finger and she jolted as his thumb brushed her nipple. "Countless times. Put your hands in back of you, rest them on my knees."

"You're bossy."

With an arch look, his lips curved into a smirk. "Do you have a problem with that?"

She swallowed; she liked to be in control. While she'd always dated alpha men, she'd kept sex playful. Dirty, yes, but still light. Something about James didn't feel quite the same way. It was the same certain something that always unsettled her about him. He didn't give her the upper hand. She licked her lips and said in a breezy tone, "Do you always have to be in control?"

"Yes." He delivered the word simply, like a statement of fact.

"What if I don't like it?"

He met her gaze. "What if you do?"

Her breath shuddered as she drew air deep into her lungs. And wasn't that what she was a tiny bit afraid of?

His attention shifted to her hands. "Do what I ask and I promise you won't be sorry."

It was sex. Just sex. It's what she'd come here for. Slowly, she lowered her arms and rested her palms on his knees. The position arched her back, thrusting her breasts forward.

"Trust me, baby girl." He murmured a sound of appreciation and cupped them in his large palms, stroking over the silky fabric, brushing back and forth over her nipples until it became the worst type of tease. She grew restless as he took his time, watching her with the type of intensity only he could manage. He leaned down and sucked one nipple through the fabric and her head fell back as her hips rocked forward.

His mouth felt so good, so right, and suddenly the fabric that separated them was too much. She wanted to be free. "James."

In answer, he switched to the other side, biting her through the fabric. His knuckles skimming up and down her peaked nipple.

"Please." The word a plea, she needed his mouth on her skin.

He lifted his head and gazed at her, his eyes glassy with desire. Slowly. Deliberately. He ran one finger over the tops of the cups, tracing the stitching on her bra, rubbing up and down the front clasp until she wanted to scream at him to hurry. But this was James and he would not be rushed.

Wanting to protest, to take control of the situation that was rapidly spiraling away from her, she bit her bottom lip, her grasp tightening on his knees while he tortured her. Touching her everywhere but where she wanted most.

Her breath grew ragged.

Time suspended.

And finally, *finally*, he flicked the clasp open with one hand, the gesture making it clear he'd had plenty of practice.

He needn't worry; she was long past underestimating him.

He peeled the cups away like he was unwrapping the finest of presents. Her heavy breasts swung free, dropping without the support of her bra. He pushed the lingerie down her arms until it fell to wrap around her wrists.

She held her breath.

He didn't attack.

He didn't say anything.

He just stared.

Under his perusal, the instinct to cover herself became too strong, and she moved, lifting her hands off his knees. The bra fell to the floor.

His jaw instantly hardened. "Don't even think about it."

She gulped and returned her hands to his knees.

And still he just stared.

She nibbled on her bottom lip.

Nothing.

He didn't even move.

"James?" Her voice soft and tentative.

"Shhh, I'm having a religious experience here. Don't interrupt."

A smile quivered at her lips. She would have thought he was joking except for the hoarseness in his tone.

At long last he seemed to shake himself from his daze. He inhaled deeply, making her aware of the expanse of his chest as she sat half naked on top of him. "You are, by far, the most spectacular woman I have ever laid eyes on."

She'd received a lot of compliments in her time, but never had one hit her like his did. "Thank you."

Later she'd worry about what it all meant, how much she cared what he thought, but for now, she relaxed.

"You should be naked all the time. Thank God I have so many years of being disciplined, or this would be over before it began." He cupped her and brushed his thumbs back and forth over her nipples.

She jolted like she'd been hit with an electric shock.

"Jesus, I love when you make that sound." He pushed her breasts together. "It makes me so damn hard."

She gripped his knees, arching into his touch.

"Soft?" He stroked feather light over her skin.

"Or hard?" He pinched, squeezing as he rolled the peaked buds between his thumb and forefingers.

A harsh gasp escaped her as she keened at the sheer, exquisite pleasure.

"We have a winner," he said, and repeated his actions.

Over. And over. And over.

Again and again.

Until she was nothing but an incoherent mess of need.

After what felt like an eternity his mouth closed over her swollen nipple. She cried out at the torment.

His tongue circled, languorous. Laved the now abused flesh. His teeth scraped over the distended bud, pulling oh so gently.

She wanted to scream. Never in her life had anyone paid this much attention to her breasts.

She needed friction. She circled her hips, belatedly realizing the way he'd positioned her hands took direct contact off her clit.

Had he done it on purpose?

She thought of all that methodical attention to detail. This seeming desire for complete control. Of course he had.

He bit down as his fingers squeezed.

Hot, wet mouth.

Ruthless fingers.

Teeth.

Tongue.

She wanted to die. The orgasm coiled, tight and desperate, but refused to tumble over the precipice. With only the slightest pressure she'd come. Unable to stand it any longer, she moved her hands.

His head shot up, his jaw hard. "No. Keep them there."

"James, you're killing me." Was that needy voice even hers?

"Don't move."

She needed to come. Was desperate for it. And that wouldn't happen unless she moved out of this damned position. She cocked a brow. "Or what?"

He smiled at her then and it was pure wickedness. "Or I'll tie you down and make this look like child's play. If you're needy now, imagine how you would feel after an hour."

She gaped at him, shocked and aroused, her need beating an insistent ache through her. "You wouldn't."

"I absolutely would." His words were sure, confident. She didn't think he was bluffing. "So don't distract me."

They stared at each other for several long moments as she tried to process this new information about him. His green eyes were unblinking. There wasn't a hint of doubt in him.

Instead of cooling, she was on fire. Her body throbbed with demand. This is something she'd never had, a man she couldn't control, and while it scared her, she found it to be the most powerful of aphrodisiacs.

Slowly she put her hands back on his knees.

Pure male satisfaction filled his expression. Arrogance hardened the lines of his strong cheekbones. "So we understand each other."

She nodded.

He sighed, running his hands down her back. "I lost my place, I'll have to start again."

She had no idea how many minutes had passed as she groaned, unsure if she was in heaven or hell.

"Please, James, now." Was that her voice? That raspy, needy growl?

Her head fell back as James's mouth sucked at her breast. He was evil. Pure evil. She'd lost track of time, of thought, lost track of everything but his mouth and hands as they relentlessly played with her breasts.

She'd moaned, cried out, begged, and still he persisted. Her hips were in constant motion, seeking a friction he never delivered.

"James, I am begging you." She clutched at his knees. The sad thing was, she didn't care about begging and she guessed he'd done that on purpose too. She'd pay him back. Later. Much, much later.

He growled, shifted to grip her hips, and toppled her to the couch. He covered her, the heat of their combined bodies an inferno as his mouth covered hers in a raw, dirty kiss.

She clutched at his shoulders, digging her nails into his skin to keep him closer.

Their tongues met, dueled.

They went at each other like they were starving. Like they couldn't get enough.

Their lips were hard and demanding. Frantic.

She wanted to crawl inside of him. The world spun, crazy and out of control, as she attempted to devour him. More hungry and desperate than she'd ever felt in her life.

She pulled at his T-shirt, wishing she could shred it off his body. He seemed to understand because he ripped away and pulled the cotton over his head before he took her mouth. Overwhelming her.

The heat of his body, his hard chest against her aching breasts, had her snarling. It was sheer excruciating pleasure, as sharp as a blade. His mouth swallowed her cry, answering back with a primal, animalistic sound. He moved, creating a friction between her nipples and his bare skin. She rose to meet his hips only to discover he'd moved away from her. She growled, conveying all her neediness in her kiss as she raked her nails down his back hard enough she had to have drawn blood.

He whispered against her mouth, "That's it, mark me."

"James, please, I need you so much."

"I know." He pulled several condoms out of his jeans, throwing them on the coffee table before moving to her zipper. With a patience that made her want to kill him, he slowly unzipped her jeans and pulled them down her legs, taking her panties along with them until she lay naked beneath him.

He stopped, stared, and shook his head. "You're a fucking walking fantasy."

She'd heard statements to that effect before, but with James it meant so much more. She went hot all over. "Thank you."

He ran his hands down her body, skimming over her waist and hips before sweeping back up again. "In my head, we take this slow. But I'm not sure I can. I need to take you. To pound into you hard and fast."

She arched off the couch. "Yes, please."

He stroked over her skin, down her hipbones to her wet, engorged center. His fingers brushed her clit. She cried out, as almost immediately a climax swelled inside her. He moved away, leaned down and brushed her lips so gently she wanted to weep from it. "You're so damn wet."

"Yes." A needy whisper. "For you."

He groaned and met her gaze. Something intangible passed between them then. It shifted the air, changing her, changing them. She reached for him, running her hands over the hard plains of his chest, tracing the muscles and thrilling when they jumped under her hands. She curled her fingers around the waistband of his jeans, her thumb already on the button.

She lowered the zipper. Through the cotton of his underwear, his erection strained. She ran her palm down his shaft and he cursed, his grip clamping down on her thighs. She pushed the fabric away, pushing the jeans down his very fine ass. His cock sprang free. She wrapped her fingers around his steely flesh, running her thumb over the tip.

A low rumble vibrated deep in his throat.

Feminine power coursed through her and she wet her bottom lip as she fisted his shaft and squeezed. "I want to lick."

He shook his head. "Later."

"Now."

"No."

She tried to shimmy out from beneath him and he gripped her hip, holding her in place. In a raspy voice she'd never heard before, he said, "I need to be inside you. Later you can play all you want. But now, we do this my way."

She settled and nodded, understanding that something inside him needed this, and she couldn't deny him. Not when she needed the same thing just as bad. "Take me."

He shook his head, already working himself the rest of the way out of his clothes. "You're killing me here."

"Good. I don't want to be alone."

"You're not." He grabbed a condom and tore open the package with his teeth, and covered his hard cock. When he was done he smiled, flashing that dimple at her, and Gracie's heart melted into a big puddle. "We lost momentum."

Only in franticness, because she'd never been more on fire.

He kissed her, covering her mouth in a hard, almost brutal kiss that had all the crazy, consuming passion rushing back. She gripped his naked hips, promising herself later she'd study every inch of this man's body and the work of art it was.

He licked a path down her throat, scraping his teeth over the pulse pounding in her neck. His skin was the best thing she'd ever felt and she found she never wanted to let him go.

She'd expected him to enter her fast, but, of course, James never did anything she expected. Instead, he positioned the head of his erection at the entrance of her core and teased along her slick center. She gritted her teeth, digging her nails into his lower back to make him go deeper.

He refused.

She groaned in frustration. "I'm going to get you back for this."

He laughed. "I look forward to it."

Slowly. Oh. So. Slowly. He entered her, only to retreat.

"I mean it," she gasped out.

Again he teased her. It was torment. "I hope you do."

"James." She arched, moaning.

And in his own damn time, he conceded and she was finally, blissfully full.

"Finally," she said on a sigh.

Jaw a firm line, he held himself still above her, his arms tensed. He shook his head. "You're so wet. And tight."

She shifted beneath him. "Please."

He answered with a powerful stroke that had her rearing off the couch.

"Yes." In invitation, she arched.

He began to move in earnest and she rose to meet him.

Their mouths met, fused. Their tongues tangled, matching the rhythm of their straining bodies. Over and over.

It was like getting lost in a dream.

The air turned thick and hot. Steamy.

The world narrowed to the feel of his mouth and his hard cock thrusting into her.

Harder.

Faster.

Her orgasm coiled tight. Oh so tight. Hanging on the precipice, for so long it refused to tumble over, suspending her in a desire-filled haze.

She clawed at his back.

He pounded inside her.

She cried out, moaning his name.

He circled his hips, catching her clit on the upstroke and she shattered.

A powerful orgasm stole her breath, robbed her of speech as it stormed through her with the most brutal force. Wave after crashing wave swept over her. Swelling and cresting as he relentlessly moved inside her.

It was endless pleasure. Sheer torture. Mindless bliss.

He shifted, angling deeper, pumping harder.

He reached between them and swept his fingers over her clit, rubbing in a hard circular motion that matched the pounding of his hips.

Impossibly another climax peaked, right on top of the first one, and she moaned as her core convulsed in violent, rhythmic contractions that had her bowing off the couch.

That seemed to be what he was waiting for because he followed her a second later, coming with a loud shout, his muscles straining as he worked the last tiny contractions of her orgasm.

He collapsed on top of her and for several long minutes they both lay panting for breath.

Wow. Holy hell. Wow.

James shifted to move off her, but she wrapped her arms tight around him and whispered, "No, not yet."

She didn't want it to be over. The desire so strong it scared her.

His mouth skimmed along her neck, sending cascading shivers over her skin, leaving gooseflesh in his wake. "I don't want to hurt you."

"You're not, you're the best thing I've felt in, well, about ever."

James raised his head, propping his elbows on either side of her. His expression so tender she wanted to look away but didn't. He flicked his tongue over her bottom lip. "That might be the sweetest thing you ever said to me."

She grinned up at him. "I was wrong."

"Hang on, I need to go mark this day down on my calendar." His voice was filled with a light amusement that made her giggle.

She punched him in the arm. "Don't ruin my afterglow."

He pulled out, and squeezed next to her on the couch. Resting his head on his open palm, he traced a path over her collarbones, down the curve of her breasts, circling her nipple.

One time with James Donovan wasn't going to be enough. But she'd think about that later. For now, she was content to revel in a bone deep satisfaction she hadn't felt in forever.

Chapter Sixteen

For a while they drifted, his fingers playing over her skin, while Gracie practically purred. She couldn't remember ever being so completely satiated. Her lashes fluttered open and she found him watching her.

"What were you wrong about?" He traced a path over her ribs, in a slow, methodical pattern. As if he was trying to learn her by touch.

"You're not a dud," she said, grinning.

He laughed, shaking his head. "You're the most impossible woman I've ever met."

"I prefer the word *challenging*."

He stroked the curve of her breast. "You are. At lunch as I watched you swoop in and charm your way into that table, I was thinking that a man had to have superhero self-confidence to deal with you."

She sucked in a breath when he circled her nipple. "Everyone says I take after my daddy that way."

She blinked. Why on earth had she brought him up? She'd meant to make some cute quip.

His fingers stilled. "What happened to him? I've never heard you mention him."

She shrugged. "He left. Did the classic going out for cigarettes routine and never came back."

He leaned down and brushed his mouth over hers. "I'm sorry."

"I'm not. I was glad. Once he started drinking, all that charm disappeared. And he drank a lot." She shuddered, remembering how he'd go out Saturday night, the life of the party, which would end with Sunday-morning bruises on her momma's face.

"Was he mean?" James asked, his voice soft.

She nodded. "Yeah, he was. He used to hit my mom."

His whole body stilled. "And you?"

"I think that's the one thing she wouldn't have allowed." As she felt her muscles going tight at the memories, all her satisfaction evaporated. "Everyone loved him."

"I didn't know. That must have been hard growing up." Once again, James began stroking her skin.

"Sam and I don't talk about it much. And once he was gone, money got tight, but I didn't care. At least it was peaceful." Where was this coming from? They were supposed to be giggling and talking dirty, not dredging up the past. She rolled into him, giving him her most seductive smile. "I'm glad I was wrong."

He cupped her chin, tilting her head to look deep into her eyes. He studied her for a long time, and when she felt the catch in her throat she looked away. He stroked her cheek. "I understand that, and I know what it's like to lose someone suddenly."

"That's different. Your dad died. And from everything I know, he was a great man." Bruce Roberts walking out on his family was the best thing that ever happened to them, although her mother mourned him until the day she died. He was like that. Knew just how to charm everyone and get what he wanted. And no matter how ugly he turned, he'd always been able to sweet-talk her momma into believing it would never happen again.

James's gaze darkened, the corners of his mouth dipping. "It may not be the same, and yes, I had a good dad, but the shock of your life suddenly changing is the same."

She shrugged. "In my case it was for the better."

Expression serious, he nodded. "I can understand. Sometimes it feels like that for me too."

She blinked, pushing back a little to look at him. "How do you mean?"

He sighed, and leaned back. "Hang on a second."

He climbed over her, his body pressing deliciously against hers for a moment before he got up off the couch. She watched him as he made his way across the room, naked, the soft light glinting over his hard muscles as he made his way to a cabinet.

He opened a drawer and rifled through it, before turning back to her. In his hand he held what looked like a picture. A moment later he returned, handed the photo to her, and slid back in beside her. "This was me, a couple years before he died."

She looked at the photo and sucked in a breath. Every piece of confusing information she'd ever received about him suddenly made perfect sense.

In the picture a young James stood next to his father. Gracie had seen photographs of Patrick Donovan and understood why everyone said Shane was the spitting image of him. But it was James who held her attention.

It was hard to reconcile the round, chubby face with the sharply drawn lines of the man next to her. She traced her finger over his image, feeling awful about all the disparaging remarks she'd made regarding his health food and exercise. His perfectly sculpted, lean frame clearly didn't come naturally.

The young guy who stared back at her, his evergreen

eyes still recognizable behind his glasses, was heavy. In the picture, James pushed the large end of chubby. His brown hair fell in his eyes, and his cheeks were overly round with none of his finely chiseled features of adulthood. His plaid button-down shirt stretched over his round belly, the buttons gaping, and his jeans pulled tight across his thighs. If he hadn't told her the photo was of him she wouldn't have believed it. She had to look closely to reconcile the man he'd become with the boy.

Everything made sense now. His dedication to fitness and health. The comments Maddie had made off and on about being worried about his need for control. The statements about how he'd been different before. It all added up, and she wondered why she'd never put two and two together.

She looked up to find him watching her expectantly. Waiting for some sort of reaction. She blinked, running her finger along the picture's edge. "Things certainly make a lot more sense."

After seeing the haunted look in Gracie's eyes when she spoke of her father, James decided to confess about his obese childhood, even though he rarely spoke about it. They were painful memories, filled with embarrassment and shame, when he'd felt powerless and hopeless.

It had been a long time, but he recalled every awkward, acutely painful emotion he'd felt on a daily basis, living in that body. Could still recall walking down the hallway at school and praying to God no one would bother him, wishing he could disappear into the woodwork. He remembered how powerless he'd felt as he waited for someone to call attention to him. To laugh. He remembered the bullies. Getting his ass kicked in the alley. The pain and humiliation of each blow. A person could put the past behind them, they could overcome it and triumph, but it was impossible to forget.

And he never had.

Gracie licked her lips and studied the picture again. "I don't understand. How it's related."

"We all changed after my dad died. This was how I changed." He issued the words with little emotion.

"What happened?" she asked, her expression filled with something he assigned to pity.

He hated that. It's why he rarely told anyone.

He cleared his suddenly too dry throat. "After he died it was like something fundamental changed inside me. Like I couldn't stand one more second of feeling powerless. My whole life I'd felt like a victim, and after the accident, my weight seemed like the one thing I could control."

It was his darkest hour. Depression had hit him hard, as it had all of them. He'd been nineteen and in his first year of college, but he'd lived at home, going to and from classes and never interacting with anyone. The day his dad died and his sister lay in a coma, it struck him how fragile life was. That he only had control over one thing in this world: himself. From that day forward, he'd started to change. He'd changed his eating habits, started exercising every day, and worked to create an identity for himself outside of Shane and Evan's fat brother. It took him eleven months to lose the weight, but far longer for the scars to fade.

Gracie ran a finger over the edge of the old photo. "And this is why you're so disciplined?"

He nodded. "It helped me focus. Gave me a place to direct my grief. And I liked it. Liked how it transformed me from someone who was afraid all the time into someone I could respect. I liked how people stopped viewing me as the genetically impaired Donovan."

She bit her lip, looking back at the picture. "Thank you for showing me. For trusting me. It explains a lot."

He ran his hand over her soft stomach, marveling that he could finally touch her. "I doubt I would have transformed my life like that if he hadn't died." He smiled, remembering his dad and all the bittersweet memories that came with it. "I think he felt bad that it was so easy for Shane and Evan and so hard for me. I can't deny he enabled me."

Gracie's expression darkened again. "Maybe sometimes we can't help enabling the ones we love. My mom, after my dad left, she cried for him. I never understood why. He was awful, but she still loved him and never stopped. If he had walked in that door five years later, she would have taken him back in a heartbeat. I was so mad at her for that."

It was hard for James to imagine. His parents had been deeply in love and made no bones about it. They all had scars, some more lasting than others. He met her gaze. "That explains some things about you too."

Her brows slammed together. "Like what?"

It was a risk, saying it, but since they were sharing secrets it seemed relevant. "It makes sense why you'd pick men who don't threaten you emotionally."

Her head snapped back as though he'd slapped her. "That's not true."

"Isn't it?"

"No," she said with an emphatic shake of her head.

Pushing wasn't the smartest move, but fuck it. With Gracie he was far past acting smart. "I think you pick men you can control."

"You think Charlie's easy to control?" She let out a snort, looking past him. "I won't tell him you said so."

Lying naked after sex, James couldn't control the

stab of irrational possessiveness that shot through him at the mention of Revival's sheriff, but he ignored it. Logically, he understood Charlie wasn't a threat and her relationship with him was long over. He smoothed a hand down the curve of her hip, both to calm her and remind himself she was here with him. "Charlie might be a badass, but he didn't threaten you emotionally. Your relationship was safe, for both of you, I'd guess. If it wasn't, you guys wouldn't still be such close friends."

A chagrined expression filled her face and the defensiveness fell away. She sighed. "Yeah, he was safe. You have me at an unfair disadvantage since you know more about my love life than I know about yours. Until I met that Lindsey Lord woman, I thought you were celibate."

A small smile quivered at the corners of his lips. "Clearly, I'm not celibate."

Pink colored her cheeks. "I kind of figured that out, Professor."

One more confession. One he thought would lighten the mood. He grinned at her. "While I was a virgin until I was twenty-one, I made up for lost time."

She looked at him with wide eyes. "You were a virgin until you were twenty-one?"

He glanced pointedly at the picture of his formerly chubby self, which she'd placed on the table. "Did you see the photo?"

She blinked, still sputtering. "Plenty of heavy guys get laid."

"True, but I had no self-esteem." He clenched his jaw. "I was teased a lot. I thought about girls, and while I wondered what it was like to go up and talk to them with the kind of natural confidence Shane and Evan had, I wouldn't have dared. Even after I lost weight it didn't occur to me. The first girl I was with came up to me. I thought she was mistaken."

"Wow, I'm shocked."

"Why's that?"

"You're so"—she waved a hand in his direction—"together. It's hard to imagine."

He arched a brow. "Is that what you call it? Being together?"

She wagged a finger at him. "No fishing for compliments."

He slid his hand up her rib cage, and over the curve of her full breasts, loving when her breath caught. Slowly, deliberately, he drew a circle over her nipple. "Baby girl, the way you squeezed my cock when you came is the only compliment I need."

Those blue eyes of hers flashed, then darkened. And he went about making her forget everything, and everyone, but him.

Chapter Seventeen

The following morning, James came downstairs, still groggy from the little sleep he'd gotten the night before, to find Gracie working away in his kitchen. She wore a dress shirt she'd clearly taken from his closet, and a pair of black leggings that clung to her showgirl legs. Too big, the shirt dipped, exposing one shoulder and the soft skin he'd tasted every inch of. He glanced at the clock over his fridge to see it was nine o'clock. After the night they'd had, he was shocked he hadn't exhausted her completely. "What are you doing?"

She whirled around, a spatula he didn't remember owning in her hand, propping one hand on her hip. "I'm baking."

Brain fuzzy from lack of caffeine, he nodded slowly. "I see."

She gave him a sunny smile that made his heart skip a beat. "Your pantry is abysmal."

He walked over to her, slid an arm around her waist, and kissed her soundly. "I forgot who I was entertaining." He licked her lips. "You taste delicious."

She melted into him, giving him a big, goopy smile that made her look so adorable he wanted to cuddle her close and never let go. Not ready to think about how he'd have to, sooner rather than later. "What are you making?"

"Well, I ran to that Trader Joe's and I have to say, it is even more awesome than everyone says. No wonder Maddie bemoans its loss and tried to proposition the mayor to bring it to Revival."

He couldn't help but chuckle. That sounded exactly like his sister. "You got up early and went to the store? Didn't I tire you out?"

"You did." She rose on tiptoes and kissed him before breaking away and turning back to her bowl on the counter. "But I'm used to waking up at five to work. I slept until seven and felt like I was back in high school."

He walked to his cabinet and pulled down a mug, then wandered to the pot she'd already brewed to pour himself coffee. A man could get used to this. "Seven, huh? Wasting the day away?"

When she didn't answer he turned around to find her staring at him, mouth hanging open.

He cocked a brow. "What's wrong?"

"Your back." She bit her bottom lip. "I, um, was a little aggressive."

He laughed. She had been, and he'd loved every second of it. He propped a hip against the counter so he could watch her. "I'll live."

"Well, technically it is your fault for driving me so crazy." She pushed a lock of hair out of her eyes, then picked up a bag of raw sunflower seeds. "You're a terrible tease, Professor."

He flashed to a mental image of her spread out over his bed, her skin pink against his stark white sheets, her gaze glassy with passion. There was an addictive quality to her, and no matter how many times he'd taken her it hadn't been enough. And each time, he'd made sure to drive her right out of her mind, because he couldn't resist watching her. Everything about her was abandoned and wild, but she had a hint of vulnerability that set his heart on fire.

With little provocation, she could become a habit.

"I'm not going to apologize," he said, thoroughly satisfied.

"Ha!" Her eyes twinkled, turning a vivid sky blue. "Figures."

He grinned at her. "Don't even pretend you didn't have a good time."

She eyed him narrowly. "You know, I never even knew you had a dimple until recently."

"Oh yeah, I didn't know I had one either until I was in my twenties." He scrubbed a hand over his jaw. "Too round."

To his surprise, telling her about his youth had lightened something inside him, almost like he'd achieved a sort of peace that had eluded him before. He never brought it up in casual conversation. In fact, he'd refused to even think about it, but now he was almost joking.

Gracie Roberts had some sort of amazing healing properties.

She attempted to look exasperated, but her huge grin ruined the effect.

"You should smile more often. It looks good on you," he said.

She poured some sunflower seeds into the bowl and started mixing with a wooden spoon.

"What are you making?"

"When I foraged in your pantry I noticed the fifty boxes of protein bars that seem to be a staple in your diet."

Fifty was an exaggeration. He shrugged, taking a sip of coffee. "I don't have a ton of spare time and it's a pain to cook for one person. Just seems easier."

She beamed at him. "I'm making you homemade protein bars that will ruin you forever."

He blinked, then said slowly, "You're making me protein bars?"

"Well . . . yeah. Good protein bars filled with natural ingredients."

In amazement, he stared at her before grabbing her by the shirt and yanking her close. "That is the sexiest thing a woman has ever done for me."

Then he kissed her.

A long, slow, deep kiss, and she responded with complete abandon, throwing her arms around his neck and melting into him. He gathered her close and sank into her warm, lush body.

Their tongues met, tangled. He angled his head, deepening the kiss, unbuttoning the shirt to reveal her naked breasts. He cupped them in his hands, running his thumbs over her nipples until she gave him that little throaty gasp he sought.

Their breathing turned ragged.

No matter how many times he'd taken her, he wanted her with a ferocity that bordered on obsessive. Never in his life had he lusted this hard after a woman, and sex with her had done nothing to abate his desire. If anything, he wanted her more.

She moaned into his mouth, and he pushed her against the counter, careful not to ruin any of her hard work but intent on having her right here. Right now.

He ran his hands up her legs, frustrated he didn't feel bare skin. Low in his throat, he growled, then kissed her harder. More demanding. Needing to consume every inch of her.

He slid his hand into her leggings and found her already wet. He groaned. Always so damn wet.

He tore his mouth away to whisper against her lips, "Too many clothes."

She arched into his touch. "Yes."

"I'm going to take you against the counter." He gripped the shirt, determined to rid her of it once and for all.

"James." His name on her lips was a needy moan that only increased the fever racing in his blood.

The doorbell rang, ripping him out of his lust-filled haze. His attention snapped to his foyer. What the hell?

Gracie yelped, pulling the shirt closed, hiding those magnificent breasts. "Who's that?"

The bell rang again.

And then it dawned on him. "Oh no."

"What?" She frantically started buttoning the shirt.

"Shit." God, he was such an idiot. The pattern was such an established routine it never even crossed his mind to cancel. He sighed and raked a hand through his hair. He supposed it could be worse; it could be Shane. "It's my best friend. We run every Sunday morning."

"You have a best friend?"

"Of course I do."

"Well, how should I know? I never even heard you mention him," she said, her tone flustered.

The doorbell rang again and then he heard the sound of keys entering the lock.

"Her," he said.

Gracie was about to meet Jane since his friend wouldn't be dissuaded by the lack of an answer.

James never missed a run.

Gracie's fingers stalled on the buttons she'd been redoing. Her eyebrows slammed together. "What do you mean, her?"

Gracie was not jealous. She did not do jealous. She didn't have a jealous bone in her body.

Never had. Never would.

She stared at the beautiful, lean, leggy, caramel-haired woman walking into the kitchen. She didn't know what to name the emotion tightening her stomach that made her want to punch James in the face, but she was certain it wasn't jealousy.

The woman—James's best friend—jumped in surprise, her hand flying to her chest. "Oh!" she exclaimed, her gaze darting back and forth between James and Gracie. "I didn't know you had company."

James shut his eyes and pinched the bridge of his nose, and Gracie downgraded her attack to kicking him in the shin at his look of displeasure. "I forgot to call."

The woman dropped her bag of things on the kitchen table and planted her hands on minuscule hips. "Well, well, well, isn't this interesting."

Gracie clenched her teeth. Did James only associate with women with less than 10 percent body fat?

James sighed, a long, exaggerated sound of a world-weary man. "Jane Conway, meet Gracie Roberts."

Gracie jumped in surprise when Jane let out a large whoop and pointed at James. "I knew it!" Before James could respond she turned to Gracie and grabbed her, hugging her close. "It's so fantastic to finally meet you."

Gracie patted her awkwardly on the back, shooting James a confused glance. "You too."

Exasperated, James shook his head.

Gracie flashed to a memory not so long ago when she had accosted Maddie in Mitch's kitchen. Was this how Maddie had felt?

Out of sorts and bewildered? Gracie wrinkled her nose, not liking being on the receiving end.

Jane released her and stood back, beaming like she'd

been awarded a prize. "You're even more gorgeous up close."

Gracie cleared her throat. "I don't remember us meeting." And she sure as hell would have remembered.

"We didn't. I saw you at Shane and Cecilia's engagement party. Of course, James refused to introduce us, but believe me, I knew who you were."

James straightened, grabbed Gracie's elbow, and shifted her away from Jane. "Well, now that the introductions are over, you should be on your way."

Jane laughed. "No way, buddy. In fact, why don't you both come over for lunch today and we can all get to know each other?"

Reality came crashing down around Gracie. Home. She had to get home, to her life. She shook her head. "I'm sorry, but I have to get back home. I have a long drive ahead of me."

A drive that would give her nothing but time to think about her weekend with James. Back to her life that didn't include him. It shouldn't matter. This wasn't a relationship, they were just . . . her mind went blank. They were just . . . well, she didn't know what they were doing. And it was fine they hadn't discussed it. There was nothing to discuss. They had great sex, but they still had no future.

Jane's expression fell. "That's too bad. Next time you're in town then."

Gracie's previous good mood gone, she mumbled, "Sure."

"We'll see," James said at the exact same moment.

Gracie shifted a sideways glance at him, trying to interpret his expression. Did he not want her to spend time with his friends? She was so confused. See, this is what happened when she had sex with someone and hadn't set the ground rules first. She didn't know what box to put him in.

She thought about being insulted at his desire to not introduce her for half a second, then discarded the notion. She wasn't exactly in a hurry to explain what was going on to any of her friends, although she had a good excuse, being that her friends consisted of his family members.

Jane's jaw hardened into a stubborn line. "I won't take no for an answer."

Gracie waved her hand. "I don't have any plans for the moment."

Jane turned to James. "Don't be an idiot."

"Stay out of it," James said, his voice taking on an irritated snap. "You're not invited to this conversation."

Despite her sour disposition, Gracie couldn't help being impressed. She'd observed James around his family when they were causing a racket, and he quietly looked on them like they were wayward children. She was coming to understand he was actually quite assertive. He just didn't beat his chest about it like his brothers.

Jane stuck her tongue out at him. "Fine, be that way." She winked at Gracie. "This is why male friends are so annoying, you know?"

Actually, Gracie did know. Quite well. She nodded. "Some of my best friends are guys. You have my sympathies."

"God, I like you." Jane turned to James and gave him a sly grin. "I might let Anne add her back to the list after all."

James pointed to the door. "Go. Now."

"List?" Gracie asked.

Jane sighed. "So you're not running today?"

"I'm not running now," James said, letting go of

Gracie's arm and ushering his friend toward the door. "You do what you need to do and I'll call you later."

Jane started slowly making her way toward the door, but only because James was practically forcing her out. "You know I need you on my long days." She glanced at Gracie. "Do you know how boring it is to run twelve miles by yourself?"

Gracie couldn't run twelve feet let alone twelve miles. "Sorry, I'm allergic to exercise."

Jane started to speak, but James cut her off. "Goodbye, Jane. I'll call you later."

"Oh, all right," Jane said as James opened his front door.

Jane paused at the threshold, turning back to Gracie to say in a too loud voice, "It was nice meeting you. And by the way, those are some impressive scratches. Nice work, girl." She wiggled her fingers. "Have a safe trip."

James slammed the door on her laughing face while Gracie stood there, waiting to die of mortification. Although why, she didn't know. She wasn't normally shy, but there was something intimate and private about what she was doing with James. She covered her face with her hands. "I'm so embarrassed."

"Don't be." James wrapped his arms around her and kissed the top of her head. "They are impressive."

Gracie smacked him on the shoulder. "Now she knows what we've been doing."

James chuckled. "She didn't need any evidence to figure that out."

She raised her head and glared at him. "And why do you have such a beautiful girlfriend?"

"She's not my girlfriend. She's my best friend."

"Whatever." Gracie let all her indignation, not jealousy, rise to the surface. "And she runs. It's sickening."

James stroked a path up her back. "She's also gay. She

lives with her partner, Anne, and my twin goddaughters. So you have nothing to worry about."

Gracie's mood lightened considerably, and instantly her agitation drained away. She would not think about her relief. "I wasn't worried."

"Sure you weren't."

"I wasn't."

He brushed his mouth over hers. "Did anyone ever mention you're stubborn?"

"Hardly ever." She rose to her tiptoes and wrapped her arms around him. "Only my momma and Sam. But everyone else thinks I'm perfect."

"You are perfect." He kissed her long and deep, until she was breathless and ready. "And stubborn."

She trailed her mouth along his jaw to whisper in his ear, "Take me."

"Whatever you want, baby girl."

They stood awkwardly at his front door as Gracie prepared to leave. That situation right here was precisely why James was a planner. He had no idea what to say to her. They'd carefully avoided all discussion of what would happen after that weekend, and now James found he had no idea what she wanted.

They'd had a good time.

Enough orgasms to lose count.

The animosity-filled tension between them was gone. They'd accomplished their goals for the weekend.

But he had no idea where that left him. Or them.

She shifted on the balls of her feet and darted a glance at the door. "I have a long drive ahead of me."

She needed to leave, but did she want to? He didn't know.

One would think he'd have a better clue after he'd soaped her up in his steam shower and taken her roughly against the tile not forty-five minutes ago, but her face revealed nothing.

Maybe he shouldn't say good-bye. Maybe he should say nothing at all. "I trust you'll have a safe trip."

Her expression darkened and her brows pulled together. She nodded. "Will do, Professor."

What was she thinking? He had no idea. He grabbed her arm before she could turn away. "I don't know what to say."

"You don't have to say anything." She jerked her arm away. "We had a nice weekend, but now it's time to get back to real life."

Frustrated, he scowled. Did she mean that? Or was she protecting herself? He gripped her wrist, and her fingers tightened on her purse. "What do you want, Gracie?"

"Nothing," she said, her voice hard and unyielding.

"Are you sure?"

Blue eyes cold, she narrowed her gaze. "What do you want?"

The question stumped him, so he answered honestly. "I don't know."

Her chin tilted. "We proved we could get along. Problem solved, right?"

That had been the goal. He ran a hand through his hair. "That's correct."

He cringed at the stiffness in his tone. This wasn't going well, but he felt powerless to stop the descent. If only he had time to think through what he wanted to say.

"Great, then things are cool between us," she said, her voice light and breezy. Like she didn't have a care in the world.

He crossed his arms over his chest to keep from reaching for her. "Is that what you want? For things to be cool between us?"

"Yep, and we solved that. The tension is gone and we worked the chemistry out of our systems."

The tension wasn't out of his system at all. Sex with her had only increased his desire. He peered deep into her eyes, which looked back at him with cool directness and no subterfuge. "So how do you want to proceed?"

She took her bag from the floor and swung it over her shoulder. "Friends. What other options are there?" Before he could answer, she waved a hand in the air. "None."

She was clearly brushing him off. Slowly, he asked, "So that's it?"

She gave him a sharp nod. "That's it. Thanks for the pleasant weekend."

Anger pricked along his skin and he narrowed his gaze. "It looked a hell of a lot more than pleasant when you were coming your brains out and screaming my name."

Color high on her cheekbones and she looked away. "It was just sex, James. I told you before, it doesn't mean anything."

He wanted to throttle her and drag her back to his room until he'd erased the coldness in her eyes; a very base, caveman-like response he didn't appreciate. It was why he'd always stayed away from her. He preferred his interactions with women to be civilized, and he felt anything but at the moment.

"Fine, glad I could take care of that itch for you," he said, waving a hand at the door. He needed her gone before he said something really ugly. "Drive safe."

She jerked around. "Great, glad we understand each other."

"You're crystal clear, Gracie."

"See ya," she said, twisting the knob.

He didn't try to stop her. "Take care."

She slammed the door on her way out.

Back to animosity it was.

Chapter Eighteen

Early the following morning, exhausted, sore, and cranky after too many hours in the car and a horrible night's sleep, Gracie dragged herself to her office with a big mug of coffee.

She slid into her chair and took a sip, willing the caffeine to do its job. Her eyes were gritty and she'd avoided the mirror, knowing full well she looked like shit. The weekend had caught up with her, but as tired as she'd been last night, sleep had eluded her. She'd kept playing that last conversation over and over in her head, wondering where it had all gone to hell.

She straightened in her chair. It was for the best. After all, they had no future. So he'd been good in bed—okay, phenomenal in bed—but so what? It didn't change anything. Yes, he made her come so hard she saw stars. So he was some sort of evil genius between the sheets. Sure, he'd given her one of the best weekends she'd ever had, and made her laugh.

It changed nothing.

They'd had great sex that ended with the weekend.

In theory, she supposed they could have the same type of friends-with-benefits relationship she'd had with

Charlie, but that didn't seem like a good idea. Somehow she doubted James would go for that type of thing.

So, yeah, the terrible end was for the best.

No matter how good he was, they weren't compatible.

Thank God she had a busy day ahead of her so she couldn't obsess. She had cupcakes to make for the annual fall tune-up event at Mary Beth and Tommy Crowley's garage. She had a batch of chocolate chip scones in the oven. She had cookies to make for the PTA, and pecan pies to make for the Lions Club luncheon.

She scanned the list she'd made before she'd left on Friday; it was endless. And she couldn't be happier. She wouldn't have time to think about James.

Or the expression on his face when she'd told him he'd been pleasant.

"What was that thought?" Sam's slow, lazy drawl ripped her away from her memories and plunged her into the present.

"What? Nothing." The words too quick. Too telling.

"Good weekend?" Sam leaned casually against the doorframe, a sly smile on his lips.

Why did she live with her brother again? Oh yeah, because he owned the house with her. She clenched her jaw and picked up her list. "Fine, thank you." A small lie, but she refused to confess, even if Sam already knew the truth anyway.

He grinned. "How was the spa? Did it relieve all that pent-up tension?"

Her cheeks warmed. Curse him. Sam knew nothing. All he knew was what his intuition hinted at, which wasn't fact. Even if he was right 95 percent of the time. She'd fibbed a little, telling everyone she spent the weekend at a spa for some much needed R and R. "They gave great massages."

An image of James's hands moving torturously over her body invaded her mind.

"Everyone needs a little stress release now and then." He pointed at the phone. "Call Maddie, she's worried about you."

Gracie frowned. "Why would she be worried?"

"She thinks you're avoiding her and being distant." He crossed his arms over his chest. He wore a black, long-sleeved waffle shirt, and faded jeans that highlighted his lean frame and set off the gold in his blond hair. This year he'd turned thirty, and had lost the last remnants of softness to his face. He was all man now. Gracie wished their mom could see her baby boy all grown up; she'd be so proud.

Gracie raised a brow. "Is that from her, or is that your assessment?"

He scrubbed his jaw. "She mentioned it Saturday night when she and Mitch came into the bar for a chat."

Gracie didn't want to be distant. It wasn't her intention. She loved her friends. But she was going through a phase. One that started with the unexpected jealousy she'd experienced when Shane and Cecilia got engaged.

With only Sam for family, Gracie had come to think of their group as hers. But marriage bound the two women together, leaving Gracie in the outer circle.

They'd be angry at her for even thinking it. Hell, Gracie was angry at herself. But rationality had done nothing to cure the emotion.

It was why she couldn't tell them about James. She couldn't do anything to jeopardize her relationship with them. Another reason it was better they'd ended things quickly.

See, the list of *why nots* was endless.

"Do you want to talk about it?" Sam asked.

Gracie jerked her head back at her brother's question. "Nope, nothing to talk about. I didn't do anything this weekend."

Sam smiled, slow and knowing. "I was talking about your distance with Maddie."

"Oh yeah." Gracie willed her expression to remain guilt-free. "I've been busy is all."

With that intense focus he had, Sam searched her face. He pointed to the phone. "Call her."

Gracie's tense shoulders relaxed; she was off the hook. She nodded. "I will."

"Good." He glanced at the clock over her head. "I've got to get to the bar. I have paperwork to do."

"When are you going to start renovating?" Since Sam had bought the bar from Mitch with the little money left from their mom's life insurance, he'd been planning to renovate. Gracie didn't understand why Sam had bought the run-down dive, or how it could possibly turn a profit, but Sam had been insistent it was the right move, and Gracie learned not to question when he got that set to his jaw. And, in the end, it didn't matter if she understood or not. For whatever reason, Sam loved the place. Only he hadn't pulled the trigger on making the business the kind of bar people would want to go to. He'd talked about plans, but hadn't executed. Whenever she asked why, he'd shrug and change the subject.

"Soon." Sam straightened and fished his keys out of his jeans pocket.

"When? Didn't you have a meeting set up with contractors?"

His knuckles whitened and Gracie didn't need to be a psychic to figure out he didn't want to talk about it. "Not yet."

She knew perfectly well he'd had meetings set up with three companies, so what happened?

"Got to run," he said, taking his leave before she could say another word.

Frowning, Gracie turned to her phone, picking up the receiver to retrieve her missed messages. She'd have to figure out the mystery another time. Five minutes later she hung up and stared at the list of names until the letters she'd written blurred.

Twenty calls. Twenty. It was only Monday. How was that even possible?

Yes, the cake had been for the mayor's chief of staff, and yes, there had been a large guest list, but she'd never expected this type of response so quickly.

Pure panic mixed with excitement raced through her blood. What was she going to do? More important, what did she want to do? The events were in Chicago. Delivering a few cakes was a pain in the ass but doable, but orders of this size would cut into her most valuable resource: time. If it continued, it would change the scope of her business.

She'd already grown as much as she could without opening up a shop, which in a town of twenty-five hundred hadn't seemed sustainable.

Nor had she wanted the commitment of a shop. She liked what she had. She worked out of her home and arranged her schedule to suit her needs, taking on as little or as much work as she wanted. She was busy, but not crazy. Her house and SUV were paid for. She and Sam split the utilities. She'd made the last payment on all her commercial baking equipment last year. She didn't have a lot of expenses and she made a decent living. It had been good enough. She was happy doing what she'd always loved.

She couldn't even wrap her brain around how she'd possibly handle these orders. The logistics alone made her head spin.

A million thoughts zipped along her neurons. She needed to talk. She always processed things better when she brainstormed out loud.

She froze, blinking at the first name that popped into her head.

James. Not her friends. The professor.

Now, instead of irritating her, the thought of all his calm, rational energy soothed her and all she wanted was to pick up the phone and call him. At the memory of their last conversation, she grimaced.

He wasn't an option.

"Okay, wait, let's go over this again," Jane said, her exasperation clear.

Situated in James's office, they were supposed to be discussing the Jane Doe case they were working on, but somehow Jane had wrangled the whole Gracie story from him and now wouldn't let it go.

He pinched the bridge of his nose. "I already told you twice. Now you're just asking me to repeat myself for sport."

Jane shook her head, as though he was too stupid for words. "No, I'm making sure you haven't left out any facts before I officially call you an idiot."

James threw down the pen he'd been gripping far too tight. He'd replayed his last conversation with Gracie a million times and he still didn't comprehend what had happened. It was like they'd imploded. "I don't see how I did anything wrong."

"That's because you're a man."

"That's not helpful."

Jane sighed and leaned forward, placing her elbows on his desk. "Let me spell it out to you. She thinks you gave her the brush-off, dummy."

James racked his brain trying to come up with a reason Gracie would possibly think that, and came up blank. "I asked her what she wanted and she said she wanted to be friends. What exactly am I supposed to do?"

"You have so much to learn about relationships," Jane said.

"I was with Lindsey for five years. I had no problem understanding her." Although he'd never really argued with her because she'd generally agreed with him. "And I'm not in a relationship with Gracie."

"Don't use that woman as an example." Jane had never been a fan of Lindsey's. She blew out a hard breath and held up one finger. "You told Gracie to have a safe trip."

"Yes, because she had a long drive ahead of her."

"You said you didn't know what you wanted."

"That was the truth."

"And then you asked her what she wanted."

"Since I was unclear on the matter, it seemed a logical question. She said friends. End of discussion." He frowned. How could she want friendship after sex like that? He didn't understand it, but he didn't see how he had any other choice but to respect her wishes.

Jane ran a hand through her hair. "James, she asked you what you wanted, and you said you didn't know."

This conversation made his head hurt. "Because I *don't* know. I haven't had time to think about it."

"Of course she's going to say she wants to be friends."

Dumbfounded, James could only stare at her.

"You gave her no indication of your feelings." When James still didn't say anything, Jane let out an exasperated sigh. "Why would she come clean about what she wants after that?"

There was a knock on the door and his research assistant, Amanda Hutchins, poked her head in. "Sorry to bother you, Professor Donovan."

"It's okay. What's up?" James gestured her to come in, thankful for the distraction.

She pointed to his computer screen. "I know you and

Professor Conway are working on the Jane Doe, and I got the lab findings on the tests you ordered. I uploaded them on the share drive. I thought you might want them."

"Thanks," James said, already shifting his attention to the computer screen.

His assistant turned to leave, but Jane held up a hand. "Wait, Amanda. Can I ask you an off-topic question? I need another female to back me up."

Amanda glanced at James and reddened before nodding. "Sure."

James scowled at Jane, who paid no attention to him. "Tell me, Amanda. If you spent a weekend with a guy and at the end of it he told you to drive safe, what would you think?"

Amanda bit her lip, shifting on the balls of her feet. "I'd assume I was getting brushed off."

"You wouldn't think he was nice and only concerned with your safety?" Jane asked.

Amanda looked at her like she'd just grown a third head. "No. Why would I think that?"

"And if you asked him about his feelings and he said he didn't know, what would you think?"

The younger girl cringed. "I'd think that's right up there with 'I'm busy' and 'We need to talk.'"

Jane gave him her best I-told-you-so smile. "You've been very helpful."

James frowned. Apparently he'd made some sort of grave error. Maybe if he'd had time he could have put more thought into what he said. He nodded to the door. "Is there anything else?"

The girl's face clouded and her hair swayed as she shook her head. "If you, like, need anything, I'll be here for another hour."

"Thank you, Amanda," James said.

When the door clicked shut Jane threw up her hands. "See!"

"You've made your point." James opened the folder that contained the data he'd ordered. So, he'd fucked up. Yes, he didn't understand how telling someone to drive safe was a mortal sin, but apparently he'd violated some secret female code. Yes, he should have been clearer. He might not know what he wanted, but it sure as hell wasn't friends.

"So what are you going to do about it?" Jane asked, tone as smug as her expression.

"I'll apologize." And now he had a perfect excuse to call her. Something he'd been searching for all day.

It wasn't smart. Logically he should leave it alone and let this weekend pass as an anomaly, but he already knew he wasn't going to do that. When it came to Gracie, reason had no impact.

"She likes you, James," Jane said, her voice soft.

"You don't know that," he said pragmatically. "She could still only want to be friends."

"I don't believe that."

"Because you're a romantic." James turned back to the computer. Gracie was hard for him to read. He'd always demanded complete honesty in his girlfriends, and gave them direct, open communication in return. But that proved difficult with Gracie, because he didn't have an established relationship with her. It limited his ability to extract information, so he was left to hypothesize about her motives. While it was possible he'd read the situation incorrectly, that didn't mean she'd been untruthful about her desire to be friends.

"What are you going to say?" Jane asked, clearly not ready to drop the subject.

"I'll figure it out." He shrugged, not wanting to talk about it anymore. "We should get back to work."

Jane sighed, scooting her chair closer while James tilted the screen so they could share.

"By the way, Amanda has a crush on you."

James rolled his eyes and opened the first file. "Don't be ridiculous."

Jane laughed. "You're so clueless. Thank God you have me."

He smiled. Thank God, indeed.

Chapter Nineteen

Gracie placed the last cupcake on the display she'd created especially for Tommy's annual customer appreciation event, and admired her work. The miniature Hot Wheels cars she'd made out of modeling chocolate were adorable perched atop multicolored frosting. She'd also gotten to use her new edible-ink printer to create an exact replica of the garage logo out of fondant.

With Maddie's help she'd created the front of a red Corvette with the hood popped, which she'd filled with four different kinds of cupcakes, including Mary Beth's favorite, a honey and banana number with vanilla-bean frosting.

She'd upped her game considerably. She thought of the messages waiting for her at home. Potential clients who wanted a website on which to view her work. Her current website consisted of her contact information and a few pictures. These new clients wanted to see portfolios of completed projects. She nibbled on her bottom lip. She couldn't ignore them, but didn't quite know what to do about them.

As much as she loved stretching her creativity, she wasn't sure how to manage all the requests.

"It looks great," Maddie said from behind her.

At the sound of her voice, Gracie experienced a pang of guilt. In all the hoopla and craziness of the day, she'd forgotten to call. Damn. With a smile, Gracie turned to her friend. "Thanks. You helped. We make a good team."

Maddie turned to the display. "I helped get the shape you wanted for the car, but that was it. You did all the hard stuff."

"You helped. And I appreciate it. I'm thrilled with how it came out." She'd done a good job and she was proud of it.

"I love the details." Fresh-faced, with her red hair tied back in a ponytail, Maddie studied the display with her artist's eye. She wore a pair of jeans and a powder-blue long-sleeved T-shirt that hugged her petite frame. She glowed with health and Gracie experienced an ache at the distance between them.

Gracie adjusted the sign that described each of her concoctions. "Thanks. I was going to call you this morning but things got a little crazy and I lost track of time trying to get into the swing of things."

Maddie smiled at her. "I understand. You've been busy. How'd the cake delivery go?"

"It must have been a big hit because I have twenty more orders."

"Wow, Gracie, that's fantastic. You must be thrilled."

Gracie reached over and straightened a cupcake so the logo was perfectly aligned with the others. "There's a lot of logistics to figure out and I'm not sure how to manage it."

"Yeah, Chicago is far enough that traveling there on a regular basis could be difficult." Maddie's head cocked to the side, sending her auburn ponytail swinging, and Gracie could practically see the wheels spinning in her head. "You could hire a delivery service. Or maybe talk to Shane. He might know somewhere in Chicago where you could rent temporary space."

After she'd finished here at the garage, she'd have to return all those calls. Maybe once she had an idea of what they wanted, it wouldn't seem so overwhelming. Gracie smiled at her friend. "I'm going to actually have to start using those reminder thingies in my phone."

Maddie laughed. "Let me know if you need anything. I can't bake to save my soul, but I have other talents, and I want to help."

Maddie had a pure heart and would bend over backward for the people she cared about. A trait that had almost led to her marrying the wrong man. But she'd learned to say no, and Gracie knew if Maddie offered now, she meant it. Gracie hugged her. "Thanks. I'm going to take you up on that just as soon as I figure out what I need."

Maddie squeezed tight before pulling back. "So, how was the rest of your weekend?"

"Oh, it was quiet," Gracie lied, and her cheeks warmed as she remembered all the dirty things she'd done with James. *Quiet* wasn't a word on the list, except if she counted the times he'd held his hand over her mouth because he'd figured out struggling excited her.

Diabolical man.

She tugged at her red top. Good thing it was over and she could stop thinking about him. And she would, any second now.

Gracie glanced at Maddie to find her arms crossed, a quizzical expression on her face. Gracie half expected her to yell, *You slept with my brother, didn't you?*

Maddie narrowed the Donovan-family green eyes and pointed. "You have a secret."

"No, I don't," Gracie said quickly. Damn it.

"Yes, you do," Maddie insisted. "Is it a guy?"

"No!" The word came out in an all-too-telling shriek.

Maddie clapped a hand over her mouth before going wide-eyed. "It is!"

"You're insane. It's no one." Gracie's heart began a rapid beat. "I had a quiet weekend at a spa, *by myself.*"

"Then why do you look so tired?"

Because your brother didn't let me sleep. "I'm perfectly well rested."

"Come on." Maddie's lower lip puffed out in an adorable pout that worked wonders on Mitch, and truth be told, wasn't lost on Gracie. "Why won't you tell me?"

"What are you two girls gabbing about? You're standing in front of my display!"

Gracie turned to see Mary Beth Crowley, head of the junior league, local firecracker, and the person paying the bill, standing there, hands planted on her hips. Gracie wanted to kiss her for the interruption.

At barely five feet, the blond, former Southern girl was a force to be reckoned with. A couple years older than Maddie and Gracie, she was the town's self-appointed matriarch. When Mary Beth spoke, people listened. She ruled her husband, Tommy, and Revival, with an iron fist.

Maddie and Gracie promptly stepped away and murmured contrite apologies.

Mary Beth snapped her Juicy Fruit gum while she framed the cupcakes with her hands. "That's better." She craned her neck and called out, "Danny, come over here and take some pictures before it all goes to hell."

The local photographer, Daniel, a cute guy with scruffy brown hair and soulful eyes, who had graduated with Sam, hustled over. Mary Beth pointed to the display. "Make sure you get plenty of shots, and don't let Tommy sneak out of getting his picture taken. You know how he is; the big dumb jock hates publicity. If it wasn't for me this place would have collapsed to the ground ages ago."

She issued a series of orders that had Daniel looking scared before she finally put him out of his misery and turned back to Maddie and Gracie. "What is going on over here?"

A bloodhound for gossip, Mary Beth could sniff out a story a mile away. She'd missed her calling. She'd be right at home as an investigative journalist in Washington. She'd wipe out corruption in less than a year.

Gracie shook her head. "Not a thing."

"Gracie's got a secret," Maddie said at the same time.

Mary Beth narrowed her razor-sharp blue eyes on Gracie. "A secret, huh?"

"I think it's a guy," Maddie offered, oh so helpfully.

Gracie huffed with dramatic exasperation, glaring at her friend. "It is *not* a guy."

Mary Beth nodded, ignoring Gracie completely. "She does look tired."

"Because I've been up since five making your cupcakes," Gracie said, her tone droll.

"And she was in Chicago this weekend." Maddie made air quotes. "By herself."

"I went to a spa." Okay, the whole thing was a lie, but Gracie had her reasons for not sharing. And if she confessed, it wouldn't be in front of Mary Beth.

Mary Beth snapped her gum. "What happened with Bill, the football coach?"

"No chemistry." Not a lie. They'd had a nice, pleasant date that ended with a nice, pleasant peck on the cheek. He hadn't called and neither had she.

"I have another guy in mind, then," Mary Beth said. "He's perfect for you. He drives a Harley, kicks ass, and beats his chest like Tarzan. He looks like sin and is a cop in the next county. He's just your type. I'm trying to get Charlie to recruit him and you'll be a perfect incentive."

A couple of weeks ago that description would have made Gracie weak in the knees, but now sounded awful.

The only thing making her weak these days seemed to be the professor, whom she was supposed to be forgetting about. Gracie waved a hand through the air. "No, thank you."

"Why?" Mary Beth shot the word out like a bullet.

"Is not wanting to be the local recruiting tool enough?"

"No," Mary Beth said.

Gracie shrugged. "Not interested. I've got too much going on."

Mary Beth and Maddie exchanged knowing glances, and said together, "It's a guy."

"Just because I don't want to be set up on a blind date doesn't mean there's a guy," Gracie said, but they weren't listening.

Maddie focused on Mary Beth, ignoring Gracie completely. "But why is she hiding him?"

Mary Beth's brow furrowed. "Who does she know in Chicago?"

Maddie gasped, her hand flying to her chest as she whirled on Gracie. "Is it Evan?"

"No! It's not Evan," Gracie shrieked, and several people turned to look at her. "It's no one!"

"I thought I caught a spark at the party," Maddie said.

Gracie sighed. God help her. "You're delusional. I wouldn't sleep with Evan."

Mary Beth's mouth curved down. "Whyever not? He's a hottie."

"He's also a man-whore," Gracie said, raising her gaze to the heavens. *Get me out of here.*

Maddie snapped her fingers. "It can't be him, he played in Miami this weekend."

Mary Beth studied Gracie. "Then who is it?"

"It's no one," she insisted.

"Did you meet someone at the engagement party?" Maddie asked.

"Can we stop this?" Gracie shook her head.

Maddie laughed. "At least I know it's not James."

Gracie had to clamp her jaw shut to keep from blurting, *Why not James?*

This caused Mary Beth to burst into a hysterical cackle. "Can you imagine? Talk about oil and water."

"It's no one," Gracie said with absolutely no vehemence. She worried her bottom lip as the two women carried on.

Her friends were merely confirming what she already knew. There was no need to get defensive. He was wrong for her. Everybody knew that.

They were oil and water, just like Mary Beth said.

But, if that was true, why did she want to talk to him so badly?

James sat on his bed and stared at the phone, aggravated to find he felt like a teenager calling a girl for the first time. An odd sensation, considering he'd never actually called a girl when he'd been a teen, so he could only guess that this was the emotional equivalent. Which was ridiculous since he was a grown man and far past his adolescent insecurities.

Or so he'd thought, until Gracie came along and messed up his head.

Ever since his talk with Jane he'd planned on calling Gracie and getting things straightened out, but now that the time had come he couldn't help wondering if Jane was wrong. Gracie wasn't like other women, so maybe she saw things differently than Jane and Amanda.

Even if the end result wasn't favorable, he needed to find out for sure. On a deep breath he picked up the phone and dialed.

Gracie answered on the third ring, breathless.

"Did I catch you at a bad time?" James asked, pleased at his steady tone.

There was a moment of silence where he thought he heard her swallow, but that must have been his imagination. "No, I just got into bed."

Not too long ago she'd been stretched across his white sheets, naked and wanting. He gritted his teeth to quell the memory and stay focused. "Why are you breathless?"

"Why are you calling?" she shot back without any hesitation.

Not willing to answer questions. Which left only one thing for him to discuss. "I spoke with Jane today and she said some interesting things."

"What's that?" Gracie's voice hitched again, but he let it slide.

"Let me start our last conversation again."

"Okay."

His reluctance to be honest about what he wanted after his weekend with her made him acknowledge Jane had been at least partially right. Self-protective and unsure, he'd played his cards too close to the vest. So close, he hadn't been able to read them until Jane pointed it out. But that was cowardly behavior and unacceptable. He'd lay his hand down, and if Gracie rejected him, so be it. He'd get over it. He'd gotten over his youth and his father's death. He could get over her.

He shifted, propping himself up against his headboard. "When I invited you to spend the weekend, I assumed by the end we'd be so sick of each other it would be easy to say good-bye. But when the time came, I found that wasn't the case. I didn't want you to go, Gracie."

She sucked in a breath, making that little gasping sound that drove him crazy. "You didn't?"

"No, I didn't. I've been informed that wishing you a

safe trip might have given you the impression that I didn't care, but I can assure you that's not the case. We conveniently avoided discussing the end of the weekend, and because I wasn't sure where you stood, I said the first dumb thing that popped into my head."

"We did avoid it."

"Yes, we did." So far the conversation was going better than he'd expected, so he plunged into the deep end. "You asked me what I wanted, and I said I didn't know, but that's not true. I'd very much like to see you again."

There was silence over the line and he glanced at his screen to make sure the call hadn't dropped. Still connected, he put the phone back to his ear.

She cleared her throat. "That sounds very proper."

Vexing woman. He dragged a hand through his hair. "Fine. I can't live without fucking the hell out of you again. Is that better?"

"Is it the truth?" Her voice all warm and husky, he relaxed marginally.

His own voice dropped. "Yes. I'd drive down there now for a chance to be inside you."

"So you liked the sex?"

"You're fishing," he said, his tone exasperated, but he smiled, feeling better than he had all day.

"Damn straight I am," she said, amusement clear in the lilt of her tone.

"Are you going to make me suffer?"

"Yes."

His smile grew wider, into a full-fledged grin. "The sex was phenomenal, baby girl."

"I like when you call me that."

"I know you do." Determined to be entirely honest, even though he could easily keep talking about their physical chemistry, he said, "If it was just sex, it would be easy, wouldn't it?"

"Yes."

"Even more than you being in my bed, I liked being with you. I liked you in my house. I liked talking to you. And I like how you make something ordinary, interesting."

There was silence over the line.

He waited.

She said nothing.

Finally, he prompted, "Gracie?"

"I'm here," she said, her voice sounding hoarse. "We should end things now before anyone gets hurt."

He clenched his hand into a fist. "Is that what you want?"

There was a long, heavy silence. "Mary Beth tried to set me up on a blind date today."

Over his dead fucking body. The vehemence of his emotions startled him. Carefully, he asked, "And?"

"He sounded exactly my type," she continued with absolutely no mercy. "But I said no."

The relief swelled but didn't quite break. "Why's that?"

Another pause. "Because of you."

He relaxed for the first time since he'd decided to call her. He wanted to reach through the line and touch her. "I'm not sorry. I have no idea what we're doing, but I want to see you again."

"Me too," she said.

"You're coming to Chicago in a couple of weeks. Will you stay with me?"

She didn't hesitate. "Yes. If you'll have me."

"I'll have you so many times you'll lose count." Talking to her was torture. The line practically crackled with the sexual tension between them. "It seems our plan has backfired."

"What do you mean?"

"Sex was supposed to alleviate the tension, not increase it."

A breathy little moan. "It's your fault, Professor."

"How's that?" His muscles finally relaxed now that he knew he'd see her again. Have her. Taste her.

"You were too good."

Primal male satisfaction seeped into his bones at her words. "So I shouldn't have given you all those orgasms?"

"Now who's fishing?"

He laughed, adoring everything about her. "Not willing to throw me a bone, are you?"

"Not today. Besides, I'm not sure you need it. I'm sure all those female students of yours fawn enough for the rest of us."

He shook his head. "Don't be silly."

"You don't think your students are in love with you?" Her voice so low and intimate he wanted to sink into the lush sound of it.

He put his hand behind his head, happy to be talking to her, content this wasn't the last time. "Not at all."

"Please, I bet they all are."

"Highly doubtful. I maintain firm boundaries. And anyone who gets another idea is sternly rebuffed."

She laughed. "Sure, because no girls have stern-professor fantasies."

"Do you have stern-professor fantasies?"

"Of course, all women do," she said, her tone light. Teasing.

She was playing, but he wasn't so sure it was a joke. He'd paid attention. She liked aggressive. Assertive. Demanding. He wondered how far those fantasies traveled and if she'd let him in enough to find out. He put a hard edge in his voice. "I don't care about all women, I care about you."

Nothing over the line but the quickening of breath. Finally she said, "And what about you? What's your fantasy?"

She'd diverted, but maybe that was because she felt vulnerable. Maybe if he opened up, she would too. "Do you really want to know? Because I've never told anyone."

"Yes, please," she said, oh-so-sweetly.

"Well, aren't you a good girl."

She moaned, and he grinned. She definitely had themes. "Tell me."

If he was going to do this, he wanted to do it right, but it didn't stop the embarrassment. And it was embarrassing. It also happened to be the truth. "It's silly. So don't get too excited."

"Tell me, tell me." And he could practically see her bouncing around on her bed. Preferably naked.

"You can't laugh."

"I'd never do that."

"It's simple, really. Boring." Now that he'd committed, he didn't want to say, but he trudged on, understanding he needed to reveal his secrets to get to hers.

"When I was growing up we had this rec room in the basement. My brothers would take girls down there and put on a scary movie. Sometimes I'd be there and they'd make a pretense of letting me stay, but as soon as the girls got scared enough to crawl into their laps they'd kick me out so they could mess around."

He could still remember the longing of wondering what it felt like. The jealousy at the way the girls would swoon over his brothers. He hated the memory, the awkwardness of being kicked out, the shame at his envy, but there it was. He blew out a deep breath. "By the time I got around to girls, they were already way past the horror movie, make-out stage. Not that it wasn't great to jump right into sex, but I never got that adolescent, desperate, touch-me-but-don't-touch-me angst. Never got to hold a pretty girl while she pretended to be scared to feel me close. I always wondered what it was like."

He paused, and when she didn't speak, he worried maybe he'd said too much. "See, I told you it was silly."

"It's not silly." Her voice was more serious than he'd ever heard it. "I'm sorry you missed that."

"I'm not sure it was that much of a hardship." It was just that the memory was acute.

"I would have made out with you."

He laughed, and the sound was far more bitter than he wanted. He'd barely been able to get her to make out with him now; he wouldn't have had a shot in hell when he was sixteen. "I appreciate the lie."

She sighed. "I want it to be true."

A smile touched his lips. "That's good enough for me. We are talking fantasy here."

"I'll tell you what's not a fantasy." Her voice a low purr.

"What's that?"

"I missed you. I thought about you all day. I couldn't get you out of my mind. And if you hadn't called me, I would have broken down and called you. Because I needed to hear your voice."

It was more than enough. It was everything.

Chapter Twenty

Gracie stared out her kitchen window, a big dopey smile on her lips as she watched the sun rise over the weeping willow trees lining her backyard. Last night she'd talked to James for two hours. She'd told him all about the orders, her worries about handling the business, the endless list in her head, and he'd listened. Really listened. Just like she knew he would. The more she talked, the more the ragged edge of her panic smoothed away, and by the end of the conversation he'd made her feel like she could do anything.

Her phone rang and she picked it up, dreamily, not bothering to look at the caller ID. "Hello."

"So, Maddie says there's a guy you're hiding from us." *Cecilia.*

Gracie sighed. The urge to confess sat on her lips and she pushed the words back down. "Wrong."

"You didn't decide to do something about James, did you?"

Gracie was just barely able to keep the gasp out of her voice. "No! God no!"

Things with James were too new. Too uncertain.

When things ended between them, when they'd finally worked each other out of their systems, it was better none of their friends and family knew.

She remembered Maddie once saying James was the brother she told her secrets to, and Gracie could understand that. He'd never tell anyone. And when they were over, she could pretend nothing had ever happened between them, and he'd let her.

"You hesitated," Cecilia said.

"I didn't." She glanced at the clock on her stove. "Don't you have anyone better to harass at 6:50 in the morning?"

"Nope. You're the only one I know is up."

"Lucky me," Gracie said.

"Would you tell me if there was a guy?"

She crossed her fingers behind her back. "Of course. What's on your agenda for the day?"

"Mostly client meetings. You're avoiding."

Gracie pressed a finger to her temple. "You should have been a lawyer like your brother."

Cecilia laughed. "I tried. It didn't stick. I much prefer cleaning up other people's messes."

And her friend was damn good at it. With her connections in the city, and Chicago's interesting political landscape, word of Cecilia's public relations skills and proven track record at damage control had grown at record speed. She already had a full client list.

Gracie's timer went off. "Ce-ce, I have to get stuff out of the oven."

A long, put-upon sigh. "Fine. I'll call you later."

"Sounds great." Gracie hung up. The heat would die down eventually, since she had no secret plans to meet James again for three weeks. Three long weeks.

She went to her oven and pulled out her cookies. She already couldn't wait.

She had plans. And she intended to make James a very happy man.

Nine days after James had talked to Gracie, he sat with Jane in his kitchen, rehydrating after their run. He'd pushed himself particularly hard, setting a grueling pace that left Jane behind at the thirty-minute mark. He'd needed a hard run; it was the only thing keeping all this pent-up sexual energy in check.

Every night, lying in bed before he fell asleep, he'd talk to Gracie for at least an hour. He hadn't known quite how it happened, but she'd become a habit. A part of his daily routine he couldn't do without.

She talked to him about everything and nothing. He'd learned about the toll her mother's illness had taken on her, how she'd given up her culinary dreams to take care of her. She talked about Sam's intuition and how she worried he kept himself distant from others because of it. She told James about her father and how abusive he'd been. About her anger over her mother staying. The hopelessness of watching her die. She talked to him about her business, her plans, and her fears.

And to his surprise he found himself opening up to her. Secrets about things he'd never spoken of. Bad memories about being bullied. Good memories about growing up in a big family. Special times when his dad would take him fishing and they'd talk. Not about football or sports that dominated the conversation when his brothers were around, but about the things James liked. Science. History. The vastness of the universe.

While his attempts to get her to watch *Firefly* failed, he had gotten her hooked on *Doctor Who* and sometimes they'd watch an episode. He'd listen to her laugh, gasp, and shriek in surprise and he'd soak it all in, learning her as he'd never taken the time to learn another woman.

He'd listened to her voice grow low and husky as the conversation turned dark and sexual. He'd listened to her groan as she brought herself to orgasm, and sigh with contentment, purring out her breathy, Marilyn Monroe thank-you in his ear.

No matter what happened throughout the day, or what they spoke about, her voice was the last he heard before he drifted off to sleep, and his dreams were increasingly carnal.

Snap. Fingers flashed in front of his face.

He blinked and his kitchen, and reality, came rushing back. He found Jane smiling at him.

"What?"

Jane pointed to the clock over his pantry. "You do realize you've been off daydreaming for the last ten minutes?"

No, he had not realized. With a scowl, he said, "I do not daydream."

"I beg to differ." She laughed, tightening her ponytail. "You've got it bad, don't you?"

He wasn't ready to discuss Gracie. He liked being wrapped in this private place with her and didn't want it to end. Couldn't help feeling once the world intruded, it would close in on them and they'd implode. He shook his head. "Nope. I'm totally in control."

"That is a crock of shit," Jane said. "In fact, I don't think I've ever seen you like this. Not even at the beginning with Lindsey."

James thought about how his heart sped up whenever he saw Gracie's number on his phone. How he couldn't wait to see her. Never once had he experienced that with Lindsey, or any other woman. James sighed. "Stop being dramatic. I spent one weekend with her. It's not a big deal."

"Why do you have to be so tight-lipped? You're a terrible best friend," Jane said, her voice turning petulant.

James took a long drink from his water bottle. "Perhaps you're confusing me with a woman. I've heard they're much better at discussing feelings."

She rolled her eyes. "You're impossible. Please, take pity on me. Anne is driving me crazy looking for details."

The doorbell rang and he stood, giving Jane a smile. "You can tell Anne we had a pleasant weekend and we were able to resolve some of our differences."

As he was walking to the door, she called after him, "You ingrate. I help you get back the girl of your dreams and you won't tell me anything."

He pulled open the door to spot a FedEx employee jumping into his truck and speeding away. James looked down at his feet to find a large box waiting for him. Odd, considering he hadn't ordered anything. He picked up the package and read the return address. It was from Gracie. He walked back into his great room and put it on the island.

Logic dictated if he didn't want more questions he'd wait until Jane left to open the package, but he couldn't, he was too curious. Like all things related to Gracie, he had a hard time controlling himself.

Jane peered at the box. "What's that?"

"Don't know." He retrieved scissors from the drawer and opened the box to find three containers packed between ice packets and bubble wrap. A note lay on the top. He picked it up and read:

> *These protein bars should tide you over until I get there and I can make you some more. I couldn't stand the thought of you eating those cardboard bars you have stashed away in your pantry like a hoarder.*

I made you three types:

Chocolate and peanut butter: Since you told me Reese's peanut butter cups are your favorite candy, my faith in you has been restored.

Raspberry: I noticed that was the only fresh fruit you had in your fridge.

Blueberry and almond: You kept going on about how they were "essential super foods" that belong in every diet, so I thought this would shut you up about them.

They'll keep in the fridge for a week. Store the extras in the freezer until you need them. For the record, I'm bringing salted caramel and fudge cupcakes with me, and you will be eating them. I'm not above bribing and/or forcing you to submit to my will. So I don't know, fast the day before on wheat grass if you need to, because you will eat cake.

~Gracie

James could only stare in amazement as he took the three containers out of the box and opened them up to find individually wrapped bars packed inside.

Jane's eyes widened. "Oh my. What are those?"

He was so stunned at the gesture he forgot to be guarded. "They're protein bars. Gracie made them."

Jane picked up the chocolate peanut butter one and took a bite. She moaned so loud it would do a porn star proud. When she swallowed she said, "There's no way these can be healthy."

He picked them up and took a bite. The flavor practically exploded in his mouth and all he could think was if she sold them she'd make a fortune. Somehow she made it actually taste like a peanut butter cup and not a pale imitation. "I think they are."

Jane got a knife from the drawer and cut off slivers of

the other two flavors, and each one was as fantastic as the last. James would never be able to eat another store-bought bar as long as he lived after this. Gracie had ruined him forever.

Jane shook her head, moaning in pure pleasure. "How does she do it?"

"I have no idea," James said, still in awe. It was the most thoughtful thing anyone had ever done for him.

Jane put down the bar and wiped her hand on a napkin before her expression turned gravely serious. "Now you listen here, James Donovan, and you listen good. Do not—I repeat—*do not* let this woman go. Do you understand me? It will be the biggest mistake you ever make in your life."

James would never admit it, but at the moment, he couldn't agree more.

Gracie had gotten into the habit of keeping her phone close since she'd started talking to James throughout the day, so when her cell rang a huge smile slid over her face. He must have gotten the bars she'd made.

Sam was in the kitchen, watching her in that way he had, so she turned her back and answered the call, unable to hide the giddiness in her voice. "Hi."

"You have been a very busy girl." James's low, smooth voice slid over her skin like a caress, warming her all over.

"You got them?" She tucked the phone between her shoulder and neck, flicking off the mixer so she could hear him better.

"I did. You have outdone yourself. Jane was with me and we got in an argument because I wouldn't give her any to take home." His voice dropped an octave. "When it comes to you, I find I'm selfish."

Her heart actually skipped a beat and heat jumped in her belly. "I could make her some."

"She'd love you forever."

Will you love me forever? The words slipped into her mind, so unbidden and unexpected, she had to grip the counter. *No. No. No.* She was the fun girl, not the forever girl. She cleared her throat. "I'd like to be on her good side."

"You already are. Jane and Anne are bugging me incessantly about bringing you over when you're in town."

Conscious of Sam behind her, she said, "That will work for me."

"Good." He paused and she closed her eyes, listening to the sound of his breathing before he said, "Thank you, baby girl. This is the best present I've ever received."

"You're welcome," she said, her breath catching a bit in her chest.

"I'll have to find a way to repay you."

"No, I wanted to." She wanted to make him happy.

"I'll think of something. Did you place the ad in the paper for an assistant?"

After much discussion and thought, Gracie had decided to hire help in order to deal with the influx of Chicago business. It was a big step—she was used to running a one-woman show—but she knew it was the right decision as soon as she'd hit upon it. "I did. So we'll see what happens."

"Good for you. I'll let you get back to work, but I had to call and thank you. I'll talk to you tonight."

Gracie couldn't wait. It was increasingly becoming a favorite part of her day. Sliding beneath her cool, cotton sheets, lying there in the dark, his incredible voice in her ear. She didn't think she could sleep without him. Which was increasingly worrisome. He was becoming a habit. More than a habit, if she was honest; he was becoming a compulsion. "Sounds good."

With a great heaving sigh, she turned back to her work only to find she had no idea where she'd left off. She was in the middle of making a wedding cake for Saturday; she remembered that much. She went to the table to grab her list, to find her brother watching her.

She flashed him an innocent smile. "So, what are your plans for the day?"

He said nothing for several long moments. He laced his fingers behind his head and leaned back in his chair. "Not ready to fess up yet, huh?"

She straightened her shoulders. "I don't know what you mean."

"Not talking to anyone has got to be driving you crazy."

He was right. It was driving her crazy. Especially when her emotions were so messed up. But still, she wasn't going to talk to Sam. Or anyone. By way of an answer, she shrugged.

He leaned forward until the chair touched the floor. "You're just making it harder on yourself."

"I'm fine," she said, and wanting to change the subject she added, "I went to the paper today and placed a help wanted ad. I also posted it online. I wanted you to know because I'll need you to meet whomever I decide to hire, since you live here too."

"And you want my read?"

She flashed him a smile. "Of course."

Sam's gaze narrowed. "But you don't want my read on this?"

Temptation ate away at her, chipping at her resolve. She'd learned over the years that Sam's premonitions were a double-edged sword and sometimes it was better not to know. But how did she know if this was one of those times? She swallowed hard and shook her head.

"All right, then. Have it your way." He got up, stretched, all lazy, and she wanted to throw something at him.

Yes, that's how she needed this to stay. Her way. At least until she figured out how she'd become so addicted to James.

And what, exactly, she was going to do about it.

Chapter Twenty-One

Two weeks later James had compulsively checked the clock at least five hundred times while he waited for Gracie to show up on his doorstep. It seemed impossible, but somehow she'd seeped through the telephone lines and become a part of his flesh and blood.

He was antsy, without even a modicum of his customary control. It both enflamed and scared the shit out of him, but right now all he cared about was seeing her.

After three long, excruciating weeks he'd finally be able to touch her. He needed inside her like she was a shot of heroin, and doubted his ability to make it to a proper bed. His desire for her bordered on animalistic, like a clawing ache that had only grown with every passing day.

She'd texted to tell him she'd be there in ten minutes. That was ten minutes and fifteen seconds ago, and he could only sit there in brooding silence and watch the clock tick by.

Was this what all-consuming passion felt like? This odd mix of uncomfortable and intoxicating? He drummed his fingers on the arm of his club chair, fixated on the clock.

Tick. Tick. Tick.

Ding-dong.

He sprang from the chair, sprinting to the door, and yanked it open. Finally she stood in front of him and he could only stare, drinking her in. She wore a black trench coat and her blond curls were in pigtails, which he'd never seen her wear before, but were very cute. Her arms were full with her signature pale pink bakery box, a big tub of popcorn, and what looked like a DVD.

She gave him a huge smile. "I'm here."

"Yes, you are." Thank God. Unable to attack her with her arms full, he took the pile from her and carefully put them on the foyer table.

He turned back, reaching for her.

She held up a hand, a peculiar expression on her face that stopped him short. She batted her lashes at him. "Thanks for inviting me over tonight, Jimmy."

Jimmy?

Before he could ask any questions, she continued. "I promised my mom there would be adult supervision. I hope she doesn't call later to check in on me."

Completely confused, and already half crazy for her, he could only blink. "What?"

She walked over to the DVD resting between the bakery box and popcorn, and held it out to him. "I've always wanted to see it but I heard it was too scary to watch alone."

He took the DVD. *Halloween.* And, finally, he got it.

It was like a kick in the gut.

She was giving him his fantasy, the one he'd told her about that first night they'd talked.

He looked at her and she gave him the most feline smile, before blowing a pink bubble in his face. When it popped, she sucked the gum back between her glossy lips, and put her hands on the belt of her trench coat.

"I hope you'll be a proper gentleman even though we're all alone."

"Gracie," he said, his voice husky with emotions he couldn't even begin to contemplate.

She untied the belt and let the coat slip from her shoulders. "I'm a good girl, so you have to promise there will be no touching below the waist."

Dressed in a red and white cheerleading outfit that would be outlawed in any high school, Gracie stood before him. The top barely covered her chest. The skirt was so short it kissed the curve of her ass. While she wore the white gym shoes he'd remembered as a teenager, she'd improvised with a pair of thigh-high sports socks. If he were a weaker man he would have fallen to his knees, but instead he only gaped at her.

Was this heaven? Or hell? He cleared his desert-dry throat. "Did you drive here in that?"

She gave him a wide, doe-eyed look. "I didn't have time to change after practice."

His chest tightened as his cock turned to steel. "You're kidding, right?"

She ran her hands over her tiny skirt. "I most certainly am not."

"Gracie, I haven't touched you in three fucking weeks."

Another dazzling smile. "We can touch, just not below the waist. I took a chastity pledge with my cheerleading squad."

He was only human, and a man could only take so much.

He growled and lunged for her, but she danced away, twirling to flash red panties that matched her outfit. "If I can't trust you, I'll have to go home. I promised my momma."

"Be reasonable."

"Where's your discipline, Jimmy?"

"I expended it three weeks ago." His voice was barely discernible as his own.

She grabbed the DVD and plastered it to his chest with her open palm. "I want you to have this. Let me do this." She rose to her tiptoes and leaned in close, intoxicating him with her clean, lightly-floral-mixed-with-vanilla-cupcake scent. Her lips brushed his ear. "Pretty please."

He groaned. "You're killing me."

She scraped her teeth along his jaw. "That's the idea."

"All right, but I'm kissing you properly first, and my hands will wander below the waist."

She shuddered against him and in that moment he knew her need was as great as his. "It will only make it harder, but I'm giving you your fantasy."

"Until the credits roll." He nipped her earlobe.

"Deal."

The DVD clattered to the floor as he slammed his mouth over hers.

It was instantly hot.

Instantly frantic.

Instantly consuming.

His tongue tangled with hers and a low, visceral sound rumbled from his throat. She arched into him, wrapping her arms around him. His hands were everywhere, running down her back over the curve of her ass. He backed her up, pushing her against the wall.

Something clattered to the floor, followed by the sound of broken glass, but he ignored it all to feast on her mouth.

He couldn't get close enough.

She rocked into him.

Since he'd be playing with her breasts for the next two hours, he bypassed them and palmed her cotton-covered mound, grinding the heel of his hand against her clit.

With a needy little gasp, she pressed into his hand.

Never in his life had he been consumed like this. He felt like a madman as he ate at her mouth. He grabbed her wrists and held them over her head with one hand.

Her head thunked against the wall as she moaned. He slid his fingers into her panties. He whispered against her lips, "You're already so wet, so how are you going to last, baby girl?"

He circled her clit and she keened and gasped, "I don't know, but I will. Oh God, you feel so good."

He slid inside her hot, tight center and pumped. Once. Twice. Three times. "Like that?"

"Yes, James." She kissed him with a dirty, wanton abandon that left him breathless and aching.

He stroked the bundle of nerves until he felt her body quicken, then he pulled away.

She moaned and broke away from him. "This is going to be torture."

He hugged her, his hands roaming one last time over her ass. "This is your game."

She shivered. "I've been planning for weeks. Don't ruin it."

He traced a path down her cheek, rubbing his thumb over her swollen mouth. "I won't."

Her tongue flicked out, licking at his skin. "This is going to be fun, I promise."

"You are always fun." He pulled away, already counting the minutes until the movie ended. He glanced around, spotting the DVD along with shattered glass from the picture frame they'd knocked off the wall. She made a move toward the mess but he took her hand, scooping up the DVD. "Later."

* * *

Gracie nestled into the crook of James's arm like a proper young lady would, and not like the raving slut she'd become in her mind since he'd kissed her.

She'd never wanted to fuck more.

Just thinking about the way his cock stroked hard and high inside her, relentless in his determination to make her come, was enough to abandon this plan and climb on top of him.

But as tempted as she was, she wouldn't. Ever since he'd told her about how he'd never had a hot and heavy make-out session as a teenager, she'd been determined to rectify the situation. Even if it killed her in the process. She shot a glance at him, and she shuddered. Maybe implementing this plan after a three-week absence wasn't her brightest idea, but she'd committed. Now it was time to execute.

He pushed play on the remote and the piracy notice came on the screen.

Time to get back in character.

She looked at him, her eyes wide and trusting. "Do you promise not to take advantage of me?"

He twirled a curl around his finger. "I promise. No touching below the waist, even if you beg me otherwise."

She scowled. "I don't think a sixteen-year-old boy would say that."

He laughed. "Maybe not."

"Play nice." How could she keep with the program if he kept acting so damn hot?

"Believe me, I intend to."

Determined to collect herself, she turned back to the screen. The classic horror movie opened with the jack-o'-lantern on the porch steps, and she grabbed the popcorn she'd bought from a nearby movie theater, even though she didn't eat any.

No, instead she obsessed about how good he felt

beside her. How happy she was to finally be sitting next to him. His body was warm. His arm strong around her. For three weeks she'd waited, and in that time something miraculous had happened. She'd grown to understand him.

The distance had forced them to spend time talking, and their relationship no longer seemed to be just about chemistry. It was real. Authentic. Men had always lusted after her, but with James it felt like he wanted *her*. More than he wanted the fantasy of her.

It scared her. Sure she knew how to have a good time, be fun and sexy, and charm the pants off a man, but relationships eluded her. She was like her daddy that way, only without the mean. But was she worse because she did it all with a smile on her face?

James's palm settled on her neck, as though sensing her troubling thoughts, and she relaxed. She wouldn't think about that now. It wasn't like James had asked her to marry him. They weren't in love. There was nothing to worry about. And, after three long weeks, she was exactly where she wanted to be.

Nothing would ruin that. She wouldn't let it.

The killer crept up the stairs and opened the door to find a naked girl.

James found the spot on her neck that was always sore, and stroked in small, rhythmic circles. She bit back a groan, tilting her head to give him better access.

"They don't waste any time with the nudity," he said, sounding like the stuffy professor she'd always assumed him to be.

Seconds later the girl lay stabbed to death on the floor. "Or the murdering."

She giggled.

James's lips grazed over her throat. She shivered in sheer pleasure as he whispered, "You smell delicious."

"Thank you," she said demurely, crossing one leg over the other and kicking her foot. Her costume was a stroke of genius, complete with Keds. His reaction had been worth the effort. She put a hand on his jeans-covered leg, loving how the muscles there tensed under her touch.

They sat like that for a good thirty minutes, watching the movie, the untouched popcorn between them. The sexual tension grew to near monstrous proportions, their abstinence mirroring the awkward anxiousness of teenage uncertainty quite nicely, if she did say so herself. She jumped at a scary part, terrified right along with Jamie Lee Curtis. She covered her face in the crook of his neck. "Tell me when it's over."

His chuckle rumbled against her lips and she was unable to help herself. Her tongue licked over his skin and he groaned, his whole body tensing.

He took the popcorn from her hands. She tilted her chin up and their eyes locked.

He stroked a finger down her cheek. "You are the absolute best."

She licked her lips. "Right back at you, Professor."

He brushed his mouth over hers. Once. Twice. "How did I get so lucky?"

She twisted closer, putting her hand on his broad chest. Throat too tight to speak, she shook her head.

He kissed her. But unlike the hard, frantic kiss at the door, this kiss was slow. Deep and sensual.

He took his time. His lips a slow tease over hers.

There was a dreamlike quality to the kiss, intoxicating as it sucked her into a sexual haze, where his mouth became her only focus.

He gathered her up, shifting them on the couch. Never breaking contact, he lowered her until she was under him.

He didn't try to touch her; his hands stayed locked with hers as they kissed for what seemed like forever. It was romantic, hypnotic, and somehow, despite its innocence, one of the most erotic kisses she'd ever experienced.

She grew hot. Restless. Her breath quickened.

The kiss changed, transformed. Softness gave way to urgency.

Her body ached. It had been too long. She shifted, opening her legs. He slid between her splayed thighs. She gripped his lean hips and rocked into his straining erection. He groaned low in his throat. The ridge of his jeans pressed deliciously against her clit with the most exquisite friction. Even with the fabric separating them, she could feel him everywhere.

His fingers tightened around her wrists as he somehow deepened the kiss even further.

His tongue stroked hers, mimicking the rhythm of their questing hips.

The air between them grew thick and humid, their breathing turning to panting.

Their hips ground together in slow, maddening circles.

He licked down her neck before biting her collarbone. He pushed up her top and unhooked her bra with a deftness no sixteen-year-old could ever manage, but she didn't bother to correct his technique. Not when she was so desperate for his touch she couldn't think. Couldn't even speak.

He circled her nipple, and then gently rolled it between his thumb and forefinger. Soft, maddening touches that enflamed her desire. He took one nipple in his mouth, rasping his teeth along the hard, sensitive peak. She cried out, tangling her fingers in his hair to keep him closer.

He was relentless. He played with her nipples, licking, biting, and sucking.

Back and forth.

Over and over.

Until she was crazy.

Their hips turned more insistent. More demanding.

His teeth sank down and she bowed up, unable to keep silent any longer. "James, God, I need you so bad."

A whisper against her skin. "I need you too, Gracie."

They were the best words anyone had ever spoken to her because she believed them. Deep down where it mattered most, she believed.

She reached for his hips, arching into him. "I'm so close. You make me so crazy."

He groaned. "Let me make you come. I've been listening for weeks, I need to feel it."

He slid his hand down her leg, his fingers brushing the curve of her panties.

She pushed him away. "You promised, no touching."

He looked at her, his green eyes hot on hers. "You have to be kidding."

"I'm not." It would kill her, but she was doing this.

A low rumble from deep in his throat.

"Don't make me go home. I'm a good girl."

He nipped at her bottom lip. "You're killing me."

She pushed at his chest. "Sit up."

With a deep sigh he did what she asked. As soon as he was settled she climbed up onto his lap, straddling him. She circled her hips as she scraped her teeth over his neck. "Where were we?"

Their lips met but this was no slow, easy kiss. They went at it, raw and dirty, putting teenagers everywhere to shame. The air turned hot as their breath mingled in ragged pants.

He gripped her ass, rocking together in a pounding rhythm.

She yanked his shirt over his head, leaning in so her breasts brushed his chest. Sensation keening through her as the oversensitive buds raked across his skin.

He surged up. Head falling back as he hissed. His muscles corded and straining. "Fuck."

She lowered her head and bit his nipple, laving his roughened flesh with her tongue.

With a guttural moan he gripped her pigtails, wrapping them around his fists and pulling her closer. The back of her neck pricked with pain, morphing instantly into pleasure.

Their mouths fused in a hungry kiss and she couldn't help it. She was crazed. It was almost the end of the movie. She reached for the button on his jeans.

She unzipped his pants and slid her fingers into his boxer briefs, stroking his erection. She whispered in his ear, "I've been dreaming about your cock and how I wanted to get on my knees and lick you all over."

"Jesus. We're done." He flipped her over, ridding her of her panties in one swoop.

Just as frantic, she pushed his jeans past his hips.

His shaft pressed flush against her wet center. She jerked and cried out as the head brushed over her clit.

He grunted and spread her open, sliding his erection up and down her slick opening.

Her back bowed. "Yes, God yes."

He pushed her breasts together, rolling her nipples, sucking first one then the other into his mouth as his cock teased her in the most unmerciful way.

The pleasure was excruciating.

His mouth wet the hard buds. His fingers plucked. And pinched. His tongue flicked over the sensitive peaks while his erection dragged across slick, swollen flesh.

She went wild. Crazed as she lost all sense of reality.

Her body surged.

Tighter. Deeper. Harder.

She burst.

The orgasm stormed through her in violent, crashing waves of bliss. One powerful contraction after another swept through her.

And then he was in her, filling her.

It was so right. So perfect. She raked her hands over his back, down to his ass, where she clutched at him. Needing to feel utterly possessed by him. "Harder. James. Take me."

On a groan, she witnessed something she'd never believed she would.

Professor James Donovan lost control.

On a low growl he thrust hard, overwhelming her.

A mad rush of crazy, frenzied passion. They were like animals. Her muscles shook uncontrollably as she came again and again as he drove relentlessly inside her. He fucked her unmercifully.

Pounded fast into her.

Demanding.

Taking her. Possessing her.

He bit her neck, hard. Another orgasm erupted. She splintered, shattered into a million tiny pieces of pure pleasure as she came harder than she ever had in her life.

He followed, coming on a loud roar as he pumped furiously inside her.

Her chest tightened as emotions swelled in time with the pounding of her heart as the aftershocks set off waves of sensation that rolled through her.

He collapsed on top of her and she wrapped her arms

around his neck. They were sweaty, their breathing fast and shallow.

She managed to pant out, "You've ruined me forever."

"Good," he whispered against her ear. "Your chastity pledge."

She laughed. "This is how all good chastity pledges end, naked on a boy's couch, your panties tossed to the floor."

He lifted his head and he gave her that smile—that heartbreaking, dimpled smile—and panic raced through her blood. She was in so much trouble. "James."

His green eyes softened. "I know, Gracie."

"You do?" *Please let it be true.*

He nodded, and cupped her jaw. "I feel it too."

That seemed to be enough for now because she once again settled into his arms, content to let everything else melt away.

Chapter Twenty-Two

"Uncle James!" Two girls with identical blond hair ran up to James, throwing their tiny arms around his legs in sheer delight.

Gracie's heart did a strange little thump at the sight and melted into a puddle of goo. An occurrence that seemed to happen at an alarming rate around him. Every moment she spent with James she fell a little bit harder, a little bit deeper. She was terrified, but nothing would get in the way of enjoying this weekend. Not when they had so little time together.

James leaned down and hugged the twins. "How are my girls?"

They beamed twin smiles, looking at him like he hung the moon.

One little girl said, "Lizzy likes a boy."

Lizzy scowled at her sister. "I do not!"

"Now what did I tell you girls about boys?" James asked, his tone serious but his mouth curved in amusement.

"They're icky," the twins parroted together.

"Right."

Lizzy planted her hands on little hips. "I don't like a boy. I'm just going to marry him."

Gracie laughed and the two girls looked at her with big brown eyes.

James straightened. "Elizabeth and Emma, this is my friend Gracie."

Gracie held out her hand for the girls to shake. "Hi. Thanks for inviting me over today."

Tiny fingers slipped into hers and the barest whisper of an image she refused to let take hold, flitted into her mind.

One of the girls asked, "Are you Uncle James's girlfriend?"

The question stumped her. She had no idea how to answer. "Umm . . ." She turned to James, hoping for a rescue, only to find him watching her with an interested expression.

She stared at him.

He stared right back.

She licked her lips.

He quirked a brow.

Jane came bounding down the stairs and Gracie was saved.

She smiled at Gracie before giving her daughters a stern look. "Girls, aren't you supposed to wait for an adult to open the door?"

Emma pointed at James. "But it's Uncle James."

Jane sighed. "You still wait. Remember."

The twins nodded. "Okay, Mommy."

"Good enough." Jane turned and before Gracie could speak, the other woman pulled her into a big hug. "I'm so glad you made it, I was worried James was going to keep you to himself forever."

Gracie flushed, although she didn't know why. Maybe because the last time she'd met Jane the woman had witnessed the marks up and down James's back.

Marks she'd put there again last night.

And she'd been marked just as thoroughly in their in-

THE NAME OF THE GAME

satiable quest to satisfy a hunger that seemed to know no bounds. It was like he'd crawled inside her, leaving her near desperate for him all the time. She wasn't even exaggerating; she'd take him in the bathroom right now if she could. It didn't matter how many times they'd already had sex.

Pulling her thoughts away from bed and James, she smiled warmly at her hostess. "Thanks for inviting me."

Jane waved them in. "Come on, let's go in the kitchen. Anne is dying to meet you."

The twins ran down the hall, skipping ahead of them in their adorable little matching jeans with butterflies embroidered down the sides. The only way Gracie could tell them apart was one wore a turquoise top and the other purple.

James rolled his eyes at Gracie. "I'll apologize now."

Jane rolled her eyes right back. "Don't let him scare you, we're actually quite nice."

James sighed and took Gracie's hand as they walked down a corridor in the updated brick townhome. Nerves danced in her stomach, surprising her. She wasn't prone to nerves, but then again, meeting James's friends mattered to her. She wanted them to like her.

They walked into an open, modern kitchen with black cabinets, vintage red appliances, and gray marble countertops. It had to be the most adorable kitchen Gracie had ever seen and she loved it immediately. A cute, very petite strawberry blonde bounced around, singing along as Dusty Springfield's "Son of a Preacher Man" played over speakers.

When she spotted Gracie she let out a squeal. "She's finally here!"

Gracie held out the box of cupcakes she'd made, an assortment of her favorites, as she hadn't known what the women might like. "Thank you for having me. These are for you."

Anne grabbed the box and peered at it with a worshipful expression on her face. "You baked."

Gracie laughed, captivated by the woman. "Of course, it's kind of my thing."

"I had the protein bars you made for James and the cake you made for the engagement party. They were to die for." Anne slid the box onto the countertop and pouted at her significant other. "And you know how it is with these health-food freaks, you can't have anything good in the house or they start going on about carbs and calories."

Gracie experienced a kind of divine, instant kinship with the other woman. "I know just what you mean. It's so annoying."

James pinched her. "Hey, I've been on my best behavior. We got pizza last night."

Gracie couldn't help the smile that spread over her lips and she could only imagine how telling her expression was. "Vegetable pizza with light cheese."

James slid an arm around her waist. "It was a compromise. If it was up to me I would have gotten a salad. And let me remind you, I ate three cupcakes."

Gracie shook her head and looked imploringly at Anne. "He had to run, like, ten miles this morning to make up for it."

"God, I know. Give me a nice walk on the lakeshore any day, but all that running. Blah," Anne said.

Gracie laughed. "Amen, sister."

"Oh no, there's another one." Jane sighed.

Anne clapped. "Now at least it can be a tie. Thank you, Gracie. After all these years I'm finally a contender."

Gracie wondered about James's other girlfriends who had wandered through this door, and figured they'd probably sided with James and Jane. A mental image of the beautiful Lindsey Lord flashed through her mind, setting off an unwelcome stab of irrational jealousy. That woman had exercise fanatic written all over her.

One of the twins, although Gracie didn't know which one, tugged on Anne's tunic top. "Momma, let's dance."

Side by side the girls were the spitting image of Anne, and it occurred to Gracie she had to be their biological mother.

Anne ruffled her hair. "Not now, sweetie pie, I'm cooking for our guest. You and Lizzy go watch Dora. We'll eat soon, then we can dance."

Emma glanced expectantly at Gracie. "Will you dance too?"

"I'd love to," Gracie said.

The twin in the purple, Lizzy, said, "We take ballet."

Very serious, Gracie nodded. "Do you have recitals? With pretty costumes?"

They nodded in unison.

Anne pointed toward the living room. "Girls, you can grill Gracie later. Let the grown-ups talk."

The twins exchanged glances before skipping off to the couch to watch an animated show playing on the television.

Gracie smiled at the two women. "Your girls are adorable." Gracie wasn't sure of the proper protocol, but she figured she'd say what she'd say to any parent when she met their kids. She shifted her attention to Anne. "They look just like you."

Anne's light blue eyes twinkled. "Yeah, they do. If you saw a baby picture of me, you'd think I was their sister."

"It's hard being the lone brunette in the family," Jane said, walking over to the cabinet. "What can I get you to drink, Gracie? Do you like mimosas?"

"Doesn't everyone? Thanks," Gracie said.

"See, I knew I was going to like you," Anne said, waving at the chairs surrounding the kitchen island. "Sit down, make yourself comfortable."

James and Gracie slid onto the bar chairs as Jane got champagne glasses and grabbed a pitcher from the fridge.

Gracie asked, "Can I do anything?"

Jane shook her head. "Not a thing."

A timer went off and Anne peered into the oven before resetting the timer. "Still not done." She turned to Gracie. "I'm so glad to finally meet you. You've been driving poor James here crazy for months."

James groaned and shook his head, looking up at the ceiling.

Intrigued, Gracie grinned. "Really now?"

"Really. I thought you were going to give the poor boy a heart attack. I mean, I can't blame him, as you're obviously spectacular."

"Thank you," Gracie said, warmed by the compliment.

Jane shook a finger at Anne. "No flirting." She shifted her attention to Gracie. "She's got a bit of a crush on you."

James laughed, and put his arm along the back of Gracie's chair. "Anne has plans to seduce you."

Anne winked at Gracie. "Just once. You don't mind, do you?"

Well, this was a strange conversation. And here she'd thought James's friends would be all stuffy and proper. Like most things regarding James, she'd been wrong; they'd fit right in with their group in Revival, who didn't know how to keep an inappropriate thought in their head. Herself included. She smiled. "Not at all. I'm flattered."

"See," Anne said, grabbing a spatula and waving it at Jane. "She doesn't mind at all. I mean, please, we'd be hard-pressed to find someone who doesn't want to sleep with her."

James curled a hand around Gracie's neck and leaned in close. "She's got a point."

"That I do," Anne said, flashing a wide, playful smile at Gracie. "You don't happen to like girls too, do you?"

She laughed, charmed and happy, liking and understanding the other woman's more forward nature. "I'm sure I could work up a little bi-curiosity for you."

James groaned. "Don't encourage her."

Gracie grinned at him, falling into his amused evergreen eyes. "I'm being entirely truthful."

"Ha!" Anne exclaimed. "So, now all we need to do is convince these two."

At the exact same time Jane and James said, "No."

Anne's expression turned hopeful. "Orgy?"

Her partner shook her head. "In your dreams."

"Absolutely not," James said, his tone deadpan. Not too long ago Gracie would have believed he was serious, but now she knew better. "I refuse to take part in any activity where 66.7 percent of the participants want nothing to do with me."

Gracie puffed out her bottom lip in a pout. "They never let us have any fun."

"Stupid monogamy," Anne muttered before turning back to the oven to peek inside.

Jane sighed. "I don't know why I put up with her."

"Because I'm awesome," Anne said, donning a pair of oven mitts.

"Yeah, she is." Jane's expression was full of love and affection as she looked at her partner.

Anne pulled a casserole dish out of the oven and set it on a trivet to cool while Jane moved around the kitchen, pulling plates from the cabinets. They moved in perfect synchronicity, possessing that special something some couples seemed to have. After witnessing it first with Mitch and Maddie, and then with Shane and Cecilia, it was easy to recognize.

For all her teasing, Gracie didn't buy for one second that she stood the slightest chance with Anne. She slid a sideways glance at James. Not that she was in any better shape. Right now, the only one she wanted was him.

"How'd you all meet?" Gracie asked, curious about the origins of James's friendship with the women.

Jane grinned. "I met James our freshman year of college. We were in the same chemistry class. Of course, he wanted nothing to do with me, so I had to force him into being friends."

That sounded about right, after what James had told her about his adolescence.

"How'd she change your mind?" Gracie slid a hand onto his thigh and his muscles tensed as though he was surprised, before he covered her hand with his own.

"Simple. She was the smartest person in class and I wanted an A. When she suggested being study partners, I'd have been a fool to pass it up."

Jane laughed and gave James a look filled with affection. "Of course, the idiot had no clue I'd asked him because I had a crush on him."

Gracie's brows rose and she glanced back and forth between the two women. "I see."

Anne winked. "I converted her."

James squeezed Gracie's hand. "She didn't have a crush. I was safe and she didn't have to think about her real feelings."

Jane blew out a long breath. "After all these years, you're still delusional. Honestly, I thought he was the gay one."

"How was I supposed to know?" James asked. "We talked about chemistry and books."

"Why do you think I kept asking you to my room?"

James shrugged. "I assumed you didn't want to leave your dorm."

Gracie could tell by the ease of the conversation this was a subject that had been discussed, and exhausted, many times over the years, with neither party changing their point of view. Although Gracie believed Jane's version. As a freshman, James had still been heavy, and it didn't take a genius to figure out he'd probably missed all the subtle girl clues.

Hell, even now he'd probably miss it. Gracie had watched him in public, and what she'd previously perceived as aloofness was in actuality lack of perception. He was good-looking, had a body to die for, and a quiet, compelling presence that made a girl feel like he saw right into her. He listened when people talked, and when he spoke, his words cut right to the heart of the matter.

She'd witnessed it countless times. In the way the barista flirted when he ordered his coffee. In the nervous fluttering of a woman's lashes as she spoke to him. In the adoration she'd witnessed on his ex-girlfriend's face when she'd talked to him in that restaurant.

It happened all the time, and James seemed oblivious to it all.

In a moment of absolute clarity she finally understood why, in all the time she'd known him, he'd never made a move on her. Why he'd never hinted at an attraction. It wasn't lack of nerve, as she'd assumed—he'd really believed she had no interest in him.

In his mind, it never occurred to him her animosity hid her attraction, because he took everything at face value. Unlike men who'd grown up good-looking, it didn't occur to James that women might be checking him out, throwing off subtle clues to gauge his interest.

She smiled sweetly at Jane. "I know how you must have felt. I've been baiting him for months, to no avail."

He jerked his head in her direction. "What does that mean?"

She ignored him and focused on his friends, who watched her with a curious anticipation. "I mean, for the love of God, I had to actually proposition the man for sex before he finally made a move."

Anne burst out laughing. "Sounds like James."

Gracie leaned over the counter, bringing the women into her conspiracy. "And even then he said no."

Jane looked at James as though he was insane. "You said no?!"

"What is *wrong* with you?" Anne asked at the same time.

James's expression turned to utter confusion. "I . . . um . . . well, I'm sleeping with her now. Shouldn't that count for something?"

Finally, at long, victorious last, she'd thrown him off his game. The poor guy was actually stuttering.

Gracie huffed, puffing out her bottom lip in a feigned pout. "I practically had to force him into it."

James pinched her. "That is not true. You couldn't stand me, and don't pretend otherwise."

Gracie sighed, a long, heavy sound. "You know how he is. It's like all romantic games are lost on him."

"I have game where it counts," James said, looking adorable and disgruntled.

Gracie gave the two women a sly, satisfied smile. "He certainly does. All that stamina and discipline leads to nothing but multiple orgasms."

Jane and Anne burst out laughing while James actually blushed to the tips of his ears. "You're the most incorrigible woman I've ever met."

She grinned at him. "But really, would you have it any other way?"

He brushed a hand over her cheek, his expression softening. "No, not in a million years."

And just like that, she teetered on the edge of the cliff, and fell.

* * *

"Jesus," he groaned, pumping hard into Gracie as he came in a mad, furious rush.

It had started as a kiss. A simple good-bye that turned hot. Then frantic. Before dissolving into a desperation that ended with him taking her against the door, her bags abandoned at their feet.

His whole body shuddered, as her inner muscles rippled down him, milking his cock, taking everything from him. He pounded his fist against the wood frame as his vision blurred and he lost himself inside her.

The weekend had passed in a blur of sex, talking, and *Doctor Who*. Nothing existed but the two of them. And now it was over.

"James." Her voice low and husky, filled with a softness that made his heart skip a beat. Her fingers tangled in his hair as she whispered against his lips, "I have to go."

He flicked his tongue over the wet flesh of her mouth, made swollen by his. "I know."

In testimony of her reluctance, she pulled him closer, her body still quivering against his.

He squeezed her tight. Never had he felt this way about a woman, and he didn't know quite what to do about it. All he could think about was the next time. "I'll be in Revival a couple weeks from now for Thanksgiving."

"That seems like an eternity." Eyes closed, her head fell back against the door. Her lips were red, her hair a wild mess, her cheeks stained pink. So gorgeous he wanted to take her again. Right here. Right now.

"I'm not sure I can go on like this." The words spilled

from his mouth before he was even aware he was going to say them.

Her lashes fluttered open and she tensed. "What do you mean?"

He slid his hand around her throat, his thumb caressing the line of her jaw. "I need to see you for more than a weekend."

She took a deep breath before blowing it out. "How?"

"I'm on break through New Year's. I can stay in Revival. If you'll have me."

She gazed up at him, but he couldn't read her expression. She licked her swollen lips. "What will we say?"

He understood why she wanted to keep it hidden. He wasn't any better. He hadn't told anyone except Jane. His family had no idea. It bothered him, and he knew he should question the secrecy, but he'd analyze it later. Not while he still had her pinned against the door. "I'll offer to help Shane with the summerhouse. I know he's driving Maddie crazy."

It was the perfect excuse. Shane was tied up in Chicago most of the time on business, and looked to Maddie to receive the construction on the second home Cecilia and him had designed. A task she didn't want and would be thrilled to pass off to him. Not something James relished, but Gracie was worth the hassle.

She searched his face, then put a hand on his jaw. "I just don't know what to say. To them. But I want you to stay, more than anything."

That was all he needed to hear. "We'll work it out."

"Okay." She curled into him like a cat. There was something distinctly feline about a content Gracie. She practically purred in his arms.

He kissed the top of her head, not wanting to let her

go. "You need to leave, before I find a way to distract you again."

She sighed and pulled away, and they spent the next several minutes straightening their clothes in between long bouts of slow, deep kisses.

"We have to stop," he said, as his hands traveled down her body.

"I know." She molded against him as though she was a part of him.

Their lips met and he was lost all over again.

He'd never had this problem before, being unable to let go. But damned if he didn't have it with her. She needed to get home; she had a long drive, and she had to get up early.

And he didn't have the discipline or the willpower to make her go.

In the dark recesses of his mind, it worried him, the way his control slipped when he was around her. But he was too preoccupied by her to care at the moment.

They finally stopped, and she turned to the door, her hand on the handle.

His heart slammed against his chest and he pulled her back, and nipped her ear. Some primal part of him needed to brand her in some way. "You're mine, Gracie. And all that comes with it. You belong to me. Understood?"

He'd never made such a possessive, caveman-like claim before, but deep down he meant every single word.

He waited, not even breathing, until she whispered back, "Understood."

Chapter Twenty-Three

Gracie's day had been far too crazy to spend much time obsessing over her relationship with James. Thank God, because she'd spent the entire ride home mooning over him and replaying every second of their weekend together. She was starting to embarrass herself.

Like a broken record she remembered his voice in her ear, the possessive claims he'd made, and her heart had thrilled.

She had no idea what she was doing. Or what they were doing.

But she refused to let the niggling fear take over. For now, she wanted to have fun and not worry about the rest.

She dragged her attention back to the pad of paper in front of her and the long, long list of what needed to be done. It was endless. She checked the clock. Her next interviewee would be here any minute. She'd had two already and hadn't liked either of the women. There was nothing wrong with them, but she couldn't imagine working with them side by side. Couldn't imagine them in her home, invading her life.

Sam walked in and went over to the coffeepot, grabbing a banana muffin on the way.

She pointed toward the door. "My next interview will be here soon."

"You want me to leave?" Sam asked, sliding into the chair at their big farmhouse kitchen table.

It was her favorite piece of furniture and she loved the old distressed wood. She could picture big family dinners there, with a hoard of crazy kids. Laughter, music, and cupcakes. She sighed, not wanting to think too much about the man she saw in her mind's eye, sitting at the table across from her.

She only saw him because of their current involvement. Yes, she'd never seen Charlie or anyone else sitting across from her, but that didn't mean anything. James was just a surprise. That was all.

She glanced up to find Sam watching her, a wide smile curving his mouth. She straightened. "No, it's fine. But skedaddle after she shows up. I don't want you making her nervous."

"I don't make people nervous," Sam said, taking a big bite. He studied the muffin for several long moments as he chewed. "These taste different than normal. What'd you do?"

She fiddled with the edge of her notepad. She had nothing to be embarrassed about. "I was, um, experimenting with a new, healthier recipe. What do you think?"

"I think"—he chewed thoughtfully as though memorizing the texture and taste—"you have it bad."

She shot him what she hoped was a menacing glare. "Shut up! Don't use your powers on me."

He laughed, shaking his head. "I don't need powers to see that you've fallen hard."

She thought about continuing the guise of denying, but this was Sam. "Please don't say anything."

"Who am I going to tell?"

The list seemed endless. "Mitch, Maddie, Shane, Cecilia, and Charlie, to name a few."

Sam scrubbed a hand over his jaw. "Do you really think I'd gossip?"

"Duh. Of course."

Sam sighed. "Your secrets are safe with me, but I have to say I don't understand. What's the big deal?"

Maybe she was being silly, but she had this ominous premonition that once the world knew, everything would collapse. That once they were public they wouldn't be able to ignore all the things wrong with them. That how different they were, how incompatible, how far apart their lives were, would be impossible to ignore.

Her throat tightened. She shrugged, waving a hand like it was no big deal. "It's a temporary blip. When it ends I don't want anyone to have to worry about picking sides."

The word *end* tasted like dirt. She wasn't ready for that.

"You've always been a crap liar. You're scared shitless."

Gracie sighed. That was her brother for her, getting through to the truth in one cutting swipe. "I'm being practical. I mean, seriously, can you even see us together?"

Sam studied her, his blue eyes intent. "Yeah, with no trouble at all."

The conversation agitated her, and she got up from the table and went to the sink, flipping on the water to run over the dishes. "We're nothing alike."

"So?"

"Basic compatibility is the key to a lasting relationship," she said, her tone flat. She didn't want to talk about this. She just wanted to go about her daydreams and ignore reality.

"If all your staring into space with a big dreamy smile on your face is any indication, you're plenty compatible."

She shrugged, rinsing the pan under scalding water. "You know I'm not good at sticking around. I'm great at all the fun stuff, but when it comes to all the emotional stuff, I'm lost." She couldn't even make it work with someone she had a lot in common with. What chance did she have with James?

She looked out the window to the backyard she'd been looking at her whole life. The leaves had turned again to the dark rusty reds and burnished orange and gold of late fall. They were starting to drop from the trees, signaling the changing of the seasons. The passage of time the only sure thing in life.

From behind her Sam spoke. "As momma used to say, don't borrow trouble."

"I'm not."

"I think that's bullshit. You stick when it matters to you—you always have and you always will. That's the way you're made."

"I'm not though," she said, her throat tight. "Not when it matters."

"Grace, you gave up your dreams to take care of Momma when she was sick. You spent all the money you'd saved on her treatment. And when she died, you still stayed."

"That's not the same thing. She was my family. You're my family. We've got to stick together, we're all we have."

Sam sighed. "I can tell you're determined to be stubborn."

The doorbell rang and she'd never been so thankful for an interruption in her life. Her emotions seemed to be barreling forward, unwilling to be stopped, and she wasn't ready for them. She flipped off the sink and dried her hands. "That's her."

When she passed the kitchen table, Sam reached out and grabbed her wrist. "It doesn't have to be that way, Grace."

She pulled her arm free. "How would you know? You're not any better than I am."

His expression darkened and he turned away.

It had been a mean, impulsive thing to say and she was instantly contrite. "I'm sorry. I shouldn't have said that."

The bell rang again.

He jutted his chin toward the door. "She's waiting."

Gracie sighed; she'd need to make amends later. She walked down the hallway and opened the door to a petite woman with shoulder-length raven-black hair, pale skin, and heart stopping ice-blue eyes. She blinked at Gracie through thick, long lashes. "Hello, I'm Harmony Jones."

"Gracie Roberts. It's nice to meet you." She stood back and allowed the woman to enter.

Even in dark skinny jeans and a black, long-sleeved T-shirt, Harmony had an ethereal quality about her and was so fine boned she appeared to almost float. A good stiff wind would probably knock the woman over, and Gracie had no idea how she'd be able to lift big batches of batter off the large mixers.

"You too," Harmony said in a light, almost musical voice. "Thank you for granting me an interview. You have a lovely home."

Everything about the woman was delicate and fine, and while she couldn't see her doing the heavy lifting of baking, there was something about her that drew Gracie. "Thanks. The kitchen is down the hall. We can talk there."

They entered the large, lemon-yellow kitchen and

Harmony gasped. "Wow, this is a dream. It's so bright and airy, it must be a joy to work in."

Anyone who commented on Gracie's kitchen with true appreciation was gold in her book.

Sam rose from the table and turned toward them, an easy grin on his lips. His expression flickered as he met the woman's gaze and the smile faded away.

Gracie waved a hand in his direction. "This is my brother, Sam. He lives here too, so you'd be running into him if this works out. Sam, this is Harmony."

The woman fingered her necklace, a thin silver chain that held a moonstone charm on it. Her hand fluttered then she reached out to Sam. "It's a pleasure to meet you."

"You too." Sam's palm slid into Harmony's. He frowned.

Oh no. Was he getting something off her? Something bad?

Harmony worried her bottom lip. Sam didn't let go and she had to shake her hand free.

Sam studied her with an intensity that bordered on rude, and Harmony shifted under his scrutiny.

"Sam," Gracie said in a sharp voice. "Don't you have someplace to go?"

Sam nodded, still watching the woman. "Yes. Nice to meet you. Good luck."

Harmony touched the gem on her necklace again. "Thank you."

"Leave." Gracie jerked a thumb down the hall and when Sam left, she smiled at Harmony. "Sorry, I guess he still needs more coffee this morning."

"It's fine," Harmony said.

Gracie waved her toward the table and got her a cup of coffee before settling in across from her. "So, tell me about yourself. Where are you from? Because I know you don't live in Revival."

A smile trembled on Harmony's surprisingly full lips. They seemed to be the one lush thing about her, and were almost too big for her delicate features. The feature made her look like an exotic pixie. "I moved here this weekend. I rented a small house over on Second Street."

"What made you pick Revival? We're hardly even on the map," Gracie asked.

Harmony wrapped her hands around the mug and laughed, the sound so musical Gracie couldn't help wondering about her singing voice. "I'm embarrassed to say I liked the name. It seemed like a good place to start a new life."

Gracie wondered why the woman needed a new life, but didn't think it was appropriate to ask on an interview. She'd find out soon enough anyway; this was a small town, after all. "Well, welcome to Revival. If you need someone to show you around, let me know. I'll be happy to help. I can tell you who to stay away from, and where to eat."

"Thank you, that's a lovely offer."

"Do you have any baking experience?"

Harmony nodded and her expression relaxed, turning a bit wistful. "My grandpa was a baker. I grew up in a bakery and worked there all through high school."

By the curve of her lips, Gracie could tell they were good memories.

Harmony met her gaze. "I still love to bake, but it's been a while since I've worked in a professional environment. I hope that's okay."

Okay? Gracie was thrilled. Out here in the middle of nowhere she had to take what she could get, and had already determined she'd have to train someone. Experience was a bonus she hadn't expected. "It's better than I hoped. What kind of work have you been doing?"

"I was an office manager for a small accounting firm in Missouri, in a town about thirty miles from St. Louis. I can provide references."

"Why not look for work in that profession? I'm sure you'd get paid more than I can afford."

"New life. New town. New job. I miss working with my hands." Harmony shrugged one small shoulder. "And not to sound silly, but when I saw your ad, it seemed like serendipity."

Gracie smiled. She liked this woman. Had a good feeling about her. "That doesn't sound silly at all."

They talked for another thirty minutes, laughing and getting to know each other. Harmony entertained her with stories of working in her grandpa's bakery. Stories only someone who'd actually had experience would understand, assuring Gracie of her authenticity.

In turn, Gracie told the younger woman about the influx of business in Chicago and her worries about the rapid growth, and Harmony offered suggestions that highlighted her business acumen.

Harmony was the blessing Gracie had been looking for. She could see working beside her. And while she proceeded through the interview like any good businesswoman would, barring any unforeseen disaster, Harmony had the job.

Sam walked downstairs and came into the kitchen. "I'm off."

Gracie said to Harmony, "Would you excuse me for a minute?"

The other woman nodded and Gracie got up and walked outside with Sam. The air had a distinct fall chill and she wrapped her arms around herself. "I love her, so if there's something wrong with her tell me now."

Sam looked past her, peering through the window with a scowl. "She seems fine to me."

"Did you get a good feel about her?"

"I didn't get any feel from her at all." Sam's eyes narrowed as he peered at Harmony again.

"I really like her, and she has experience." Gracie couldn't imagine finding anyone better.

Sam shrugged. "Then follow your instincts."

"You don't have any other problem with her?" Because he seemed like he had a problem.

"Why would I?" Sam's jaw tensed.

Gracie rubbed her arms. "I'm going to hire her then."

Sam's gaze slid once again toward Harmony. "Sure."

He didn't sound sure, but Gracie couldn't figure out what his problem could be. Harmony was lovely, and Sam said himself he didn't get anything ominous from her.

Gracie went back into the house and shut the door behind her. "Sorry about that."

"Is everything okay?" Harmony asked, her expression clouding.

"Everything's great," Gracie said, putting her hand on the counter. "Here's what I'm thinking. I've got a bunch of stuff I need to get done and I think this would be a good test. Do you have time?"

Harmony held out her hands. "Nothing but."

"Perfect. Why don't you make one of your recipes and one of mine. I figure it will give us a good idea how we'd work side by side and I can get an idea of your skills. Sound good?"

Harmony jumped up, her light blue eyes dancing. "I'm ready."

"Then let me show you the pantry."

Late that afternoon, James sat in his office at the university reading research papers when Jane knocked on the door and plopped down on the chair without waiting for an invitation. "We've got to file our report on the Jane Doe. The precinct called."

"It's on the list." James put down his pen and rubbed the bridge of his nose under his glasses. "What did you tell them?"

"That they'd have it by Monday," Jane said, offering a crooked smile.

"We'll have to work over the weekend."

"Is that okay? Or is the blond bombshell going to be here?"

Unfortunately, no. And talking over the phone wasn't the same as being able to touch her. He shook his head. "I won't see her until Thanksgiving."

"Too bad. Anne and I love her and can't wait to see her again."

The three women had practically ignored him all afternoon as they became fast friends. He noticed Gracie had that effect on people. Outside of her gorgeousness, there was something vibrant and warm about her that people gravitated to. He'd never run across a person who hadn't liked her on sight.

"So . . . ," Jane said, her voice turning sly. "What's going on with her?"

The real question was, what *wasn't* going on with her? Cautiously, James said, "We're taking it slow."

Jane laughed, shaking her head. "Is that what you call it?"

"Yes, that's what I call it."

"James, you guys are crazy about each other."

He feared he might be more than crazy about her. He feared he might be in love with her.

He scowled at the thought that had been popping into his mind over and over again like a bad penny. It was crazy. They hadn't spent nearly enough time together to make that deduction. Love required time and commitment. It required being together for more than forty-eight-hour intervals. He was merely infatuated, which wasn't the same as love. He shrugged.

"Don't think I don't know what you did to her when you took her down to the wine cellar. You know exactly where I keep that bottle of Pinot Noir."

James grinned at the memory. He couldn't help it. "Yes, well, I do enjoy her company."

Jane threw her hands in the air. "You're impossible!"

There was an incessant loud banging on the door followed by his older brother yelling, "Jimmy, are you in there?"

James shot a warning glare at Jane. "Not a word about her. Understand?"

Jane frowned, but nodded.

James called, "Come in."

The door flew open and Shane entered the room. He wore a dark navy suit, white shirt, and a red striped tie.

James cocked a brow. "You look like a politician."

Shane slammed the door behind him. "Goddammit. That's exactly what I said. I swear that woman is out to get me."

Jane gestured to the empty chair as though it was her office instead of his. "Take a seat, you look exhausted. Everything okay?"

"Hey, Jane." Shane rid himself of his jacket and ripped off his tie, rolling up the sleeves of his dress shirt. "Long day of bureaucratic bullshit. You know how it is—typical."

Jane nodded. While Shane owned a ridiculously successful commercial real estate company and they worked in academia, they weren't strangers to bureaucracy. "And who's this woman out to get you?"

Shane looked at her like she was a bit dull witted. "Cecilia, of course. It's like she's looking to get me riled up."

James had been a witness to Shane and Cecilia's relationship since the start, and he had to side with Shane on this one. Cecilia routinely devised plots to challenge him. But, in fairness, Shane couldn't be happier. His brother needed that in a woman.

Jane gave Shane a long once-over. "I can't say I blame her."

James let out a long-suffering sigh. "Don't encourage him. What are you doing here?"

"My last meeting ended early and I need a game of no-holds-barred racquetball to relieve all this stress. I'd have called first, but you've been avoiding me, so I figured I'd make an in-person visit. You game?"

His brother played a vicious game, with no rules, and blunt force. Seeing as how James was pretty pent-up himself, it sounded damn good. "I'm in."

Shane cocked his head, studying James before shifting his attention to Jane. "Do you know why he's avoiding me?"

"I'm not avoiding you," James said, shaking his head. "I've been busy."

Jane's expression turned innocent. Too innocent. "I saw him this weekend, so I haven't noticed."

Shane scrubbed his jaw. "Ce-ce thinks it might be a woman."

James said nothing.

Jane shrugged. "With him, you never can tell, can you?"

"Isn't that the truth?" Shane stood and grabbed his abandoned suit jacket. "Ready?"

Jane smiled, craning her neck to look up at him. "Could you give us a minute? I have to ask him a quick work thing."

"Sure, I'll pull the car around and meet you out front," Shane said, and gathered his tie.

They said their good-byes and his brother left. James started straightening his papers. "What's up?"

"Why are you doing this?" Jane asked.

"Doing what?" His mind on racquetball, he couldn't figure out what the problem might be.

"Keeping your relationship with Gracie a secret from your family."

Even as his stomach tightened, James shrugged. The secret had started innocently enough. He'd expected them to have one date, declare it a disaster, and move on. Secrecy seemed prudent under those circumstances. But now it seemed that Gracie wanted to keep it that way and he hadn't fought her on the issue. "You know how they are."

Jane stood and narrowed her eyes. "Why, though? Who cares if they know?"

"There's nothing wrong with keeping things private. I'm a private person. You know that."

"But she's not, and neither were you when you were at our house."

He knew why. It was a preventive measure to prepare for the end of their relationship.

Jane pressed her finger to her temple as though he gave her a headache. "Keeping your relationship with the head cheerleader a secret feels a little too much like you think you don't deserve her."

"That's ridiculous." The words were calm, but inside his defensiveness grew.

"Is it?" Jane put her hand on his arm and he had to force himself not to wrench away.

"Yes," he said through gritted teeth.

He knew Jane thought that this was some leftover issue from his youth, but she was wrong. He deserved her.

He just didn't have faith he could keep her.

Chapter Twenty-Four

Gracie couldn't decide if she was in heaven. Or hell.

After all these weeks, James would be here any minute. Thanksgiving had arrived and she'd finally see him. Only she wouldn't be able to touch him, because the day was already in full swing at Mitch and Maddie's house.

Maddie opened the oven door and waved her over. "I think this is looking pretty good, don't you?"

Gracie put down the dish she'd been drying and peered into the hot oven. The turkey was golden brown. "It looks great. We should put some tinfoil over the top for a while to keep it from getting too brown."

Maddie shut the oven and gave her a hip bump. "I'm so happy you live next door."

Gracie put her arm around the smaller woman and squeezed. "Me too, baby doll."

Maddie's green eyes filled with tears and Gracie frowned. "What's wrong?"

Maddie sniffed. "Nothing. I'm just so happy."

Gracie studied her suspiciously. Her red hair was tied back and her skin glowed with health. Gracie surveyed her small frame, still as tiny as ever, in a tan miniskirt and a long, burnished red top. "You're not pregnant, are you?"

Maddie laughed and wiped under her lashes. "No! God, nobody tells you when you get married that anytime you have an emotion or don't feel well everyone assumes you're knocked up."

Gracie waved at Maddie's outfit. "Well, in fairness, crying over happiness and wearing a long, belly-concealing top does give one thoughts."

"True, but no." Maddie covered her heart with an open palm. "We're still waiting. We agreed to talk about it again on our first anniversary."

Gracie handed her friend a glass of wine. "Then we'd better drink up now."

Maddie took a sip and glanced around her kitchen. "I feel like I'm supposed to be doing something for dinner, but there's nothing to do."

"It's one of those hurry-up-and-wait type of meals. Let's go relax with the rest of them while we have a chance."

Maddie bit her bottom lip. "Before we do, I have a favor to ask."

"Of course, anything."

"It's our first Thanksgiving as a married couple. Do you think you could try not fighting with James, just this once?"

Gracie willed the heat flooding her face to cool. If Maddie only knew how easy it was to make that promise. In fact, she planned on being more than nice. Gracie sighed, as though this would be a great struggle, because that's what her friend expected. "I will be on my best behavior. He's staying until after Christmas and I vow, for your sake, to be nice to him the whole time. I even offered up the garage apartment. See how nice I am?"

"Thank you. It will be a big weight off my shoulders not having to oversee Shane's summerhouse construction when he can't attend to things because of work. He's so demanding, I don't know how Cecilia puts up with him." Maddie shot her a megawatt smile. "I wish you could appreciate how great James is."

Oh, she appreciated it. Nightly. They might have been apart but they spoke every day. More than once, and every night before bed. She'd grown dependent on his low, calm voice being the last thing she heard before she went to sleep. Her fingers clenched in anticipation. She was going to tear him apart.

Oblivious to Gracie's insatiable desire for James to arrive so she could start being *nice*, Maddie continued. "I mean, how many brothers would come during their break to help their little sister?"

"He's practically a saint," Gracie said dryly.

"I'm just saying, be nice."

"I promise." She'd be so nice he wouldn't know what hit him.

They strolled into the hallway at the exact same moment James opened the door, brushing snow from his shoulders. Gracie's heart leapt into her throat as her belly heated.

Good God, the man looked awesome. Tall and lean, his green eyes vivid behind his black frames, his brown hair tousled. She sucked in a breath at the sight of him and had to resist the urge to throw herself into his arms. He wiped his boots on the mat and their eyes locked.

I want you. I want you. I want you. A chant in her head.

His gaze turned hot, skimming down her body. She wore a short, black, pleated skirt, black knee-high boots, and a matching top. She also wore thigh-high tights because, surrounded by people all day, they'd need easy access. She wanted him, like, right now, and had no intention of waiting for privacy.

Maddie didn't seem to notice the long, tension-filled stare because she ran to James and threw her arms around him. "You're here!"

James hugged her back, giving her a kiss on the cheek. "How's my little sister?"

His voice. She loved his voice. Loved the way he whispered all sorts of dirty things in her ear. The sound of her name as he stroked inside her. The way he moaned when she went down on him. The catch of his breath—

She sucked in a lungful of air as her body heated. She was already wet. Ready and needy. *Okay, get it together.* She could handle this. She'd have him soon enough.

Gracie walked slowly toward him, trying her damnedest not to smile as he watched the slow sway of her hips with hungry appreciation. She nodded. "James."

He nodded back. "Gracie."

She jerked a thumb toward Maddie. "She made me promise to be nice to you."

His lips quivered. "I see. I hope it's not too much of a hardship."

She flicked her gaze to his mouth, letting her tongue lick over her bottom lip before shrugging. "I'll survive."

Maddie looked back and forth between the two of them. "Just for today and Christmas. Is that too much to ask?"

James's brow rose. "Anything for my little sister."

"Awww," Gracie said, her voice oh so sweet. "Aren't you a good brother?"

Before James could speak, Shane walked over and clapped him on the back. "Just in time for the game."

"A day watching football. What a joy," James said, his voice wry.

"Hey, it's your brother," Shane said.

"But what about the other six games?" James asked.

Shane laughed, shaking his head. "It's only three."

In an effort to be "nice," she asked, "What would you rather be watching, Professor?"

James's attention traveled down the length of her body. "There's a *Doctor Who* marathon on."

"Really?" she asked hopefully, forgetting to play it cool. The damn man had gotten her addicted. He'd already seen all the episodes, but he watched with her because, as he said, he liked the way she got all excited.

"Really." His voice lowered an octave. "Twelve whole hours. With special bonus mini episodes."

"What channel?" Gracie said, shivering.

Maddie laughed. "I said be nice, but let's not go too far."

Shane raised his brows and pointed to Gracie. "I don't think she's faking, Mads."

Maddie's expression flashed with surprise. "Really? Since when?"

"Umm . . ." Gracie tucked a lock of hair behind her ear, remembering the last time she'd watched it with James. They'd played their own *Doctor Who* drinking game. A combination that included shedding their clothes, melted chocolate, and champagne that James had licked from her nipples every time the doctor said "TARDIS." "I . . . um . . . caught an episode one night and got hooked."

James gave her his most evil smile, telling her with one look he knew the exact memory she recalled. "Something we have in common."

Gracie swallowed. She couldn't last. She needed to get him alone. "Will wonders never cease."

"Come on," Shane said, waving them in to the living room, taking his seat next to Cecilia.

They were a small group. Sam was coming later. Charlie worked. Maddie's mom had decided to stay with

Aunt Cathy, and Mitch's mom had gone on a cruise in the Greek isles with friends. Gracie had invited Harmony Jones since she was new in town, but she'd declined, saying she had too much to do as she settled into her new home.

James took off his coat and hung it in the foyer and Gracie said, "Maddie, I'm going to give the turkey a quick baste before I sit down."

"Thanks," Maddie called.

Gracie walked through the swinging door and didn't even breathe as she waited for James.

He'd follow her.

She knew he'd follow her.

Seconds later the door swung open and she turned to face him. And then he was there. Crushing her to him, his mouth slamming over hers.

He walked them back, pushing her against the countertop.

Devouring her.

His tongue in her mouth.

His hands everywhere. Hot and demanding.

Between hard kisses he said, "Jesus, you look so fucking good."

"So do you." She pulled out his shirt and ran her hands up his chest. "I want your cock."

He growled, pushing her against the counter and lifting her leg over his hip, thrusting his erection against her already swollen center. "Now."

"Yes."

"Gracie," Cecilia called out.

They broke apart, their breathing ragged.

"Yeah," Gracie answered, never taking her eyes from the man in front of her.

James's mouth was wet, his lips full from the force of their kiss.

"Can you bring beer?"

Gracie sighed. "Sure."

James pulled her back and kissed her again. "Maybe this isn't the time."

"When?" She leaned on tiptoes. "I'm desperate."

"Good." He ran his hand down her hip and under her skirt, freezing when he met bare thigh. He groaned. "Why are you torturing me? You know how I feel about these."

"I do," she said, licking his throat. She was pretty sure he had a fetish for them, and she took full advantage.

He pulled her to the table and moved to stand behind her. "You are the worst kind of temptation."

He placed a palm at the base of her spine and pushed her down so she leaned over the table, lifting up her skirt. He slid her panties down her legs. "Step out."

She didn't even hesitate. In this, he was exactly her type, scarily so. She'd worry, if she weren't so desperate for him.

He kicked out her legs and she clenched at the wood table, her breath coming in little pants. His fingers slid between her legs and she trembled at the sheer pleasure. He leaned over her, whispering into her ear, "Someone's wet."

She pushed her hips back, needing him to deepen the touch. "For you."

So light it was nothing but a tease, he skimmed his fingers over her aching flesh. "I know how you like our games. I could practically feel your excitement when you remembered our *Doctor Who* adventure. So let's see how far I can push you until you break, shall we?"

She'd never wanted anyone more. He was like a drug in her system. "I'm already there."

"I think you can take more." He pulled her up and slipped her panties into his pocket. "I'll hang on to these."

Oh man, it was going to be a long dinner.

Every ounce of discipline and control James had ever possessed had been used up over the course of one evening. He'd been hard for hours, as he'd tortured Gracie, and himself, in every possible way. The last time he'd touched her she'd been so wet it coated her thighs.

The sound of her begging still rang in his ears.

It was hell, but damned if it wasn't fun watching her squirm. Keeping her on edge and desperate.

With a glass of wine in one hand, he dragged his fingers through his hair and tried to catch his breath in the now empty kitchen. He wouldn't be able to wait much longer.

The swinging door blew open and Shane entered the room. "What are you doing here all by yourself?"

James shrugged, taking a sip of wine. "Just needed a moment of silence."

Shane nodded, a grin spreading over his face. "So, how long have you been sleeping with her?"

James straightened, his wine sloshing around in his glass. "I don't know what you're talking about."

Shane laughed, leaning against the counter and kicking one foot over the other. "I suspected after Gracie didn't stay with us both times she was in town. And there was also Ce-ce and Maddie's suspicions that Gracie was seeing someone. But tonight confirmed it. You guys are doing a shit job of hiding it."

James had actually believed they were being discreet, but with too much wine and too much lust clouding his perception he couldn't be sure. "You're delusional."

Shane scoffed, shaking his head. "Please. Don't insult my intelligence. Most women don't look orgasmic at the mention of *Doctor Who.*"

Surprised laughter burst from James's mouth, coming

out like a bark. "Maybe you don't know the right type of women, Shane."

Shane rolled his eyes, but before he could speak Mitch came into the room. He walked over to the fridge and pulled it open, grabbing a bottle of beer. He twisted off the top and tossed it onto the counter, kicking back against the counter much like Shane. He raised a brow. "So, you finally took care of that, did you?"

"See, I told you," Shane said, before shifting his attention to Mitch. "He's still denying it."

James hadn't actually denied as much as he'd evaded.

"Don't even bother. The only one who doesn't know is Maddie, who thinks it's cute you guys are making such an effort." Mitch rubbed his jaw. "Must be some effort. You have Gracie almost speechless and I never thought I'd see that."

James experienced a swell of satisfaction, knowing deep down he'd wanted her marked, needed to be different from the other men she dated, but he still avoided their questions. "I promised Maddie I'd be nice and I'm fulfilling my promise."

Shane laughed.

"I'd say you're going above and beyond the call of duty." Mitch raised his beer in a toast.

The door swung open again and Cecilia came in.

James sighed.

She pointed at him, putting one hand on her narrow hips. "All right, what did you do to make sure she didn't tell me?"

James shook his head. "I have no idea what you're talking about."

Cecilia scowled, looking very disgruntled as she appealed to her fiancé. "I'm one of her best friends. I can understand Maddie, but me—Why me?"

"I don't know what game they're playing, Ce-Ce." Shane reached for her and pulled her next to him, sliding his arm around her waist. "Now you've gone and upset her."

James opened his mouth to speak but then Maddie entered, flying into the room like a mini tornado. "What's going on here?"

Cecilia pointed at James. "Your brother is violating Gracie."

"Wait, what?" Maddie's attention flew to James.

James once again opened his mouth to calmly explain, but then Mitch said, "Gracie and James are sleeping together."

"But that's impossible." Maddie shot him a confused glance. "You don't even like each other."

When Shane jumped in, James leaned back and let the conversation swirl around him, since nobody seemed to be interested in what he had to say about the subject. He should have known they couldn't keep it discreet; this group was far too nosy.

"You're just too blind to see it because he's your brother," Shane said.

"He's your brother too," Maddie responded. "Maybe you're wrong."

"He's not wrong, Maddie," Mitch said.

Maddie shifted to her husband. "How do you know?"

Mitch grinned at her. "They sat next to each other at dinner."

"I asked them to be nice," Maddie said.

"Oh, I'd say he's having no trouble there," Shane said.

Maddie glanced at Cecilia. "Do you think it's true?"

"Yes. I'm sure," Cecilia said, frowning. "But I don't understand why she didn't tell us."

They continued on, all talking over each other as they hashed out what they believed was going on, and James leaned back against the counter, drinking his wine, and didn't say one word.

The door swung open again and Gracie strolled in on

those spectacular boots that he intended to wrap around his waist very soon. "What is going on in here? Why are you all yelling?"

"Why didn't you tell us?" Maddie shouted, her expression flashing.

Gracie's eyes slid guiltily to James's, and she asked in a low voice, "Tell you what?"

"I knew you weren't staying in some spa by yourself!" Cecilia raised her brows, shaking her head and sending her hair flying.

Gracie yanked her attention to James and demanded, "What did you tell them?"

Thus confirming all their suspicions.

Maddie and Cecilia gasped and the men laughed.

Gracie's eyes went wide and James saw the exact moment she'd recognized her mistake.

James spoke up for the first time. "I have *literally* not said one word."

"Well, you must have said something," Gracie said, taking a warrior's stance, committed to the line of questioning now that she'd given away their secret.

"I have not," James said, calmly. "None of them would even let me speak."

Gracie chewed on her lower lip.

Maddie stepped forward. "Is it true?"

Gracie met his gaze and he shrugged, taking a sip of his wine. She sighed. "Yes."

"Why didn't you tell us? We're your best friends," Cecilia said.

"It's complicated." Gracie took a deep breath. "But now that you all know, get the hell out. I need to speak to James alone."

Maddie's expression creased with concern. "Oh no, don't be mad at him. He didn't do anything. It was all us."

"Maddie, I love you, but you need to leave," Gracie said.

James crossed one foot over his ankle and grinned into his wine glass. He knew damned well what she wanted. And it wasn't to yell at him. He gave his sister a somber look. "Don't worry, I'll be okay."

Shane snorted and Cecilia elbowed him in the ribs.

Gracie's expression flashed and she narrowed her gaze on him. "Don't encourage her."

Maddie wrung her hands, clearly not caught up to the fact that Gracie and James's relationship had changed so drastically. "Okay, but promise me you won't be too hard on him."

Gracie raised her gaze to the ceiling. "God help me, I haven't had sex in nearly a month! Get out!"

James chuckled, enjoying himself too much to be embarrassed.

Mitch scrubbed a hand over his jaw. "I'm not sure that's the kind of help God provides, Gracie."

She curled her hands into fists and stomped her foot and screamed, "Get out!"

"Geez, chill," Shane said, turning a sly smile on James. "What did you do to her?"

She pointed toward the door. "Now! Or so help me, you'll regret it."

With both amusement and surprise they all filed out of the kitchen, finally leaving them alone.

James shot her his most cocky, arrogant grin. "I'd say you've finally reached your breaking point, baby girl."

She stalked over, grabbed him by the shirt and hauled him toward her. "Shut up and fuck me."

He growled and kissed her.

It was out of control. She clawed at his shoulders, as he feasted on her mouth.

She fisted the fabric of his shirt and practically tried to crawl into him, rubbing and rocking against him.

He'd always been the quiet one, careful to never call attention to himself, but he threw that to the wind and pushed her back, knocking a chair over in the process. Her ass hit the table and he pushed plates and dishes out of the way. Loud crashing filled the air but they didn't even break stride.

She groaned and fumbled for his zipper while his hands slid under her top and cupped her breasts. He rubbed his thumbs over her nipples and she arched into him. Her head fell back as she put her hands on the table in back of her. He yanked up her shirt, flicking over the clasp of her bra with one hand and peeling the cups away from her spectacular breasts.

He leaned down and sucked the peaked buds into his mouth, hard and urgent. She gripped his head, her nails digging into his skull as she pressed him closer. He bit and she let out a mewling cry and a second later another dish shattered on the floor.

He knew they were making a lot of noise, that as soon as they left this room there'd be a million questions, and he just didn't give a fuck.

All he cared about was her.

He swirled his tongue over first one nipple then the other, pinching and plucking in a way that drove her wild. "James, yes, God . . . I've missed you so much."

"I missed you too, Gracie," he murmured against her breast.

He slid his hand around her throat, brushing his thumb over the pulse hammering in her neck. He'd think about how much later. Much, much later. After he managed to quench his impossible hunger.

Chapter Twenty-Five

With a batch of vanilla-bean cupcakes and oatmeal-raisin cookies in the oven, and James asleep upstairs in her bedroom, Gracie sat at her table and wrote out her list of the things she needed to get done this week, including things she could delegate to Harmony, who was a godsend.

She'd mulled over the list of her Chicago orders, which seemed to be growing by the day.

The logistics of getting products to Chicago continued to be the problem. She'd checked with some local distribution companies and the costs were too high. And even after hiring Harmony, who'd made some kick-ass pumpkin cupcakes and duplicated Gracie's red velvet ones so well she hadn't been able to tell the difference, it wasn't feasible to continue to travel back and forth to Chicago. She kept waiting for the orders to slow down, but it never happened. She was going to have to think of something, but at the moment she was at a loss.

There was a knock at her back door and Gracie glanced up and waved Maddie inside.

Maddie smiled as she entered and said politely, "Is this a good time?"

Gracie sighed at the distant, cordial tone. "Just because I'm sleeping with James doesn't mean we're strangers."

Maddie shut the door behind her. "I'm sorry, I just . . . I don't know. I'm not sure what to say."

"There's nothing to say. Nothing has changed between us." Gracie swallowed hard. This was exactly why she hadn't wanted to say anything. Her best friend was already treating her differently.

Maddie grabbed some coffee and sat down at the table. "But that's just the thing, it *has* changed things between us. You've been acting different for weeks. You won't talk to me. I knew something was going on and you didn't trust me enough to tell me." She shrugged. "I thought you felt like you could tell me anything, like I tell you."

Gracie put down her pen and took a deep breath. Of course, Maddie was right. Gracie had been acting differently. Maddie had tried again and again to break through, but Gracie had avoided her. Now it was time to rectify the problem she'd created. "I'm sorry. I have a confession to make, but you're not going to like it."

Maddie frowned. "I'm listening."

Gracie ran her hand through her hair, hating that she had to admit it, but not seeing a way around it. "Ever since Shane and Cecilia got engaged, I've been fighting a bad case of jealousy."

"Because they're getting married?" Maddie asked.

Gracie shook her head. "No. Because you and Cecilia get to be sisters."

Maddie's hand slid across the table, touching Gracie's. "You are my sister. Just as much as Cecilia."

Throat tight, Gracie nodded. "I know you feel like that, but you guys are so close now. And I got it into my head you have a special bond that doesn't include me. You were family, while I was a friend. I love Sam, but it's just us, and I guess I wanted what you guys had."

When Maddie's eyes turned too bright, Gracie's own eyes welled. She shook her head, blinking the wetness away. "I hated that I felt so petty, so I hid it."

Maddie squeezed her fingers. "I wish I'd known. I love you, and no matter how big my family gets, you are always a part of it."

"I love you too, Maddie. I'm sorry I didn't tell you. I should have trusted our friendship more."

"I understand." Another last squeeze before Maddie's fingers slipped away. "And James?"

Gracie blew out a long breath and took a sip of coffee to compose herself. "In my own stupid way, I was protecting our friendship. Since I was already worried, I didn't want to put you in the difficult spot of having to choose between your brother and me when things end between us. It seemed easier to keep it private until things played out. Then life would go on and things wouldn't change."

Maddie cleared her throat. "What *is* going on with you guys?"

Gracie's heart started to pound fast in her chest. Last night had been awesome, and since they hadn't had to hide, he'd stayed over and they'd talked and made love until the wee hours of the morning. It scared her, how she felt about him, the look in his eyes when he watched her, and how damn good they were together. They didn't speak about the future. In fact, they actively avoided it, but everything unspoken sat between them, rife in the air. She said softly, "I don't know."

"Gracie," Maddie said, her voice turning soft. "Please don't break his heart. He doesn't deserve that."

Her chest squeezed. "I know he doesn't."

Maddie worried her lower lip. "The way he looks at you, the way he acts, I've never seen him like that. He's always been so . . . well, you know how he is."

"I do," Gracie said.

"I've never even seen him touch another girl. He's never engaged in public displays of affection. But last night, with you, he wasn't being at all shy."

"Is that bad?"

Maddie gazed at her, her eyes wide. "You broke half my dishes."

Gracie had the good grace to flush. She'd been a touched crazed. "Yeah, sorry about that. I'll replace them."

"It just didn't seem like him. Does that make sense?"

Gracie nodded. She couldn't pretend it wasn't something she'd wondered about before. He barely seemed like the man she'd come to know over the last year. She was changing him like he changed her. But she didn't know what it meant. She swallowed. "Maybe he's loosening up. You've always been concerned about how controlled he is, so isn't that a good thing?"

"I think so." But Maddie didn't really sound sure.

"Are you upset?" Gracie's throat tightened.

Maddie shook her head. "No, I just don't want him to get hurt."

Gracie didn't blame Maddie for her worry. After all, she hardly had a good track record when it came to relationships. But it hurt all the same. "I don't want that either."

Maddie blew out an exasperated breath. "It's just that you're the girl everybody loves and James is as susceptible as the next guy."

"But that's the thing, Maddie," Gracie said, her tone angrier than she wanted it to be. "I'm not the girl everybody loves. I'm the girl everybody *wants* and that's sure as hell not the same thing."

Surprise flashed over Maddie's expression. "That's not true."

"Yes, it is. Plenty of guys want to sleep with me but they

don't want to know me. All they want is who they think
I am. They don't care about the real me."

It wasn't the guys' fault. She'd always let that be
enough, because deep down she feared she didn't have
it in her to go the distance. Yes, she was nicer and didn't
have a raging drinking problem, but how was she really
different from her father? Everyone always said they
were exactly alike. He'd been a snake charmer, capti-
vating his audience, but behind the mask, there wasn't
anything there.

Maddie frowned, her expression concerned. "And
James is different?"

And wasn't that exactly the problem niggling away
at her? He was different. In some ways she felt more
herself with James than she ever had. Somehow, the
man she least expected to, had managed to work past all
her defenses. He saw past her charm, saw past the sex
kitten—but what if there was nothing there?

"Yes, I'm different," James said from the doorway of
the kitchen, his voice stern. "Now stop worrying."

Gracie's shoulders tensed. How much had he heard?

Maddie averted her gaze from her brother's bare
chest. "Well, this is awkward."

"It's only awkward if you make it that way. But back
off, you're upsetting her."

"Am I?" Maddie frowned.

Gracie shrugged. Didn't anyone understand James
wasn't the only one who could end up hurt here?

Maddie's green eyes, so much like her brother's,
clouded. "I'm making things worse, aren't I?"

"Yes," James said.

"Cecilia told me to leave it alone for a while but I
wouldn't listen," Maddie said, her expression tight with
concern.

Gracie didn't want to discuss this anymore. "It's fine,
don't worry about it. I understand."

"I'm sorry," Maddie said, straightening in her chair. "Just give me a chance to catch up, okay? I mean, in fairness, I spent the last year trying to keep you from murdering each other. This is a bit of a shock."

James sat down at the table and raised a brow at Gracie.

"It will be fine," Gracie insisted, putting on her happy face. "How about we go to Big Reds tonight, just the girls?"

Maddie's expression brightened. "Really?"

"Yep, we'll have guys buy us drinks all night."

With a smile, James winked and opened his iPad to scroll through the morning news, as usual, and Gracie released a pent-up breath she hadn't known she held.

That's what she loved about him. Most guys would kick up some sort of fuss about being abandoned after twenty-four hours so she could make peace with her girlfriends, but James just took it in stride. Not remotely fazed that she planned to pimp other men for free drinks. A man couldn't fake confidence like that.

"I'd love that," Maddie said.

"Great—you, me, and Ce-ce, just like old times."

Maddie shot a wayward glance at her brother, then cleared her throat. "I should let you get back to work."

The timer dinged and Gracie laughed. "It seems it's about that time."

There was still a touch of awkwardness between them, but hopefully by tonight it would be gone and they could go back to normal. Maddie waved and took her leave as Gracie pulled her cookies from the oven.

From behind her, James said, "I didn't know you felt that way."

"What way?" She tested the doneness, deciding the cookies were perfect.

"You're not a fantasy, Gracie." He came up behind

her and put his arms around her and she melted into his strong chest. "Admit I'm different."

She took a deep breath. "You are."

He kissed her temple. "We're going to have to talk about us soon."

All her muscles tensed and he ran his hands up and down her arms, soothing her.

"I'm not ready."

"You're afraid." A simple, straightforward statement; like the man himself.

"Yes." Why bother denying it, he already knew the truth.

He squeezed her tight. "Me too."

She twisted, turning to face him. "You are?"

He nodded. "This is more complicated than I expected."

"Yes, it is." Her other timer dinged. She pulled back. "Duty calls."

"Saved by the bell." He released her and she moved to her ovens. Behind her he asked, "Have you given a Chicago bakery any more thought?"

She pulled the sheet cake from the oven and put it onto the cooling rack. He'd made the suggestion a couple times but she didn't see how that was possible. She shrugged. "Not really."

There was a long moment of silence before he said, "Okay. I'm going to go for a run."

Happy to change the subject, she put a smile on her face and turned to him. "How many miles?"

He shrugged. "I'm thinking ten."

"Ten! That's insane." She moved to the oven and pulled out her cupcakes. "What is the matter with you? Didn't I wear you out last night?"

He laughed. "Actually, I've never had more energy."

"You're sick and demented."

"So you keep telling me."

She grinned. "I'll make you the peanut butter and chocolate protein bars while you're gone. I have just enough time to make sure they're set before you get back."

He grabbed her wrist and pulled her back, giving her a long, hard kiss. "God, I adore you."

And just like that all the air sucked from her lungs.

She was in love with him.

For the first time in her life she was completely, head over heels in love. And she had no idea what to do about it.

James observed the progress the construction team had made on his brother's vacation home, while Shane panted for breath next to him.

Shane put his hands on his knees and heaved out, "You fucking suck."

James grinned, and leaned up against a tree. "It's good for you."

"You're a sadist," Shane said, sweat trickling down his temples.

"So I've been told." James wiped his own sweaty face. Sure, it had been a hard ten miles but it hadn't been that bad. Given his late night, he'd actually gone at a more leisurely pace. "I took it easy on you."

Shane rolled his eyes and finally managed to catch his breath. "Whatever."

James chuckled. "If you ran with me more often maybe you'd be in better shape."

"I'm in fine shape, compared to normal people."

True, Shane didn't have an ounce of fat on his body. He'd always been blessed with the good genes and hardly had to work at it at all. Unlike James, who, even after all these years, would go flabby in an instant if he didn't work at it.

James pointed to the house, a white frame home that sprawled over the large lot, with a big wraparound porch and plantation shutters. "They've made good progress."

"Yeah, should be done soon. They started on the drywall last week," Shane said.

They were silent for a bit, and the cold November air chilled James's skin.

Shane finally cast him a sideways glance. "So, what's going on with you and Gracie?"

Something. Although he was unclear how to define their relationship. But it was clear this wasn't the easy, uncomplicated fling he'd envisioned. Nor was she going to wear off given enough time.

If it ended, or when it ended, it would be messy.

He was starting to need her. She was the last person he talked to each night and the first thing he thought of when he woke up. He wanted more, but she seemed content to drift along, and he didn't want to push it yet. He understood her now, how she thought and felt. What she believed. He'd learned enough about her past to figure out that commitment terrified her, and instinct warned him to take baby steps.

But he already knew his own truth. He was keeping her. He just had to figure out how.

Realizing his brother watched him, James shrugged. "Nothing that concerns you."

Shane laughed. "You always were a talker."

"Want to show me around inside?"

"Is it serious?" His older brother was the mother hen of the family and couldn't quite break the habit of worrying about them even though they were all grown, successful adults.

Normally, James would shut down this line of questioning, but he wanted something from his brother and he would have to pay to get it. James jutted his chin toward the house. "Can we at least get out of the cold?"

"Wuss." Shane grinned and pulled the key out of a hidden pocket in his pants.

They bounded up the stairs and entered the house, with its wide-open spaces and high ceilings. Even with the drywall only partially installed, James could tell the house would be spectacular. His brother would have it no other way.

They walked across the plywood to the back of the house where the kitchen would be. It had floor-to-ceiling arched windows that overlooked the backyard. Shane had the trees cleared away so the river was visible. The view was scenic and peaceful and James could imagine working for hours in the quiet tranquility.

He smiled. "Dad would have loved this."

Shane propped himself up against the structure that would be an island. "Yeah, he always talked about a place where he could experience small town life."

Truth was, their dad would never have been able to afford anything like this. Finances hadn't been his strong suit, but none of them held it against him, not even Shane, who'd worked to the bone to ensure they didn't lose everything.

"Has mom seen the house since the frame was completed?"

Shane rested his hands on the plywood where a countertop would eventually be. "Are you going to avoid the question forever?"

Reprieve up, James sighed. "I think it might be serious."

"I'm not surprised," Shane said.

That got James's attention. "I sure as hell am."

"She turned Evan down at Maddie's wedding. After that I knew it was a matter of time."

James didn't want to think about his younger brother hitting on Gracie. He could handle the countless men who constantly wanted her, but the visual of Gracie and

Evan, their heads close together, was still an unpleasant memory.

He looked out the window. "I need a favor."

"Anything." The word was absolute. That was the way Shane was. If it was in his power, he'd walk through fire for any of them.

James turned away from the window and faced his brother. "You know Gracie has been overrun with orders from Chicago."

Shane nodded. "Cecilia told me."

"I think she should consider opening a storefront in Chicago." The idea had germinated soon after her first visit, but no matter how many times he suggested that as a possible solution to her current problems, she'd rejected the idea.

Shane cocked a brow. "And it puts her in Chicago."

"I won't pretend I don't have ulterior motives." If James wanted a relationship with her, it made logical sense she'd have to move to Chicago. She had the beginnings of a thriving business, a clientele already recommending her, and James couldn't move to Revival. He had tenure at one of the most prestigious universities in the country.

"Have you talked to her about this?" Shane asked.

"I've suggested it, but she's reluctant to discuss it."

Shane scrubbed a hand over his jaw. "Have you pressed?"

James shook his head. "As you've pointed out, I can hardly be objective."

"And how do you think I can help?"

The truth was, James didn't know how Shane could, but he had to start somewhere. "You are one of the most successful businessmen in Chicago. Maybe you could talk through the options with her? Then it's not me wanting to change her life, but one business person to another."

Shane tilted his head to the side and got that faraway

expression he wore when working something out in his head. James waited patiently and didn't interrupt.

After what seemed an eternity, Shane said, "Even though she's got an established business here, she can't make much money. This is a small town and though she has no overhead, people can only eat so many cakes. Even if she's open to the idea, I doubt she'll have the capital to open a storefront. Chicago is an expensive place to do business, especially when you're used to the cost of living in a small town."

James scrubbed a hand over his jaw. See, this was why he stuck to academics. He'd been so focused on getting her to discuss the possibility he hadn't thought through the business side of the equation. "I hadn't thought about that."

"Business 101, Jimmy."

"I missed that class in school." The flare of hope burning in his gut died a quick death. "So you don't think it's feasible that she could move her business to Chicago."

Shane shrugged. "I don't know her financial situation, but it's doubtful. I do, however, have a solution."

"What's that?"

"I'll front her."

James blinked and shook his head. "I can't ask you to do that."

"She's Gracie. People are already clamoring for her. She bakes like she's got magic in her hands, everyone that lays eyes on her loves her, and my future wife happens to be some sort of public relations guru." Shane's expression turned pleased and satisfied. "I'll get the money back and even if I don't, I can eat it."

Said with the confidence of the very rich.

James wasn't quite sure how much money his brother actually had, and never asked, but he made their pro-football-player brother look like he made peanuts.

That hope once again flamed anew. It was a solution

and James needed a solution. "Do you think she'll go for it?"

Shane nodded. "We'll devise a plan she can't refuse."

James mulled it over, liking the idea more and more. If they did the work for her and gave her the financial support to make it happen, as a businesswoman she'd have to consider the opportunity. James nodded. "All right, what's the next step?"

Shane grinned and rubbed his hands together in almost maniacal glee. "I'll put Penelope on it first thing Monday."

Penelope had worked as Shane's right hand for years, but she was also Maddie's best friend.

"Can we trust her not to say anything?" That James asked that particular question should have been a warning, but he was too intent on finally hitting on the perfect solution to care.

Chapter Twenty-Six

It had been a crazy couple of weeks and Gracie had worked like a madwoman. She smiled at Harmony, who'd been by her side through the whole thing, helping her in ways Gracie hadn't even imagined. "Have I told you how happy I am you came to town?"

Harmony laughed, the sound like music. "Only every day. You're getting lax on the compliments." She walked over to the mixer, flicked off the lever, and silence descended over the kitchen.

"I'll try and show more appreciation." Gracie grinned at her.

She couldn't be happier with Harmony's performance and she was a dream to work with. She was good-natured, hardworking, and blushed easily, giving Gracie endless hours of fun teasing her. They worked side by side in both companionable silence and friendly camaraderie. Harmony had taken over almost all of Gracie's routine baking duties so she could concentrate on the two elaborate cakes she had to deliver to Chicago.

Two more cakes and she'd be done until after Christmas. At the beginning of the New Year she'd have to put serious thought into a business plan. This constant traveling wouldn't work as a long-term solution.

Her phone beeped, signaling an incoming text from James. When will you be done?

Since he was a man who liked silence and her house was nothing but a racket, he'd set up the garage apartment as an office space so he could work on the publications he needed to complete over the school break. Despite the craziness, they spent every last minute with each other, and her fear about the depth of their relationship continued to mount. Another subject she was putting off until after the New Year.

Gracie smiled at his text and Harmony chuckled. "There's only one person who makes you smile like that. The professor must be out of his cave."

Gracie texted back. I'm finishing up, maybe fifteen minutes. Was it ridiculous that it seemed like a lifetime? Probably, but she didn't care. She loved him and she was going to enjoy it. While he was here, she'd vowed to throw herself into him, unreservedly and freely, until he forced her to deal with the future.

She'd worry about that later; now she just wanted to see him. Gracie beamed at Harmony. "Is it that obvious?"

"Yes, but it's adorable," the other woman said.

Her phone beeped again. Good. Please report to my office in 30 minutes, dressed appropriately.

Hmmm, what did that mean? Something good, she was sure. A rush of heat washed over her. How was it possible he was this much fun? To think, six months ago she'd believed he didn't have a fun bone in his body. Appropriately?

Almost panting, she waited a full minute for his response. I'm very disappointed with your term paper, Ms. Roberts. Proper discipline is required.

Instantly her professor fantasies sprang to mind, and

if she hadn't been leaning against the counter, she would have melted into a pool of butter on the floor.

Harmony whistled. "Ohhh . . . What's that about?"

Another text. I trust you won't be late, or suffer additional consequences. Professor Donovan.

Gracie's knees actually weakened. She licked her lips. All that control—she shivered—when properly channeled, was the most delicious thing she'd ever experienced. "Um . . ." Gracie looked around as a low throb took up residence between her legs. "Could you finish up here?"

Harmony raised one dark brow. "With the look on your face, I'd be cruel not to."

"You don't mind?"

Harmony waved her toward the door. "Go have fun with your dreamy boyfriend."

The term gave Gracie pause; she'd never heard anyone refer to him that way before. Something else to ponder when she wasn't raging with desire. She sighed. "He is dreamy, isn't he?"

Harmony laughed. "Yes, and apparently very creative."

"He has his moments." Gracie clutched her phone in her hands.

"Go, go, before you pass out."

Gracie practically flew upstairs, searching frantically through her closet for the perfect outfit. She had the perfect top in mind but she couldn't find it, and she flung clothes from her dresser like a madwoman as she raced around her bedroom to get ready. Fifteen minutes later it looked like a mini tornado had torn through her room, but damned if it wasn't worth it.

She slipped on her coat and was out the door. Ready and willing for whatever James dished out.

* * *

Exactly twenty-five minutes after he sent his last text, Gracie was at the garage-apartment door. James affixed a stern expression on his face and waved her in from his position behind the desk. He'd debated long and hard about what he was about to do, but now he was committed.

She entered the room in her trench coat, her hair in a ponytail, her cheeks a pretty pink from the cold.

He raised a brow and said in his most serious voice, "Ms. Roberts, good of you to be on time."

She gave him a pouty smile, made all the more obscene by the pink gloss on her lips. "I didn't want you to think I didn't take my grades seriously."

His lips quivered with the desire to smile but he repressed it, gesturing toward the seat he'd arranged in front of the desk in preparation for her arrival. "Have a seat."

She nodded, and slowly undid her coat, unfastening each button with elaborate attention to detail. Clearly she was intent on being a tease, and James leaned back in his chair, enjoying every minute of it. When the coat dropped to the floor he almost had a heart attack, and it took every ounce of his self-control to maintain his distant facade.

She was right out of a professor's wet dream.

She wore the thigh-high tights he loved so much, and a red, black, and gray pleated skirt so short there was a gap between the hem and the exposed flesh of her thighs. His gaze locked on her skintight black top, and the words in red glitter over her magnificent chest. *Spank me.*

Funny, that was just what he had in mind, but it no longer surprised him when they were on the same page. For two people with supposedly nothing in common, they thought remarkably similarly.

"I said sit, Ms. Roberts." Letting the hard edge of lust into his voice.

She gave him a smug, knowing smile and sat down, crossing her legs and letting the hem drift up to show the edge of her panties. White cotton. Gracie always remembered the finer details.

She licked her lips. "I'm prepared to do whatever is necessary to improve my grade."

"Good. You'll need to if you intend to pass." He opened the bottom drawer of the ancient desk and pulled out one of the large textbooks he used in his classes. "I've prepared a three-part exam. Are you ready to proceed?"

She gave him a sly little smile. "I'm sure there's an easier way to make up my grade. Maybe something a bit more fun."

He'd always been a controlled person, and until Gracie, had never really thought about how that extended to sex. The more she'd seemed to like his control in the bedroom, the more fascinated he became with the idea of taking it a bit further.

When she'd first confessed her professor fantasies, he'd done some Google research and decided on something he hoped she'd like—something a bit more forceful than they'd been skirting around. After careful planning and research, he'd developed his plan and he didn't intend to be dissuaded at the first seductive glance. No matter how tempting. He injected as much sternness into his voice as he could muster. "I asked a question, Ms. Roberts. I suggest you answer, or suffer the consequences."

Her blue eyes darted to him, the Lolita seductress still firmly in place.

He placed a palm over the cover of the book and tapped his finger. "Do I need to ask again?"

She grinned, clearly liking the game and believing herself in full control of the situation. "I'm ready."

Lately he'd come to understand how much she relied on her dazzling personality and nonstop sex appeal, and while he couldn't blame her, he also suspected she used it to hold herself back.

Something he intended to rectify today, if his research paid off.

"Good. If at any time during the exam you feel you're unable to continue, please tell me to stop and I'll end the test immediately. Of course, you'll receive a failing grade, but that will be your choice. Understood?"

She giggled, uncrossed her legs, and splayed them wide. "Oh, I understand."

He shook his head. "The correct answer is 'Yes, Professor.'"

Her eyes widened and her breath seemed to stick in her throat.

He smiled. Excellent.

Oh, so he wanted to play it that way, did he? Well, she could do that. She crossed her legs again and tugged down her skirt to affect the role of a nervous school girl.

She had to admit that with the look in his eyes and set of his jaw, tapping his fingers on the book, he was quite convincing. She gave him her most demure look. "Of course, Professor."

He raised a brow. "Are you finally going to take your grades seriously, Ms. Roberts?"

He was doing an excellent job of playing the character because her body bought it hook, line, and sinker.

"Yes, Professor." She lowered her voice. "I'll do anything to get an A."

His lips quirked, and an expression she'd never seen before passed over his features. "Anything?"

She licked her lips. "Anything."

A slow nod. "Very good. But if you need to stop, tell me at any time."

She purred. "I'm quite positive I can please you."

"I'm counting on it." His tone was stern and exciting.

Boy, he was really committing to the role. Of course, she'd played games like this before; but it felt a touch different with him. Maybe it was because he mattered.

She offered her most sultry smile and said in a light, flirty voice, "I'm sure there's something I can do to convince you of my dedication."

He smoothed his open palm over the textbook. "Your only way out of this is to do what you're told. Do you understand?"

A flare of heat spread over her chest and beaded her nipples. "Yes."

He crooked his finger. "Please, come here."

She bounded out of the chair. "Yes, Professor."

He twisted in his seat. "Come stand in front of me."

Now was the fun part. She walked over to him, stopping directly in front of him as he'd instructed.

His gaze traveled over her body until her skin tingled as though he touched her. "I understand you believe your pretty face can get you out of any mess you find yourself in, but I can assure you that will not work on me. Manipulation will be met with consequences. Are we clear?"

The statement made her pause. She wanted to make a joke, something fun and sexy, but her mind was an utter blank. And she found that all she could do was nod.

"The first part of the exam will test your stamina." He tapped a finger on the desk. "Lean down and rest your elbows on the desk."

Something stuttered inside her as hot desire pooled in her stomach. He was very good at this. And it was so hot. She knew it was just a game, not even an unfamiliar one, but she'd never felt like this before. Was he just that good? Or was it because she loved him?

When she didn't move, he said, "I don't like hesitation, Ms. Roberts."

She couldn't seem to move, because something quivered and niggled inside her. What, she wasn't sure, but it was definitely affecting her performance.

"I suggest you don't make me ask again," he said, his voice filled with authority.

And suddenly she understood. She thought of all the times they'd been together. The ways he'd tortured her at Thanksgiving until she'd been insane. That quiet, steady command. The way she'd never been able to charm her way out of something with him. This wasn't quite an act. This was *him*. Unleashed.

She shivered. Her nipples beaded into tight, hard buds as the thrum of her heart became too loud.

"You're hesitating." Clipped, calm words.

The command spurred her into action, and she slowly leaned over the desk in the position he'd indicated.

"Good. Now spread your legs."

She did, her pulse a rapid beat in her ears.

"Wider." His voice a hard bite.

She complied, her breathing fast and shallow. Her nipples rubbed against the desk and she stifled a low groan. She liked this. Like, really liked this.

He stood, walking behind her.

She closed her eyes, leaning her cheek on the table, ready for whatever he gave her.

"Up on your elbows."

Her lids flew open and a giggle escaped. She grinned back at him. "You sure are taking this seriously."

His lips quirked but didn't break into a smile. "Your education is important to me." He grabbed a fistful of her hair and tugged. "Here's how this is going to work.

Every time you hesitate I'll add five minutes to your test. Understand?"

Something needy and desperate took hold, intoxicating her. "Yes, Professor."

"And what did I tell you to do?"

She had no earthly idea. She licked her lower lip. "I forget."

He sighed, a long, exasperated sound, as he tsked. "Ms. Roberts, what am I going to do with you?"

She wiggled her ass. "I have some ideas."

His palm skimmed down her back and he kneaded it roughly, and she had to bite back a moan of pleasure. "That's not going to work on me."

Why wasn't he going for her naughty school girl act as the game dictated? She tried again and puffed out her bottom lip. "Are you sure about that?"

He frowned at her. "Up on your elbows, Ms. Roberts."

Okay then, he wasn't playing around, and somehow that made it that much hotter. Slowly, she rose to her elbows.

"Good." He straightened and picked up the book with one hand, while pressing the palm of his other down on the curve of her spine, exerting pressure until her back bowed and her ass lifted. He stroked over her spine. "Very nice."

Her breath hitched and she decided to give up thinking and just go with it.

He flipped up her skirt and ran his hands over her round, cotton-covered cheeks. She sucked air into her burning lungs. He ran his fingers over her hip, sweeping up her back before running down her other leg. "Have you ever been properly disciplined?"

Her thoughts scattered as she tried to sort through her answer. Sure, she'd been smacked on the butt before, but somehow she didn't think that was what he was talking about. She hesitated too long and he clucked his tongue. "What am I going to do with you? We'll have to add another five minutes."

"But—"

He squeezed her hip. "Do you want to make it ten?"

God, it was too much. She started to hyperventilate.

"Answer me," he barked, and she jerked in shock and a near debilitating desire.

"No, Professor."

In answer his hand started to move again, ever so slowly, ever so deliberately over her skin. He trailed a path over her ass and then slipped the spine of the book between her legs, rubbing it against her clit. She clenched her hands into fists as she moaned. Impossibly, despite the barrier of her panties, she felt the first telltale sign of an impending orgasm. She fell out of position, pushing her hips back to increase the friction.

And then he was gone.

She turned and glared. "Don't stop!"

He shook his head as though he was totally disappointed in her. "You have no self-control."

She opened her mouth to speak, but he stopped her with one arched brow. "That's ten minutes."

A type of desperate, panic-filled desire fired through her blood. "You can't be serious!"

"I'm quite serious. Now I suggest you be quiet." He tapped her forearms with his fingers. "Elbows up, Ms. Roberts."

She gulped, and returned to the position he'd put her in. She'd often fantasized about what it would be like to be helpless, with no control. And while she'd played at it, it had never actually happened.

She was always in control, especially with men, but there was something implacable about James in this moment. Something that had her shaking inside.

She trusted him implicitly, but she was far out of her comfort zone and she suspected he damn well knew it.

Emotion welled inside her and she broke character. She whispered, "James?"

He leaned over her, his large frame solid and safe. "What's wrong, baby girl?"

Her fingers tightened on the wood of the desk. "I-I don't know."

His hand stroked over her back, fingers running along the curve of her spine. "You're not sure if you love it or hate it."

She nodded.

"It scares you."

She closed her eyes. Right again.

A whisper in her ear. "But, deep down, this is something you've thought about."

"Yes," she said, her voice so thick she hardly recognized it.

"Me too," he said, sounding exactly like the James she knew and loved.

She looked back at him. "It is?"

He stroked her hair. "Yes. I think maybe this is something we both need. But at the end of the day, it's still you and me."

She nodded, her unexpressed love heavy in her chest, making her ache.

He trailed a finger down the nape of her neck. "All you need to do is tell me to stop and it will be over."

"Okay." The reassurance was exactly what she needed to continue.

"Are you ready to continue?"

She didn't understand why this was making her so emotional; it should be just a fun little sex game, but it was so much more. She didn't want to stop. "Yes, James."

Without a word, he straightened and once again began his slow seduction, running his hands over her skin. Down her legs, over her ass, over her core, up her back until he became the worst type of tease.

She squeezed her lids together and clenched her teeth in an effort to keep from crying out and falling out of position.

He stepped behind her. She pressed back, hoping to tempt him, but he didn't seem to notice, nor did he heed her silent demands.

He ran his hands down her hips, skimming her panties down her thighs to rest at her knees. Her legs started to quiver as the elastic bit into her skin.

His fingers slipped between her legs and it was like an electric shock.

"My, someone's wet."

Her head fell forward as he stroked her clit and a powerful orgasm, which threatened to tear her apart, began its upward climb.

He pulled away.

She cursed.

He slapped her ass, hard enough to bring the sting of tears to her eyes as fire exploded over her skin.

So. Damn. Good.

He slapped her again and leaned down. "In fairness, you are asking for it, aren't you?"

She'd forgotten all about her cute little top she'd thought would be so funny. "Yes, Professor."

His hands started the slow journey all over again. Up and down her legs, over her hips, circling her ass, stopping to rub over her clit, working her up only to stop when she was about to come.

She whimpered in protest.

His erection pressed against her hot skin as he hovered over her. With an arm around her waist he stroked her, and she was so wet it was almost embarrassing. He whispered, "I've only just begun."

A low sound emanated from her throat and she shuddered.

He straightened and pressed on her back with the

flat of his hand until she was once again in position. He picked up the book and balanced it on the curve of her bottom and stepped away, sliding into the desk chair next to her. "Here's how this is going to work. You're currently at ten minutes. Every time the book falls to the floor, we'll add another five minutes to your test. I suggest you stay still or we'll be here for a long time. Sound simple enough?"

Actually it did. The textbook was large and not hard to balance. "Yes, Professor."

"Good." He turned his chair and straightened the papers on his desk, before grabbing a pen.

She frowned at him. "What are you doing?"

He didn't even glance up. "Editing my publication."

"But . . ." She trailed off.

A tilt of the head, and a raised brow. "Yes?"

"Nothing," she mumbled, and stared down at the desk, mildly disappointed. This wasn't going to be hard at all.

She'd expected more of a challenge. She scowled at the wood between her splayed hands.

James made a notation on the paper.

She let out an annoyed huff.

He ignored her and continued reading.

She glared at a TARDIS paperweight.

He highlighted a few sentences.

Her back started to ache from holding the position so long.

She glanced at a clock. Six minutes had past.

He didn't seem to know she was alive.

She tapped her nails against the wood.

He abruptly smacked her ass, surprising her so much she jerked and the book tumbled to the floor. He laughed, low and evil. "That's a shame. And you only had a couple minutes left too."

"Hey!" She fell out of position as she turned to glower. "You did that on purpose."

"Me? Never."

"Liar!" She'd been so close to the end. "That's not fair."

He clucked his tongue and picked up the book. "Imagine that."

"You're mean." She pouted, and as much as she hated him in that moment, she couldn't deny the tiny kernel of satisfaction.

He jutted his chin toward the desk. "Back in position, Ms. Roberts."

She shivered, and seconds later the book was once again balanced across her ass.

He returned to his papers. She huffed.

Without looking up, he reached between her legs and rubbed her clit. She gasped, lust instantly roaring in her head. And then he was gone. He trailed his now wet fingers over her inner thighs. "I can tell how much you're hating this."

She sucked in a breath. "Jerk."

He chuckled and went back to his work.

"You can't possibly be reading."

"Maybe I should read it out loud, Ms. Roberts. Then I can quiz you on your concentration."

"At least I'd have something to do." The second the words left her mouth she knew her mistake.

He sighed and got up from the chair.

And gave a whole new meaning to the word *torture.*

An hour later, Gracie cried out as he denied her yet again. Her back ached, her ass was sore, her clit was on fire, and she'd never been so turned on in her whole life. She felt insane, completely depraved, as James assaulted her body with such delicious torment she thought she'd die from it.

He was implacable.

Hard.

Driven.

Methodical.

And absolutely ruthless.

She loved it. Hated it. She wanted it to never end and couldn't wait for it to stop.

She was a wreck. Sweat dripped down her temples, her makeup a thing of the past, her hair a wild, tangled mess. She'd begged. Pleaded. Cursed him. Worshiped him.

And still he wouldn't give in to her demands for release.

"Face me and get on your knees," he said, his tone impenetrable.

Far past hesitating, she turned and dropped to the floor, between his knees, looking up at him in expectation.

As he stared down at her, his expression softened and he trailed a finger over her cheek. "You're a good girl."

Her throat tightened unexpectedly. "Thank you."

"I love you," he said, and her heart skipped a beat. "I think I've been in love with you forever."

Tears filled her eyes and spilled down her cheeks. He loved her. Not the fun, fantasy girl, but *her*. The real her. The words trembled on her lips, but she said them anyway. Because, despite her fear, they were true. "I love you too."

"Do you trust me?"

She nodded. All pretense of playing gone.

"Then give me what I want and you won't regret it."

"What do you want?" Her chest so tight she thought she might explode.

"Everything."

Chapter Twenty-Seven

Gracie's fourth orgasm exploded through her with such a violent shock she burst into tears. The tears came from out of nowhere. One second she shuddered with the most exquisite pleasure she'd ever known, and the next, she was crying. Deep, soul-wracking sobs that shook her to the very core.

James pulled out, scooped her up as though she weighed nothing, and sat down in the office chair, nestling her into his lap. He stroked her back in slow sweeps, making soothing sounds into her ear.

On and on she cried. She cried for everything that was wrong in her life and everything that was good. She cried for the business she'd grown that now seemed to be spiraling out of her control. She cried for her dad. For his abandonment, but also for the way he used to pick her up and swing her in the air. The way he taught Gracie and Sam to climb the tree by the river and jump off the thickest branch before they came home sunburned and tired, to sit at the kitchen table and eat oatmeal cookies.

She cried for all the dreams she'd lost, and the ones she'd found. For the hopes of her childhood. And her future. For her friends and brother. For all the ways she'd been blessed in life and for all the things she had left to accomplish.

And most of all she cried for James. This man she loved, who had the ability to bring her such shattering pleasure and heart-stopping joy. He was everything she'd never known she wanted in a man. Against all odds and probabilities, he fit, and he seemed to love her unquestionably. Unreasonably. With all her flaws, and even more scarily, all her strengths.

He terrified her. What he'd just done terrified her. He'd stripped her of all her barriers, all her defenses, until she was nothing but a mass of dependent need. He'd made her want to follow him forever. To believe in forever. To want to take hold of that image she'd been keeping at bay. The idea of them, and kids, sitting around the farm table in her lemon-yellow kitchen, eating homemade cookies and laughing.

She'd never dreamed that about anyone before, and as much as she wanted it, she was desperate to push it away. Too afraid of what it all meant.

He rubbed her back in methodical circles. "Shhhh. You're okay. You'll feel better soon."

She hiccuped against his chest, his skin damp from sweat and endless tears. "H-how do y-you know?"

"I came across this in my research. You're over-whelmed, but it will pass. Just take some deep breaths." His voice so calm and reasonable she couldn't help but believe him.

She did, drawing air into her lungs, and slowly exhaling as she clung to him. The sound of his low, smooth voice instructing her to breathe, calming her the way nothing else could.

He didn't ask her to explain. Didn't question her

outburst, he just sat there and comforted her, as she continued to weep like she hadn't since her mom died.

It seemed she had something profound and important to tell him, about love and life, but her brain was too muddled to follow the thread, the thoughts floating away as soon as she had them.

She had no idea how much time passed. It could have been five minutes or five hours for all she knew, but finally she settled. The tears dried, and a bone-deep relaxation took their place. She sank into his warmth, all her limbs impossibly heavy.

He trailed a finger down her cheek. "That's it. Just relax. I'm going to move you to the bedroom, but you don't have to do a thing."

She stirred, managing to move her lips enough to mumble, "Don't leave me."

"Never." That one word, so certain it settled into her heart and became a part of her as the rest of the world melted away.

James sat next to Gracie as she slept, watching her. She didn't stir. Her blond hair was a mess of tangled curls against the white pillow, and her eye makeup smudged her cheeks, but she'd never looked so beautiful. Or peaceful.

All the violent emotions that had stormed over her had calmed, and now her face held a softness that hadn't been there before.

It hadn't been his intention to push her so hard, so fast. He'd intended to give her a taste of what they'd been hinting at since they'd started their sexual relationship.

She'd needed what he'd given her, of that much he was positive, but he wasn't sure he'd done the right thing.

In the moment, he'd been acting on pure instinct,

guided by some gut understanding that she needed to release all that pent-up emotion. But now he wasn't sure if it had been too much, too soon.

Gracie was a strong, determined woman. She liked being in control, almost as much as he did. She liked the upper hand because it gave her power and kept her safe. It had been part of their mutual antagonism. She had tried to mold him into what she wanted him to be, and he'd stubbornly refused to bend. Now, in retrospect, he understood the struggle between them. How much Gracie depended on her natural, near-blinding charisma to keep a wall between her and other people.

And he'd gone and stripped it away. Took her power and control, smashed all her walls, overloaded her senses, and she'd broken.

As right as it had been, as much as he thought she'd needed to release all that emotion, now that he'd come down from his high, he knew that there would be repercussions. He'd have to back off and give her some space as she sorted through her feelings. And he'd do it, because he loved her and she loved him.

Everything else would just have to sort itself out.

Chapter Twenty-Eight

"Where are we going?" Gracie asked, her tone more snappish than she'd intended as she sat in James's car, blindfolded.

He stroked a hand over her knee. "Just be patient. We're almost there."

Gracie huffed and pressed into the seat of the car, crossing her legs in a hopeless attempt to get comfortable. They were back in Chicago for the weekend so she could make a delivery, and she was in a foul mood.

It had been five days since their encounter in the garage apartment that had changed everything. He'd tied her up in so many knots she didn't know what to do about it. After that night—she shuddered—that night in what she now thought of as *his* office. He'd taken her to places no man had ever touched. He'd stripped her bare, emotionally and physically, and it changed something fundamental in her. In them.

The worst part was how much she craved it. It was like the most addictive drug, and the strength of her desire for him terrified her.

It also embarrassed her, how badly she wanted what he'd given her. She'd always been bold when it came to sex, but for some reason, she couldn't find the voice to ask him for it. It set her on edge. She couldn't understand why she desired it so much, when she'd always strived so hard for the upper hand. But since she seemed incapable of asking, over the last couple of days she'd taken to childishly goading James in hopes he'd exert that control over her again.

To no avail.

If anything, he'd backed off. And his implacable calm was driving her crazy.

She wanted him to explode at her, so she'd be justified to explode back and release this god-awful tension that had taken up residence in her body and wouldn't shake free.

She needed something, because she was all over the place. As though she rode an endless roller coaster of staggering drops, unexpected dips, and pitch-black tunnels. One second she loved him so much, needed him like he was her next breath, the next she couldn't wait to get away from him. Desperate for space, she'd push him away, but as soon as he left, she felt lonely.

Her emotions were so out of control she'd secretly taken a pregnancy test, even though James had always been ultra careful, never once taking her without protection.

She'd stood in the bathroom, watching the digital clock on the stick turn around and around, praying to the gods it wouldn't be positive. Then, ironically, the second the test read "not pregnant" she'd been filled with a gut-wrenching sadness. Locked in the bathroom, she'd cried for thirty minutes.

In short, she was a mess.

The car turned, ripping her away from her turbulent thoughts and she asked again, "Where are we?".

"You'll see," he said, tone amused.

Unreasonably, Gracie wanted to scratch his eyes out.

She bit her bottom lip. Maybe she needed a break. Some space to get her head screwed on straight so she could stop acting like a lunatic.

Before she could think any more about it, the car pulled to a stop and James turned off the engine. She could hear the cars on the busy street, but other than that there were no clues as to their location.

He got out of the car, and seconds later he pulled her from her seat by the hand, and guided her up the sidewalk. She heard the fumbling of keys, and then they were once again walking.

When they stopped, he stepped behind her and ran his finger down the curve of her neck. "Shane called in a favor so we could be alone for the tour."

She frowned, having no idea what he meant. He'd obviously gone through a lot of trouble to plan something, the least she could do was be grateful. She touched the blindfold and attempted to inject levity into her tone. "I'll need to see where I'm going for a tour."

"Soon. We're almost there. I hope you like it." She sensed a slight tremor of nerves in the cadence of his voice.

What could he possibly be nervous about? She shifted on the balls of her feet as her stomach dropped. He wasn't going to propose, was he? No, he wouldn't. He planned, talked things out. He was methodical. They'd barely said they loved each other, and they'd only said it that once during all the crazy intensity of the scene in his office. The M-word had never even been spoken. They hadn't even discussed their relationship. So surely he wasn't going to propose.

It was too soon for that? Wasn't it?

Her mind raced as she searched for another explanation for his blindfolding her, *and* his nervousness.

No, she was being crazy. There had to be another reason. There were too many things they hadn't discussed.

He couldn't.

Would he?

She didn't know.

Palms sweaty, she clenched her hands, hardly even breathing as she waited.

With slow, methodical movements he carefully untied the knot holding the fabric over her eyes. He whispered in her ear, "If it's not to your taste, there are others to choose from."

Her throat went dry. Oh God. This was it.

She was going to pass out.

The blindfold came off.

She blinked into focus an empty room. What? Where?

James walked in front of her, a smile on his face, and held out his arms. "What do you think?"

What was she supposed to think? She looked around. It was a big, empty, dilapidated room with high ceilings and big windows at the front where the sun beamed rays of light across hardwood floors that needed to be refurbished.

Totally confused, she frowned at James. "What is this place?"

While he still wore a smile on his face, the corners of his eyes were creased, like they got when he worried. "It's a storefront."

The words slammed through her. This wasn't a proposal at all. Her spine snapped ruler straight.

Of course, she was relieved.

That would have been insane. Something James was not.

But, still, she couldn't have heard right. "Excuse me?"

"A storefront. A potential spot for your bakery."

Stunned, she could only stare at him as his words sank in. When she didn't speak, he stepped forward and put his hands in his pockets, as though he resisted the urge to fidget. "It's in the heart of River North. Prime real estate. Shane made sure of it. He believes it's the best on the market right now, but if you don't like it, there are others we can look at."

Well, didn't he have it all planned out? James and his brother. She balled her hands into fists. How could he? And her friends. Did they know about this? Had they all planned this behind her back? Certainly Cecilia must know; after all, Shane wouldn't have kept this from her.

James continued on. "There are four other contenders, so say the word and I'll arrange for us to see them."

All Gracie could do was stare at him as fury, disappointment, and betrayal sank deep into her bones.

She'd been looking for a reason to explode. And he'd just handed her one on a silver platter.

Gracie's expression revealed nothing, but some ancient male instinct warned James he didn't have a happy woman on his hands.

Although, in fairness, he hadn't had a happy woman on his hands since she'd woken up the morning after he'd taken her so completely. Since he'd anticipated that, he'd been prepared. Per his plan, he'd backed off, giving her space to breathe, but it seemed to have had the reverse effect. Instead of relaxing her, she'd grown more agitated.

After the bakery site tours, when she understood how

serious he was about their relationship, he'd intended to talk to her and get everything straightened out.

But now the plan that he'd concocted with Shane all those weeks ago didn't appear quite so foolproof.

Since she still hadn't said anything, he continued to relay the information Shane told him about the location, hoping that once she saw how perfect it was, she'd get excited by the idea. "The block is filled with restaurants and shopping, in a high-traffic area. There's not another bakery in the neighborhood. The closest one is four miles away and has mediocre reviews on Yelp. So this would be perfect."

Blue eyes, filled with icy coldness, stared at him, unblinking. Not excited at all.

No, this certainly wasn't going according to his plans.

She crossed her arms over her chest.

He cleared his throat. "Shane said the lease is also priced to get the place filled, and it's not technically on the market until the first of the month. If you want it we'd need to move fast."

A muscle worked in her jaw as though she ground her teeth, but still she said nothing.

With a sinking feeling, he asked, "So, what do you think?"

Expression hard, she tapped the toe of her brown knee-high boots. When she'd pulled them on over skinny jeans this morning, along with a matching sable sweater so soft he couldn't stop running his hands over it, he'd joked that she looked ready for riding. Then he'd tumbled her to the bed, stripped her jeans to her knees, and licked her to orgasm.

"Gracie?" Her name on his lips sounded as uneasy as he felt.

She tapped her finger on her chin. "You and Shane

have all the answers, so you tell me. What should I think?"

Okay, so he'd clearly made a mistake. "You're not happy."

"Gee, Professor, what was your first clue?"

"Let me explain."

She blew out a hard breath, sending a curl flying. With a jerky movement she yanked it behind her ear. "Please explain to me how you and your brother took it upon yourselves to meddle in my business without even discussing it with me."

The knot in his stomach tightened. "I didn't think of it that way."

"Tell me, James, is there anything else you decided for me?"

Somehow he didn't think telling her about the draft Shane had drawn up was a good idea. Cautiously, he said, "We were only trying to help."

She planted her hands on her hips. "How incredibly thoughtful of you." Her words dripped with sarcasm.

"Let me explain my thought process and we can talk."

She shook her head and her blond curls floated around her cheeks. "No explanation will justify your actions. Did it ever occur to you to discuss this with me? I mean, after all, it's only my life." She waved a hand in the air. "But, ha, what do I matter?"

James blinked, and suddenly the stupidity of his plan came into crystal-clear focus. He was an idiot. Why had he talked to Shane, of all people? James pinched the bridge of his nose under his glasses. He knew why. Because his brother was a man who took whatever he wanted, and ruthlessly bulldozed any obstacle in his path. If James had any brains, he'd have discussed the idea with Jane and Anne. Surely they would have stopped him from making such a drastic mistake. But he hadn't done that, because deep down he'd known they wouldn't approve and he hadn't been able to think of another way.

He took a deep breath. Okay, he could handle this. He'd just calmly explain what he'd been thinking and why, and apologize. "Of course you matter. I was trying to be helpful."

Her hands clenched at her sides. "How exactly is this helpful, James?"

His only recourse was to be honest. "You were overwhelmed, and I knew the logistics of traveling back and forth to Chicago was wearing on you. Opening a storefront seemed like a viable option, but when I tried to talk to you about it you wouldn't discuss it. I thought if we did all the legwork for you and came up with financing solutions, you would see it as a possibility."

She flushed, with what he was pretty sure was rage. "Revival is my home. It's where my family and friends are. Where my business is. Did it ever occur to you I don't want to move to Chicago?"

"With all the orders you're getting it seemed logical. All I wanted was for the possibility to be on the table. I knew you were busy. I had the time and resources. I didn't see the harm. Is that so wrong?"

"Yes."

"It's not like I signed papers for you; I just gave you another option to consider."

"For me, right? And you don't factor in this at all?"

There was no right answer here. He could see that from the hard set of her mouth. Instead of its normal lushness, it was pursed into a thin, angry line.

"I thought if we saw each other more, our relationship would have a better shot at survival."

She shook her head "Did you run it through a proper experiment to determine the statistical odds?"

"Don't be caustic."

Arms rigid at her sides, she screeched, "Caustic? Caustic! You're lucky I'm not throwing knives at you. I can't believe you!"

Anger spiked hot in his blood, but he couldn't let it out, so he pushed it down. "I'm not saying it was my smartest move, but it's not as horrible as you're making it sound."

She pressed a fingertip to her temple. "You're busy making decisions about my future and you haven't even talked to me about a relationship. Don't you see how crazy that is?"

His brow furrowed. "I was only giving you more options."

God, he sounded stuffy, pompous, and stubborn, but he couldn't seem to stop. As though he stood apart from the situation, he watched as he opened his mouth and dug a deeper grave. "I mean, it's not like I can move. I'm a tenured professor."

She let out a scream. "We've never even discussed our relationship! We've never talked about our future."

He was compelled to point out the obvious. "You said you didn't want to discuss it. What was I supposed to do?"

Her eyes went wide as though she couldn't believe he was so stupid. "Oh, I don't know, wait until I was ready?"

"And when would that be?"

"I don't know."

He met her gaze and said softly, "We love each other."

"So what?"

The casual dismissal of those words was like a stab in the heart. *"So what?"*

She held up her index finger. "We said it one time during sex. Big fucking deal."

"It was a big deal to me." His tone turned icy.

Her expression twisted with fury. "That's not the point. The point is, you went about deciding the future of my life and business without even discussing it with me."

"I wasn't looking at it like that. I was helping you."

"Bullshit!" she yelled. "You were helping yourself, trying to get what you wanted because it suited you. You didn't discuss it with me. You didn't even treat me like I matter. I'm just an afterthought in your plan to make our relationship mathematically possible."

"Don't be ridiculous."

"You're ridiculous."

"I asked, you wouldn't answer."

"You didn't ask, you hinted." She jabbed a finger at him. "You said we'd need to discuss it soon. You didn't lay out what you wanted, or tell me you wanted something more. Or that you were, I don't know, wanting me to pick up my whole life and move to Chicago. It's just like that first weekend. You didn't have the balls to say you wanted to see me again, you just skirted around the issue, hoping I'd take the risk for you. And when I didn't you calmly told me to have a safe trip."

A sinking sensation filled his chest. Fuck. She was right. She had the capability to bring him to his knees. He understood she was leery of commitment, and he'd been afraid to push her. So instead of being direct, he'd been maneuvering her in hopes she wouldn't notice he was pulling her deeper and deeper into a relationship.

All the frustrated anger drained away, leaving him shaken. There was only one thing left to do. Lay it on the line, risk his heart, and hope she could see the truth. "I'm sorry. I do love you and I need to be with you for more than a few days at a time. I want you to move to Chicago so we can be together all the time."

She stared at him for several long, tension-filled moments, before shaking her head. "Well, that's not going to happen."

He took three steps and bridged the gap between them, grabbing her arm. "You don't mean that."

She wrenched her arm away. "I do."

He narrowed his gaze, feeling desperate and mean. "You don't think I know you've been waiting for this? Looking for some excuse to run away from what we have?"

She reared back as though he'd slapped her. "Well, you certainly gave me a good one, didn't you?"

He pointed at her. "All your talk about being wild and crazy, but you're just as scared as I am. You don't want to be vulnerable. You don't want to make a commitment. Maybe I wasn't direct enough, but every time I mentioned anything that would hint at a future, you'd change the subject."

"So this is my fault?"

"It's both our faults."

"How diplomatic of you," she said with a sneer. When he opened his mouth to speak she held up a hand. "Just stop. Stop being so goddamn reasonable. Rage at me, tell me I'm a bitch, but stop trying to fix it."

He wanted to, more than anything, but the more helpless he became, the more tightly his control clamped down around him. He'd trained himself so well, now he didn't know how to turn it off. When he spoke, he sounded completely calm. Which he wasn't. At all. "So, what? That's it? One tiny slip-up and it's over?"

"One tiny slip?" she screeched, and started to pace. "You went behind my back and planned my whole future without me."

"I apologized."

She came to an abrupt halt. She shook her head. "I'm leaving."

No. She couldn't leave. "Wait—"

"No. Just leave me the hell alone."

And with that, she turned and stormed out of the building. Five seconds later, because of the fucking high-traffic area, a cab pulled up and she was gone.

James stood motionless in the cold, abandoned room and watched his future walk out of his life.

She didn't even look back.

Chapter Twenty-Nine

She would not cry. Gracie stood on Shane and Cecilia's doorstep and rang the bell insistently. She was furious. And heartbroken. But she refused to think about that now. Instead she focused on the rage seething in her belly.

Because if she stopped and thought about what had happened, James's betrayal, she'd crumble. And she didn't know how to put herself back together again.

Through the glass panes she watched Shane storm to the door, expression belligerent. Just to annoy him, she rang the doorbell two more times. A small, petty gesture, but she didn't care. She was too angry, at him, at James . . . at everyone.

He threw open the door, that you've-got-some-explaining-to-do expression on his face. "What the hell, Gracie?"

"You!" she spat, jabbing him in the chest with her finger. "How could you?"

Cecilia padded into the grand two-story foyer in bare feet. "Gracie? What's wrong?"

One look at her friend and bile rose in her throat, making it hard to talk. "How could you?"

Worry creased Cecilia's brow, and she glanced at Shane. "How could I what?"

Gracie stomped through the doorway, boot heels angry jabs on their shiny hardwood floors. "I can't believe you guys would go behind my back like that."

The confusion on Shane's face instantly cleared before flashing with guilt, while Cecilia's face remained blessedly befuddled. She shook her head. "Go behind your back?"

A flash of relief filled Gracie as she realized her friend had no idea what the two idiotic brothers had done. She glared at Shane. "Are you going to tell her, or should I?"

Cecilia swung around to her fiancé, with narrowed gray-blue eyes. "What have you done?"

Shane held up his hands. "I can explain."

"Explain what?" Cecilia's tone was like the snap of a whip.

"Yeah, Shane, explain how you and your stupid brother took it upon yourselves to decide the future of my business without even consulting me." Thank God, Cecilia hadn't been involved; she wasn't sure she could have handled that. But what about Maddie? No. Maddie would never agree to something so stupid. They'd been friends too long. But just to be sure she added, "What, did you have Mitch draw up the contracts too? Did the three of you decide to sign the lease for me?"

Shane shook his head. "I didn't mention it to him. I didn't get that far. I did draw up a few plans."

"You what!?" Gracie screeched, her hands balled into fists. She was going to hit him. One good pop in the jaw. "You're a dead man."

"Look, I didn't see the harm in helping," Shane said, his tone defensive.

Her nails were digging into her palms. *What is wrong with these Donovan men?* "Help? How is it helping me?"

Shane shrugged, running a hand through his blond hair. "I thought it was a good idea at the time."

"What is wrong with you?" Gracie's head began to ache. "What if I did something like that to you?"

Shane's expression turned to chagrin and he rubbed the back of his neck. "I was trying to help my brother. He needed help and I gave it to him. What did you expect me to do?"

Not even slightly moved by him playing the I-did-it-for-my-family card, she yelled, "Oh, I don't know, say no!"

Cecilia shook her head. "I'm so confused. What is going on?"

"Now, baby—" Shane started, but Cecilia held up a hand.

"Don't even think about it." She turned back to Gracie. "Okay, what did they do?"

James called the only person he knew who wouldn't ask any questions: his younger brother.

Thankfully, Evan had a home game this week. As football was the only thing Evan took seriously, he left most of his wild antics to the off season, which is why he ended up being home on a Friday night instead of out with one of his supermodels.

Evan opened the door to his penthouse bachelor-pad apartment with panoramic views of the city. "Hey."

"I need liquor and lots of it," James said. He'd had only one thought since he'd locked up the storefront and returned the key to the real estate agent: get as drunk as possible.

Because he couldn't think about Gracie, or what had transpired between them. Or how their relationship was over.

Evan's gaze widened and he stood back. "What happened to you?"

"Don't want to talk about it," James said, walking in.

Evan shrugged, and closed the door. "I've got anything you want."

Which is why James had come. He needed to forget and he couldn't go back to his house. All her stuff was there. She'd invaded his life. There wasn't a room in his house that didn't remind him of her. She was probably packing her stuff as he sat here.

He clenched his jaw. He'd have to move. There was no other way. Which was a shame because he loved his home. Had begun to think about Gracie in it, permanently. And now that wasn't going to happen.

He'd think about it later. Now he'd get drunk, sit on his baby brother's couch, and play video games so he wouldn't have to think. Normally he was a red wine drinker, but that wouldn't cut it, so he decided on a family favorite. "Whiskey."

James sank onto Evan's leather sectional sofa, which dominated the room along with a ridiculously large eighty-inch flat-screen filled with the scenes of an action movie already in progress. There was a huge explosion that vibrated through the surround sound and James winced. "Don't your neighbors complain?"

"Soundproofing," Evan said, walking into the industrial, ultramodern kitchen and opening up a cabinet.

James yelled over the sound, "Bring the bottle."

A second later the bottle and a glass were in front of him. James picked up the liquor and poured a healthy drink before downing it in one big gulp. He poured another. "Can we turn that down?"

The gunshots were too loud in his head, reminding him of the carnage he'd left behind. He shot back another two fingers and the alcohol burned down his throat. He let out a hiss as it hit his stomach and poured some more.

Evan sat down and lowered the volume, his expression actually concerned. "What's wrong?"

James tossed him a dirty look. He'd specifically come to Evan because he didn't want to talk. "What's the most violent video game you have?"

Evan raised one brow and said slowly, "I have *Dead Rising*, and *Ryse* for Xbox One."

James took another long drink and waved the controller toward the television. "Do you mind?"

"Nope," Evan said and grabbed the remote.

Thirty minutes later they'd spoken in nothing but monosyllabic words and James was well on his way to drunk. He'd killed his fair share of enemies, staying competitive despite his rapidly diminishing hand-eye coordination. He still felt like he'd been run over by a truck, but at least he didn't have to think. And, as predicted, Evan didn't press. Didn't ask questions.

James didn't have to explain how he was in love with a woman who didn't love him back. Yes, she'd said the words, but now he knew they hadn't mattered to her. She'd said them in the heat and passion of the moment.

He'd finally had a woman he didn't want to live without. That mysterious puzzle piece that eluded him with other women had finally shifted into place; until he discovered Gracie didn't feel the same way.

Fuck. What was so wrong about what he'd done? Okay, maybe he should have talked to her, but he'd truly had good intentions. He took another sip of his drink. She'd just been waiting for an out and took the first one he gave her.

Well, good. It's better he know up front. It would never last if one tiny screw-up would send her out the door.

Another gulp. The whiskey no longer burning as it went down. He should have stuck with his first instinct about her and stayed the hell away from her.

The intercom buzzed and James's gaze flew to the offending speaker. With slurred words he asked, "Who's that?"

"Don't know." Evan went toward the intercom.

James had one brief flash of something that disgustingly felt like hope that Gracie was at the door, before dismissing the idea. Besides, she'd never think to look for him here. James scoffed. "I hope it's not a hooker."

Evan grinned, walking backward. "In my price range they're called escorts, but you know I never have to pay for sex."

James stabbed a soldier through his armor, leaving a blood-soaked puddle in his wake. Of course, Evan didn't. He was six-five, too good-looking for his own good, and played professional football. Like Gracie, the opposite sex seemed to be unable to resist him, and women lined up for the chance to be in his bed.

That kind of life had never appealed to James, but at the moment, through his liquor-filled haze, it pissed him off. Some people, and he wasn't going to name names, had it so easy.

Evan pressed the button and barked, "Yeah."

The refined voice of the doorman came over the line. "Mr. Donovan, a Mr. Shane Donovan is here to see you."

Oh, great. His culprit in crime and the last man he wanted to see. James shook his head. "Don't let him in."

"Send him up," Evan said, then walked back to the couch. "You know he won't leave until he gets what he wants."

"I don't want to talk to him." James slid a sword right into the enemy's chest and gutted him.

"What's wrong with you?" Evan asked.

James paused the game and shook his head. "Get rid of Shane and I'll be fine."

Evan snorted. "Have you met our brother?"

"Just do it." James took another drink and eyed the bottle.

"He's already on his way."

James had already drunk well past his comfort zone, and hopefully it wouldn't be too long before he passed out. "Can I sleep here?"

"What's wrong with your place?" Evan asked, walking to the door Shane pounded on.

James thought of Gracie sitting on his couch, curled up with her feet tucked under her, wearing no makeup, her hair wild after all the things he'd done to her the night before, and shuddered. He couldn't walk into an empty house. "It's being fumigated."

Evan opened the door and Shane stomped in, carrying a brown grocery bag with him. He nodded to the bottle on the table. "Good, you've already started."

James scowled.

"Cecilia kicked me out of the house," Shane said, putting the bag on the table. "I guess the conversation didn't go well."

James experienced a moment of camaraderie until he remembered that for Shane, this was temporary. Even if they argued, Shane was still marrying Cecilia. Unlike James, who had been permanently removed from Gracie's life. "Don't want to talk about it."

"Fine."

There's no way it would be that easy. "I'm serious."

"Understood," Shane said.

Evan looked back and forth between them. "What's wrong with him?"

Shane sat down. "He's in love with Gracie."

The words were a knife in the chest, and James viciously slayed another soldier in retaliation.

Evan patted James on the back in a consolatory gesture. "Sorry she turned you down. If it makes you feel any better, I didn't fare much better."

The statement enraged James and before he could process his actions, he stood. Clenching his hands into fists, his vision blurred and he lunged at his younger brother in a cloud of fury.

"What the fuck?" Evan rolled out of the way, falling to the ground. James tackled him and wrestled him onto his back.

James raised his fist to coldcock him, but Shane grabbed his arm and twisted.

"Let go," James roared, suddenly realizing what he really needed was real-life violence instead of game simulation.

"No. You're going to hurt him and yourself," Shane said calmly.

Even drunk, James saw the logic of Shane's argument. With a sigh, he climbed off Evan, letting him go.

"Dude, what is your problem?" Evan scrambled up from the floor with the grace of the athlete he was.

James glared at him. "She didn't turn me down, asshole."

Evan's expression widened in surprise.

James shook free of Shane and stumbled back onto the couch like the athlete he wasn't. "That's right, she turned *you* down, not me. You think I'd be upset over a stupid infatuation?"

"Geez, chill, man, I didn't mean it that way," Evan said, slumping back and looking at Shane. "What the hell happened? And why did Cecilia kick you out?"

Shane sighed and returned to his own seat. "James and I decided to help Gracie open a bakery in Chicago."

Evan's brow rose. "And?"

Shane scrubbed a hand over his jaw. "We . . . kind of . . . forgot to mention it to Gracie."

"That was a stupid move," Evan said, kicking his feet up onto a coffee table that probably cost more than James made in a month.

"We were just trying to help," James and Shane said at the same time.

Evan rolled his eyes. "Have you met Gracie? She doesn't want a couple of guys coming along poking their noses into her business."

"That's not what I was doing." James's mouth was like mush and he had a hard time forming the words. "I was giving her options."

"Stupid," Evan said, shaking his head.

"What do you know about relationships?" Shane snapped.

Evan scoffed, laughing. "I know enough not to treat smart, strong, independent women like they need to be rescued."

Shane and James just stared at him, unblinking.

Why did that actually make sense?

Shane said, "Just shut the fuck up and look pretty."

Evan shot Shane the finger. "Like you'd ever do that to Cecilia."

James frowned at his older brother.

Shane's gaze slid guiltily away. He asked, "What was I supposed to do?"

James clenched his hands into fists. "So, what, you were just trying to fix it?"

Shane shook his head. "No. I wanted to help. You never ask for shit, never want any help, and never talk to anyone. So when you did, I wasn't going to say no."

Evan nodded. "He's got a point."

James clenched his jaw. "Stop acting like an adult, it's annoying."

Shane grinned. "I'd agree, but you're on my side. For once."

"You're both pretty much idiots," Evan said, picking up the Xbox controller. "If you need advice about women, you should have come to me, Jimmy."

James snorted.

Shane leaned forward on his elbows. "Your last girl-friend didn't last a month."

"It was a good month, one for the record books," Evan said, although he didn't look particularly pleased.

"Didn't Gracie turn you down?" James said, feeling a bit smug in his drunken state.

Evan laughed and elbowed James in the ribs. "Yeah, she did. I've got to hand it to you. You landed one of the top ten hottest girls I've ever laid eyes on. And I've seen a lot of gorgeous women. She wouldn't even let me get close enough to make a move, and believe me, I tried."

James frowned. *Had* landed. He'd lost her quick enough.

Shane chuckled. "That must have been a novel experience."

"Fuck you," Evan said, but his tone was good-natured. "I chalked it up to too many ties between us. I didn't realize who I was competing with."

Shane turned to James and raised a brow. "True."

James pondered the idea that he was finally a contender on par with his brothers. It shouldn't matter, and really it didn't, but he still remembered how he felt as a teenage boy, all those years ago.

Shane grabbed the paper bag he'd brought, pulling out a bottle and setting it on the table.

James squinted at the label. "Is that what I think it is?"

"Yep," Shane said.

It was a bottle of 1951 Knappogue Castle Irish whiskey. The mythical vintage their father had always wanted to try.

"One of Cecilia's relatives gave it to us as an engagement present." Shane shrugged. "I figured I might as well waste it on you two."

Evan vaulted from the couch. "A couple of sips shouldn't hurt my game day performance."

A smile tugged at James's lips, when he'd been sure he'd never smile again.

Evan returned with three glasses and set them down on the table.

Shane grabbed the bottle and twisted off the cap. "I wish Dad could see us."

They all glanced away, looking off at an unseen horizon. James swallowed the tightness in his throat, understanding his brothers did the same.

The moment passed and Shane poured the amber liquid into the glasses. When they each had one in hand, Shane raised his. "To brothers."

A long tradition they'd carried on since they'd gotten drunk in a dive pub three blocks from the house they grew up in after their dad died. The bartender had known their father and looked the other way at James's and Evan's underage drinking.

"To brothers." They clinked glasses in a toast, as they had all those years ago. As they would in all the years to come.

Chapter Thirty

So this was heartbreak.

Gracie had never been so miserable in her life. In Cecilia's guest bedroom, she'd tossed and turned, unable to sink into sleep. Sometime in the middle of the night, she'd heard Shane come home. He'd clearly been drunk, making too much noise and calling out Cecilia's name. The last thing Gracie heard him say before their bedroom door had closed was that he loved her and he was too old to sleep on a couch.

Gracie had turned over and wept into her pillow, irrationally wishing James would come banging on the door and demand entry.

But, of course, he hadn't. And why would he? She'd made it clear she wanted nothing to do with him.

Early this morning, eyes gritty from crying and lack of sleep, she'd dragged herself out of bed and snuck out of Shane and Cecilia's house so she wouldn't have to face them.

She'd had no choice but to go to James's to get her stuff, but he hadn't been there. She'd cried some more before she finally pulled herself together and loaded her stuff into her truck.

It was over. Really and truly over. She tried to tell herself she'd known it would never last, but her heart wasn't buying it. The more time she spent with James the more she'd begun to believe in them.

But it was over.

It was the right move. He'd interfered in her business. He'd planned her life and hadn't even bothered to consult her.

She couldn't forgive that.

Now she stood in a room at the Drake Hotel, people milling around her in preparation for the wedding reception that would take place a couple of hours from now, and she'd never been so miserable.

She studied her work, a five-tier red velvet wedding cake covered in white frosting, with thick black ribbons, big crystal snowflakes, and topped with roses. It looked beautiful and sophisticated, but Gracie took no joy in her creation today.

All she wanted was to be done so she could get out of Chicago.

"I remember you," a delicate feminine voice said from behind her.

Gracie turned around and blinked.

Of all the people in the world she could run into, it had to be the one person Gracie least wanted to see. In front of her, like a bad nightmare, stood Lindsey Lord, James's physicist ex-girlfriend. She looked spectacular as ever in a red taffeta bridesmaid dress. The spaghetti straps showed off her dancer's frame, graceful neck, and fine bone structure.

Gracie clenched her teeth. There was no justice in this world. She was at her absolute worst and Lindsey looked like a freakin' prima ballerina.

When Gracie didn't speak, Lindsey gave her an elegant

smile. "We met at the restaurant. You were with James, right?"

"Yes," Gracie said, willing her voice not to crack.

"How funny, running into you. This is my sister's wedding. I promised her I'd come check everything. You know how brides are."

Gracie nodded, unable to speak.

"What a small world. I had no idea you were the wedding-cake designer she's been raving about. She was thrilled to get you after the place she'd ordered from originally closed up shop without a word to any of their customers. Ashley was in a panic and you came to her rescue."

"I'm glad I could help."

Another serene smile. "The cake is lovely. My sister will be so happy."

"Thank you." Gracie's throat was so tight that's all she could manage to say, and an awkward silence thickened the air between them.

Lindsey's hand fluttered to her clearly defined clavicles. "How's James?"

Gracie felt tears well in her eyes and she blinked them frantically away. "I'm sure he's fine."

Lindsey's arched brows drew together in concern. "Are you all right?"

"I'm fine, thanks." Gracie attempted her most dazzling smile, but she could feel the corners quiver.

Lindsey frowned. "I know that look. I wore it myself for too many months to count after James. It's the worst thing about him. He's such a heartbreaker and he doesn't even know it."

Gracie's dull, sleep-deprived brain tried to wrap itself around what the other woman was saying and she managed to squeak out, "He broke your heart?"

"Yes," Lindsey said. "Terribly."

Gracie was so confused. Had she missed something? "But I thought you broke up with him."

Lindsey shook her head. "No, everyone assumed I was the one, and he was kind enough to never say anything. But the truth is, he broke up with me."

"I'm sorry. I didn't know." It was so infuriatingly like him. Why bother setting the record straight?

"I was devastated. I thought he was the one. I can't deny I harbored some hope." Lindsey offered a ghost of a smile. "But as soon as I saw you in the restaurant I knew you were the one."

Gracie frowned. They'd barely been speaking in the restaurant. She should end this conversation, but she was too curious. Too greedy for information about him. "Why? We weren't together."

Lindsey smoothed a palm over her dress as though smoothing out imaginary wrinkles. "I guess it was the way you couldn't stop watching each other."

"Gracie!" James's voice echoed through the large room, loud enough that everyone working stopped to gape at him.

She whipped around, her heart leaping into her throat at the sight of him sprinting through the hall, weaving through tables. He looked terrible. His hair was a disheveled mess. His clothes wrinkled, his shirt untucked.

As he drew closer, Gracie could see the bags under his eyes and a sickly pallor to his skin. She'd never seen him look so awful. He came to a crashing halt and put his hands on his knees, gasping for breath.

He reeked of alcohol.

"James?" Gracie was so startled by his appearance she forgot to be angry. "Are you okay?"

He shook his head. "No. I'm not."

"What's wrong?"

His head shot up. "You don't know?"

Gracie shot a sidelong glance at Lindsey, who watched them with avid interest. "Well, I meant, apart from the obvious."

He took more deep breaths and sat down at a table, dropping his head between his knees as he panted. "Give me a minute."

"What happened to you?"

He raised his head, and his green eyes were bloodshot behind his glasses. "I'm dying."

"Of alcohol poisoning." Gracie waved a hand in the air to encompass the room behind her where they were starting to draw a crowd. "James, I'm working."

"I know. But it couldn't wait." He glanced sideways, and his expression twisted as he seemed to notice Lindsey for the first time. "What are you doing here?"

Lindsey blinked, her eyes going wide with what could only be shock. "Ashley is getting married today."

"Oh." James turned green, and dropped his head into his hands. "Kill me."

"Are you going to be sick?" Gracie asked, frantically scanning the room for a trash can.

James shook his head. "I'm okay. I couldn't get a cab, so I had to run. I threw up three times on the way over, so I think I'm done."

A smile quivered at her lips. He was a mess. A complete, utter disaster. Even worse off than she was. God bless him. "I see."

James sighed and ran his hands through his hair. "Gracie, I know what I did was stupid. I should have talked to you and I pretty much screwed up in every way a man could, but I'm sorry, I can't let you go. You're just going to have to find a way to forgive me."

"James," Gracie said, her heart swelling.

"No, Gracie. I won't take no for an answer. I love you and that's final. We're going to have to work it out."

"I—" she began, but he cut her off.

"And when I mean work it out I mean find a way to be in the same fucking city for more than two goddamn seconds."

He was yelling and people were starting to stare.

"We—"

He pounded his fist on the table. "Do you want me to quit my job? Is that it? If you want me to, I will. I don't think the junior college by your house has a forensic program, but I could switch to consulting full-time." He scratched his head. "But I might have to travel more."

"Let's—" Gracie said, only for him to hold up a hand.

"What can I do to make it up to you? Can't you just give me the benefit of the doubt? Is that so hard? I've never done this before; I'm lost. And all this drama is making me stupid." All of a sudden his eyes narrowed and he gave Lindsey a sharp glance. "Do you mind?"

Lindsey blinked.

Gracie gasped. That was so unlike him. "James, you're being rude."

James stood and threw up his hands. "Well, I'm sorry, but I'd prefer not to grovel while my ex-girlfriend enjoys the show. Is that so damn hard to understand?"

Gracie pressed her lips together. "Um—"

James glowered and yelled, "I mean I know how you love to make all the men you sleep with into best friends, and I understand I'll have to hang around with Charlie for the rest of my life, but can't I just have this one thing? Or do I have to start inviting her over for dinner to prove I'm liberal enough?"

Gracie had no idea what he was talking about. But all the crazy emotions that had been riding her hard for weeks settled into something peaceful.

James—reserved, conservative, never-make-a-scene

James—was a basket case. He was drunk. Irrational. Impossible.

And making a huge scene. God, she loved him.

Pretty much everyone had stopped what they were doing to enjoy the show, so Gracie really couldn't blame Lindsey for hanging out to see what would happen next.

"What do I have to do, Gracie? You make me so crazy. Since the day we met, you have been a pain in my ass." He raked his fingers through his hair, making it stand up on end, giving him a deranged, wild look. "Do you understand how difficult you are, woman?"

Gracie shook her head, wondering what twisted part of her loved him more every time he yelled at her.

He turned to Lindsey. "What does she want from me? She's moody, scared of commitment, doesn't like to talk about her feelings, is irrational, and gets hit on everywhere we go. I mean, I haven't paid for a drink since I started seeing her."

Lindsey seemed speechless.

Gracie knocked him in the shoulder. "Hey! Do you think you're any sort of prize, buddy?"

"Yeah, actually I do!" he hollered.

"Ha!" Now she turned to Lindsey. "He tried to open a bakery for me and didn't even tell me. He's bossy, arrogant, annoyingly calm when I disagree with him, runs ten miles a day, and counts carbs. Do you know how irritating it is to stay up half the night and have someone bound out of bed the next morning and put on exercise clothes?"

"Um—I—um . . ." Lindsey trailed off, offering up one of her peaceful smiles.

Gracie huffed and scowled at James.

He pointed at her chest. "Don't even pretend you don't like when I'm bossy. You loved it."

With every moment that passed, their fight slid further

and further out of control, and she felt better. Hopeful. "During sex, sure, but not all the time."

"So you *did* like it," he said, tone accusing.

"Of course I liked it, you idiot. What's not to like? But then you had to go and get all nice on me and I won't have it."

"I was taking it easy on you!" He roared loud enough that the whole room stilled.

"Who asked you to?"

"For Christ's sake, Gracie—"

"Excuse me." An older man, with dark hair and graying temples, stood there in a navy suit, his hands clasped behind his back. "I'm the banquet manager here at the hotel, is there a problem?"

"Go away," James bellowed. "Can't you see I'm trying to apologize to my woman?"

Gracie couldn't help the smile on her lips. So James had a caveman streak; she could live with that.

"Sir," the man said in a soothing, reasonable voice. "I'm going to have to ask you to calm down or I'm afraid you'll have to leave."

James looked at Gracie, and all of a sudden whatever color he had in his face drained away. "You're right, that is annoying."

Then he passed out, falling flat on his face on the floor.

"Wow!" Lindsey exclaimed to Gracie, staring down at James lying in a heap. "He really loves you."

"Yeah, he does." Gracie giggled.

Professor James Donovan was crazy after all.

James woke up in his bed disoriented, with a pounding headache and no recollection of how he came to be home. He moaned and rolled over, as jackhammers pounded against his temples and his stomach rolled.

He squeezed his eyelids together and thought back. He'd been at Evan's, he hadn't slept, he'd definitely drank. In the wee hours of the morning Shane had gone home, Evan had gone to bed. James stayed up playing video games, analyzing the situation. The more he thought, the more crazy he became, until suddenly it was like something broke in him, and he'd determined the only thing to do was find Gracie.

And he had, at the Drake Hotel. He'd made a huge scene. He'd yelled. She'd yelled. He frowned, and it hurt his skull. Was Lindsey there? Why was she there? Had it been a dream?

Then he remembered the manager threatening to throw him out, and the smile on Gracie's face. As though she was proud of him, which made a strange kind of sense—she did like her grand gestures.

That was the last thing he remembered, the brilliant smile she reserved just for him, before the world went black.

He crawled out of bed, pulling on sweats and a white T-shirt, before splashing water on his face and brushing his teeth.

He stared into the mirror. Did he tell her he'd quit his job? Yes, he had. He sighed. Well, he didn't know how, but they were going to have to work this out. Because he couldn't live without Gracie Roberts driving him crazy.

Now he had to find her again.

Lucky for him, he didn't have to search far.

He walked downstairs and there she was, sitting on his couch. Evan, Shane, and Cecilia were there too. Evan had his arm draped over the couch, and he rubbed Gracie's back.

"Get your hands off her," James said in a growl, his voice far louder than he'd intended.

Four surprised faces stared up at him.

Shane cocked a brow. "Someone woke up on the wrong side of the bed."

"Shut up." James stopped at the bottom step and gripped the railing. "I mean it, Evan, get your fucking hands off her."

Evan held up his hands. "Dude, I was comforting her."

"I don't care. Stop it." Apparently, James wasn't entirely sober yet because this was highly unlike him. Or was it? Hadn't he had thoughts like this before and repressed them?

Gracie shifted more fully to face him, and James relaxed. Her blue eyes danced and she waved a hand through the air. "I guess drinking turns him possessive."

"Wrong. I've always been possessive of you. I just didn't want you to know it." And there was the truth. He'd just unleashed it.

"I see." Her lashes fluttered up at him, and she smiled. "I should probably discourage this type of behavior."

He shrugged. "I don't see why, since this kind of thing is right up your alley."

Shane, Evan, and Cecilia laughed.

Gracie scowled. "Hey!"

Cecilia crossed her legs and snuggled up next to Shane. "Well, he's kind of got you there."

James worked his face into a stern expression he didn't really feel. "I accept that I have to put up with total strangers hitting on you, but I draw the line at my friends and family. I think that's fair."

Evan frowned. "I wasn't hitting on her."

"I'm just making myself clear," James said, his tone implacable.

Gracie ran a hand through her hair. "What about Anne?"

James pretended to contemplate this for several seconds before he nodded. "Fine, I'll let you have Anne."

Her head tilted as though deep in thought. "Deal. See, I can compromise." ·

James gave her a droll look. "Jane will be so pleased."

Gracie raised her gaze to his.

He crooked his finger. "Come on, we have things to discuss."

He didn't miss the hitch in her breath or how she scrambled off the couch. He turned his attention to his family. "I trust you'll get the hell out of here."

Cecilia smiled up at Shane. "Your quiet, mild-mannered brother is kicking us out of his house."

Shane rubbed his fingers over her neck. "Looks like it."

James didn't bother listening to the rest of the conversation. Instead, he grabbed Gracie's wrist and dragged her upstairs like a caveman. He shoved her into the bedroom, slammed the door shut, and pushed her to the bed.

"James," she said, her tone admonishing, but her eyes were dark with heat.

He flicked a gaze over her. "Let's stop pretending, shall we?"

"I don't know what you mean."

He climbed onto the bed, straddling her. He manacled her wrists with his hands and brought them over her head.

Her breath came fast.

"We both know me bossing you around in the bedroom makes you so hot I could light a match off you."

She moaned and arched. "Okay."

He leaned down and nipped her neck, scraping his teeth over her sensitive skin. "If you give me free rein during sex, I figure it will help curb my controlling tendencies in the rest of our lives."

"Deal," she said, breathless now.

He licked her collarbone, his tongue dipping into

the hollow of her neck, loving the way she practically purred under his lips.

Releasing her wrists, he raised his head and waited until her lashes lifted and she met his gaze. And then he spoke from his heart, with no protection, and no reserve. "I'm sorry, Gracie. I should never have gone behind your back. I have no good excuse. I was afraid. I wanted to find a way to keep you and I didn't know how. I know I'm not what you envisioned as the love of your life, but I promise, if you'll let me, I'll make you happy."

Her blue eyes brightened with unshed tears. She reached for him, stroking her capable fingers down his cheek. "Oh, James, you're wrong. You're exactly what I envisioned, since the moment I met you. I was too stubborn to admit it."

He kissed her fingertips. "Good. I will never go behind your back like that again."

She smiled. "You'd better not, or I will make your life a living hell."

He laughed. "Been there, don't want to go back. You're right, you know, I was protecting myself. I wanted you to take the risk. I didn't push you to talk, even when I knew I should, because I didn't want you to think too hard about the fact that you were in an actual relationship with me."

She tangled her hands in his hair, pulling him down to nip his bottom lip before she said, "I'm sorry too. I guess after all this time, you bought the story I kept telling you about how wrong you are for me. But it's a lie. I need a man like you, even when it's hard for me. I wanted what you gave me so bad, I pushed you away when the truth is, I've never loved anyone more."

God, he adored this woman. "Gracie, you mean everything to me. I love you and I need you in my life. If that means I have to move to Revival, I will."

Her curls splashed across his white pillow as she tilted her head. "You know, when you were sleeping, it occurred to me that we were thinking about this all wrong."

"How so?" He ran his hand down her stomach. "Take your shirt off."

Her gaze fluttered over his chest. "You too."

He stripped the cotton T-shirt over his head and dropped it to the floor. A second later she followed suit. He jerked his chin. "Bra."

"You're really taking this bossy thing seriously, aren't you?" she said, her tone amused as she reached behind and unclasped her bra and peeled the cups down. The lace dangled from her fingers for a moment before falling to the floor.

In answer he glanced down at her spectacular breasts. "Your nipples are hard."

She punched his arm, and everything jiggled deliciously.

He clasped her hand and held it down on the bed. "That's going to cost you."

He laughed when she shuddered under him. "Now what were you saying?"

She licked her lips like a hungry cat. His little temptress. "Well, you're a professor, so you have flexibility. Right?"

He nodded, slid down her body and licked her nipple.

Her fingers tightened on his. "Stop. I can't concentrate when you do that."

"Go on," he said, sucking the hard bud between his lips.

She gasped, her nails digging into his skin. "I have Harmony to help me now. She's talented and her skills in business make her the perfect fit. The Chicago orders are piling up, and I can't deny I don't want to turn them down."

"I'm listening," he said, moving to her other breast to play.

"So, it occurred to me, why do we have to choose?"

He raised his head and looked at her. "How?"

"We can split our time between Chicago and Revival. While you were out cold, Shane apologized but then went on to explain how he thought a storefront was possible. I'm not sure how I feel about him backing me, but Cecilia was on board by then, and you know how convincing the two of them together can be."

"I do know," James said. "Do you think it would really work?"

"I've been thinking about it a lot, and I don't see why not. Sometimes we'll need to spend more time in one place than the other, and I'm sure that as I'm getting the bakery up and running I'll have to spend more time in Chicago, but I think it will even out."

James turned the idea over in his mind, liking it. He could live part-time in Revival. He had family there, ties. And so did Gracie. Ties he wanted to support instead of sever. "I like it. And we'll make it work."

She tugged him down. "We will."

He brushed his mouth over hers. "I wish my dad could have met you. He'd have loved you."

Tears spilled over her lashes. "My mom too."

He wiped the wetness from her cheeks. "I love you, Gracie."

"I love you too," she said, tilting her head up for a kiss.

It was going to work out. He'd get to keep his girl. She'd be his, and damned if he wouldn't make sure everyone knew it. His mouth settled over hers. Their lips melding in a promise of the life they'd build together. Satisfaction and peace settled deep into his bones. He understood now.

Sometimes a man could have his cake and eat it too.

Love the Donovans?

Don't miss Evan's story in

AS GOOD AS NEW,

available in April 2016.

Penelope Watkins surveyed the crowded dance floor with a weary gaze as her best friend tugged her hand and whined, "Please, come dance with me."

Penelope turned her attention to Sophie Kincaid—who looked like a rogue Disney princess in a powder-blue spaghetti-strap dress that set off her blond hair and doe eyes—with a heavy sigh.

Was she the only person ready for the wedding of the century to end? She scanned the room, still crowded with guests. Even after midnight, the music was cranked up to concert decibels and the dance floor was packed. Apparently, she was.

Her head ached. She'd already taken three Advil. All she wanted was her bed, but as a bridesmaid at Shane and Cecilia Donovan's wedding, and Chicago's hottest power couple, she had to stay until the bitter end. Not that she wasn't ecstatic for them, because of course she was. Shane wasn't only her boss but her friend as well, and over the last year she'd grown quite close to his new wife, Cecilia.

She just wanted to go home.

Penelope shook her head, glaring at her best friend's four-inch heels. "Aren't your feet killing you?"

"Hell no, come on. I need you to do a slutty little dance with me. I'm trying to drive Logan mad with lust." Sophie gripped Penelope's hand a little tighter and peered over her shoulder at the man in question, sighing.

Penelope couldn't blame her. Logan Buchanan was the very definition of tall, dark, and dangerous. With sharp, watchful blue eyes, and a commanding presence that filled a room, he was the kind of man a woman was supposed to get excited about. Unfortunately, he had no effect on Penelope. Nope, she had to be stubborn and pine away for the first boy she'd fallen in puppy love with at the age of six.

If she'd had any brains at all, she would have befriended Tiffany White, who had all sisters, the first day of kindergarten, but no, she had to sit next to Maddie Donovan.

But how was she to know she'd take one look at Maddie's older brother and become instantly infatuated? Up until then, she'd thought boys were icky.

Unable to help herself, she scanned the room for the man in question. At six-five, Evan Donovan wasn't hard to pick out of a crowd, but he was nowhere to be found.

She took a drink of water. Good. At least she didn't have to look at the Barbie doll he'd brought to his brother's wedding. Penelope was still cringing at the blond girl with the minuscule dress, mermaid-extensioned hair, and flotation-device breasts. Some football groupie—a wannabe model, if Penelope had to guess.

Aka, his normal type, otherwise known as Penelope's exact opposite.

She shook her head. No. She would not start down that road.

She turned back to Sophie, who was standing there expectantly, and smiled. "If you want to drive Logan crazy, I'm not your girl. We are strictly in the friend zone."

Besides, she wasn't really the type to drive men mad with lust. She was attractive enough, with classic bone structure and well-formed features. Tired of wearing glasses, she'd treated herself to Lasik surgery six months ago and she'd been told by numerous dates that her blue eyes were startling against her rich, dark hair. At five-seven she had a nice, trim figure that she kept in shape with workouts at the gym, yoga, and running along the lakeshore. Overall, her looks were nothing to complain about. She had a nice face and a healthy, fit body, but being sexy wasn't important to her.

Sophie puffed out her lip in a pout that would sway most people, but had little effect on Penelope. "Isn't this just my luck? Since I really wanted to cause a scene, I tried to coerce Gracie, but stupid James said no." Sophie released her grip and threw her hands up in the air in frustration. "And she listened! I mean, what the hell is that?"

Since Gracie Roberts was one of the sexiest women on the planet, it was a smart choice on Sophie's part, only she hadn't considered the middle Donovan brother's hold on the other woman. A pairing Penelope had never seen coming, but damned if it didn't seem to be working. James hadn't tamed the sex goddess per se, but when he spoke, Gracie paid attention.

In sympathy, Penelope sighed. "I guess that's what happens with new love."

"Well, it's annoying." Sophie grabbed her hand again. "Now come dance."

"I've got a headache."

Sophie rolled her eyes. "I don't expect you to put out after."

Penelope grinned. God, she loved her friends. Needed them to remind her to do something other than work.

Remember how to have fun. It wasn't that she didn't like fun, she did. It was only that so many other things required her attention. Between her demanding work schedule and watching over her parents, fun wasn't a priority. And that's where Sophie and Maddie came in, to reset her priorities. Why, if it weren't for the two of them, Penelope would have spent her childhood getting into no trouble at all.

Well, except for one thing, but Penelope refused to think about that.

As if Maddie sensed her thoughts, she ran over to them, her heavy auburn hair spilling from the topknot after the long night of dancing. The long skirts of the jeweled, deep purple bridesmaid dress, which matched Penelope's, flounced as she came to a stop. She grinned. "What's up?"

Sophie huffed, jerking her finger toward the dance floor. "Penelope won't dance with me so I can seduce Logan."

Maddie threw an arm around her and squeezed. "I'll dance with you. We'll give everyone a show."

Sophie's face lit with excitement. "Mitch will be jealous."

Maddie laughed, waving a hand. "I know. I'm in the mood for dirty sex and this is just the kind of thing that sets him off." Maddie gave a little shudder, obviously thinking about the dirty things her husband had already done to her.

Penelope laughed. Okay, she needed to shake off this mood, put her headache aside, and go party it up with her girlfriends. With Maddie living in the small town of Revival miles away from Chicago, they didn't get this chance very often, and Penelope refused to waste it.

She looked at her friends, who wore twin expressions filled with the same reckless, excited anticipation that had convinced her to ditch seventh period and hang out at the forest preserve with a bunch of bad boys from the public school, and smiled. "You guys go. I need to run to the ladies' room and then I'll come find you on the dance floor."

Maddie rocked on her heels. "Promise?"

"Yep." And everyone knew her word was gold.

Sophie winked and skipped off with Maddie, the two of them holding hands and laughing. A surefire sign they were up to no good, and Penelope had no doubt she'd return to find them gyrating on the dance floor, causing quite the scene. If Logan would notice was anyone's guess, but Maddie's husband, Mitch, was bound to enjoy himself.

Penelope weaved through the crowd, pausing a few times to talk to a coworker, before she finally reached the hallway. Instead of heading to the bathroom, she veered right and headed toward the balcony, needing to clear her head.

She pushed open the door and the cool spring air washed over her. She breathed in deep, her pounding head instantly easing with the music now only a distant, muffled beat. Small clusters of people filled the expanse of the balcony, enjoying the first hints of warm weather after a long, frigid Chicago winter.

Penelope searched the area for a secluded spot where she could be alone. She didn't want to talk. She wanted quiet. To stand by herself and let the night air and view of the skyline soothe her aching mind. She finally found what she was looking for, tucked into the corner: a concrete structure that partially obstructed the view. She walked over to it and tucked herself into the corner, resting her elbows on the rails. She closed her eyes as a breeze blew over her skin and ruffled the strands of hair curling around her face. Finally, some quiet.

And that's when she heard a giggle.

Penelope's shoulders stiffened and she craned her

neck, dread already pooling in the pit of her stomach. When her gaze locked with Evan's, she wasn't the least bit surprised.

Even in the dim glow of the lights, she could see his vivid green eyes boring into hers. His tux jacket was undone, along with his shirt, exposing the cords of his neck and barest hint of his strong chest. With his dark hair and strong, chiseled features he was so sinfully gorgeous it was nauseating. He was also wild, reckless, and didn't care about anything but football and screwing as many women as possible.

The girl he'd brought was on her knees, working at his belt buckle. She peered over at Penelope and smiled with glossy, over-collagened lips. "Oops, busted."

Evan's eyes didn't leave Penelope's. "Hey, little Penny."

He knew she hated when he called her that. She wanted to scream at him. Throw something. Kick him. But that wasn't the role she played. So she swallowed her emotions and turned, keeping her expression cool and impassive. She flicked a dismissive glance at the woman, who didn't have the decency to get off her knees, and smirked. "Evan. I see your girlfriend's mom let her out past curfew."

This wasn't the first time this had happened, and it wouldn't be the last. Sometimes Penelope wondered if he did it on purpose. Just to hurt her. Although, in fairness, that probably gave him too much credit. Penelope doubted he thought that deeply.

The girl rose, and plastered her hands on spandex-encased hips. "I'm twenty-two."

Penelope laughed, and let her eyes go wide. "Wow, twenty-two, you're practically ancient."

"Who is this woman?" the girl asked, her voice filled with scorn.

Penelope shifted her attention back to Evan. "I'm nobody."

"Evan?" his date asked, slithering alongside him.

His expression flickered. "She's my sister's best friend."

"Nobody you need to concern yourself with," Penelope said.

"I didn't think so." The girl flipped her hair, but her eyes were wary behind her overly mascaraed lashes. The girl might be young but she was no fool, and she sensed the undercurrents lacing the air. She looked back at Evan, who still watched Penelope as though searching for something in her expression. The girl's lips curled. "You're hardly his type."

True, since he never seemed to date anyone over twenty-five. Penelope gave the child her sweetest smile. "Of course not, I'm an adult."

The girl opened her mouth to say something, but Evan shook his head and encircled her wrist. "Go wait for me inside, babe."

She pouted. "But Evan . . ."

"Go. I'll be there in a minute."

Penelope held up her hands. "No, don't let me bother you. I'm leaving."

He looked like he was about to say something, but then he stopped, and shrugged. "Suit yourself."

The girl curled into Evan, draping her perfect *Playboy* body all over him, and giving Penelope a smug smile. "You didn't forget your walker, did you?"

Evan's jaw tightened, and for a fraction of a second Penelope thought he'd be decent and put the girl in her place, but then his expression smoothed over to impassive.

His response stuck like a thorn in her side, reminding her just how much she didn't like him. She shifted her attention back to the twenty-two-year-old. "By the way, he doesn't know your name."

The girl blinked, and her smugness fell away. "Um, yeah, he does."

Penelope shook her head. "Nope. Sorry. He always calls you girls 'babe' when he doesn't remember." She flicked a glance at Evan. "Have fun."

Then, before she could get caught up in any more of his crap, she turned and walked away.

Last thing she heard was "babe" asking Evan what her name was, but Penelope didn't have to stick around to wait for the answer. She knew Evan, and he had no idea.

Of course, being as he was a famous, bad-boy football player who was reported to be notoriously insatiable and wild, Penelope knew it wouldn't matter. Evan would get his blow job, and probably a hundred other things before the night was through.

Little things like names didn't matter in the NFL.

Penelope slipped back inside and hurried down the hallway, searching for a place to collect herself. When she found a tiny alcove at the end of a corridor, she rested against the wall, squeezing her lids tight.

For a smart woman, she sure was stupid.

She had everything she could want from life. A great house, success, respect, friends, and a family who loved her. She had an MBA from Northwestern, and was admired by her colleagues for her logical, analytical brain, which could solve even the toughest of problems.

And what was she doing with all these brains of hers? Still pining for Evan Donovan.

It was so ridiculous and frustrating. Crushes that began at six were supposed to end. They weren't supposed to plague her at thirty-one.

She rubbed at her temples. She'd tried countless times over the years to talk herself out of him, but it hadn't worked. Ironically, her heart seemed to be the only impetuous, self-destructive thing about her.

And she'd tried. God knew how hard she'd tried. She'd dated plenty of men—good men who appreciated her and treated her the way she deserved—and still she couldn't forget Evan, or the past that meant more to her than to him. He lingered in the back of her mind, always present.

She didn't even like the man he'd become—if he could even be called a man. More like an overgrown frat boy. The grown-up version of Evan, she could get over. Only her memories wouldn't allow that. No matter how many times she'd told herself the boy she'd known was a figment of her imagination, her heart refused to believe. And, thus, like every bad country song ever written, she pined for a man who would never love her in return.

She hated it, but didn't know how to stop it from being true.

The one saving grace was that nobody knew. Not her friends. Not her family. No one. She refused to even write his name in her diary, for fear someone would discover the truth. She hid it well. She never reacted. Always played it cool. And no one had ever guessed. In the long list of humiliations she'd suffered at the hands of Evan Donovan, this wouldn't be one of them.

This secret would follow her to the grave.

Books by Bestselling Author
Fern Michaels

___**The Jury**	0-8217-7878-1	$6.99US/$9.99CAN
___**Sweet Revenge**	0-8217-7879-X	$6.99US/$9.99CAN
___**Lethal Justice**	0-8217-7880-3	$6.99US/$9.99CAN
___**Free Fall**	0-8217-7881-1	$6.99US/$9.99CAN
___**Fool Me Once**	0-8217-8071-9	$7.99US/$10.99CAN
___**Vegas Rich**	0-8217-8112-X	$7.99US/$10.99CAN
___**Hide and Seek**	1-4201-0184-6	$6.99US/$9.99CAN
___**Hokus Pokus**	1-4201-0185-4	$6.99US/$9.99CAN
___**Fast Track**	1-4201-0186-2	$6.99US/$9.99CAN
___**Collateral Damage**	1-4201-0187-0	$6.99US/$9.99CAN
___**Final Justice**	1-4201-0188-9	$6.99US/$9.99CAN
___**Up Close and Personal**	0-8217-7956-7	$7.99US/$9.99CAN
___**Under the Radar**	1-4201-0683-X	$6.99US/$9.99CAN
___**Razor Sharp**	1-4201-0684-8	$7.99US/$10.99CAN
___**Yesterday**	1-4201-1494-8	$5.99US/$6.99CAN
___**Vanishing Act**	1-4201-0685-6	$7.99US/$10.99CAN
___**Sara's Song**	1-4201-1493-X	$5.99US/$6.99CAN
___**Deadly Deals**	1-4201-0686-4	$7.99US/$10.99CAN
___**Game Over**	1-4201-0687-2	$7.99US/$10.99CAN
___**Sins of Omission**	1-4201-1153-1	$7.99US/$10.99CAN
___**Sins of the Flesh**	1-4201-1154-X	$7.99US/$10.99CAN
___**Cross Roads**	1-4201-1192-2	$7.99US/$10.99CAN

Available Wherever Books Are Sold!
Check out our website at **www.kensingtonbooks.com**

VISIT WARNER ASPECT ONLINE!

THE WARNER ASPECT HOMEPAGE
You'll find us at: www.twbookmark.com then by clicking on Science Fiction and Fantasy.

NEW AND UPCOMING TITLES
Each month we feature our new titles and reader favorites.

AUTHOR INFO
Author bios, bibliographies and links to personal websites.

CONTESTS AND OTHER FUN STUFF
Advance galley giveaways, autographed copies, and more.

THE ASPECT BUZZ
What's new, hot and upcoming from Warner Aspect: awards news, bestsellers, movie tie-in information . . .